BUDDHA'S
BAD BOYS

Praise for Alan Chin

First Exposure

"The level of emotional honesty is unavoidable, it's so real. At some point during all of this, I realized I wouldn't be able to ever forget these characters. Beautiful, sweet, carrying their burdens, frightened, hopeful and working to survive. Again, it's the writing. It brings inspiration and darkness to life."
—*Prism Book Alliance*

"Chin has really created a character that we so badly need in gay literature. This is a book that cries out to be read and reading it is an experience that you do not want to miss. It is an 'upclose and personal' look at how we live as gay men and how we relate to those around us."—*Reviews by Amos Lassen*

"Chin has given us an irresistible page-turner about friendship, protectiveness, and tenderness. The author's brilliance is his ability to write authentically and entertainingly about the human condition, while simultaneously exposing the wide range of often-conflicting emotions and tragic imperfections that are part and parcel of our humanity."
—*Queer Town Abbey*

The Plain of Bitter Honey

"Mr. Chin gives us an unrelenting, breathtaking work, sympathetically beautiful and riveted to an unhinged life, which could realistically evolve if we allow prejudice and obsession to overtake a sense of humanity. Despite its powerful pace, the novel is character driven and superbly written. Mr. Chin always makes strong statements in his work, but *The Plain of Bitter Honey*, to this reader, is his most powerful to date."
—Edward C. Patterson, author of the Jade Owl Series

"I've said in the past that Alan Chin is my favorite author, and that is still the case with this new book. It is best described as a sci-fi/speculative/political novel, so unlike any of his previous works I have seen, and he handles the genre with mastery. The story is action-packed, well-constructed and expertly told, with a diverse, developed cast of gay and straight characters working together in situations that risks not only their lives, but perhaps the future of this country. Bravo…five stars out of five."—Bob Lind, *Echo Magazine*

By the Author

The Plain of Bitter Honey

First Exposure

Buddha's Bad Boys

Visit us at www.boldstrokesbooks.com

BUDDHA'S BAD BOYS

by

Alan Chin

A Division of Bold Strokes Books

2015

ISBN 13: 978-1-62639-244-1

This Trade Paperback Original Is Published By
Bold Strokes Books, Inc.
P.O. Box 249
Valley Falls, NY 12185

First Edition: February 2015

Credits
Editor: Greg Herren
Production Design: Stacia Seaman
Cover Design by Gabrielle Pendergrast

Most of these stories and characters are pure fiction,
yet some are based on real people and events.

CONTENTS

MONK FOR A MONTH   1

HANDCARVED ELEPHANTS   41

EMPTY CHAIRS   87

ALMOST ENOUGH   143

WHITE MONKEY   187

DEATH OF A STRANGER   237

The best way to find yourself is to lose yourself in the service of others.

—Mohandas K. Gandhi

MONK FOR A MONTH

I sat at the bar sporting saffron robes and a shaved head, sipping a Singha beer and listening to the bartender, who was clearly agitated. I couldn't tell whether the man was upset over the recent murders, or because the hard rain was hurting his business, or if he simply didn't like serving alcohol to a monk, even a Caucasian one.

"His name Somchai," the bartender said. He spoke English, but with the usual Thai singsong clip that I had come to adore. "He kill American expatriate named Warren. Tony Warren."

I had seen a dead body only once, a gruesome spectacle. It took an effort to settle my nerves as the bartender glared at me, as if, also being an American, made me an accomplice. I had never learned the invaluable art of staying detached in the face of tragedy, of not identifying with the victim. I had no way to shield myself from the reality of how brutal humans can be to each other, what ruthless lengths they will go to, and the pain they are capable of inflicting on each other.

Across the street, four soldiers trudged along in the rain.

"When did Somchai kill Warren?" I asked, my voice scarcely a whisper.

The bartender didn't know exactly, sometime at the beginning of the afternoon that had now come to an end. At the same time that he killed Warren, Somchai had also slain Warren's Thai girlfriend. Both victims had been found two hours earlier at the apartment belonging to Warren.

The barroom was already dark, due to the lateness of the hour and another power outage. Candles flickered on the bar and at each table; their yellow light mingled with the blueness of the dying day.

The shower stopped as suddenly as it had started, as it often does in Thailand.

"How old was she? The girlfriend, I mean," I asked.

"Very young. Nineteen." Regret passed over the bartender's face. "A real beauty."

"I would like another Singha," I said, "but I have no more money. Can I buy on credit?"

The bartender's look of regret turned to disgust. As he walked away, a customer two stools over ordered beers for me and himself, and also shots of cheap Thai whiskey.

The bartender prepared our drinks while the customer moved to the stool beside mine. He introduced himself as Ty Poe, and did not shake my hand, as it is considered disrespectful to touch a monk. Poe was courteous, offering the customary *wai* gesture of respect. He was somewhere in his forties, and had a smoking-induced cough. The polluted streets of Chiang Mai didn't help his lungs any more than his chain-smoking, I thought. I gave him my name, Reece Jackson, and told him I was from America, San Francisco in fact.

"I overheard your talk about the murders."

"Why haven't they caught him yet?" I asked. "Chiang Mai's a small town."

"They have him trapped within the walls of the old city, but you should know how it is," Poe grunted. "We're talking about an American expatriate and his whore who got themselves killed by a homeless gay kid. I mean, there are limited resources available to the police department. The police force, as a rule, is not well trained. Officers have to buy their own uniforms, their own guns. They are poorly paid. Not much would be happening now except that this dead girl happens to be the daughter of an army major. The army is doing what they can but they do not know the town as well as Somchai."

Poe was right, I thought. What could anyone reasonably expect of this situation? The unvarnished fact was that in this country, any given police station's cases were ranked according to priority. And priority in Thailand had to do with wealth and status. Those on the low end of the spectrum were unlikely to receive much attention. And for a homeless gay kid with no family who happened to murder a bit of riff-raff, then it was probably the victim's fault. Why bother figuring out all the sordid details?

I felt thankful that I came from a country where every death warranted respect, every victim merited justice, no matter how far down the social and economic ladder that victim might fall. At least I liked to believe that bit of hype.

The bartender placed the beers and shots before us. I lifted my shot in a toast to Poe and knocked my head back, taking the drink in one hot swallow. Poe stared at me in obvious surprise.

"I've never seen a monk do that," Poe said.

"I'm not really a monk. My partner and I paid good money to enroll in the Monk-For-A-Month program here at Wat Phra Singh. He's on some damned spiritual quest that I, frankly, don't understand. Me, I'm just an IT geek along for the ride."

"So you're not alone," Poe asked, exhaling a stream of smoke.

"Technically, no. But it often feels like I am."

The bar stood only a few doors down from Tha Phae Square, which spread before one of the four main gates of the old city, and where two of the town's chief avenues collided. The square was bordered by the city wall, built of ancient brick, and butted against by the city moat on the north and south sides. The top of the wall was wide enough to walk on, and just then a flock of children scampered along the wet brick, heedless of the danger of slipping. Among them ran Archer, my adopted son, also sporting a shaved head and wearing the saffron robes. The children looked down on the tourists who gathered in the square, clutching their umbrellas in case the rains returned.

It must be between six and seven in the evening, I thought.

Another shower started and people in the square ran for cover.

Archer hopped down the wall steps and dashed across the road like a fleeing deer. He entered the bar and huddled against me, giving Poe a cautious glance. Archer was a handsome seven-year-old with a round face that gave way to a large jaw and a brilliant set of teeth. He had an impishness and good humor in his eyes, and was strong for so young a boy. But what I admired most about him was his gentle and trusting disposition. Unlike most boys, he was incapable of hurting anything. His only flaw was that he was fathered by two gay men, which made him an outcast back home, someone to be pitied, stared at, whispered about, laughed at, and occasionally beaten up by his peers.

Strokes of lightning lit the sky, coming so close together that they seemed like a ceaseless illumination. The thunder was continuous. The noise burst like metal fireworks, and then would immediately rise again; its modulations grew less and less defined as the shower let up, until there was only the sound of rain striking paving stones.

"This rain will last all night," Poe said, lighting another cigarette from the butt of his previous one.

Moments later, the shower stopped. Poe left his stool and pointed at the leaden sky, patched with massive blotches of somber gray so low that it seemed to brush the rooftops. "Don't let that fool you."

I finished my drink, motioned for the bartender to set up another round for Poe and me, and I nudged the slim stack of Poe's money closer to him.

"It's my husband who wanted to vacation here," I told Poe. "I would have preferred anywhere else."

"Such as?"

"Africa. I'd love to see the Okavango Delta in Botswana, and track gorillas in the Virunga Mountains of Zaire, and see the migration at the Masai Mara in Kenya. Don't pay attention to what I say; I'm a dreamer, always fantasizing of what is beyond my reach. Actually, I adore this town. I'm just feeling a little...neglected."

Poe picked up a shot glass and handed it to me. He paid the bartender and patted Archer's shoulder as if he were a pet dog, which told me he no longer considered us monks, as well he shouldn't have.

During our conversation I scrutinized the square. The police had come out again with the end of the rain, and I listened to the harsh whistles that rang out from every street.

The sun had set behind the end of the main avenue, although it wasn't quite as late as it seemed. The storm had scrambled the hours, bullied them on, but now the sun appeared again, spreading red hues across the bellies of clouds.

"And where is your husband now?" Poe asked.

"Reading in our room at Wat Phra Singh, no doubt, or perhaps he's gone to the evening chant by now."

Poe nodded while seeming to study the cigarette between his fingers. "I recall seeing another white monk roaming the town. It must have been him."

The sky grew dark again. A new phase of the storm was gathering. Another black, ocean-like mass crawled over the town. It came from the east, leaving only enough light to see its threatening color.

When I didn't respond, Poe turned to stare into my face. "Look, your eyes are not as blue now," he said, "because of the clouds."

"I can't go back yet," I said. "Look what's coming." I wasn't looking at the sky. I watched the barefoot children splashing through the gutter in front of the square. The water running between their feet was saturated with dust from the wall's bricks, giving it a muted red color that matched much of the town and the earth around it. The boys sang as they played, a sound I found sweet as it pierced the grumbling clouds. The sky opened, and an ocean spilled onto the streets. The square disappeared. Tourists scurried into the bar, soaking wet and snorting. Even the police rushed in to escape the deluge.

"Tell me more about Somchai," I said.

"He and the American were lovers, but it seems Warren had a girl on the side," Poe said. "Then today, he found the American with her. People who heard the shouting said Warren was throwing Somchai out so he could marry the girl. I don't blame Somchai. Who wouldn't have done the same thing? He would be acquitted, no doubt, if it were not for this father who is an army major."

I sipped my beer. "You mean, because it was an American he killed, and a woman, they would slap his hand and let him go?"

Poe nodded.

I pushed my beer away. The conversation had turned my stomach. "Where do you think he is?"

"Who can say? If it were me," Poe said after a moment's hesitation, "I would take refuge in one of the temples. Trust in the Buddha, always."

He leaned toward me, and we smiled at each other. We were so close I thought he might kiss me. He moved away, but I could still feel the warmth of his breath on my neck, still smell the thick, gingery scent of his hair. I stared after him, noting that his lips were smooth, beautiful.

"You think the monks will hide him?"

"No," Poe said, and laughed. "I'm just repeating what I heard. No one will protect him. He's as good as caught. I don't know why he doesn't give himself up."

"There'll be trouble in the town tonight," I said.

"Probably not as much for you as there will be for Somchai," Poe said, shuffling away to talk with the police.

An argument about the crime had started at the back of the bar between an Australian tourist and a police officer. It grew loud when one of the bar girls joined in, siding with the Australian man. "The bitch threw herself at American," the bar girl spat, "and he too weak to say no. How you push away a slut who jumps in your arms?"

Yes, is it possible to be that strong? To summon the will to resist young passion?

The shower ended, and with it the nerve-racking noise of rain pounding the metal roof.

"Americans," the bar girl spat, "they fuck any dog they find. Poor Somchai. He deserve better."

Suddenly furious, I jumped off my stool and charged the woman, my pent-up anger now fixating on a concrete target.

A policeman caught hold of my arm; his other hand grabbed my saffron robes. He shouted something in Thai that I didn't understand and pushed me back. The girl fled the premises. Given our reputation for serene indifference, I suppose she hadn't expected to see an irate monk ready to rip her face off.

Once more, with the end of the shower, tourists and children ventured onto the square. I could see all the way down the long avenue to the mammoth white shapes of Wat Phra Singh, the town's main temple.

Another customer—an American tourist, tall and heavyset with a wattle of fat under his chin—stepped up to the bar and offered to buy me another whiskey.

Archer scowled as I accepted and the bartender poured another shot. How long had I been in Chiang Mai? Twenty days, I said. Did I like being a monk? It had its hardships and joys. Does this boy belong to you? I've adopted him. He doesn't say much, does he? Monks generally don't.

"Now that the rain has stopped, I should go back," I said, although my words sounded more like a long, continuous sigh.

"To my place?" the American asked, followed by a nervous laugh.

I laughed too, but not as much as I would have liked. I shook my head.

"One more beer?" the American said.

I had already consumed too much. I lifted myself off the barstool and took Archer's hand in mine.

"Will you be back..." the American asked, using a hopeful tone, "tonight?"

I didn't know. It was possible, I thought.

Archer and I took to the sidewalk leading to the wat. The clean scent of rain blew through the town. The night would be cool, a good one to huddle indoors, cuddling with Darren under double quilts. Archer skipped along beside me, splashing through puddles of blushed water. We passed police and troops at every corner. The entire town inside the walls seemed locked down, people watching each alley, peeping from behind every door. There was still no electricity, and that would probably last until tomorrow. I squeezed Archer's hand and told him to hurry. The boy didn't listen. He was off in his own world again. *A chip off the preverbal block.*

❖

Wat Phra Singh monastery and temple complex was a sprawling affair inside the ancient walls of the town. Three large temples, a bell tower, and an impressive stupa sat at the center, with the main temple situated closer to the front gate, near the main road with its traffic congestion and vehicle clamor. It was the place where we congregated for morning and evening chants and held most of our public affairs and festivals. The smallest temple, beside the stupa, was northern Thailand's oldest abode of worship and enshrined the town's principal Buddha image. Surrounding these main buildings were four three-story dormitories where we students lived, two dozen smaller houses called *kutis* where the senior monks resided with a bit more solitude, a dining hall, and an open-air pavilion where dharma lectures on the Lord Buddha's teaching were given.

By the rear wall, near the dormitory where I lived, stood a large Bodhi tree, the kind under which the Lord Buddha had sat in meditation when he achieved enlightenment. Every monastery had one, and beneath its sprawling branches were scattered several Buddha statues. It was a favorite gathering place for monks and visitors, and also a popular shady spot where a dozen temple dogs slept through the hot afternoons.

Trees were abundant, but there was little grass to speak of. Concrete footpaths wandered among the buildings, and there was a large parking lot where the boys played soccer following their afternoon lessons and before the evening chant.

As Archer and I entered the front gate, I spied them sitting together, opposite each other at an open window in the dining room. They had become nearly inseparable. They waved as Archer and I drew near.

"We've been waiting for you," Darren said.

Darren Prewitt had pitch-black eyebrows below the sallow skin of his shaved head that looked like a newly laid egg. A pale ghost, yet too sharply focused, I thought, remarkably attractive but not affected by it. He never flaunted his sex appeal, but rather, expected you to discover the matrix of his greater beauty that was hidden within. Below his arresting exterior was an unfathomable intellect. Yet, there was more; when he engaged you in conversation, he seemed to hear and see more keenly than anyone else, understanding each word and gesture as if he could see it germinating within your soul before you spoke it.

I sent Archer to our bedroom to change into dry robes.

"It is nice like this, cool I mean," Noy said as he watched Archer trundle up the stairs to the dormitory's third floor. He struck a match and lit another candle in the center of the table.

How lovely Noy looked in the quivering candlelight, dark and thin and supple as a silk scarf floating on the breeze. The soft light on his face turned his skin a pale brown. He seemed to breathe in the light as he inhaled, which fed him from within and shone through his black eyes. "Brother Salisangwaro," I said, willing my face into neutral, "you look happy tonight. The weather must have lifted your spirits."

I glanced over his head, scanning the dining room. The rain had driven all the monks indoors, and the room was filled with brown men in orange garb. Even our venerable abbot sat among them, leaning over a table, deep in conversation.

"Please call me Noy."

My gaze returned to Noy, a seventeen-year-old who had come to the temple a year earlier than Darren and I. He had been homeless, and had come here trying to overcome a drug addiction. I knew of four others who were currently trying to kick their habits cold turkey, with nothing more than meditation and a belief in the Buddha to help them. Whenever I sat in the temple for prayers or chanting, I found myself being watched by their haunted eyes as they struggled to stop trembling and control the need surging through their veins. Noy had been one of those boys, and after he had beaten his habit, he stayed on and became a disciple of the Buddha.

Right then Noy grew unnaturally pale, as if suddenly in desperate need of a blood transfusion. Yet he was so striking, like looking at a point on the horizon where the relationship of shape, texture, color and space fall into perfect harmony. I felt a jolt when he looked into my eyes, peering through me.

"Where were you?" Darren asked.

"At a bar by the square."

"You've been drinking?" Darren's voice held an edge, making his words an accusation. "So those vows we took meant nothing to you? It's only for thirty days, for christsake."

I shot him a level stare—a warning that I was done with this charade he'd gotten us into—and held it for a few heartbeats. "I'll go see what's keeping Archer." I strolled toward our dormitory stairs. I could feel their eyes on my back even when I entered the room to find Archer putting the finishing touches on his upper-body robe that draped across his chest and fell over his left shoulder. We smiled at each other, and I felt a flash of gratitude that he had such a warm and accepting nature. I waited, letting him finish dressing himself.

To him these robes, this whole adventure, had turned into a grand escapade to savor until he would find himself back home and stuck in a classroom for another year.

While I waited, I inhaled the room, our room, Darren, Archer, and I: the dim light from two candles, the muted colors, Darren's Gibson guitar with the pick trapped between the strings, the photographs standing on the only wall shelf. Our sleeping cushions stretched almost the full length of the far wall, with light cotton blankets and pillows nestling between the wall and the wardrobe in a secure, inviting way. This was where we lay, our cocoon. A Buddha statue sat in the lotus position on a small table in the corner, with an electric fan and a few books—Sartre, Camus, Graham Greene, Isherwood, Maugham, and Mary Renault's *The Persian Boy*. He, Darren, immediately surrounded me. He was the gravity that held our family together. But at the same time, I noticed there was an additional sleeping cushion and blanket on the floor, and I knew it belonged to Noy. That boy had invaded our space with the intention of staying. There was also an additional chest, small and colorful, beside ours.

Rather than let myself get distressed, I moved a candle closer to the photos on the shelf as a way to remember happier times. In one, Darren and I stood on a beach, both wearing boardies and holding surfboards. We were deeply tanned, and his long hair was streaked by salt and sun. In another shot, we sat together holding an infant, Archer, and before us was a cake with a single candle on it.

I opened the wardrobe and pressed my face against the folded garments, Darren's civilian clothes, searching for his smell, the one he had before we came here. I found the scent of his skin, an indecipherable script that only I could read. I held it in my chest for a long minute, wanting to turn back time. The moment I pulled my face away, I began to miss him.

I glanced back at the chest on the floor. Though it was not mine, I had to investigate. I knelt before it and opened the lid. Underneath a set of robes and an iPod, I found a bag containing a syringe, spoon, lighter, and a baggie that held a white, powdery substance. So Noy had not entirely kicked his heroin habit, I thought. Had he given some to Darren? Were they sharing that needle? And where did the money to buy it come from?

I set everything back in place and moved to our wardrobe again, checking the shoebox where we kept our wallets. Much of our money was missing. I felt my heart stop, and then start again a moment later to a different, more fragile rhythm.

Archer finished adjusting his garment. We walked onto the third-floor balcony of what I called "our barracks." I watched him brush dust from his hands. He was a very neat and deceptively slim boy in bright orange robes that were still fresh from the previous day's washing.

We both leaned our elbows on the balcony ledge and gazed down at the familiar compound. I began to feel a half-sheepish affection for this vantage point that I would soon be leaving.

Below me, I could see into the vast open windows of the dining hall, lit bright by many candles, and I saw Darren and Noy in the same spot. They had not noticed me, for they were leaning across the table, talking softly, intimately, with their hands discreetly linked together. Not a trace of fear or regret marred either face. It was still early. It seemed as though midnight had come and gone, but it was only the storm darkening the sky. Although the rain had stopped temporarily, the storm was huge, spreading over the entire valley, and the downpour would no doubt continue soon.

Somewhere along the edge of darkness between the railing and the dining hall, this place became my heritage. I was multiplied by each sound of grumbling monks and tuk-tuks racing by on the street beyond the walls and by each shape and each splash of color within the walls. I could not deny any of this without denying my own existence. Yet now, I told myself, I am denying it all by renouncing this place and all that it has given me, along with all it has taken away.

Darren's head turned toward the open window and his hands pulled back from Noy. I grabbed Archer's shoulder to steady myself, and we marched down the steps. As we crossed to the dining room I saw Archer was now afraid of the storm. The sky rolled over on itself, hanging low over the town and threatening to burst open.

Darren had become pale, so much so that his complexion seemed even more surprising than the fear it revealed. Noy, on the other hand, seemed immersed in the memory of Darren's touch on his fingers, those caresses up his forearm that had occurred only minutes before.

I glanced at Noy's arms, checking for needle marks, but could find no trace in that dim light.

Before I could scrutinize Darren's pale skin, his arm swung out and around Archer's waist, pulling him close for a long hug. At the same time Darren's other arm reached out to me, lacing his fingers with mine, me, his rightful husband.

Darren smiled. "I missed you."

I stepped closer to him, clutching the back of his chair. I closed my eyes and began to speak while remembering the last time he had been unfaithful. "Once, in Rome…"

Noy had no way to know what was coming. His voice rose above the other voices in the room, cutting a bright path. "Rome? Wow. What happened there?"

Before I could continue, Darren said, "There was a brutal storm and we slept badly." He leaned into Archer and kissed his face.

I stroked the back of Archer's neck, and decided to say nothing more. Archer swiveled his head around and stared at me with puppy-dog eyes, begging.

"Daddy," Archer said, "my tummy hurts."

Hunger was the worst hardships here. No monk was allowed to eat after the noon meal; however, for the children there was always congee, rice gruel, to be had in the kitchen. It was neither tasty nor very nutritious, but quelled the belly pangs.

"Run to the kitchen," I said. "See what you can find."

He took off, skipping between the tables.

Noy concentrated on what was going on in the dining room. Behind his thoughtful expression lay a smile. He was gloating to himself. Darren, wincing, raised his eyes to meet mine—the same eyes as Archer—and I returned a knowing smirk.

The turmoil in the dining room began to settle. Yet there were more flashes of lightning on the horizon, and more thunder. The storm was gathering again.

The shorter the time between the flash of lightning and the sound of thunder, the closer you are to the actual lightning—so they say.

"One crocodile, two crocodile, three crocodile," I counted. Yes, I confirmed the storm was moving toward us. There was little time before the next wave.

Police whistles continued to shriek beyond the walls. Whenever they were heard close to the dining room, conversations would die down and everyone would listen. Moments later, the monks continued to discuss the murders. Some declared that Somchai would soon be captured, while others said never. It would no doubt be a difficult night.

"He's hiding at one of the temples," I said, but nobody paid me any attention. I walked out of the room and ambled to the front gate that opened onto the main street in old town. Another shower was in the making. The horizon was lurid, and seemed very near. The storm had grown bigger, more violent.

"Squalls go as quickly as they come," Darren had said only moments ago.

I glanced around the temple compound. Except for the dining hall, the place seemed deserted until a squad of military men in formation marched into the compound. They halted outside the dining hall and the leader spoke with our abbot. I went back to join Darren and Noy. When the abbot came back into the hall, he announced that the army intended to search every building, every room.

"As we all know," the abbot said, "a crime was committed in our town earlier today. We are all very sorry, and we will all cooperate to the fullest."

I thought about Noy's heroin, and prayed the soldiers would find it, but I realized that even if they did, they would most likely say nothing and keep it for themselves.

❖

Eight soldiers rushed through the dining room carrying automatic weapons at the ready. Their boots and belts gave off a nauseating smell of wet leather and sweat. Others climbed the stairs to the dormitory while still more men searched the individual houses inside the walls. I became afraid that the soldiers would frighten Archer, and was relieved when he came running from the kitchen to clutch me around the waist. At the rate the soldiers were moving, I knew it would not take long before they were gone again and we were left to ourselves.

"If Somchai is here," I said, "then he's either hiding in a temple or he's on a rooftop."

The monks resumed their chatter. The officer in charge of the troops shouted orders to soldiers who jumped to obey. The monks listened carefully to what the officer said, watched the soldiers coming and going, worried, gained or lost hope as to the outcome of the search. They all seemed to agree that it was horrible that Somchai had killed a nineteen-year-old girl, a mere child with a full life ahead of her. No one seemed to care that he also killed the American.

Calls could be heard rumbling down the corridors of the dormitories. The soldiers were calling his name. "Somchai." In plaintive, nearly tender tones, they begged him to surrender.

Darren took hold of my arm and forced me to sit beside him. I did so obediently, and pulled Archer onto my lap.

"He's here," I said again, "hiding behind one of the Buddha statues. I just know it."

"Funny," Noy said softly, "I don't care at all. If he's here, I hope he escapes." He had a dark look in his eyes. He had a small Buddha image hanging from a chain around his neck, pressing against his bare chest. He brought this to his lips and kissed it. "Not that I approve of what he did, of course."

My back stiffened. For most of the evening, I had remained appropriately detached and calm, even after seeing the evidence of betrayal. Noy's words, however, cast my thoughts back on another gruesome night so long ago back in the States, and a strange sort of grief took hold of me. That night I had witnessed a fourteen-year-old boy shot. A runaway, too young to work a job, he had been cruising for johns at a street corner near my apartment, like he often had done to feed himself. But then bullets erupted from a passing car. The boy's white shirt became red, and more blood trickled down his face from the hole in his forehead. I could still see him lying on the ground, his straw-colored hair gathering in the gutter. I was still appalled by the horrible unfairness of it, shocked by how violent people—we all—could be to each other and to ourselves.

My eyes never left Noy. Hadn't I come here, taken these robes, partly to cope with what I had seen that night, to restore my shattered faith in humanity? Yet, here it was again, staring me in the eye.

"If he murdered two people," I said to Noy, "I should think you'd want to see justice done."

Noy gazed across the table, his lips lifting into a grin. "To see with true understanding, one must look from the heart; what is just is often invisible to the eye."

I hugged Archer closer to me and kissed the top of his head. "Noy, you would be surprised at what my eyes can see, even on a night as dark as this."

"Then you know that it is impossible to escape justice. One can only avoid it for a time, then karma grabs you by the throat with a heavy hand."

I took Darren's hand in mine. "I don't want to stay here. Let's go to a bar and have a drink. I miss being alone with you."

"You've already had enough."

"Not by a long shot, Mom," I teased. "Come on. Noy can watch Archer. We'll listen to music, share some laughs. Just you and me."

Darren sat silent for what seemed a long time. He finally stood and said he would go to the room and get some money.

While I waited, the troops finished their search, fell into formation, and marched away. The rain had stopped momentarily. The lightning flashes and thunder continued, but from a distance.

"Do you think Somchai loved the American?" Noy asked.

"Why else would he kill him, kill them both?" I said.

Noy laughed, which made me feel foolish because I realized I still knew so little of his culture.

"Listen to me, Noy," I said. I leaned across the table, coming so close to him that he leaned back, away from me. "I want to tell you something important, something you should know."

"I'm listening."

"Most murders in the world are crimes of passion. Do you understand?" I asked. I was about to continue down a path that no doubt would be a threat, but before I could, Darren strolled to the table.

He spoke louder than usual, and with a beautiful voice, always precise, with a rolling fastidiousness that was almost oratorical. "You stay here. I'll go out and buy us a pint of Thai whiskey and some Singha beers."

A smile danced in Noy's eyes. I knew then this change in plan was a way for Darren to build up his courage with liquor, yet not be away from Noy for most of the night. So be it, I thought.

"I'll put Archer to bed," I said.

"Great. Wait upstairs for us. We won't be long."

Plural? He planned to take Noy with him. I didn't object. Many of the children were climbing the stairs to their rooms. Some were already in their beds, asleep. I took Archer by the hand and led him upstairs, lit an oil lamp, undressed him, wrapped him in a blanket, and let him lie on the sleeping cushions beside the wall. Normally, Archer would have pushed me away and put himself to bed, but my sweet child must have understood that I needed something to keep me busy, something that would bring us closer together. When he was bundled in warm blankets, he looked up at me with that dear perfection and told me he loved me. It nearly broke my heart.

I waited for Darren to return, and for Archer to fall asleep. I waited a long time.

❖

So much time had passed that the dining hall had nearly emptied. The children were asleep. I stood on the balcony, staring down at the black puddles in the compound.

"Do not expect electricity tonight," said an old monk in passing. "Utility workers are lazy and inept. We will be blessed to have it restored by this time tomorrow."

No electricity and more rain on the way. The sky was still low and whipped by strong gusts of wind. From the balcony, I could see the whole expanse of the storm, and there seemed no end to it. Behind me, Archer slept, his body outlined in the yellow light of an oil lamp hooked on the wall.

It was now past ten o'clock. Policemen and army troops were still stalking the streets beyond the temple walls. I heard them dragging their feet through the mud puddles. The crime had been committed almost a dozen hours ago. They must be tired, I thought. By now they must be more concerned about the weather than about catching Somchai.

I glanced along the walls of the main temple, half expecting to see the culprit crouching at the doorway. All I saw was stillness. Through the dining hall windows, I spotted Darren sitting with Noy. They had somehow slipped back into the compound without my noticing. Amid the cleared tables, and oblivious to my scrutiny, they sat across from each other, staring, motionless. The barracks were full and the temples were shut up for the night. They had no other place to be alone, where they could stare so longingly at each other.

More whistles screeched from the streets, but not much happened. Troops gathered on a corner, flashlight beams searched all directions, and they moved off again.

I knew I should go down to the hall, sit between them and talk more about Somchai and my growing certainty that he was in the temples hiding among the Buddha statues. Perhaps he was even sitting in a lotus position, a Buddha effigy himself, flesh turned rigid as his mind entered nirvana.

More rain began to fall, harder this time. I left the balcony and lay beside Archer, the only one left who belonged to me. I kissed his head.

"Now you are my life," I whispered.

He stirred, and, with a sigh, fell back into a calm sleep.

I intended to follow Archer into slumber, but I craved another drink. I could taste the cheap whiskey, feel it burn my throat only to be soothed by cold beer. I forced myself not to move, but I couldn't keep my gaze from traveling beyond the yellow and vacillating screen of the oil lamp, out the open doorway and balcony, to the moving sky.

I rose up from the blankets, still hesitant about going back to the dining room where they would still be immersed in their overpowering desire, still alone in the midst of the empty tables. I walked onto the balcony and smoked a cigarette. There was a break in the rain. The sky moved slowly now, brooding. Monks moved along the corridor, talking softly so as not to wake the children. From everywhere came the sound of muted voices, regularly interrupted by the fateful police whistles.

At last the sky opened up, torrential. It filled the streets in a few seconds; the inadequate sewage system couldn't drink up that much rain so quickly. Trees in the compound bent before the wind. Ten yards away, lightning struck a tree on the outside of the compound wall. This close, the thunder was not a rumble but a white, detonation crack. The force knocked me back against the doorway and into the room. Archer lifted up on one elbow, threatening to cry. I held him, soothing him back into sleep.

When I walked back onto the balcony, more lightning lit up the courtyard, and in its livid illumination, I saw a body clinging to the upper branches of the Bodhi tree. Somchai was not among the Buddha statues; he had taken refuge from the police within the protection of the sacred tree's foliage.

The shower lasted another ten minutes. Calm returned as the strength of the wind collapsed. A vague glimmering, so long hoped for, descended from the appeased sky. The glimmer increased, as I hoped it would, but I knew it would quickly fade with the beginning of the next phase of the storm. But while it lasted, I could clearly see the shape of a man clinging to a branch.

When the rain subsided the police came into the compound again for another search. I leaned over the balcony railing and heard one of them laugh. When I glanced back at the dining hall, I saw them, Darren and Noy, pressed together, kissing. My throat went dry and my pulse went haywire. I moved a step or two back into the shadows, but I could not take my eyes off them.

This must be their first kiss, I thought. While Darren mouthed Noy, his hand roved over hairless chest. The hall was dim but I could see them fully outlined. They seemed to break apart to talk, no doubt speaking the first words of love—irrepressible, passionate words that came to their lips between kisses.

Lightning made the scene more livid. The brilliant light struck with irregularity, and every time it made their kisses livid too. Their single, nearly blinding shape was etched onto my retinas. Was this truly their first kiss, or had it been going on for days, perhaps weeks? How could I know?

Opposite these kisses, perched in the tree a dozen yards away from me, Somchai, drenched and no doubt trembling, waited for the night to end. At dawn, it would be over.

I suddenly felt a bond with him, Somchai. He had killed in a fit of jealousy, and I felt that same dangerous emotion surging through my flesh. And like him, the morning would bring the end for me as well. The end of what I wasn't yet sure, but I knew what I'd had was over, dead.

I was alone with my adopted son, in a foreign country. Still, a glimmer of hope refused to die out.

A hand gripped my shoulder and I jumped. I turned to see Brother Chitakhutto. I immediately offered the customary *wai* gesture of respect. "Pho," I said, using the affectionate word for "father."

Of all the temple monks, he was my favorite. We were not supposed to show partiality, but I couldn't help myself. Chitakhutto was forty years my senior, and had joined the monkhood when he was fourteen. His left leg had been crippled thanks to a bout of childhood polio shortly after he had lost both parents. He had lived as a street urchin for a few years before entering the monkhood. He was scrupulously learned in the sutras and in advanced meditation techniques, yet he often acted like a wondrous child, always eager to laugh or tell a joke. He sometimes joined the boys at kicking the soccer ball.

He was my mentor, had taken me under his wing and taught me how to meditate.

He regarded me with warm eyes. "Young Brother, you are uneasy tonight. Is it the storm?"

It was customary for novices to make confessions to an elder monk, a practice I had use often with Brother Chitakhutto since coming here. I inhaled deeply, mustering my courage. "Pho, I'm feeling betrayed this night."

He glanced toward the dining hall, and then his eyes found mine again. "It is foolish to cling to things of the material world, even when those things are people. It impedes the goal of attaining Nirvana. If you wish to travel fast and far down this path to enlightenment, you must travel light. Discard all your envy, jealousy, unforgiveness, selfishness, and fear."

I bit my lower lip. My aspirations had nothing to do with enlightenment.

"Perhaps you should meditate on why you feel betrayed, why you demand someone love you exclusively when the sutras command us to love everyone equally?"

"Pho, I shall do as you say." I bowed in the *wai* gesture, and he returned it.

He patted my shoulder, and there was true warmth in his touch. As often happened in his presence, I felt he was seeing into my heart, perceived every nuance of my being, and even though there was much to dislike there, he still saw only the worthy.

As he hobbled down the long hallway checking other rooms, candle held high, I watched his hips go up and down in that strange gait, one leg shorter than the other, one leg strong with overdeveloped muscles and the other skinny and weak. For some reason, it made me think of Darren and myself, one strong and one weak. Together we formed a complete person, yet both wounded in our own ways.

Could I give up Darren? I had been working on giving up my attachments, or more accurately, learning how not to be attached, since coming here. But losing Darren was not in my game plan. Perhaps someday when I was close to perfect understanding, no longer ensnared by desires, floating in Nirvana with no need for earthly pleasures, but that wasn't going to happen tonight, and probably not in this lifetime or the next.

I glanced at the sky again. Another few minutes and the next wave of the storm would sweep over the town. Glancing back at the dining hall, the candle at Darren's table went dark. Through the dim, I saw them step further back into the shadows, no doubt so Darren could hold Noy, united for the first time, their happiness intensified by the suffering they created in my soul.

More waiting. My impatience for them to reappear grew so intense it reached its climax, and at last calm set in. I imagined Darren's hands moving over Noy's tawny skin while his erection found the warmth it craved. It was done now, I knew, forever.

Moments later, the next wave of rain doused the town. My chest seemed to implode, and within its bloody confines, there was no longer any room for love. I continued to thirst for it, but I remained unfulfilled. Flashes of lightning kept illuminating the shape of their desire. They were still there, folded into each other's bodies, mouth pressed to mouth. Noy was devouring him.

Those same flashes also lit up the irregular shape in the tree, the killer, Somchai. Was he truly a calculating murderer, or simply a victim of uncontrollable rage at the American's duplicity?

The wind grew stronger, swept into the room and over my sleeping Archer. The lamp blew out. The temple, the entire town, stood dark and asleep. Even the whistles had fallen silent. Only the howl of the wind and the rain pounding the earth could be heard now. The air smelled of rain, that ineffable, lifeless scent. That odor was everywhere, in the streets, in the temple grounds, and no doubt in the kitchens and the bathrooms. There was no getting away from it. For me, it became the fragrance of their passion.

The dawn was hours away with nothing to do but wait. I needed a drink. The downpour lasted longer than all the others. It kept coming with force, hammering the roof, echoing horribly throughout the barracks. It was a wonder anyone could sleep.

"We waited in the dining hall for you," Darren said.

I turned toward the door as they entered the room. Darren relit the oil lamp. In the light, I saw that Noy held two large bottles, one beer, the other Thai whiskey. Both men seemed like huge shadows.

"We thought you would come back," Darren said. He held out a cup, and Noy poured two fingers of whiskey into it.

"I stayed here in case the storm woke Archer."

Darren smiled as he passed me the cup. He walked to the balcony and leaned against the door frame, staring out at the wind-driven rain. Noy set the bottles on the nightstand and followed him. I took a hot swallow and felt that glorious burn warming my throat.

"Hopefully it will end by daybreak," Darren said.

Even if I had not seen it, I would have known from his voice—trembling, almost apologetic, affected by his desire for Noy. I had no doubt now; their love had been fulfilled. I was foolish to have hoped otherwise.

Noy turned his head and gave me a small, lopsided smile. He looked radiant; his eyes glowing like a new bride; the youthfulness of his skin showed clearly as it stretched over the clean lines of trim muscles. I knocked back the rest of my drink and poured a full cup of beer.

A whistle rang out on the street. *Are they still searching for Somchai?* I glanced past Darren to the shadow in the Bodhi tree. *Should I tell?* We all waited for a second whistle but it never came.

Darren yawned, and I knew then these two would soon lie on the sleeping mats, next to each other, separated while torn and tortured by yearning. But just now, both were smiling, equally guilty, anxious and happy.

"You should have come back to the dining hall," Noy said. "We waited for you."

Gloating. The little bitch was gloating. He was looking at the future, the days to come when he would have Darren to himself. I glanced at Darren, whose hands now dangled at his side, hands that had caressed my body for many long years. Now Noy had stepped into the misfortune that radiated from those fingers. So be it.

"I'm going to sleep," Noy said, and he removed his robes and wrapped himself in a blanket, stretching out on the mat below the oil lamp. Darren watched him, but he did not move.

Noy lifted his head to stare at Darren. "Aren't you sleepy?"

Darren stumbled to the chest, removed his robes, and pulled a brown blanket over his shoulders. He lay on the mat, but on the other side of Archer. Disappointment marred Noy's face.

I turned my back to them to study the Bodhi tree. *Could Somchai still be there? Yes.*

"Good night, Reece," Noy said.

"Sleep tight, bitch," I mumbled to myself.

Darren lit a cigarette. I heard his regular breathing as I sipped my beer and inhaled the smell of the rain, waiting for the dawn. I kept watching the shadow in the tree, thinking that at daybreak Somchai would be caught, perhaps even be killed.

A gust of wind blew out the oil lamp, again. In a soft voice, Darren asked me if I wanted him to relight it.

"No. I like it like this."

"I like it too," Noy said.

I turned to see the red glow of Darren's cigarette, and I wondered if he was feeling the least bit embarrassed. Now that we were all together—husband, son, lover—was he becoming gloomy for fear that I knew? Now that he had satisfied himself, was he dreading what would come next, and what he would lose? Or was he disturbed at the thoughts of my new loneliness, tonight, compared to what I had felt before?

The shower let up. A last cloudburst fell on Somchai, and I

could hear the police in the streets, talking while sloshing through the puddles. The barracks grew quiet. I wanted to tell Darren that as crazy as it sounded, Somchai was a dozen yards away, clinging to a tree, and with the daybreak he would surely be caught. But I said nothing. I began to wish the night would last forever because I wanted Somchai to slip away.

I walked to the nightstand and lit a cigarette.

"You remember," Darren whispered, "Rome?"

"Yes."

He reached out for me but I moved away, gliding back to the balcony. I recalled Rome perfectly, how could I not? It was a time of glorious lovemaking, and also of deceit. It had rained there too. I remembered the earthy smells of those wet city streets, endless, the scent of tears, and under that hid the odor of wet, ripened wheat. I could smell it so intensely, even now. The monastery was bathed in it. Could Somchai smell it as well? What did he smell? What did he feel in those moments before he shot the American who betrayed him?

I finished my cigarette on the balcony. Noy slept soundly, but then he moaned, and I knew he was dreaming of hands caressing his skin, of a cock splitting him in two. I waited to hear more but it was over. Noy turned over and fell silent.

"Why did you mention Rome?" I asked.

"You know I love you."

"Yes, I believe you do," I said.

"Rome was the last time I knew for sure that you still loved me."

Is that what this thing with Noy is, a test? And what will be the outcome? Will I pass? Do I want to pass?

I leaned against the door frame and stared at the Bodhi tree. It seemed so much brighter than moments ago. *What is happening to the air? Is this really the end of the storm?* Water still poured from the rooftops, and I could see the distant flashes of lightning and hear the faint echo of thunder.

"Come to bed, Reece. Try to sleep."

I can do it. I can lie with him, even make love before the dawn breaks, then at sunrise, we can pack up Archer and leave this place, just the three of us. My memory of Noy would grow dim over the next year to the point where I would seldom see them pressed together, consuming each other.

Noy moaned again, no doubt still dreaming of Darren's mouth locked to his.

I slid into the room and crept to Darren's side. "Somchai is outside," I whispered, "in the tree." Darren didn't hear. He had fallen asleep as suddenly as a child. He had always been like that.

I crept back to the balcony. With everyone asleep I felt a mixture of loneliness, freedom, and of being abandoned. But outside, clinging to a branch, Somchai was still there, still with me. We, together, would face the night and await the dawn. I could see him more clearly now that the storm had moved on. Sodden and shivering, he waited for the rosy light to appear in the east, which would bring his death.

❖

The sky rose above the town, but on the mountain slopes it seemed flush with the rice paddies. I thought it was the end of the storm. The lightning had moved far off and the thunder had grown weak. In three hours the sun would arrive, albeit a veiled dawn, and a bad time for Somchai.

There was no longer any sign of the policemen roaming the streets. They were, no doubt, guarding all the town exits, waiting for the daylight to continue their search.

Everyone in the temple compound was asleep, everyone but me. I had dozed for a time, but the need for another drink had pulled me from unconsciousness like a fish on a line. I had polished off all the beer, but still had a half bottle of whiskey. My desire to drink, to stay drunk, was strong, even though I grew to dislike the burn in my throat. But each hour of the long night pushed me further into the weariness of this next, unavoidable day. The anticipation of it coming made my arms and legs feel like lead weights. I would have to face Darren, and perhaps with the light, his appreciation for me, for our family, would brighten and he would turn away from Noy. Perhaps.

I lit another cigarette and walked onto the balcony again. I took a hot slug, feeling the fire in my raw throat. I stayed there, even as more rain shrouded the town. It soaked my skin but I was beyond feeling the cold.

The Bodhi tree was being drenched, as was the dark shape that clung to the branches like a malignant growth. It hadn't moved all night. It was the same shape, the same size it had been at nine o'clock, in that first flash of lightning. The rains stopped after several minutes, but the shape was still wrapped in darkness. I stared at it for a long time, until I began to doubt that it was human. Perhaps it was a growth or a large hornet's nest. Yet, when the lightning had lit up the sky, I had momentarily seen the shape of a man.

"Somchai," I called out. The possibility that he might answer made my pulse pound at my temples. "Hey, I know you're there," I said, slightly louder as I gestured toward the tree.

Nothing moved. Why did I think this shape was really a man? I had only gotten instantaneous glances. I had not seen his eyes, or any other part of him that would confirm my suspicions. It was possible, I knew, and with that possibility a thin thread formed between us, that shape and me. If it was indeed a man, then it had to be Somchai. Who else would sit in a tree through a lightning storm? Yes, wasn't the proof right there in front of me, only a dozen yards away? The proof was urgent. Real. Or had I simply invented him clinging to that trunk because of my own world collapsing?

I took another swallow. The burn in my throat made my voice sound funny when I said, "Hey, Somchai, answer me."

It continued to drizzle on him, and on me. The shape didn't move. It was waiting for the pale red of daybreak.

Why does he stay there? Does he want to die? I leaned against the iron railing of the balcony. I felt the metal beating, but soon realized it was my pulse, my heart growing stronger as hope grew thin, became minute, vanished. I would know with first light, but it would be too late.

"Answer me, Somchai, I'm begging you."

Nothing. It probably was not a man. The only thing I was sure of was that I wanted it to be him, the murderer.

The drizzle stopped altogether. The clouds to the west parted and the moon appeared, pouring bushels of light over the town. Within the Bodhi tree, nothing moved, but with the light I could see more clearly. It had sharp angles, long and supple enough to be human, with a round nub at its top—a small head poised above a body. It was a man. Did he plan to surrender at dawn? Or wait for the army snipers to pick him from the tree?

"Somchai, I want to help you."

I leaned out over the balcony and began to softly sing, "We are family..." Being a gay man, even a Thai gay man, he would know that song. He would identify. He would have danced to it at the boy clubs by the university.

I stopped singing and waited. Still nothing. The sky was clearing fast now. The storm had moved on and the dawn would be pale and beautiful.

"Somchai, I have whiskey. It will warm you." I lifted the bottle and took a hot swallow. My throat was still raw but I hardly noticed the burn this time. "Let me help you." Even as I said the words, I had no idea what I could possibly do. The words meant nothing to me or to him. They were only an attempt to ease this beastly pain surging through my veins.

In the room behind me, Noy whimpered, rolled over and fell quiet.

Two trucks charged up the street and screeched to a halt outside the front gate. Army men—no doubt reinforcements—poured from the rear of both. They formed into small patrols and moved off in different directions. Their boots sounded loud on the still wet pavement and beams from their flashlights pierced the darkness.

A jolt of anger rushed from my gut and I shouted, "You're an idiot, they'll kill you."

A lamp kindled in the window of one of the senior monk's houses. An old monk tottered on to his porch, scanned the area, and then retired inside. The window went dark.

I would not call to him again, damn it, even though the anger still boiled in my chest. If I had a rifle I would have shot him out of that tree myself, just so it would be over. I couldn't stand the waiting, but it seemed I must, letting the seconds tick by like months, for Somchai's death.

I stepped back into our bedroom. I could see them clearly, Darren and Noy, sleeping on either side of Archer. That cruel separation. That barrier to fulfilling their love. I could almost feel sorry for them, but what I felt was admiration for their patience. For them the passing seconds brought them closer to fulfillment, so they had something to hold on to, to anticipate. Perhaps they were more in love with the anticipation than anything else? Perhaps this temporary obstacle—me and Archer—was making their love grow stronger.

I took another swallow and moved back to the balcony. The storm had dissolved, little by little, and now stars spread across the sky, stars so bright they could make you cry.

I opened my mouth to call to Somchai one more time, but I couldn't. Time was getting old, buried. I would not try again, but I would lean over that railing until first light, to share his vigil. I would not abandon him in his last hour. I realized what I waited for was a signal from him to acknowledge me, as a last act of kindness on his part. I offered him a chance to pull back from absolute despair and remember for a few fleeting moments what it means to be human, to share in this thing we call humanity, to experience the ordinary reasons for living, to share yourself with someone else. I would keep offering this until the end. Even if he wanted to die, even if he demanded this particular fate, he could still share himself with me, to be human one last time.

A patrol of soldiers trooped by outside the walls. They seemed in high spirits, talkative, laughing, anticipating the approaching day's capture, and perhaps killing.

I stared at that dark shroud in the tree, and saw something white turn toward me. A hand? No, a face! He now stared back at me. He had finally acknowledged me, and I fell prey to a sudden joy. The waiting had finally burst open; the tension I felt in my shoulders released. I lifted a hand and waved. Within the tree's shadow, a hand slowly lifted and made a similar gesture.

As our arms fell to our sides, a warm wind blew through the compound. I glanced at the horizon. The coming day would be warm and bright. The night, however, would cling to its darkness for another hour or so, and within that span of minutes, I had to find a solution to this problem of conscience.

I raised my hand, again. He answered, again. I gave him a signal to wait there. His head emerged from the shadows and he nodded. There were a dozen yards between us with only the moon to illuminate the thread of understanding that linked our souls. Did he understand? Yes, he knew that I wanted to help. "I'm coming to you," I said very softly.

I entered my room, snatched up the whiskey in one hand and the cigarettes and lighter in the other. They were all asleep. I moved soundlessly. Archer slept on his back, and he wore a smile. He must be caught in a blissful dream, I thought. Noy and Darren both slept on their sides, facing one another with the boy between them. I could feel their sexual need pulling them closer together even in slumber. The door creaked as I opened it to slip into the corridor. Darren stirred, grumbled something unintelligible, and settled back into stillness.

I hurried down the hallway, but slowed my pace to descend the three flights of dark stairs. The steps were made of wood, and groaned under my weight. The doors to the barracks were wide open, which I found strange with a murderer on the loose, but then it had been a crime of passion, a one-time act of violence by a man temporarily driven mad. There was no need to lock the doors.

I stepped onto the compound. The soft ground was cold and wet on my bare feet. A patrol entered the front gate, making a swing through the area. I pulled back into the shadows. I watched them carefully. They checked the grounds, but their heads never looked up at the trees. The idea must not have occurred to them. As they passed me I heard one of them grumbling, and I imagined he was complaining that they weren't paid enough to be on duty at this hour. They were so caught up in conversation they didn't notice me. I waited until they had made their search and marched back out to the street, the entire time the cold seeping up my legs.

I hurried to the Bodhi tree and began to climb. It was difficult because I still held the cigarettes and whiskey bottle, but I soon pulled myself level with Somchai. There seemed to be a peacefulness to the temples from our vantage point. I felt like a bird, perhaps an owl, perched high on a branch, watching the world wag on below, and not caring what happened.

I lifted the bottle, and he snatched it from my grasp, taking long, enormous gulps. For courage? He passed it back and I swallowed a mouthful. It burned so much that I had to close my eyes with pleasure. With that warm feeling, came a wave of clarity, a plan of how to get Somchai from harm's way and free of the town.

My eyes pooled with water, brimming, and I felt grateful for the darkness so that he could not see the emotion boiling in my head. I could hide my sadness and fear from him; if only I could do that for myself. I was terrified, and told myself that if I did this thing, there would be no going back. I would become a criminal, a beast roaming outside the law in an alien country, but at least I would be free of my current prison. I had successfully kept myself in ignorance for God knows how long, and now that I saw the situation clearly, what was there to do? And because of this sudden, invisible bond that I now felt with Somchai, this path seemed as good as any.

I lit a smoke and passed it to him. As he took a drag, I leaned toward him, my face so close to his we could almost kiss, and I whispered, "There is not much time. The temple comes awake in a few minutes. I can sneak you out of here and get you by the police, but first we must shave your head."

Understanding blossomed on his face. He took another long slug of whiskey, finishing the bottle.

We scrambled down, but before reaching the ground he slipped and fell. A branch had broken under his weight and had made a shattering noise. Somchai's groan when he landed was an even louder, obscene racket.

A window lit up with candlelight. Someone shouted. A whistle shrieked on the other side of the wall.

I pulled Somchai to his feet, checked for broken limbs, and led him to the washroom. His legs, stiff after a long night braced in a tree, were clumsy and I had to support him. He stayed hidden while I raced to my room to get a bar of soap, razor, and my extra robes. Each monk is allowed two sets of robes, and I intended to sacrifice half of all I owned for Somchai's freedom.

❖

The monastery's gong rang at four o'clock. The temple dogs howled before the ringing stopped, as if they had been waiting for the chance to use their voices.

The day began.

I finished tightening my sarong around Somchai's waist. His shaved head glistened but his dark eyes seemed lifeless, which made me wonder if he was suffering from shock. After what he had done, who could blame him? On the other hand, it could have been the whiskey, which most Thai people never drink.

I showed him how to fold the upper robe, which was basically an orange sheet, and properly wrap it over his left shoulder and around the strong, beautiful lines of his torso, leaving his long neck and right shoulder exposed. Dressing in the first few days here had been a nightmare for me, and my robes had often fallen off my shoulder or from my hips, leaving me, literally, exposed to ridicule by the other monks. But I had gotten the hang of it. By the time the first monk came into the washroom, I had us both looking like properly dressed monks.

In the lamplight, I could now see that he was about twenty, and handsome. More pleasing than most of the bar-boys I had seen roaming the town. He would fit in seamlessly with the other young monastics.

Monks began filling the large communal bath, standing in rows before the earthen jars. Ladling rainwater with wooden bowls, they splashed their shoulders and shaved heads, and gave their bodies a good scrubbing.

Realizing this might be the last time I would partake in this cleansing ritual, I found that I had grown to love these men, even the cantankerous, unhinged ones. They had become my family. There were times, during moments of weakness, when I played with the idea of not leaving them, of staying on and making this my life. I imagined Archer and I living out our days among them, truly becoming one of them. Of course, that was a romantic whim, not a practical life solution.

While the others prepared for the morning chant, I led Somchai to the temple to pay homage to the Buddha. We fell to our knees and bent forward, pressing our foreheads to the floor three times. This humble ritual, for me, represented paying reverence to the Buddha spirit that resides in all beings and binds us together. I bowed my head to the virtuousness in all, and gave thanks that there was still a spark of it within me, and within Somchai. Yes, that morning I was more grateful than I could have imagined, given how much I'd lost the previous night.

Part of that feeling stemmed from the fact that I was caught in this new adventure with a criminal, which felt like I was fleeing the life I had known to this point, that safe life. I remembered what it was like to sleep with Darren, making love, whispering the words that only lovers could bring themselves to express. Those images tormented me, stirring up lust and desire while I knelt before a Buddha shrine. That desire, for the first time, somehow began to focus on Somchai. My mind offered up endless fantasies about what it would be like caress his curves, nuzzle into his softness, and experience the pleasure of his touch.

As exciting as those images were, reality, I knew, would likely be much different.

We were soon joined by the other monks, including Darren, Noy, and Archer. Somchai sat beside me during the morning chant, and not one person seemed to notice there was a stranger among us. My hopes rose. If the monks could not detect an impostor, then surely we would be able to slip by the police as well.

I soon became absorbed by the chanting; my mind freed itself of all thought, following along with the Pali words. After, we sat in meditation, and I enjoyed the ritual for what I've always loved about it—calm, soothing, quieting.

When the meditation ended we lined up with the other monks and ambled out the front gate on our morning alms rounds. They all paired in twos and threes, going their own route, which did not overlap with any others. Archer stepped to my side and offered me a shy smile. We had always walked together on our morning rounds, me holding my begging bowl and him carrying a red plastic bucket that held the overflow from my bowl whenever we had a particularly good haul.

I say begging bowl, but in truth, no monk was allowed to beg. On the contrary, we presented ourselves to the town's lay people, inviting them the opportunity to earn merit by giving us food and the necessities of life—soap, toothpaste, candles, even coins. Townsfolk stood in front of their homes and businesses in the predawn, waiting to exchange offerings for our blessings.

I told Archer to make his rounds with Darren and Noy this morning, that I would be showing this new monk the ropes. He shot me a look that felt like a slap. His child's intuition saw right through my lie.

I gripped his narrow shoulder and gave him a loving shake. "Please, son. Just this once. It's important."

He dropped his head and ran after Darren, who was already halfway down the block.

Somchai trailed me and we both kept our eyes down, walking barefoot, and without talking. We followed my usual route, three blocks along Ratchadamnoen Road and then we turned onto a *soi*, or alley, with numerous shop houses and parked cars and motorbikes crowding the side of the pavement. The street was lined with the Buddhist faithful, mostly women with their children, who stood waiting for us.

I stopped before the first believer. She offered a *wai* of respect and asked if she might be allowed to give me food. She dropped two rice balls into my bowl, being careful not to touch me. I offered her the customary blessing, and moved on. The process repeated itself as we worked our way toward the Chang Phuak city gate.

Somchai had spent a hungry night in a tree, and now he snatched food from my bowl and wolfed it down.

A motorcycle screeched to a halt beside me. The driver, a bar-boy no doubt returning home from a night with a client, tossed a wad of cash in my bowl and asked for a special blessing. We both knelt in the street while I offered atonement, then he jumped on his bike and sped away.

A few minutes later an army patrol came marching down the *soi*. I stopped before a lady offering alms. The soldiers must have thought it strange that only one monk offered a begging bowl because they slowed and looked us over carefully as they passed. They stopped further down the road, under an open window, and called Somchai's name. I froze, fear gnawing my gut. But they went on to the end of the *soi* and turned onto the street.

It took more than an hour to make our way to the city gate, and the coming dawn had lightened the sky. Army vehicles crowded the road crossing the moat and a dozen men were checking each car coming out of the old city. We kept our shaved heads bowed and walked a tranquil pace between the vehicles. My fear disappeared, leaving only a fresh, flowering memory of what it had been. The army men moved aside, offering a clear path to freedom, and they each gave a *wai* of respect as we sauntered past.

But then an officer stopped us, shining a flashlight beam into each of our faces. "Who are you and where are you going?"

For a moment, I didn't know if my voice would work properly. But I remained calm, telling him we were brothers at Wat Phra Singh and were on an errand for the abbot. Did he believe me? He studied me judiciously, but had no reason not to believe. I asked him what was going on, and he waved us by, telling me he had no time to explain.

Once we were free of the army, I hailed a tuk-tuk on Mani Noppharat Road, which took us east to the Waroroot Market at the banks of the Mae Ping River.

We zipped along the main road, the wind in my face, cooling the fire burning in me. The dawn was almost upon us, and the sky was light enough that I saw the contours of Somchai's face clearly, and what I saw frightened me. His face had fine, beautiful lines but his eyes, dark and comatose, held no expression at all. His face looked blurred in the morning's blue light.

The driver cut down some alleys and we emerged at the town's largest covered market, four square blocks. Even at that hour, the streets were jammed with people and carts unloading everything imaginable— whole hog carcasses, bundles of flowers, sweaty earthen jars holding slithering eels, dried insects, ducks and chickens and frogs and dogs waiting for the butcher's knife. The place hummed with activity.

I paid the driver with coins the faithful had dropped in my bowl that morning, and jostled our way between the stalls, literally pulling Somchai along in my wake. No one gave us more than a glance. We pushed past the flower market and crossed the road to the banks of the river. There was a footbridge that crossed the water, and below it was a stretch of riverbank with a half dozen boats crowding the muddy shore. The river was swollen from the storm so there was not much bank, but there was enough to hide Somchai for the time I needed.

The surface of the river was smooth, but the current ran swift. It gave me a chill staring at that brown mass. I saw shapes drifting along, raped by the swirling current.

We dropped down onto the sodden clay, and our feet sunk into the mud. I pulled a pack of cigarettes from my shoulder bag and he pounced on them. I lit one for him. His hands trembled so violently that he had to hold the cigarette with both hands so as not to let it fall.

He would not look into my eyes, but I studied him for a long time. "Damaged" was the word that came to mind, severe emotional impairment, which I suppose was no surprise. Who wouldn't be?

He looked up and down the river, and for the first time he spoke. "Where you take me?" he said in passable English.

"We'll steal a boat and get you downriver, then make our way to Bangkok. You'll be safe there. No one will find us."

He didn't say anything more. Neither did I while I guided him into one of the boats and lit two more cigarettes, passing one to him. As the sun peeked over the horizon, we sat smoking in silence until we finished our cigarettes. His expression remained vacant, reduced to his concentration on smoking.

"Is there some place you'd rather go?" I asked.

He didn't answer immediately. He looked at me as if from very far away, without caring. "It no matter," he mumbled. "I already dead."

A haggard expression came over his face, but in his eyes there was nothing. He held no emotion, and had no strength left for anything beyond smoking. Why had he come with me? Why didn't he give himself up after the shooting? Did he do it for me, one last gesture of human compassion to help me through a difficult night? Was I saving him or was he saving me? I became confused. My head began to throb. I wanted to devour his injured spirit, to somehow restore this black flower that had bloomed in the night within my heart. I suddenly felt an immense love for him.

As a pale light blew over the river, Somchai leaned his head against the smooth wooden bow and closed his eyes. His mouth dropped open and I could tell he was already asleep. I watched him as he dozed, thinking he would sleep for as long as I needed to get back to the monastery to retrieve my regular clothes, money, and Archer. I couldn't leave Archer. The round trip could take as much as an hour, but surely Somchai would sleep that long without stirring. He was done in, spent. I felt the weight of my own exhaustion, and wanted nothing more than to curl into his sleeping body and feel his warmth as I dozed off myself. But there was work to do.

As I gathered my strength to leave him, I noticed his slightly open mouth form a quivering smile, an unmistakable expression of joy. He was dreaming, and those visions had lifted him over his troubles on feathered wings. I could see it clearly now, the spark of life thriving within his unconsciousness. There was hope for him, for us.

My fatigue vanished, replaced by this slender thread of optimism.

I watched the dawn move over him, little by little. When the sun was full up, the vivid light had covered his entire body, warming us both. He looked beautiful wrapped in my robes, and yet I wanted more than anything to see him naked, to caress his amber skin with my fingertips and with my tongue. The sky took on more color, changing the hue of his skin, making him even more alluring. I glanced up at the golden horizon, greeting the day that was rising on my new love.

A pack of boys tromping over the footbridge above our heads reminded me that I still had work to do, much as I wanted to curl up beside Somchai.

I took a last look at his peaceful face. His eyelids trembled, yet they remained sealed in sleep. He no longer smiled.

After I had climbed to the top of the bank, I heard a soft cry, a long moan coming from the boat. I turned to find him sitting up straight, but not looking at anything. I could tell from his expression that he was remembering everything.

"I need to return to the temple," I said barely loud enough for him to catch. He gave no indication of hearing me. He was still caught up in the horror of remembering the last twenty-four hours.

"I have a child," I said in a louder voice. "I need to get him. I'll be back within the hour. I promise."

He glanced up at me with heartbreaking eyes—heartbreaking because there was nothing behind them, a void.

"Rest here." I gestured with my hands that he should stay put, as if he were a pet dog.

He nodded and shifted his body so that his left arm flopped over the side of the boat. His fingers caressed the water, making little ripples in the current. The sun hammered him now, casting his perfectly black shadow over the surface of the river.

❖

By the time I got back to Wat Phra Singh the morning air was already warm. I knew that it would grow hotter in the next few hours and stay that way the rest of the day. With the sun on my scalp my head throbbed with an almost lethal combination of fatigue and hangover. Each time I felt I could no longer fight off sleep, the memory of Somchai waiting at the river got me moving again.

The police were still searching the town. The ones I saw looked discouraged. Their uniforms were crumpled and muddy, and they moved as wearily as I did.

There was nobody in my room. The balcony door stood open and sunshine bled obliquely into the austere interior. It shown on the red, glaring floor tiles, and was reflected onto the walls.

I began to feel quite nauseous, but I fought it down. I hurried to the cabinet where we kept our street clothes and changed into jeans, T-shirt, and sandals. I snatched up a few personal items and the box where we hid our money, and stuffed them into my shoulder bag.

"Reece?"

I spun around to find Darren at the doorway.

"Where have you been?" he asked.

"Where's Archer?"

"He's in morning class. What's going on?"

For a moment, I thought he had said "mourning class." I felt bile rising to the back of my throat again, and I swallowed it down. "Can you bring him to me?"

Darren stepped closer. He took my hand in his. "Is this about Noy? I've already asked him to move to a different room."

I glanced down and noticed for the first time that Noy's sleeping mat and chest were missing.

Darren squeezed my hand and looked at me insistently. "Nothing happened. I only kissed him. I couldn't go through with it."

I pulled my hand away, my mind swirling in a chaotic fog. I pressed my hands to the side of my head. The pain. The throbbing became overwhelming.

"It's too late," I mumbled. "I have to leave and I need to take Archer with me. Please bring him here."

"Nothing happened!" he shouted.

"Just do as I asked!" I shouted back, and I thought my head would implode. The pain grew monstrous. All I could think about was getting away from there. Had I found a graceful way to back out of my decision, I might have curled into Darren's arms and cried away the pain. But whenever confronted with a fight-or-flight situation, I had always chosen flight. It had forever been my strongest survival mechanism. And besides, Somchai needed me.

Darren gripped my arm and pulled me to him. My hands moved to his face, caressing those contours that had once been so beautiful to me. He was lovely still, but less so. The way I moved my hands over his skin—with little feeling and without caution—broadcast that I would not be swayed, and I saw in his eyes that he had accepted defeat, perhaps forever.

"If you could only drink less," he said, giving a last feeble attempt, "we could make this work."

When I didn't answer, he released me and went to retrieve Archer.

A few minutes later, they strolled into the room, and Noy was with them. He glared at me, his eyes burning with triumph. His desire for Darren had grown even stronger. It followed him into the room like a shadow. It seemed as though he was shouting at me when he asked, "Where did you go this morning?"

I ignored him, telling Archer to change into street clothes. I had already packed all his belongings into my shoulder bag. He looked confused, taking the news like a blow to the gut. Children need to see things coming from a long way off. They don't deal well with abrupt changes. He dropped his head, pulled off his upper robe, and reached for his T-shirt.

I wanted desperately to hug him and tell him how sorry I was, but Darren pulled me into his arms again. "Reece, Reece," he begged, "at least tell me why."

He held me at arm's length to stare into my soul. He must have slept well during the night because the rings that had been under his blue eyes for the past week had vanished.

I assumed that Somchai was now sleeping in the boat, but he would wake soon. I wanted to be there when he did so that he wouldn't think I had abandoned him. Yet, I believed Darren when he said that nothing had happened, so even though I couldn't turn back now, I felt he deserved an explanation.

"Last night, while you were sleeping, I found Somchai, the man the police are searching for."

"You were drunk," Noy spat.

Darren's face grew serious, and I could tell he wanted to hear more.

While Archer changed, I told the story of last night, of Somchai in the Bodhi tree, of me sneaking him beyond the patrols dressed as a monk, and my intention to drift down river and smuggle Somchai as far as Bangkok. Once I had started, it all poured out in one, calm and continuous stream. When my words came to rest, Darren ripped off his robes and grabbed his jeans. He intended to come with us, and for Archer's sake I would not put up a fight.

"Darren," I said, not knowing how to continue, what to say.

"There's no choice," he said. "You've placed us in a situation where we have no choice."

"I didn't mean to ruin your vacation," I said, stupidly.

Noy rushed from the room and down the corridor. I knew then he would take my story to the police as a way to keep Darren here at the temple. I gathered up Archer and rushed out to the street. Darren came running after us and we all jumped into the first tuk-tuk parked outside the temple gate.

While we raced through the streets toward the Waroroot Market, Darren held my hand and Archer sat between us, squealing as we dodged through heavy traffic. Darren sat with his back straight, but he looked much less majestic in street clothes. The wind in my face burned my eyes and made them tear; two streams flowed down my cheeks.

I kept asking myself: What have I done? But no answer came back from the void that I had sunk into. It was all such a colossal fuckup. The only thing I knew for sure was that I needed to get back to Somchai before he woke.

I glanced over at Darren and realized that he had been shouting at me but I had not heard a word over the noise of the tuk-tuk. I leaned closer, pressing into Archer.

"*I love you, dammit!*" he shouted again.

I felt the urge to yell back that it was too late, but I couldn't. Darren, Darren, forgive me. I truly didn't know what to do.

I heard a siren shrieking over the tuk-tuk's roar, and I knew the police were racing to the river. That fucking Noy!

My exhaustion, that felt as heavy as a planet, fell away as a surge of adrenaline shot through my veins.

Our tuk-tuk slowed to a crawl at the edge of the market, caught in tangled traffic. I leaped from my seat and ran, weaving between stalled trucks and motorbikes, pushing women and old men out of my way. I could hear Darren and Archer's footsteps right behind me. I reached the river, gasping for breath, and stared down the bank at the line of boats.

They were all empty.

Darren and Archer ran up and stopped beside me. I pointed at a boat and gasped, "I left him there."

"He couldn't have gone far," Darren said. He turned to scan the crowded market.

I was certain, however, that Somchai was not among the shoppers. Voices murmured from the flower stalls and the drone of traffic grew louder. I looked up at the footbridge to see a small-headed man holding a fishing pole out over the water. He wore yam-colored shorts and nothing else on this hot morning. Even from this distance I could count the ribs on his gaunt frame. He stared at me and nodded, and I felt a chill at the base of my neck. Then he glanced back at the brown water again. How fortunate he is, I thought, to be doing something as simple as waiting for a fish to bite. Sooner or later he would catch his dinner. I, on the other hand, was a failure. I was no longer a monk or a husband or a father or savior to a lost boy. I had failed everyone. And now a voice beyond the range of my vision was telling me that if I had chosen a simpler path, some other place to vacation, some other circumstance, like fishing from a bridge, then perhaps I could have been a success.

I called out, "Somchai." My voice echoed back from the far bank.

I clambered down the embankment until my legs were ankle-deep in water. Clay oozed between my toes. The water was cold, but not unbearably so. I searched the river for a boat, thinking perhaps he was already floating down river. Nothing. I methodically scanned the far bank, thinking he might have crossed to the other side. Still nothing.

Suddenly the hot, humid air was suffocating.

I felt immensely sorry for them all, these men I loved—Somchai, Darren, Archer. And feeling this sorrow my eyes cast downstream to the bridge that stood a quarter mile away. Under the rumble of cars and trucks, and flowing just below the surface of the river, I noticed a smudge of orange. At first I thought it might be a trick of the morning light reflecting off the water, but no, it was unmistakable. I waded awkwardly out into the river until the cold touched my crotch. The river bottom was mucky, and I sank into it.

The yellow surface of the river (more yellow than brown when seen looking into the sun) showed those swirling orange robes an inch below the surface, no doubt caught on the bridge piling. Here, then, was a moment of pure awareness, a man wearing only shorts fishing from a footbridge and the smudge of orange under the surface of the opaque water. The entire universe stopped cold, seemingly holding its breath. Could this have been my moment of supreme understanding, my enlightenment? If so, they could keep it.

I stumbled forward, thrashing the water with my arms, only to feel myself yanked back. Darren had a hold of me. He had come after me, pulling me toward shore. I fought him with all my remaining strength but it was no use.

"He killed himself," I said, to no one in particular.

"Yes, I saw. Let's not talk about it now."

We stayed in the water, sinking into the muck, facing each other. We were both waiting for the other to say a word that would serve as a conclusion, a word that did not come. After a minute he hauled me onto the bank.

The police arrived, with Noy leading them. A policeman shouted something in Thai. When we didn't respond, he shouted in English. "Where is Somchai?"

Two dozen people had crossed the road from the market and gathered around the police. They were all staring down at us. Others were rushing to join them. Somchai's name must have sped from mouth to mouth in the marketplace. They were glaring, serious, and the police were the most serious of all.

I leaned into Darren for strength. "Everyone's staring," I whispered, becoming afraid.

"We don't know what you're talking about," Darren shot back. "We're only here for a morning swim."

Someone in the crowd translated. Every face in the throng changed; they began to laugh. They made funny faces and pointed at us, howling with amusement. "Fucking Americans," one policeman barked. The crowd began to disperse. I held on to Darren, still not sure if I would be arrested or taken to an asylum.

The officer in charge turned to Noy and spat a harsh sentence in Thai.

"He's lying," Noy said. "They must be hiding him."

The officer spoke again, so cruel and so fast it sounded like a long burst from a machine gun. He waved his arms and walked away in obvious disgust.

"I'm sorry," Darren said.

I didn't know if he was apologizing for kissing Noy, or because Somchai had died, or for making me a laughingstock. I didn't care. "We could have had a good life. I might have loved him."

Archer stepped down the bank, throwing his arms around us both. He was crying.

"Yes, perhaps a very good life," Darren said.

"What will happen to him?"

Darren shrugged. "They'll find him eventually. In the meantime, let's get back to the temple and get you cleaned up."

"Then it's over?" I asked, not altogether sure what "it" I was referring to.

He closed his eyes to squints, and glanced up the bank to see Noy better. Noy stood there, alone. The crowd had dispersed. I followed Darren's stare, and in that light all I could see of Noy was his dark eyes. They were ice hard.

"Yes, it's over," Darren said.

One lesson I had learned at the monastery was that important changes that are thrust upon us define the new being we become. I had lost everything. Right then, I felt like a planet ripped from its orbit, left searching. What could I possibly become?

We climbed the bank and walked through the market, leaving Noy at the river. Darren suggested we catch a tuk-tuk back to the temple, but I wanted to walk, hoping the exercise would help my debilitating hangover.

Somchai's suicide on that early morning was foreseeable. He was disturbed by the horror he had committed, and exhausted by the long night in the Bodhi tree. I should have known better than to leave him alone. I was such a fool.

"How tired I am," I said to Darren. "I think I can stand almost anything but this ghastly fatigue."

He spoke gently, using his voice to comfort me, telling me it was the hangover that made me tired. He suggested we stop at a bar and share a Singha beer, hair of the dog or some such nonsense. I knew, however, that this tiredness pulling me down came from very far away, had accumulated over time, and was made of many kinds of things, everything. Drinking would only add more weight to the heap. I had overestimated my strength to carry such a load.

"No," I said, "let's not stop. I don't want a drink."

We did stop. He jerked me to a halt right there on the road in the midst of the traffic, and he kissed me. A tender, loving, hopeful kiss. He kissed me for a long time, while Archer hugged me from behind. We all seemed to merge like drops of water coming together. The irreplaceable perfume of Darren's power enveloped me, blending with it his breach of love, his wishing me well, and the slight stench of my dead love.

When our lips broke apart, we smiled at each other.

"He might still be alive," Darren said. "All we could see were his robes in the water. Perhaps he chucked them off in order to swim to the other side. He could be running bareassed through the rice fields, hell-bent for Bangkok."

He was humoring me. It was a one-in-a-million chance. Still... perhaps.

"Kiss me again, and again," I whispered, and he did. I had no idea what would come next. Did he know? He groped my crotch with his usual lack of shame and I pulled back, still not knowing if that was what I wanted.

We walked again. I couldn't wait to get back to my sleeping mat. I knew I would sleep well, perhaps for days, or weeks. Archer didn't have to be back to school for another month. We could stay on at the monastery a while longer, enough time to get my mind clear.

When finally I lay on my mat and closed my eyes, Archer lay with me, offering me his body for coziness. Darren sat on the balcony, his back against the door frame, as if standing guard over us. I fell into a deep sleep and dreamed of a naked youth sprinting through rice paddies like a springbok, while the morning sun glistened on his amber skin. Perhaps.

HANDCARVED ELEPHANTS

The humid sea breeze pounded my face as I staggered to the bow. I leaned against the railing where port and starboard forged a spearhead to cleave the sapphire plain, and, with my back to the ship, I saw the immensity—sea and sky, and the sun hovering inches above the vanishing point. It silenced my racing mind and weighed on my chest with such force that I struggled to take in air. Shouts echoed from behind me, angry and belligerent, and to me they no longer mattered. The passengers' rage was directed at me, but they would have to sort it out themselves. All I could think of now was how to lose myself in that gigantic yellow disk as it touched the water. I stared at the sun until my eyes burned and I had to look away, anywhere but behind me. Due east I saw a small and insignificant slash of color on the horizon that I knew must be the island of Phuket, Thailand. The yacht under my feet dipped, plunging down then up, yet the island stayed its course, became the only solid, immovable point of reference in my world.

My eyes locked on that strip of land as I stepped back from the railing, spread my feet across the teak planks, and leaned into the wind. I raised my arms like angel wings, as if I were a second jib, balancing resistance against gravity until it felt like I was soaring above the ship's mainsail, leaving all behind and vaulting over virgin territory. It felt epic, a sensation of freedom I'd never experienced before. My feet, however, never left the deck.

The island was not our ship's destination, but at that moment I knew it held some power over me, a place that could either free or kill me. Perhaps in my case death was the only freedom. The unknown quantity of "X" in the equation of my sordid existence.

Below decks, the incensed voices grew in volume. At the same time I heard the sandpaper scuff of deck shoes trundling toward me, and realized it must be the captain. I glanced over my shoulder to confirm what I already knew. Captain Mike MacDougal had a large, unattractive head, and his body was as stout and chunky as a Shetland pony. He was a swarthy man in his mid-sixties, affable and rapaciously lusty for someone his age. I knew that for a fact because I had shared his cabin—his bunk—since the day he hired me as first mate of the *Wanderbird* seven months earlier. He wore khaki cargo pants and a blue denim shirt unbuttoned to his belly. Just then, he was panting, sweating, and wild-eyed. Captain Mike was Black Irish, and when his temper was up, his face boiled a scalded red.

"Leave me the hell alone," I hissed through clenched teeth.

"Corbin," Mike said with a level voice, "come below and tell those miserable Christian bastards that this is all some mix-up, that you never touched Jason Starling."

"I said leave me be, and for God's sake button your shirt."

"Corbin, you can't ignore this. Jason is underage. His father is demanding that we put in at Patong tonight so he can hand you over to the authorities. If you're convicted, it means ten to twenty years in a Thai prison, and you can't imagine what kind of hell that is."

The ship steadily sailed toward land, and Phuket began to take shape, the edges soft and muted, the colors more distinct. I realized Mike had already decided to make harbor. Fear settled in my gut like fine silt. "Unlock the liquor cabinet," I said, "I need a stiff belt."

"If you start drinking now, you won't stop," Mike said. "It'll be just like the last time." He paused in the same instant that the voices below hushed. All I could hear was my heart beating in reckless, liquid gushes and the wind streaming past my ears. "If you won't tell them, at least tell me. Did you fuck the kid?" When I didn't answer he shouted, "Dammit, I need to know. Is it true?"

Was he protecting his passengers like a responsible captain of a third-rate cruise ship, or was he simply a jealous lover? Did it even matter which? I knew already that he and I could not go on as before. After feasting on ambrosia, how could I return to the swill he offered?

The deck pitched and I had to seize the railing to stay on my feet. Mike grabbed my waist, trying to steady me, but I couldn't stand to have him touch me now, not after what had happened. I shoved him away.

A wail floated up from below, sounding vaguely like a wounded hyena. It had to be Mrs. Starling, Jason's mother. That three-hundred-pound medusa could turn a man to stone with a single glance. Her voice ran up the scale until it was so high it could only be detected by bats.

"A drink, dammit. I need it to steady my nerves."

Mike turned to one of the Malaysian deckhands. "Huay Nam, fetch a Singha, chop chop!" Huay Nam took off along the deck.

"Beer? Might as well be mother's milk." I needed something industrial strength to battle the demons that young Jason had whipped up in my gut, not to mention the visions of Luke now circling my head. This was not a case of merely dabbling with a teenager, this was the weight of a decade of mistakes crashing down on my shoulders, crushing me.

Mike grabbed my arm. "Fifteen years I've been takin' out parties, from Shanghai to Calcutta, and this is the worst thing that's ever happened." He obviously wanted to say more, but his voice gave out.

I saw Mr. Starling crawl from the hatch. He and his wife led a sizable congregation and a Christian high school in the heartland of Oklahoma. Pretentious assholes, both of them. The whole damned party, all eleven, were a football squad of pious, Republican charlatans.

I glanced into Mike's eyes. "You've got to help me. Tell these mealy-mouthed twits that I'm a man of the cloth, ordained by the Catholic Church, and a servant of God himself. Tell them I could never do such a thing to an innocent boy."

"Shit, Corbin, you haven't worn the collar in six years, and besides, Catholic priests lost their currency on that topic decades ago. Everyone knows you all diddle boys every chance you get."

Huay Nam ran up with an open bottle. I pressed it to my lips and tilted my head back, guzzling beer so cold my chest burned all the way to my stomach. I kept swallowing until I tossed the empty bottle over the side.

"Why, Corbin?" Mike asked, no demanded. "Why him?"

"Innocence. Purity," I said, searching for the truth within myself. "I love boys because they live outside the realm of cynicism and irony."

"Christ, if you wanted chicken you could have had Huay Nam or Ye Min. They've been wiggling their fannies under your nose since you came aboard. But no, you've got to chase after a lily-white, Baptist, paying customer. I mean, what the fuck!"

"Huay Nam and Ye Min aren't Luke. I saw something of him in Jason."

"Right, that boy ruined you once, and you keep letting him drag you back down every time you stand up."

"Perhaps I was seduced by Jason's beauty. Surely that's something you can understand."

"Beauty is a whore. I like my freedom better. Once you're rotting in a Thai prison, you'll know exactly what I mean."

I already knew. Two years in a Texas state prison, convicted of the same crime, had not only stripped me of my vestments, it had taught me a valuable lesson: I was weak. I had barely survived Huntsville. A Thai prison would no doubt kill me. I had been spiraling downhill for years, until taking this job, which I had presumed was rock bottom. I loved being on the water, but letting the captain slobber over my thirty-year-old body every night had made it a living torment. During sex, he was a pig at a trough, clumsy and often brutal. It wasn't that much different than Huntsville. I had put up with his ill treatment as a form of atonement, which at that moment seemed a ridiculously empty gesture.

Yes, I had assumed this was rock bottom, the seventh rung of hell, but thinking of Thai prison, I realized there were deeper levels to fall to, more anguish to experience before the freedom of death.

"Mike, don't anchor until we can talk these folks down. We've got to stick together. It's a test of strength between them and us. You know that, don't you? Don't give in. Don't let them win."

Mike shook his head. "We've got to dock sometime, and when we do those Bible thumpers mean to see you hang. You flew too close to the sun, my friend, and you've charred your wings but good."

"Would it do any good to tell them I didn't touch him?"

Mike looked past me, out over the vast ocean. "What's got this whole ship rucked up is Jason bawling like a baby, saying how much he loves you."

"So nobody actually knows anything for sure?" I asked, trying to see a thread of light through the gloom.

"Look, as long as he keeps sobbing, everybody has convicted you. Sooner or later, they'll drag the truth out of him."

Then I'm screwed. We're all screwed. That last glimmer dimmed. *Why? Why did foul luck chase me across the globe like a bloodhound on a scent?* "How long do I have?" I asked, my voice feeble, defeated.

"We should anchor at Patong before midnight. I'll take you ashore at dawn."

I hung my head, staring at my deck shoes in the fading light, feeling the wind on my face. *Would I have shoes in prison? Would I be able to feel the wind? Would I have a view of the water, or just some brute pushing my face into a squat toilet?* "I never meant to hurt you, Mike, you or your business. Please believe me."

He turned and walked along the deck, leaving me to the breeze and the galloping motion of the ship. I called after him. "Can a condemned man at least get a real drink?"

"No!" Mike yelled over his shoulder.

"It's not like you've never broken the law." It was too true. I had been aboard long enough to know that when there were no paying customers, Mike ran the white powder from Burma to Singapore to Hong Kong, although I had never seen it with my own eyes because Mike made those long trips alone in case his boat was seized by authorities.

❖

I hurried to the captain's cabin and ripped off my shorts and T-shirt. The sun had set and the sky had turned lavender, darkening the cabin to the point I needed to switch on the overhead lamp. I tore through my locker and pulled out the one set of priest's clothing I'd kept hidden for six years. I dressed meticulously, as if I were preparing for Easter Mass where every movement must be performed scrupulously if it's to succeed, finally donning a coat much too heavy for the weather. I stood in all my raiment at the bottom of a long downhill slide. I had once been quite handsome in these clothes, with my black hair and blue eyes, olive complexion and muscular physique. I had been the pride of my parish, but no more. I had lost thirty pounds since then, and now these clothes hung on my slender frame like gunnysacks. I felt like an actor in an oversized costume playing a part where I didn't know my lines.

At last I lifted a jeweled crucifix from my locker. It was roughly the size of a saucer, and hung on a golden chain. I draped it over my head and arranged it on my shoulders so that the cross dangled over my heart. It had belonged to Luke, a family relic passed from father to son for six generations. It felt substantial, almost too heavy for me to stand upright. I knew I would need more weight for my purpose, so I rummaged through my drawers looking for my box of spare coins. I filled my pockets with silver from America, Singapore, Malaysia, and Thailand.

I left the cabin, shuffled along the passageway, scaled the ladder to the deck, and walked purposefully toward the stern, certain of what

I would do. I became distracted by the sight of the lights far off; a town spread over the land we were passing, incandescent, tinged with a faint hint of starlight, trembling under a darkening sky. I paused, watching the lights and the sky, and then walked on.

Voices murmured behind me. I couldn't tell if they were the voices I carried in my head (the voices of breathless boys calling to me in the heat of passion) or the passengers still arguing below decks. It really didn't matter now. I marched past a deckhand manning the wheel, Huay Nam or Ye Min, I couldn't tell which in the dim light. He glanced at me, nodded, and stared back at the horizon. As I passed him I thought of how successful he was, how fortunate to be working a simple job, without a desire in the world beyond steering the ship through calm waters, and with no goal greater than reaching port. I myself had failed. I was neither a priest nor a sailor, had no religion or any other damned thing to cling to in desperate times. I was merely an eccentric, an ex-con haunted by the faces of my past, faces staring up at me, wide-eyed, while I took my pleasure.

My deck shoes rasped as I staggered along the deck, and growing louder were the voices, not the belligerent voices below deck, I knew now, but the seductive ones muttering indistinctly just beyond the range of my vision. And following the voices would surely, as night follows day, come the migraines, days of blinding pain. But no, I thought as I reached the stern and stepped over the wire railing, not this time.

The coins in my pockets jingled like Santa's sleigh bells.

I fingered the cross over my heart, knowing my faith had run dry, but I lifted it to my lips and kissed it anyway, a gesture of gratitude for that brief time in my life that I had felt fulfilled. I couldn't help but notice the medallion's cold feel, and its color, tarnished gold with spots of red where the rubies were inlaid. I returned the cross to my breast and inched closer to the edge.

It seemed a crime that at age thirty I should have no future. I had experienced so much in my life, seen so many places, yet accomplished so little. Achievements alone are not the true measure of a man, but when I looked back on my life, I found nothing there to gauge beyond the agony I'd caused others.

The ship hissed at the waterline as it cut through the waves. The voices grew louder. The water looked as solid as a highway that extended to the shoreline where the lights glimmered. Almost involuntarily (at least it felt that way) and without removing my deck shoes, I stepped into the empty space behind the ship.

The frigid bite of seawater sent a sudden chill through me, but it was not unbearable.

After the shock of cold, I knew true silence for the first time—a divine quiet I felt in every cell of my body. Even the voices had hushed. I thought of Luke. I saw his lovely hands and his face, the dimples accenting his perfectly formed smile. I had once heard that we punish the ones we love the most, and in those seconds of plummeting into the blackness, I knew that it was an absolute truth, perhaps the only one. I also knew that it was a two-way street, that the ones we love bring the most pain back to us.

As I sank, I thought of the other boys I'd seduced, each one an expedition to find what I had discovered with Luke. None had measured up, or perhaps I had been lacking. I suddenly felt immensely sorry for them, each one, and I imagined ripping the cross from my neck and the coins from my pockets so that I could swim to the surface. I could live on, and do something to make those boys' lives more bearable. But as my lungs began to burn, I knew that was impossible.

The water grew frigid, but all I could feel was the fire in my chest. The panic of survival became a roar. The current wrapped itself around me and tumbled me with muscular force, as if a strong man were brutalizing me. It felt personal.

I saw my body being borne along, as if I was several feet away. I appeared to be flying. Coins trickled from my pockets like raindrops falling from heaven. Arms spread, hair streaming, my coat billowed like Batman's cape as the current worried me, twisting and untwisting and twisting me again. A crushing pressure in my head became unbearable. I folded one arm against my chest and fingered the crucifix one last time.

I heard music, and a voice called to me. I saw myself adjusting the sails of a schooner on a day vivid with sunshine—one hand on the wheel, one holding a rope taut. I was wearing rust-colored boardies. The wind, cool and crisp, soothed my sunburned skin.

Through the hatch leading below deck, I saw Luke in the galley. My Luke. The joy and torment of my life. Nuzzling his side was Castle, his Springer spaniel puppy. They made a perfect pair, both energetic and lovely and still awkward with youth.

Biting the end of his pencil, Luke studied the map spread out on the tiny dining table.

He jotted a few calculations on a notepad, then meticulously and confidently charted our course. His lips parted, revealing the trace of a satisfied smirk. Removing his glasses, he rubbed the bridge of his nose, and glanced up at me. "We're utterly lost," he said. His grin blossomed into a full-on smile. I waved to him, and he snatched up Castle and scrambled up the ladder, crossed the cockpit, and leaned into my side. He offered me a playful kiss, which turned passionate, drawing blood. I tasted the deep, rich sweetness. With us, every act of love was yet another razor cut. I lingered in the pain with happy contentment.

The smell of his hair, a faint lavender scent, made me pull him closer. That hug and the blood varnishing our lips bound us, collectively, forever.

Then I saw only glacial blackness.

❖

I tumbled within a void, like falling with no place to land. After what seemed an eternity, I felt something lift my head. My body was too numb to feel pain, too traumatized for anything beyond my mind saying *am* and *now*. As my mind grew more aware, I realized that I lay in a fetal position, caught in a rhythmic wash of gushing liquid. My thoughts slowly progressed to *I am now*. Everything that came before was obsolete, irrelevant. My eyelids crept open, and a flash of light burned my eyes, blurring everything into a cold white haze. As my vision cleared, I realized I lay in the surf under a morning sky, watching the turquoise water lap over my limbs while molten webs of sunlight tumbled over the blue waves.

I glanced up into a brown face, surrounding the kindest-ooking black eyes I had ever beheld. *This must be the face of God. Is this heaven?* Through my numbness I could feel fear tweaking my vagus nerve, a sick shrinking from the knowledge that I was dead, and having no clue what lay before me.

God's face lowered until those beautifully formed lips touched mine and air blew past a blockage in my throat. I began to cough, retching seawater. As if standing at the edge of a sheer cliff preparing to plunge, my mind delayed, caught for a moment in a membrane freeze, struggling with the shock of being alive. Sweet air poured into my lungs. I glanced up at God's face again, noting his shaved head, unblemished coppery skin, and an expression of determination that seemed almost comic. He cradled my head like a newborn, smiling at me—a smile that warmed my chest. I focused on his slender neck that grew out of a nude shoulder. His other shoulder was wrapped in the orange robes of a Buddhist monk, which held a spicy scent of incense that overpowered the salt smell of the sea. I tried willing him to press his silken lips to mine once more. I wanted to lose myself in them.

Instincts took over and I began testing my body: legs stretched, back arched, fingers clench into fists and relaxed. Every part of me obeyed my mental commands, yet I couldn't shake the feeling that all this was an illusion, that I must be quite dead, drifting over the ocean floor.

That impression, that certainty of being drowned, caused my name to pop into my awareness, and with it came my entire history, like a ton of shit falling on my abdomen. I struggled to inhale.

Two other men standing over us, both monks, helped the youth haul me to my feet. They half led, half carried me up a beach to a temple that was as opulent as the grand hotels of Europe, but with a distinctly Thai architecture.

We made a dreamlike entrance upon a scene of monks gathered in the center of a massive hall, chanting in guttural voices. They were all dressed in the minimal concessions of a monk, and all were bronzed, splendidly physical, and supple as stalks of bamboo. At one end of the hall sat a dais, and behind that stood a golden statue of the Lord Buddha. The dais was carved from sandalwood in the shape of a lotus flower, and on it sat a monk, old, like a piece of yellowed ivory. Judging from the elegance that radiated from that pencil-thin body, I first thought it might be a woman, but I knew there were no female monks in Thailand. At that point, however, I was still convinced this was either Heaven or, more likely, Hell.

A smirk adorned the old monk's face. Incense sticks burned near his feet, sending spirals of perfumed smoke toward the ceiling. He wore a voluminous saffron cassock and held a knife in one gnarled hand. A sizable carved elephant lay in his lap. While his pale eyes stared into space, the fingers of his free hand roamed over the elephant feeling for the next place to shave off a sliver of wood. Those hands, more than anything else, made me guess his years were on the far side of eighty.

A Caucasian acolyte, a year or two shy of adulthood, sat in the lotus position to the old monk's right. In that musty room lit by chandeliers that were a rainfall of crystal and light, he seemed to glow, to exude a faint light from his hazel eyes, shaved head, pursed lips, and the delicate curve of his neck. I wondered if everyone could see his shimmering aura; it seemed impossible that it could go unnoticed. We made eye contact, the acolyte and I, and I felt suddenly naked, my soul exposed. Something jumped in my gut, pulling me off balance. I stumbled and nearly fell.

My three saviors hauled me onto a large cushion beside an altar. On the wall to my right hung a phoenix painted on silk, and below it, a mirror was propped on a small table. I wanted to thank my porters, but I knew no words of Thai. They offered nothing more than beaming faces. I began to understand why Thailand is called the Land of Smiles.

Gilded light poured through the windows. The autumn breeze drifted in via the open doors to mingle with the sonorous voices of the chanting monks. What a thrill, a shock, to be alive to witness a sunrise in October, being aided by lovely, bald, saffron-robed men in a temple of piety. I became conscious of my appearance. I still wore my priestly attire that included the crucifix draped around my neck, albeit wet with bits of seaweed clinging to it. Dressed in Catholic drag, I felt a fool sprawled before a statue of the Buddha, a milkweed bloom in a field carpeted with poppies. I pulled the cross over my head and tucked it into my coat pocket.

I glanced into the mirror on the table. My face held an expression of predicament. The glass revealed what I had done to myself, the clusterfuck I had tried to end but only made worse, expressed in terms of a dull, distraught stare and a face drawn into a pinched grimace. I resembled a distance runner who is utterly spent, but who keeps plodding one foot in front of the other because life won't let him stop. In that face I saw my history—the boy, the teen, the young man, the hopeful clergyman, the fallen angel—all preserved with fossil-like rigidity in a lifeless outer shell. I swallowed. *Yes, I'm dead. This is Hell. What's there to fear now?*

I stared and stared at that mirror, not trusting the image it bore. My lips parted. I breathed through my mouth, having no idea what was expected of me now.

The chanting softened to a whisper, and then ripened into silence as everybody scrutinized me. Above the stillness was a tranquil singing of the wind accompanied by muffled, measured booms that could have been pounding surf or distant shellfire.

My body shivered. "I'm freezing," I croaked in a voice alien to me.

The monk carving the elephant spoke a burst of Thai. As if his words had been a command, the acolyte to his right, the one with the penetrating eyes, jumped up and came to me. He placed both hands on my chest and pushed me to a prone position. He unbuttoned my shirt, bared my chest, and pulled his robe off his shoulder to expose his own torso. He sprawled on top of me, clinging to me in a full-body embrace. It only took a moment to realize he meant to warm me. His body was blazing with energy as only the young can, and that delicious heat had an immediate effect. I hugged back, absorbing all of that glorious warmth into my chest until it leached outward into my limbs.

As my body relaxed my thoughts focused on the feel of sumptuous skin pressed against me, and the tickle of his breath curling on my neck. I must have dozed off, drifting in a dreamless zone, because when I woke with a start the acolyte was sitting beside me in the lotus position. The old monk was still seated on the dais carving his elephant statue, but the hall stood empty of other people. The acolyte had draped his upper robe over me, and his delicate white shoulders and chest gave him a look of naive purity. I placed his age at seventeen or eighteen, but his eyes were much older. Underneath his Zenlike tranquility lurked something wounded…and dangerous, at least to me. He sat with such a casual, dignified ease, however, that he could have been the Buddha himself.

"You washed ashore on Nai Harn Beach, Mr. Edwards," he said with perfect, American-accented English. He had the pristine, singsong voice of youth. I lifted myself to face this Caucasian Buddha. We sat with our knees almost touching.

"You know my name?"

"While you slept, the *Wanderbird* anchored in our bay. Your shipmates came looking for you."

He reached out and began to massage my neck and shoulders, his fingers competent and gentle, his touch as soothing as running a silk scarf over my skin. "Ah, Christ…" I muttered to my mortal god as sexually charged messages rushed to my groin.

"I'll send word to them that you're awake."

"No," I gasped. "I mean, I've got to hide."

He scrutinized me for a long time while his fingers continued to work their magic. "You're a criminal?"

"Let's say I had a carnal run-in with a minor on that ship, and I'd like to avoid prison."

"So you corrupted a young chick and now the old hens are squawking?"

"An eighteen-year-old, less a few months. But he asked for it, begged for it actually. He's an emotionally precocious brat who lured me into his web."

"And daddy blames you?"

"Not just him. They're a clutch of evangelical zealots, over here searching for a spot to establish a mission. It's bad enough that they've ruined America with their pious blight; they have to spread it around the globe. I'll bet they're on the beach right now holding a revival meeting, and after all the amens and before there is a chance to escape, Miss Aurora Goodwin will no doubt lead the flock in an earsplitting rendition of 'When The Saints Go Marching In,' completely out of tune, of course."

He snickered. "Well, sir—" he said as his hands returned to his lap.

His calling me "sir" made me feel old, or at least old in his eyes. The other thing I found odd was that he didn't use the hip slang that had become popular with teens in the States, giving me the impression that he came from a well-heeled family living in a rural area or abroad. "Call me Corbin."

"Well, Corbin, I find your views of Christians interesting, considering you're dressed as a Catholic priest."

"I was a priest, once. But six years ago I realized that there is no God, or if there is, you won't find Him in any human hearts. It was a rude awakening, and a very long story."

"I have nothing but time, sir, literally. Your shipmates know you're here. They've no doubt gone to the police, but you're safe from the law as long as you stay here under the protection of the Buddha. So try to sleep again; regain your strength. I'll bring some soup, and you can tell me about your rude awakening."

"What I need is a drink. I don't suppose—"

He shook his head.

"An elephant is the symbol of distance!" the old monk said in a cracked voice that sounded weary. "Yes, distance is the steady, measured march of elephants."

I was quite surprised he spoke English, albeit with a heavy Thai accent. The acolyte jostled my elbow, and with hand signals let me know that the old one was blind. "His name is Khun Thammarato," he said, using the standard Thai honorific *Khun* to show respect, "and I'm Griffin Toller. My friends call me Griff."

Khun Thammarato's ivory-colored eyebrows perched high on his elongated face, over pale eyes set between two enormous ears. He scrunched up his features and continued, "Distance, and also unconquerable strength. That is why a pilgrim should carry a picture of an elephant close to his heart, to remind him of the distance that he has traveled, the expanse he has yet to journey, and the strength he must spawn to continue his path."

Above the old man, a wooden plank had Thai letters carved across it. I leaned closer to Griff. "What does that inscription mean?"

"Long live those who practice mercy."

Outside the tall windows came the soft, urgent cries of parrots. Their wings beating the air caused flickers of white radiance on the glass, as though morning light were a snowy dove caught in a net and struggling to escape.

Griff helped me to my feet, and I shuffled to a window. Beyond a line of roadside shacks that must have been restaurants, a luxury hotel terraced halfway up the hillside. Each room opened onto its own patio that overlooked the bay. I stared out over the beach. The morning was like true summer, with the sea smooth and bright under the sun and a slight breeze off the water to soften the heat's edge. At the horizon, a line of dark cumulus clouds galloped toward shore from the northwest.

Griff shifted beside me. His eyes followed my gaze. "You see it, sir? Should hit us within the hour."

"Mr. Edwards," bawled a voice from outside the temple.

"For God's sake, Griff, hide me."

Before I could move, Aurora Goodwin charged into the temple leading a posse consisting of Captain Mike and two Thai policemen. Aurora pointed an accusing finger at me and barked, "There's your man, officers. Arrest him."

Griff spoke a few sentences in Thai, his voice as light and fresh as a spring shower. The officers smiled, bowed to the statue of the Buddha, and retreated out the doorway. Aurora grabbed at their shirtsleeves to stop them, but they shook her off and walk back toward town.

"Miss Goodwin," Griff said, "you charged up the hill! Never exert yourself like that in a tropical climate."

Miss Goodwin, panting and visibly furious, looked ethereal, almost ghostly, suggesting a Gothic cathedral image of a saint, but overly animated. She could be thirty or as old as fifty, with a sassy face and buckskin-colored eyes. She wore a cotton print dress with a woven dirt-brown bag slung over her shoulder. "I don't need advice from a heathen. What did you say to those officers that made them refuse to arrest this molester of children?"

"I told them Mr. Edwards has entered into the service of the Buddha, and therefore, as long as he takes the vows and stays within the temple compound, they have no authority to arrest him."

Taken aback, she was momentarily at a loss. She quickly recovered. "What kind of backward shithole is this where rapists can shave their heads and go free? Is this man paying you to protect him?"

Griff pouted. "I'm a monk, Miss Goodwin. I have my robes, begging bowl, a clean bed, a bathroom with real plumbing, and enough food to keep me healthy. What could he possibly offer me that I don't already have?"

Miss Goodwin, still panting, dug into her shoulder bag and pulled out a handkerchief, no doubt aware that her face was flushed and sweating. She dabbed her neck while scrutinizing my open shirt and Griff's still-naked torso. "Yes, what indeed? Just what the hell has been going on here?"

Griff sighed. "Miss Goodwin, and you call yourself a Christian. You should be ashamed." He stooped to retrieve his upper robe off the floor, wrapped it over one shoulder and around his waist in the customary way, and left the hall. He walked like a rope uncoiling, carrying his head high and exhibiting a quiet dignity that left me entranced.

Captain Mike glared at me. "Button your shirt," he said, finally finding his voice. "Are you so vain you have to flaunt your body to the world?"

"Bite me, Mike. I no longer take orders from you."

"So you got all dolled up in your religious duds," Mike said. "You planning on going back to the Church? You gonna write another letter to your bishop, confessing everything and begging for forgiveness? You've caused that bishop enough embarrassment. What makes you think he'd take you back?"

"There is no forgiveness in the Church anymore, even if I wanted to return. And speaking of returning, why don't you two run back to the *Wanderbird,* find your spot to open a mission, and vomit your morals onto somebody else. You've done enough damage here."

Miss Goodwin shook a finger at me. "We are not leaving until you are behind bars. You might as well give yourself up."

"Miss Goodwin, I'd like to confess something to you. As you well know, I was once a man of the cloth, but for some time I've been at the end of my rope. When our young Romeo seduced me, I was vulnerable. I regret everything—"

"Seduced you?" she spat. "Jason would never!" Her face blistered red.

"Where is your compassion, Miss Goodwin? Please don't shatter everything left of my faith in essential...human...goodness!"

"Human goodness?" Her voice rose an octave. "Why, just plain human decency is beyond anything in you. You're vile, Mr. Edwards, and I mean to see you put away—I don't care what it costs. I'm staying here until that happens. I'm—"

"Oh, Miss Goodwin, the real reason you're agitated is plain as day. Why don't we talk about your true motivations here?"

Miss Goodwin balled up her fist and charged me. I tried to defend myself but I slipped and fell back onto the cushion. Luckily, Captain Mike caught her arm and held her.

"Swine," she hissed through clenched teeth as Mike led her toward the open doorway.

I turned away from them, facing the golden Buddha. It stood thirty feet high, and light from the windows on the far wall caused its shadow to fall across me. She was right, of course, I couldn't sit on that cushion forever. When I glanced back they were gone. Griff shuffled across the polished floor carrying a steaming bowl with both hands, a blanket slung under his arm. "You must be relieved, sir. You look like you're feeling better."

"Better? My head's bursting, the room is spinning, and I'm freezing to death. Hard to believe this is better. And stop calling me 'sir.'"

He sat facing me and placed the bowl between us. He lifted the blanket. "Peel off your damp coat and shirt, and wrap this around you."

I did as he asked, pulling the blanket snug under my chin.

"Chow down on this broth. It's been simmering all morning so it's strong enough to put sap in your muscles and grow hair on your balls."

"Leave my balls out of this," I said, a bit surprised. "I need a stiff drink and a bottle of painkillers."

"Soup first."

Steam rose from the bowl and a savory aroma infiltrated my nostrils. The smell caused me to realize that under my pain there raged a voracious hunger.

"I call you 'sir' because I used to love those fifties sitcoms like *Leave It to Beaver* and *My Three Sons*. Those boys always called their father 'sir,' and if you don't mind, I could use a father figure just now."

I was much too young to be his dad, but I smiled, wondering what his story could be.

Once he saw me yield, he said, "She'll be here every day until you're in prison, sir. That woman is nearly hysterical and very determined." He dipped the spoon into the rust-colored liquid and blew on it to cool the broth.

I nodded. "Hysteria is a biological phenomenon, the common denominator of the feminine nature. It's a woman's most potent weapon, and the test of a man's mettle is his ability to cope with it. Besides, she's furious I screwed her dreamboat before she could. Now she knows she never will, and she blames me for that." The pain in my head ignited as I tried to sit up at a better angle. "Thanks, but I can feed myself."

He ignored me, holding the spoon close to my mouth. "Let me do this. I'm working on building up my good karma."

He placed the spoon in my mouth and I swallowed. The heat felt divine. "That's brilliant. So, why are you here?"

Griff drew another spoonful, blew, and fed me.

"A year ago, I came to Phuket with an older man I trusted. After a few days, he tried to rape me. He wouldn't give me any money or my passport unless I let him fuck me, so I ran away. He's probably back in the States now, and I'm stuck with no money and no way to get home."

As Griff filled the spoon again, I asked, "Can't you call your folks? Surely they'll wire you money."

"That older man was my stepfather, so no, I can't. I don't have anyone. I became a novice monk because they feed me. It's the only way I've been able to survive. If I can get to Bangkok I'll go to the embassy. They'll help me. I don't suppose you have a few hundred to spare?"

I sighed, knowing I had jumped overboard with nothing but coins in my pockets and the crucifix around my neck. That cross had been a gift from Luke. I would rather give up my life than lose it. Griff held out the spoon, and I took more broth.

"Then we're both prisoners," he said.

"With one difference. You're here because you kept your honor. I threw mine away."

Griff dropped the spoon into the bowl, reached for my hand, and squeezed gently. His intimacy was touching, but the pain in my head was still intensely present. It seemed to reflect the sudden hurt I saw on his face. His agony made me think that if I could somehow fly him to Bangkok, he might sacrifice his honor.

The light outside rapidly weakened until lightning flashed over the temple. The hall went brilliant white for an instant. A clap of thunder shivered the room. Rain fell from the sky in huge, glistening droplets. It steadily grew heavier until it looked like a solid waterfall out the windows.

Griff fed me more soup. "An autumn squall. They only last an hour or so." He lifted the end of his robe and wiped away some soup dribbling from the corner of my mouth.

Khun Thammarato laid his carving knife aside and held up a branch of orchids at eye level, gazing at a bloom with such intensity that the connection between them seemed palpable.

"I thought he was blind," I whispered.

"He is, but that doesn't mean he can't see."

"With no eyes?"

"Bats fly two hundred miles each night, zero in on tiny insects, and return to their cave, all without sight."

"Point taken, but what's he doing?"

"He's delivering a silent lecture, demonstrating the nature of the human spirit. It's very Zen."

"I don't get it," I said, my voice rising with frustration over the sound of rain pounding the roof tiles.

"Of course not. You see a monk staring at a flower. But flowers are more fleeting, more ethereal, more delicate than the plants out of which they emerge, and they give off fragrance, which is invisible. They're a bridge between form and the formless. Seeing the nature, or beauty, of a flower awakens the splendor that is an essential part of your own inner being, your true nature. Simply put, he's demonstrating enlightenment."

"Really, that's all there is to enlightenment?"

Griff stared at me for a half minute before shaking his head. "I'm going to call you Rock."

"Like Rock Hudson?"

"Rocks are the densest of all forms. The good news is, even some stones can undergo enlightenment, alter their molecular structure and change into crystals or even diamonds."

"You think I'm dense? No, don't answer that. How do you know all this?"

"The monastery has no TV, no Internet, no phone service. I read a lot, and Khun Thammarato gives me hour-long lessons every morning and evening."

"Well, just to show that I'm not completely stupid, let me tell you something about your name, Griff. According to Stephen Friar's *New Dictionary of Heraldry,* a griffin's claw was believed to have medicinal properties and its plumes could restore sight to the blind. So perhaps that's how Khun what's-his-name can see. You've given him your chicken feathers." I also knew that griffins, being a union of beast and bird, were seen in Christendom as a symbol of Jesus, who was both human and divine, but I would keep that bit of information to myself.

"He doesn't need feathers or eyes. He doesn't need anything," Griff said with an impish grin. "He's the only person I've ever known who hasn't tried to take something from me. He gives without expecting anything back."

Love shaded his voice, pure and unintended, and I felt my stomach turn a slow somersault. I don't know why I didn't see it before then, but, as if a veil had lifted, I saw Luke sitting before me with a shaved head. The similarities were uncanny, particularly those penetrating eyes that were much older than his years. I felt my own eyes tearing up, and as I reached out and took hold of his hand, I had to look away. I couldn't let him see the emotions boiling in my head. What caught my attention was that old fool still staring at the lotus blossom as if all eternity depended on his merging with it.

"What about me?" I asked in a voice rougher than I intended. "I haven't asked for anything."

He squeezed my hand. "I've upset you. Rest now. I'll come back later." He stood, whisked away the spoon and bowl, and disappeared through a side doorway.

I sat alone, wishing I had said something to make Griff stay. I felt a glimmer of understanding lurking just outside my reach, something having to do with comparing Thammarato's blossom to my Luke, but I couldn't quite grasp those fleeting images. It became clear that Griff had reached out to me because everyone here was so alien. He was searching for an authority figure, and because of our similar backgrounds, he would cling to me as if I were a life raft on a stormy sea. He would place himself in my hands, not realizing that I was more unstable than he, that I was the one who needed saving.

Shouts came from outside, joyous and masculine. I lifted myself off the cushion and staggered to an open window. Inside the courtyard, a group of twenty young monks—some wearing underwear, others nude—bathed in the wild rain. They scrubbed themselves and each other from scalp to toes while leaning into the wind-driven rain, letting the water sluice away the suds. I smiled at the sight of so many naked men drenched in lather.

I leaned out the window, feeling cold drops buffet my head and run down my face. Rain. The clean scent of it reached into my lungs and lifted my heart. *Yes, even this remote village has an element as untainted as rain.* I tilted my face up and opened my mouth, gathering the freshness.

I shook the water from my hair like a drenched spaniel, then turned my attention back on the bathers. They had deeply tanned bodies; all except Griff, whose alabaster skin stood out in that sea of amber like a beacon of blenched light. Nude, he was slightly slimmer than Luke had been, yet more lithe, and yes, more beautiful because of his supple grace. As I watched him move, seeing another man soaping his glistening back, I realized he felt no embarrassment, no awkwardness from being naked among them. And he gave no consideration to his superior beauty. It was the sexiest thing I had ever witnessed. My soul, my entire being reached out to him, wanting to devour him in minuscule bites.

Griff rang out with laughter, which fused with the sound of my own breathing. He turned and stared at me with those hazel eyes, no doubt seeing the part of me that no one else sees. Our eyes locked through the slashing rain. I leaned over the windowsill. Raindrops pummeled me.

A joyous excitement animated the bathers, as if the men were all happily drunk. Swept up in the energy, I surprised myself by laughing out loud. I felt reluctant to join them, but I yearned to stand beside him. He merged into the crowd to let someone scrub his head. My hand reached out on its own, wanting to caress that soapy skin.

A voice behind me, rough and demanding, barked, "Corbin!"

I leaned back into the temple and turned to the massive double doors at the head of the hall. A drenched Captain Mike stood there looking like Poseidon rising from the sea.

"Corbin, I've got all our churchgoing passengers checked into a budget hotel between here and town. Nobody's aboard but the crew. Come back with me now. We'll leave them here, and head back to Singapore, then maybe up to Hong Kong."

I had a brain freeze, not moving for several heartbeats as my mind wrapped around this new escape route. The idea of leaving those pious bastards high and dry tickled my fancy, but then I glanced out the window again. The sun had broken through the cloud cover and the light caused the raindrops to gleam silver. I inhaled sharply and held my breath. The bathers seemed to dance in molten light. The spectacle of them being pelted with silver droplets made me exhale slowly. I saw Griff emerge from the bathers, drenched in that shimmering vision, and I realized that someone now depended on me.

"There's a boy, an American. No passport, no money. He comes with me."

"Underage, no doubt?"

I shrugged.

"Fuck that. I'm not taking an undocumented minor on the *Wanderbird*. Christ, Corbin, that's human trafficking in this part of the world. We can't risk it."

"If you won't take him, then give me enough money to get him home, or at least to Bangkok so he can get a passport at the U.S. embassy. A few thousand, that's all I'm asking."

"Be reasonable, Corbin. I'm already losing my shirt if we leave those sons-a-bitches here. Come back to me. This kid can find his own way. They all do in this part of the globe. He just needs to spread his legs for the right people. Easy as pie."

I stared out the window again. The rain had turned to drizzle and the sky grew brighter. Griff now stood under a canopy, adjusting his robes. I admired how his thin neck merged with his shoulder, and I saw my escape route vanish.

"Screw you, Mike."

"I'll be aboard, Corbin, waiting. The fanatics aren't budging until you're in prison, and sooner or later, you'll see I'm your only chance out of this train wreck. So come to the ship after you've figured out your options."

Without turning from the window, I waited until I sensed his presence leave the hall. I felt as if a giant bird's talon—or was it a Griffin's?—clutch my gut, squeezing, and I wondered how long I would hold out before I ambled to the shore and swam out to the ship.

❖

I stood at that window for what seemed hours, long after all the monks had disappeared into their dormitory or wherever the hell they went. I watched shadows move across the courtyard where they had bathed in the rain, sorry now that I had not stripped off my clergy garments and joined them.

The whole time I stood there, Khun Thammarato sat carving his elephant, staring into space without a word or a care.

Griff glided into the hall, fresh and smelling of rain. "I've made up a room for you, Fred's old cell, next to mine."

"If you don't mind," I said, "can we refrain from calling them cells?"

He smiled with his eyes. "I can't really call them rooms, they make a broom closet seem like a suite at the Ritz, but you could do worse. I've also laid out some comfortable clothes on the bed, and a good pair of sandals that Fred left. He wore a size fourteen shoe, so they may be loose on you."

"Yeah, I could do worse," I said, "especially if Miss Goodwin has her way. What happened to him, Fred I mean?"

"Fred's dead. Pneumonia. He didn't leave much, but what you need, he had."

"A gallon of vodka? Lead me to it."

"I said 'what you need,' not 'what you want.' "

"You expect me to wear a dead man's clothes, walk in his shoes?" I could feel droplets of sweat running down my temples.

Griff's back stiffened. "I expect you to take what's offered, humbly and gratefully, but suit yourself if you'd rather sweat to death in that morbid get-up. Just shoot me for trying to help."

I felt my anger rising and I wanted to unleash it, if only to show that I was still alive, that I wouldn't walk in a dead man's shoes because I had come so close to death myself, that I still mattered in a world that had abandoned me years ago. Noticing his immaculate robes and proud posture, however, I realized that he was a bit of a showman. There is a good kind of pride, an innocent, childlike vanity, and he had it. He carried it like a banner wherever he went. My anger deflated, replaced with the desire to reach out and touch his face. I involuntarily lifted my arm, fingers reaching, but I caught myself and stepped backward. "Which way to the dorm?"

His expression changed slightly, standing there with a proud person's hope of acceptance when it is desperately needed.

"You won't regret it," he said. "Your cell...er...room overlooks the sea. If you're a painter you can create a masterpiece from that view."

"If I were a painter I'd be back in the States right now, enjoying the good life."

Griff nodded. "Somehow I can see you wearing an artist's smock, picturesquely dabbed with paint, and holding a brush and palette...or not." He sprang forward with the nimble movements of a springbok. "We'll take Khun Thammarato back to his...er, room, and then I'll show you yours." He breezed behind the altar and came back a moment later pushing a wheelchair. He climbed the dais, took the carved elephant from Thammarato's lap, and helped him to a standing position. They tottered off the dais arm in arm, and Griff lowered Khun Thammarato into the wheelchair. Again, I could see love radiating from Griff; he handled the old monk with a tender, almost sensual esteem. Griff glanced at me. "He's normally scampering around like a mountain goat, even though he's ninety-seven, but he took a turn about a week ago. No worries, his recuperative powers are legendary." He leaned down so his lips were an inch from Thammarato's ear. "Mr. Edwards will be our guest."

"Did he make a reservation?" Thammarato mumbled.

I cleared my throat. "This is the first time in twelve years I've arrived at a destination without advance booking. And I'm afraid I have no money. I can't pay."

Khun Thammarato held up a finger, pointing toward the roof. "In that case, welcome." He craned his neck to speak to Griff. "Tell him if my disgraceful longevity continues, I will begin carving him an elephant as soon as I'm finished with yours."

As Griff pushed the chair through the temple, he explained that Thammarato was a master sculptor, highly revered in Thailand, and each of his works sold for thousands. He was currently working on his masterpiece. He intended to give it to Griff, once it was finished, to sell it and pay his way back to the States. He had been carving this elephant for the last two years, and it was nearly finished. Word had spread and art dealers were already making offers. Griff was obviously thrilled, but I saw it as a two-year sentence in lonely hell. Still, I knew that was somewhat better than a ten-year sentence of being some Thai brute's prison bitch.

We meandered into a courtyard bathed in coppery light. The heavy foliage gleamed with wetness from the recent squall. Dotted about were several wooden statues of the Buddha in all positions—standing, walking, sitting, reclining. Griff told me that Thammarato had carved each one.

"In my youth I carved only the Buddha's image," Thammarato

said as we trundled toward a long, two-story dormitory, "but then I could no longer visualize the holy one in my head. Now I carve elephants. Them I see lucidly, from a vision I saw as a child, a line of elephants lumbering single file through the morning mist." He laughed heartily. "Of course, I see more than elephants. I now see three men, each passing from one of Shakespeare's seven ages to another."

For a moment I thought Griff was about to lean down and clamp a hand over his mouth.

"From schoolboy to lover," Thammarato continued, "from soldier to justice, and one temporarily into the final age. It is a picture most vivid."

I was more amazed at his familiarity with Shakespeare than his senile predictions, but what really caught my attention was the vision of Griff becoming a lover. I glanced at him but saw his eyes saying "*no*" in big hazel letters. I looked away, noticing the courtyard for the first time. Now that the rain had stopped, townspeople were erecting booths for what would surely be a festival.

A woman setting up a food cart brought us a plate of mango slices, offering them as she bowed. Griff handed one to me and took one for himself. Thammarato gave her a blessing. Griff stuff the whole slice into his mouth and chewed. Juice ran down his chin and onto his throat. I couldn't stop from staring as I nibbled little bites, one after another, relishing the sweetness.

A monk, the one with the kind face who had held my head above the surf, came rushing past, brazenly bumping Griff on his way, almost knocking Griff off his feet. Griff shot me a wry smile. "That's Khit. He doesn't like us together because he has a crush on you. If you'd like, I can have him show you to your room instead of me."

"You little pimp. Don't do me any favors, okay?" A patch of bright sky caught us, and I turned to stare between two buildings. The alley opened onto a bone-white beach. Beyond the sand lay a backdrop of sea and sky, a tableau of blue and white lines as strict as a Rothko canvas.

When I turned back I almost crashed into Griff, who had stopped cold. In our path stood a gray-haired clergyman, Reverend Starling. His back was ramrod straight, his long-nosed face held a stern expression. To his right stood his elder son, Wayne Junior, and to his left towered Bud and Scott, two missionaries who seemed more like East L.A. thugs than God's chosen followers. I swallowed, thankful that the reverend's youngest son, Jason, wasn't there to create a scene.

The reverend raised his chin and looked down the length of his nose. "I sent a woman to do a man's job. My mistake. This is your judgment day, Mr. Edwards. You're coming with us."

Before I could answer, Griff said, "He's under my care. I'm taking him to his room to recuperate."

Reverend Starling's back stiffened even more. "You seduced my boy, Edwards. Now you'll pay, one way or another."

"Seduced? Is that what Jason told you? Did he tell how he stole the key to my cabin, how he snuck in while I was asleep, how he begged for it like an addict begs for heroin?"

"He's seventeen, for God's sake! You have the unbelievable gall to suggest it was his fault?"

"No," I said, dropping my head. "I'm to blame."

"You degenerate pig," Wayne Junior barked. "Like Pop said, it's time to pay. There's no point in prolonging this. Let's go." He jerked his head toward town.

I stared Wayne Junior straight in the eye. "You're calling me a degenerate? That's rich. I was a priest, remember; I heard confessions. I know a little something about brotherly love."

"Shut the fuck up!" Wayne Junior clenched his fist and stepped forward, as did Bud and Scott.

Thammarato raised a hand and stopped them with the force of his voice. "We do not abide violence. Leave us in peace, or I will have you arrested."

Reverend Starling glanced around, no doubt seeing the dozen or so monks milling about and the townspeople setting up their carnival booths and food stalls. I could almost see the wheels turning in his head. Wayne Junior, I was confident, could only see blood. He was breathing loudly through his nose because his teeth were clenched as tight as his fists.

"Gawd, what's a father to do?" the reverend said. "As a former man of the cloth, perhaps you'll understand my predicament. I'm the head of a vast congregation that spans cable TV and the Internet. We're double-digit millions in donations. I'm seen not only as a leader, but also as an example. Now everyone on that ship knows you had sex with Jason. The word is out, and if they believe he's a fruit then I'm done for. Who would follow a man who can't even teach his own children to live a moral life?"

I glanced at Wayne Junior again.

"So I'm offering a deal," the reverend said. "You come back to the

Royal Palms Resort with us and make a confession to my congregation. Tell them all that my boy's no fag, that you manipulated him, forced him. That way they'll understand he's a good boy, led astray by Satan. You tell my people you stole his virginity against his will, and I'll let you go. We'll sail tomorrow, and you're free to rot in this Godforsaken shithole."

They must have thought I had just fallen from the cradle only hours ago. Any fool could see it was a lie to lure me away from this place and haul me to the police.

"I didn't take his virginity," I said, glancing at Wayne Junior again, "or his virtue." But then I thought about what happened to my Luke, and part of my chest caved in. "I'll tell you what, you bring your people here tonight, and I'll tell them it was my fault, that I raped him. I'll lie, not to shelter you, Reverend, but to protect Jason."

"No," Wayne Junior hissed. "You're coming with us now, or I'll gut you like a trout." He moved his right hand, and I noticed for the first time he was holding a switchblade knife. He meant business, but I knew with the crowd that had gathered to watch, he was powerless to act.

"Wayne, are you sure you want me to make a full confession?"

He growled, guttural and menacing.

The blade sprung open but Reverend Starling seized his arm. "Later," he hissed, and he pulled his son a few steps back. He drew a wad of sweaty bills from his pocket and held it out. "I'll make a donation to your temple if you hand him over quietly."

A silent pause stretched into something awkward before Griff said, "Shove that money in your pie hole. We're not Christians; we don't buy and sell souls in this country."

Reverend Starling locked eyes with me. "We sail tomorrow. If you don't give yourself up to the authorities, I'll let Wayne and the boys have their way with you. It's our moral duty to ensure you can't corrupt another youth ever again, and I intend to do that or God strike me dead."

I stared him down, not knowing what else to do. Perhaps that was the answer. Let them kill me. I had tried and failed. Wayne Junior and his chums, I suspected, would finish the job admirably.

With infinite grace, Griff pushed Thammarato's chair forward, parting them like the Red Sea. We left them staring after us. The people around us gawked. I heard cries from bathers on the beach. The afternoon light now had an almost horizontal slant.

Griff squinted up at the sky. "Looks like you're staying the night. But maybe just one."

"I'll sneak out of here before they get back."

Griff chuckled. "You think you'll blend in wearing those clothes? Better to hide here and let the monks protect you."

We had that exchange of words without looking at each other, and continued with downcast eyes until we had deposited Thammarato in his cell on the first floor. We climbed to the second story where Griff led me to my room. The walls were brightly colored in reds and purples and greens, but the room held only a bed and a nightstand with a lamp and a golden statue of a Laughing Buddha. Even in its austerity, the room seemed somehow noble, or at least it touched something deep in my being that still felt vaguely noble.

A military-green tank top, shorts, and underwear were laid out on the bed, no doubt dead-Fred's contribution. One corner of the bed was soaked. I walked to the window that overlooked the bay, and stared out at the *Wanderbird* at anchor. I could run now, swim to her, and be beyond the horizon before Reverend Starling knew what hit him. I didn't need to worry about Griff, because Thammarato's elephant would soon give him the money he needed.

"The roof leaks," Griff said, "but the rains won't return tonight. Considering what you've been through, a damp mattress won't concern you." He laughed, and I felt compelled to turn and stare, but I resisted the urge until he said, "By tomorrow night it won't matter."

I turned.

Griff stood in the doorway, blocking my exit.

"You think its funny that my lifespan should be counted in hours instead of years?"

Griff shook his head. "Years, hours, minutes, the only thing that counts is what we do now, tonight."

Is that an invitation? Is he flirting?

"If you won't use a damp mattress," he said, "then have my room. I'll sleep in here."

Kindness. It's such a simple thing for some, and so effortless. Yet it touches every fiber in a man's body, for the giver and receiver. It had been so long, seemingly eons, since someone had given a gift with no thought of getting something in return. I shook my head. "I'm fine here, but I'm not wearing a dead man's clothes." I turned to the window again, suddenly angry with myself but not knowing why. I gripped the windowsill and glared into the blazing sun as if it were a personal enemy, wondering if this would be my last sunset.

Griff clutched my arm, guided me to the bed, and pushed my chest until I folded over the mattress. I half expected him to join me, but he flashed me a benevolent grin and told me to sleep, that he would return at sunset. My fatigue embraced that suggestion and I closed my eyes. Come what may, I didn't have the strength to pull myself from that damp bed.

❖

I woke to the feel of a breeze caressing my face and something tickling my right foot. Coming fully awake, I realized I was naked, but covered, cocoon like, with a yellow blanket. Griff was giving my leg a sponge bath. He breathed deeply as he labored, pushing his bare chest up and down, working the muscles of his abdomen. I stared at him, so groggy and confused that I couldn't even form a question. As if reading my mind, he said, "I put a sedative in the soup I fed you. That's why I was able to get your clothes off without you waking. I've given you a bath already." He dropped the sponge in a bucket of water.

I felt embarrassed and betrayed. I glanced around the room, searching for my clothes, but they were missing. I noticed that Griff looked different. He was not wearing his monk garb, but rather, dead-Fred's shorts and sandals.

"What the hell's going on?"

"Are you hungry?" he asked.

"Where are my clothes? Why are you wearing Fred's duds?"

"Now that you're clean, I'll shave you. Then we'll grab some food at the festival. The merchants will feed us in return for a blessing. Once you're fed, we'll go swimming. All the monks skinny-dip at night when there's nobody on the beach." He lifted Fred's tank top from the bed and slipped it on.

"Shave me?" I noticed a pair of scissors and a straight razor lying on the nightstand. Beside the statue of the Buddha lay my jeweled cross and chain. Good, I thought, I still had something of mine, something from Luke.

"Your head," he said, and pointed to a stack of folded saffron robes at the foot of my bed.

"You want me in monk drag?" I snapped. "Is this a joke?"

"You said you wouldn't wear Fred's threads, so wear mine. If you look like a monk, the townspeople will protect you from those thugs. And Khun Thammarato says an outward disguise has the power to obscure inner flaws."

"I won't."

"You can't walk around naked. Your clothes won't be back from the laundry until Monday. Besides, I don't need these robes any more. Thammarato finished his elephant. Soon as we sell it, I'll be back in the States before you can spit."

Startled, I said, "You can't leave me here," but then I realized his freedom meant my freedom. With Griff taken care of, I could run back to the *Wanderbird* and sail away with a clean conscience, or perhaps there would be enough money from the elephant that he would take me with him, at least as far as the American embassy in Bangkok.

He left the room and came back moments later with a straight-back chair. He ordered me to sit, and when I did he draped a towel around my shoulders. I felt rather foolish sitting there naked while he lifted the scissors and began to crop my hair. What the hell, I thought, disguised as a monk, perhaps I could give Reverend Starling the slip and fly to Bangkok with Griff.

Much as I wanted to not think about anything, having Griff within a foot of me had my senses sizzling. I could feel the energy radiating from him like a furnace. My temperature rose to meet his. The sound of his breathing mingled with the sound of the wind outside. I leaned closer and inhaled his spent breath, which had the fragrance of toasted sugar. I focused on his fingers sliding across my scalp as my eyes took in the paler skin of those soft areas under his arms. My heart began to race. I so wanted to pull him onto my lap and kiss him, and I somehow knew that he would let me. The moment had become, I knew, intensely sensual for both of us. At the same time, I didn't want him to stop. I gave myself over to him, placing myself in his will and giving him my complete trust. It felt delicious to let go, to give up control and simply experience whatever happened. It felt like stepping off the stern of the *Wanderbird,* not caring what came next.

"It won't take long to learn the routine," he whispered. "The monks are obliging. You might even like it."

His voice so close to my ear was like hearing a rainstorm form words. I scrutinized him with an unflinching stare. I longed to tell him to take me with him, but what I said was, "Living as a monk is impossible. I can't undo who I am. Why don't you just ship me off to the Black Hole of Calcutta or the Siberian salt mines?"

A shadow passed through the room. I leaned closer and inhaled, absorbing his intoxicating sweetness.

Griff set aside the scissors, lifted the towel from my shoulders, leaned out the window, and shook the towel. My hair flew away like a swarm of insects. He laid the cloth around my neck again and soaped my stubbly head, face, and neck. "Thammarato would say, becoming a monk doesn't change who you are, it takes away everything that is not you, to reveal who you are."

"Sounds like he's full of shit."

He opened the straight razor and inspected the edge, no doubt hoping there was still some cut left in it. "Hold still."

Griff was adept and meticulous, making slow, graceful sweeps with the razor. My eyes closed on their own as I focused on the scrape of the blade. I felt somewhat relaxed as he hovered above me, shaving away my stubble. The process seemed to take an eternity for my scalp to emerge from its cocoon.

Without opening my eyes, I said, "That feels glorious."

Griff wrapped a hot towel around my head and went to work shaving my face, including my eyebrows. I remained motionless, but I scrutinized him through the slits between my eyelids. I was fully hard now, but he didn't seem to notice. That amazed me because I'm impressively endowed. There was no way he couldn't have seen, and not been even a little overwhelmed. He showed no embarrassment at all, and surprisingly, neither did I.

It was difficult to tell which felt better, my newly shaved head or my proud cock. The two feelings reached across my body for each other and fused somewhere in my chest. The sensation was beyond carnal, like stars are beyond the clouds.

Five rapturous minutes crawled by before he laid aside the razor, unwrapped the hot towel, and replaced it with a cool one. When the cloth touched my head, I moaned as if I were eating something delectable. Griff mixed a concoction of herbs and water from the pan into a paste and began to rub it into my scalp, neck, and shoulders. It smelled like turmeric. This haircut was getting positively flirty by my reckoning.

Staring out the window, I noticed a large birdcage suspended from a Bodhi tree. Trapped inside was a raven, coal black and about the size of a dog's head. Its alert face had a sharp beak and two solid black eyes that stared intently at me. Its face expressed a vast contentment, as if it was enjoying the tranquility of evening's cooler temperature, safe and secure within the confines of rusting wire.

I stood, unwrapped the cloth from my head, wiped my face with it, and tossed it to Griff. He bowed low, as if I were the Buddha himself. *Is he mocking me, or is he paying homage to my impressive cock?* Either way, he became utterly, dangerously charming. He dropped the towel into the pan next to the bed and made a quick departure while I continued to stare at the raven.

My mounting lust had me confused and curious. Griff was not pretty like Luke, so it was not a question of beauty. I wondered what qualities he possessed that could kindle this severe desire in me. Could it be only his youth, a thin connection to vitality at a time when my life could be cut short? Perhaps I saw something in him of what I had once been—innocent, wholesome—and I wanted to devour that as a way to recapture my past. Or was it simply the reflection of Luke I saw at his core? As the silence grew, I wondered if it was my move; had he purposely led me to the brink and now expected me to do something?

Griff entered the room again. He froze, blazing in my glare like an exposed power line. It seemed that there was a penetrating blue light illuminating my naked body and stiff cock. Griff offered a visual counterpoint. He clenched his eyes shut, and when they opened a moment later, they displayed a look of stoical despair for the refuge he had unsuccessfully struggled to repair.

I felt myself begin to deflate, but I had yet to give up hope.

As he came toward me, I slipped my arms around his waist, pulled him to me, and touched my lips to his. The softness consumed me.

He pulled back only a little. His fingertips caressed my cheek as though he was reading Braille, and his voice, when he finally spoke, was a whisper. "Please don't."

"Why are you doing this?" I murmured.

"Because you seem so sad, the saddest man I've ever known. Sadder than my stepfather, sadder than me."

Good Lord, how can anyone with so much poise and promise hold even a kernel of sorrow in his heart? To face the world as he did, locking his sadness inside and not letting it affect him, showed remarkable spirit. Certainly more courage than I could muster. The bond between us grew—fortified by our bound grief—even as my lust subsided.

I stepped back and dropped my arms to my sides, now as limp as my dick. A silence stood between us like a fortress wall. Outside, I heard the raven calling and the chatter of people in the courtyard.

"Let me show you how to arrange these robes," he said.

Once that dreadful silence was broken, I could feel my body relax slightly. I stood there naked, having given up everything except my crucifix necklace. Even my hair had drifted away on the wind, but I was still reluctant to don those robes. Griff folded the lower gown and wrapped it around my waist. I said, "I feel like a phony wearing these. I don't believe in anything now, and it's too late for me. I've done too much sinning, spoiled too many lives."

Griff stayed silent for the time it took him to fasten the lower robe and fold the upper one. He laid the upper gown on my left shoulder and draped it across my back. "It's not about being good," he said, "whatever that means. I'm not at all religious, but I've become spiritual as hell."

"What's the difference?"

"According to Khun Thammarato—"

"Him again?"

"Being spiritual has nothing to do with what you believe, or being good, and everything to do with your state of consciousness." He wrapped the cloth under my right arm, across my chest, and folded it over my left shoulder.

"Meaning?"

"Religion is believing in a higher power. Being spiritual means giving up your past and future, and tapping into your inner-being to experience the world here and now."

I wanted to argue that if I gave up my history and future, then who would I be? Nothing. Memories and dreams of the future are what make a man, but I wasn't certain of that. I wasn't sure who I was even with those memories and dreams intact, so I stepped back and asked, "How do I look?"

"Different," he said, with the wisp of a grin. He moved to my bedside table and lifted my necklace. "You want this?"

I nodded, not wanting to leave it in the room and having no pockets to carry it.

He placed it around my neck and adjusted the crucifix in the middle of my chest. "Not ready to give up your past yet?"

It was both a rhetorical question and a true statement. Yet, I wanted to defend myself, tell him I had tried to commit suicide. If that's not giving up everything, then what is? "I've lost my life. It's the one thing left."

"The Buddha said, 'You only lose what you cling to.'"

I held my tongue. I had the distinct feeling he had suddenly turned into a smug little bastard, but I also knew I was being too defensive after having lost everything.

He took my hand and led me into the hallway, down the stairs, and onto the veranda. The carnival was in full swing. Hundreds of tourists and townspeople rubbing elbows while wandering from stall to stall, eating, playing games, listening to music. It all sounded like the singing of giant mosquitoes. Villagers from the hills arrived carrying baskets of handicrafts. They displayed their knickknacks on straw mats spread under trees, while happy-faced children gathered around a storyteller. Stalls spilled over with cooked foods, flowers, and raw fruits. The spicy odor of Thai chilies clung to the air, and the flicker of sparklers burst in the dark like shooting stars.

A shrill voice called my name. I glanced over my shoulder to see Jason charging toward me. I ducked into the nearest room and slammed the door shut so quickly that my robes got caught. I was trapped.

"Corbin," I heard him call from the other side of the door, "I know that's you in there. You can't fool me with that getup."

I held my breath, foolishly praying he would give up and leave.

He pounded on the door. "I'm staying here till you come out," he shrieked. "Please, Corbin, my father is looking for me. We only have a few minutes. Let me in."

"Stop shouting and I'll come out."

After a moment of silence, I opened the door and stepped onto the veranda again. Jason threw his arms around me, hugging me so hard I thought he would crack ribs. I pushed him back to arm's length and held his shoulders.

Griff moved to the far side of the porch, but not quite out of hearing distance. I took note of his unsmiling eyes juxtaposed to his gentle grin.

"Jason, we can't do this. It's over. You should have never told them."

"I overheard my brother saying they were going to kill you tonight. That's when I realized that you didn't drown. We've got to get away from here. I have money. I can pay our way."

My attention divided between the two young men—one tranquil

and perfectly stationary, the other wriggling with passion—mentally comparing the two opposite attractions to my simple, sensual nature.

"For God's sake, Jason, if they find us together we're both screwed. Go back. Forget about me."

"But I love you."

"The worst thing in the world for you is to get mixed up with a man in my unstable condition. It's not too late to save yourself."

"Fuck that! I—"

"Look at me. Take a good look. I've lost everything, even my hair, all because of you. Haven't you done enough damage? Let it go."

"We can—"

He stopped in midsentence, glaring at the edge of the porch. I turned to see Miss Goodwin climbing the steps. "Jason," she said, "I think you should heed Mr. Edwards's advice and leave. Go back to the hotel. You'll only enrage your family more by staying."

Jason muscled his way closer to me, wrapping an arm around my waist. "No! I won't. You don't understand. Nobody understands."

Miss Goodwin arched her spine, making herself appear a foot taller. "Jason, I'm not an old maid. I understand perfectly." She inched closer, holding out her hand to him. "What you don't appreciate is that you're placing Mr. Edwards's life in jeopardy. You know what your father is capable of, and this costume he's wearing will not help him in the least. If you feel deeply for him, and I know you do, then you'll come with me now, before it's too late."

We stood for a moment in silence as Jason shook his head. Tears trickled down his cheeks. Miss Goodwin glanced at me. The hate I had seen in her composure earlier had softened into something like pity. I had no doubt she spoke the truth regarding Jason's family.

"He doesn't want you, dammit," she spat. "He just said so. I do. I want you with all my heart. I'll take care of you. Come, now. Obey me!" She stepped closer.

He glanced at me with eyes pleading. I turned my head away.

Jason retreated like a well-trained dog, led by Miss Goodwin. She looked over her shoulder as she wrapped a protective arm around him. "I'll do my best to stop them."

They had walked twenty feet when I called to him, "Jason."

He stopped and whirled around, but I could think of nothing to say. We stood there for an instant, silent. His tears flowed freely now; the pain on his face seemed to match the burn in my chest. "I'm sorry," was all I could think to say after that awkward pause. They continued on, swallowed by the crowd.

Griff took hold of my arm. He coaxed me into action and led me to the steps. "Come on, you'll feel better if you eat something."

He steered me through the throng, passing one food stall after another. I noticed one selling dried cockroaches as big as my thumb. "You ever eat iguana meat?" he asked as we stopped before a fire pit where a rotund woman was roasting four huge lizards, each on its own bamboo spit. The look on my face must have shown my revulsion, because he chuckled.

"I'll bet you're going to tell me it tastes like chicken."

"Jesus, sir, don't be such a wuss. Besides, they do taste like chicken breasts. And I don't mean these scrawny Thai chickens that taste like whatever they scavenge; I mean good old Texas, grain-fed hens." He smiled, and for a second I completely forgot about Jason.

Griff spoke a few words of Thai to the lady. She bowed to me with her hands pressed together at her forehead. I felt like such a phony. Nobody should bow to me no matter how I was dressed.

Griff lifted one of the cooked creatures from the flames and handed it to me. "Let's get a beer to wash that down."

"What about you. Aren't you hungry?"

"We can share, sir. She can't afford to support too many moochers."

As I followed him, I held the carcass to my nose and sniffed a gamey tang. My hunger overrode my repugnance, and I ripped off a hunk with my teeth and chewed. I had never tasted a Texas chicken, but I'm willing to bet they taste nothing like an iguana slathered in a Thai-chili sauce. My mouth seared. My stomach, however, seemed to rejoice after so long a time of being empty. I ripped off another hunk, and this time it tasted palatable.

We stopped in front of a large tub of ice water. Griff spoke a quick sentence to a man who was sucking on a bottle of Singha beer. The man waved at the tub. I was relieved to see he didn't bow. Griff plunged an arm into the water, drew out a can of Tiger beer, and popped the top. "Let's take this to the beach. We can swim after we eat."

I exchanged the remains of the lizard for the beer and began to follow him toward the sound of the waves hitting the shore. I raised the can to my lips but the odor of beer, for the first time in my life, was beyond revolting. I had to fight to keep the lizard in my stomach. As we neared the seawall, I turned the can and began to empty the contents, but he snatched it from my fingers and downed the remains in three long swallows.

"Oh shit," he gasped, "that's so cold my chest hurts." He stared at me expectantly, then threw his head back and laughed. "That was a test, sir."

I cocked my head. "Test?"

"To see if you would object to my drinking beer. Most adults would. They put themselves in a special status and screw the rest of us."

"I'm nothing special."

"Yes, sir, but Khun Thammarato would say, nothing *is* special." When I didn't respond he asked, "Are you really going to swim with me?"

"Will you save me if I start to drown?"

With a bark that could have been another bout of laughter, he vaulted off the seawall and landed nimbly on the beach. I clambered over the rail, a bit stiffly, and dropped to the still-warm sand. I fell to my knees and he helped me up. During my ascent, our bodies jostled against one another, briefly and roughly. Now that we were away from the temple, I felt our relationship evolving into something different, something new.

He ran for the surf. I followed as fast as I could. Already the carnival lights, however bright and colorful, seemed far behind me as I pursued him to the water's edge. I could feel in my chest the boom of the rollers crashing to shore, but out to sea the waves were invisible. If there were other monks swimming, I saw no sign of them. Beyond the rushing surf, the blackness seemed immensely forbidding, almost suffocating. A small and very cold tickle crept over my scalp. My body didn't want to do this.

Shrouded somewhere in that blackness, the *Wanderbird* lay at anchor. It meant freedom. All I had to do was swim past the breakers. I could see the dim lights atop the masts on each boat in the bay, looking like bright stars on a pristine night. I knew the tallest of them was the *Wanderbird*. I also knew it would be an easy swim. We could be on the high seas within an hour.

As I hesitated, Griff tore off his clothes and charged the waves with a wild whooping cry—fearless, confident, and bursting with animation. Seeing his slim, naked form frolicking in the water disintegrated my thoughts of freedom. Twenty-four hours ago I had plunged into the depths to end my pitiless life. Now I found myself stripping off my robes in order to chase after life. It seemed somehow appropriate that this night I would end up neck deep in seawater.

I waded straight in, determined to show Griff I had some vivacity left in me as well. I floundered, however, over rocks and broken shells until I felt smooth sand under my feet. Then a stinging slap of cold hit my groin, and a bolt of electricity shot to my brain. Undeterred, I moved further out, up to my waist. I was about to plunge when Griff came out of the darkness, riding a wave on his belly. He shot past me without a glance, a dolphin absorbed in his acrobatics.

That same wave bowled me over. I tumbled under the foam with a nose full of water. Gaining my footing again, I choked out a laugh while suddenly drunk on the exhilaration of it all. I glanced out to sea again, only then appreciating how large the waves actually were. That close, they seemed tremendous, towering over me, dark movement unrolling itself out of sheer blackness. It was thrilling and terrifying, but I was too intoxicated to be afraid. I thought of the *Wanderbird*— of freedom—once more, but before I could react, another black wall rolled over me, catching me in a thundering wallop of foam. It pulled at me with a powerful undertow. I faltered for a minute more, until I saw Griff sailing down on another toppling precipice, intent upon his own rite of passage. I stood in awe of him, my mind coming microscopically close to the true meaning of life. I had that revelation on my tongue, but then I received another stunning baptism of wild surf. It washed me away, my thoughts, speech, desires, whole sections of my history. It all flowed from me as the undercurrent pulled me further out. I didn't care. For the first time since Luke, I felt happy, clean, and yet less than I had ever been.

Total freedom was not to be, however. I felt something grip my neck, and moments later I realized Griff was pulling me toward shore. My joy at finding such freedom was doubled with the sudden realization that I was sharing this amazing experience with him. The night, the cold surf, the colorful lights up the beach were all being played out for our pleasure alone. Again, I felt so close to understanding the thing that had eluded me all my life. I could feel it, but I couldn't put it into thoughts. All I could think to do was stay afloat while being hit by pylons of water until everything made sense. I put myself in his capable hands, and simply enjoyed the ride.

A great and apocalyptic tower grew out of the darkness, tumbling in on itself with a roar that sounded like the ending of the world. We were still too far out, well out of my depth, struggling against the receding flow. *This is it, our Thelma-and-Louise-at-the-Grand-Canyon moment.*

We rocketed toward heaven, up the face of that monster, and were hammered down to hell, pitching head over heels. I had the breath knocked out of me as I pounded the sand. I held on to him. As long as he pressed against me I had no fear.

The next thing I knew, Griff was hauling me up the beach while I vomited seawater. I took a gasping lung-full of salty air before he said, "That's enough for tonight, sir," in exactly the tone of voice that nanny Perkins had used when I was a child.

"No. I'm all right," I rasped. "Let's do more." I hated the fact that he thought he had to protect me, that we had fallen into a nanny/child relationship. Moments ago we were two stallions racing through a universe of liquid omnipotence. I refused to squander that sensation. I had been so close.

He cocked his head and laughed, a big throaty roar, and the sound of it made me laugh too.

Within that joyful howl, I seemed to shrink while everything about him grew larger: the white of his smile, beads of water clinging to his shaved head, narrow hips, heavy sex, and his shoulders that had begun to shiver.

"Time to"—he gulped down his giggles—"go back to the dorm?" His voice calmed to a whisper.

"What else?"

He leaned into me, his face hovered close to mine, and he kissed me on the lips. It was not an act of passion, but one of searching, and done with such profound tenderness that I was stunned. He tasted of salt, like a two-hundred-proof margarita. My heart began to thump. Suddenly, we were stallions again, equals, racing the wind.

His face pulled a few inches away, not so far as to lose the scent of his breath, and he stared into my eyes. There was nothing either of us could say. It felt like moments ago when we tumbled through the surf at the whim of the current. But then, on the periphery of my vision, I noticed a shadow moving toward us, something large, and I knew we were not alone.

They skulked out of the darkness like hyenas prowling through heavy brush. One by one their shapes became visible. I heard the tick-tick-tick of what little time I had left slipping away. The sound was quieter than my heartbeat, but it seemed like slow detonations, a gradual explosion in the making. At my back lay the *Wanderbird*, no longer a viable escape route, and I silently cursed my stupidity.

With a tired grace, we rose from the sand, Griff and I. My right hand lingered on his shoulder. I pushed him away, hoping he would run for help, but he would not leave me. Reverend Starling confronted us. A few feet to his right, Wayne Starling stood with one hand clenched around a knife. Bud and Scotty hovered on the reverend's left.

"You see, what I tell you, boys," Starling said to his posse, "he's already corrupting another one. This is why God commands us to put an end to all his kind."

"Run for it," I told Griff.

He faced them, ever defiant. "Will you kill me too? What was my sin?"

"You better leave while you can, boy," Wayne hissed.

I stepped forward, putting myself between Griff and them. "I don't ask for your forgiveness or understanding because I don't think you're capable of that, but I do ask for your recognition of what I am in each of you, in all of us."

Wayne bent his knees, lowering his center of gravity like a cat preparing to pounce. "You're a cancer on humanity, faggot, and the only way to deal with a tumor is to cut it out."

"That's interesting coming from you," I said. I glanced at Reverend Starling. "I told you once before I didn't take Jason's virginity, but I know who did."

"Liar!" Wayne lunged at me, the knife whooshing as it made its arc. I leaped to one side, but felt the sting of the blade travel up my arm. At that same moment, Bud tackled Griff and held him well back, though he fought like a lion.

Anger swelled up in me, becoming overpowering. Before I could get my balance, Wayne's knee smashed into my solar plexus and I doubled over with the wind knocked out of me. I saw green spots in front of me. As I fell, he cracked my jaw with an iron fist. I tasted blood, which made me even angrier.

"Fucking animal," I spat. I seldom cursed, but it felt like the right thing to say, the kind of thing the hero of an action movie would proclaim before dying. He hauled me up and pressed the blade to my cheek, dangerously close to my left eye.

"I've had it with you fucking fudgepackers," he said in a calmer voice, "always throwing it in people's faces while spreading your disease to innocent boys."

My anger detonated, and I let it take over. It was time to fight back, to kill or die. I tensed my body, ready to spring, but Scott kicked my calf and I fell again, landing on my butt.

Wayne collapsed against me. He slammed me to my back and straddled my chest with the knife pointed at my heart. I held his arm with both hands, trying to force it away. I clenched my jaw and strained with all my capacity. It did no good. The blade slowly fell.

"Fuck you," I gasped between clenched teeth.

He barked a laugh.

Fear replaced my anger. It crawled up my spine and I felt tears burn my eyes. There was no escape. No hope. Ever so slowly, the blade sunk until the point pierced my skin directly below where my crucifix still hung. I knew this was how my life would end, and I accepted it. His mouth moved as if he was chewing something bitter, and I wondered if he felt justified in killing me. Yes, if the eye-for-an-eye rule related, then tonight I would die.

I watched his animal face, bright with lust and filled with hate, or could it have been jealousy?

But then it all ended. Wayne's father grabbed him by the collar and yanked him off me, chucking him onto his back and then standing over him. The reverend's foot pinned Wayne's knife hand to the sand.

My body went limp as I gasped for air.

"Don't believe him, Papa. I never fucked Jason. I never did."

There was a moment of stunned, heavy breathing. Griff broke free of Bud and rushed to me. He hauled me to a sitting position and held me up by my shoulders in a protective embrace.

"He never said you did," Reverend Starling hissed in a voice as cold as mercury, "but the truth is undeniable." He took a great gasping breath, as if recovering from the wind being knocked out of him. "Why in Christ's name? Why? You could have had any girl!"

"He's lying! Don't believe him." Wayne tried to rise up, but as his face rose to the level of Reverend Starling's crotch, his father cut the air with his fist, hammering Wayne's jaw. I heard the snap of bone from six feet away. Teeth flew across the sand like popcorn from a popper. Wayne lay on his side shrieking like a gut-shot animal. The reverend signaled Bud and Scotty. They grabbed Wayne by the arms, snatched him to his feet, and led him up the beach.

Reverend Starling faced me. It was too dark to see the pain in his eyes, but I heard it in his voice. "How long did it go on, between my boys I mean?"

"Three years."

He bowed his head. "You fucking queers destroy everything. Children. Marriage. Morality. Even a father's love. This doesn't make what you did right, but you'll have no more trouble from me as long as you stay the hell away from my family. You hear?"

I nodded.

"And if you open your mouth about this to anyone in my congregation, I'll track you down and gut you myself."

I closed my eyes, grateful to be alive.

He staggered away with a visible fatigue. I felt a stab of pity as sharp as the slash on my arm. Griff snatched up his shirt and wrapped my wound. We sat for a long time staring at the sea before pulling on our clothes, as if not willing to let go of what we had shared in the water. I noticed out of the corner of my eye that the movement of his breathing slowly grew gentle. His body relaxed again. His hand reached for mine and we laced our fingers together. At that moment, it was all I needed. Any more would have been too much.

❖

Our walk back to the carnival calmed us both. We were no longer water-creatures frolicking in the surf, but we became happy. He held me up by wrapping an arm around my waist, even though there was nothing wrong with my legs. I didn't resist.

When we reached the edge of the carnival I realized that we had reverted back into a thirtyish, defrocked priest being helped by a young Prince Valiant. Some of the stalls were already packing up. The crowd had thinned.

Griff became self-conscious and almost curt. "Let's go to the washroom and rinse the salt off, then hunt up some antiseptic for your arm. It may need stitches."

"That's bound to hurt like hell," I said, trying to lighten his mood.

"I read once that when the Mexican painter Siqueiros did a portrait of the American poet Hart Crane, he had to paint him with closed eyelids because he couldn't paint those eyes. There was too much suffering in them."

I looked away. "Should I close mine?"

"I know your torment," he said. "I can stand it. What was his name?"

I glanced back at him, wondering how he knew. Had I talked in my sleep? Was he that perceptive? Or was I so transparent? "Luke," I mumbled. Then louder, "His name was Luke, and he was about your age. I was younger then."

"You were defrocked because of him?"

"Defrocked? I was put in prison. I had been a priest only a year when Luke asked to see me privately in my study. He was a beautiful soul, innocent, but too young—I thought there was no chance in the world. But he threw himself at me, declaring his love."

"And his young, hormone-charged lust?"

"Don't make fun of me."

"Sorry."

"I was such a prig back then. I suggested we kneel and pray for guidance, and somehow that turned into rolling on the floor. I swear I didn't even know I was gay until he kissed me." I noted Griff's grin blossoming into a full-on smile. "It was love, pure and full, for both of us. The great difference between people in this world is not between rich and poor or good and evil. The biggest difference is between the people who give humble pleasure in love and those who can't. The ones who can't are people who can only stand back and watch true love with a sickened envy. I don't mean sex. I'm talking about soul mates, two people merging into one."

"What happened to him?"

"We were found out by one of his chums. Word went around and then got back to his parents. They did a number on him, that abhorrently ignorant family, to the point where they had him so mortified that he hanged himself from their garage rafters with a noose made of his father's Arman, silk tie."

He touched my arm. "I'm so sorry."

"That day I walked away from religion and all those smug, disapproving, accusing, God-fearing frauds."

"They couldn't fault themselves, so they blamed you."

"They all see God as an angry, petulant, peevish old man. A senile delinquent who punishes people for faults he created in the first damned place, and of course, they acted just like their image of Him."

"And you've been searching for something to believe in ever since."

"No. I believed in Luke. I still do. But imagine all your dreams and hopes dissolving away in an instant, being blacked out like a lovely poem washed off a blackboard by a wet sponge, just some accident of fate. So after that, and a two-year sentence in hell, I cracked up, my nerves did—nightmares, drinking, waking up to a strange face over and over, and now I'm here with nothing but a cross around my neck and a gash on my arm. More often than not I feel more dead than Luke."

"My savior's name is Eddie Flores," Griff said. "He's three years older than me, and his family came from Tulum, Mexico. Even though I'm straight and we never had sex, I think we shared that same kind of love. That's why my stepfather thought he could have his way with me. He assumed Eddie and I were lovers."

I stopped and stared at him. There were people chatting all around us, yet between us there stood a deep silence as we took each other in. I so much wanted to hug him, as an offering of comfort for both of us. Then I remembered something else about the Griffin myth: When they mate, they mate for life. And if their true love dies, they never take another, which explained why there was no passion in that kiss on the beach earlier.

"Have you called him? Why isn't he helping you get home?"

"His phone is offline. I called his folks and they told me he came over here looking for me, but they wouldn't tell me how to reach him."

I draped my arm over his shoulder and we walked on. I thought about how lucky he was, because at some point they would surely find each other. That would only happen to me if there was indeed an afterlife, which I wasn't holding out any hope for.

❖

A windy murmur drifted from the surrounding trees and a flicker of light from lanterns cast golden spots on the ground, like a hushed scattering of shiny coins. The sound of distressed voices grew loud. Two monks raced to us and one spoke a few words of Thai to Griff. He took off running toward the dormitory. I followed him all the way to Khun Thammarato's room.

Griff turned on a light fixture that was suspended from overhead. A pearly moon of a low-watt, bare light bulb gave an unearthly luster to the room. Within seconds, the shining globe was decorated by insects, large gossamer moths that immolated themselves on its surface. The light through their wings gave them an opalescent color, a flash of fantasy.

Khun Thammarato sat in his wheelchair, impeccably dressed in burnt-orange robes. His shaved head gleamed under the light bulb. Griff kneeled before him, taking his hand that was already stiffening with rigor mortis. A carved elephant lay on his bed. On his lap sat a solid block of wood with a few slivers shaved off the top. His other hand still clutched his carving knife. Griff remained silent, dry-eyed.

I took the knife from that withered hand, lifted the block of wood from his lap, and stepped back onto the veranda to let Griff express his sorrow alone.

An elderly monk scurried up the steps and hobbled into the room. As I waited, a sharp bursts of Thai echoed from the room. The tones of Griff's voice no longer held sweetness or purity. A moment later, he stormed outside.

Even though he stood a few yards away, under a porch light, I could see his eyes were hazel inside and red and puffy outside, as if he'd been crying. He looked through me, not at me. He clenched his fists and stared without seeing, breathing hard like he was trying to push his pain away by beating it with his lungs. The scariest part was that I recognized that pain. He had been reduced to helplessness against a cruel world. I had been there too many times myself not to see the outward signs of it.

I stabbed the block of wood with the knife and tucked it under one arm. I draped my other arm over Griff's shoulders and led him up the stairs to my room. He was still in some other world when I sat him on Fred's bed and leaned his back against the cinder-block wall. I laid the block of wood on the floor, sat next to him, circled an arm behind his neck, and pulled him into a hug.

"Whatever it is, you'll be all right," I said, already knowing what it was; what else could trigger such a response? I guessed it would not be okay, not for Griff, not for me. My words sounded as hollow as the sudden void in my chest.

He confirmed my suspicions a minute later when he said, "They intend to cremate him with the elephant that he carved for me. I'm screwed."

"We'll find a way. Trust me."

"Trust you?" I could see him attempting a smirk but he couldn't manage it. "I woke up this morning owning nothing but my robes, a begging bowl, and a sliver of hope. I've lost everything."

I swallowed the lump in my throat. "I've been holding on to things that I thought mattered for so long that I'm dead tired. I have no strength left. Right now, having nothing to carry around seems like a godsend."

"Lucky you. Not sure if you realized it, but now we're in the same boat, or should I say, sinking ship?"

We had entered a new phase, though in his despair he probably hadn't realized it yet. We had gone beyond the symbolic dialogue relationship to this new phase of communication that was very much heart to heart, deep calling to deep.

I inched closer, snuggled into his hip, and pulled his head so it rested on my shoulder. I wanted to tell him we had each other, but that sounded like such an exhausted cliché that I said nothing, gently stroking the now-prominent veins on his arm, tracing each deviation in the skin. We sat in the dim gloom, waiting for God knows what. I certainly didn't.

Deep into the night, Griff slept, his head still supported by my shoulder. I sat in the dark, wrestling with something that kept me awake: an itch in my blood and the nerves of my groin that needed scratching. The moon rose into the sky, and clouds passing over its face caused shadows to come and go through the window, making parts of his body appear and disappear, as if temptation was being given and then withdrawn.

I thought about that kiss on the beach. I knew he felt abandoned, and now he would devote his full attention to me, probably cling to me as tightly as he did now. I was confident he would let me comfort him. He was mine for the taking. But as I felt his spent breath curling on my skin, I knew I would not disturb his sleep. I thought about the weeks, perhaps months, ahead of him and me traveling together, working our way back to the States. It was a rare show of strength for me not to wake him so we could make love, but I also knew my restraint wouldn't last. If we traveled together or even stayed here, it was only a matter of time.

I leaned my face to him and lightly kissed his bare head, while dreading that time in the not-too-distant future when I would demand more.

❖

The sky turned an astounding shade of pale cerulean that left only one star hanging in the western firmament. It was so lovely my throat went thick and tears caught themselves in my eyelashes. I wanted to wake Griff so we could share this splendor, but I didn't. His head still leaned against my shoulder. He hadn't moved as I held him through the night.

I knew what I would do now, and as the idea matured, I realized I would do it out of love. Not love for Griff, which I did feel after only a day, but love for Luke. My Luke. The light of my soul. My adoration for him was the only thing I could relate to now, and every action I would take from now until the end of my days would be for him, done in honor of what we had shared.

The call to prayers sounded at the temple, which woke Griff. I heard stirring in other rooms and the sound of bare feet plodding along the corridor.

Griff stared out the window as that last star vanished before the new day. He made no move to leave my embrace. We sat there, battered and bruised, my arm throbbing, not quite knowing what to do.

As the sky brightened, he mumbled, "Awesome."

Watching him, holding him, feeling his warmth, I had to agree. I took his hand and brought it to my lips. It was stained with my dried blood. I kissed it. Then I lifted the crucifix from my neck, wrapped the chain around the cross, and placed it in that bloodstained hand. "Walk into town and sell this. The cross and chain are twenty-four-karat gold, the gems are seven rubies and one fine amethyst. It will bring twice what that elephant would have. Then get your butt to the airport and jump on the first flight to Bangkok. This should get you home."

"I can't. It's all you've got."

"If you don't take it I'll toss it out the window." I ripped it out of his fingers and raised my arm to throw it, but he caught my hand to restrain me.

"Tell you what," I said, "I'll trade you your begging bowl and that old monk's carving knife for it. Even-steven, and you're on your way."

"But you're coming with me?"

I shook my head.

He was silent for a minute, and I saw comprehension light up his eyes. He cleared his throat. "This cross is the last of your past, your personal history. Who will you be now that you have nothing left?"

"That's what I intend to find out."

He smiled with his eyes, as only he could. I knew they were hazel, but dawn's light had turned them a gentle orange. I promised myself that I would never forget how they looked into me that morning.

"I'll pawn this in town and send you the claim ticket so you can redeem it." When I shook my head again, he continued, "Because you'll want it again when you've overcome your fear."

He kissed me, a lingering press of lips that seemed to merge with the sunrise and the silence. I vowed to carry that kiss as I had carried that crucifix.

"Someday, when we meet back in the States," he said, "we'll get a good laugh out of this."

He sprang off the bed, seized his begging bowl, and handed it to me. "Don't be late for prayers on your first day."

I took his hand, letting him pull me off the bed. I snatched up the block of teak and carving knife, and I carried them downstairs with me.

In the courtyard, we shared a final embrace.

Griff cocked his head to one side. "You're not staying here because I spilled the beans about Khit having a crush on you? Could it be mutual?"

I smiled, remembering that sexy boy with the kind face who had resuscitated me on the beach the previous morning. "No promises."

Griff's laughter filled the courtyard as he began walking toward town.

I entered the temple for the first time as an acolyte, and spread before me were the temple's inhabitants, a field of brilliant orange robes fluttering in the morning breeze that drifted though the open windows. I sat on a pillow in the shadow of the Buddha and placed the block of wood before me. Taking the knife in my right hand, I closed my eyes. As I listened to the sonorous chanting, I tried to envision an elephant rambling out of the mist on a cool morning. Then I moved my hand, shaving a sliver from the teak block.

EMPTY CHAIRS

Sometime after midnight, he dreamed of bodies falling—familiar faces, and others, half-forgotten but still recognizable, and still other ones unknown. The images played on for hours, until he felt himself falling with them, tumbling through silent space with no place to land. He woke in the darkest stretch of night, that fulcrum before the sky begins to pale. He was well acquainted with this hour, the musty aroma, the feel of clammy air on bare skin, the creak of wooden beams as the temple prepared itself for the dawn. He kneaded his neck muscles; to his fingers they seemed unyielding and sweat-covered, but not painful. As he moved his head they creaked like a rusty door hinge.

He reached for his pipe and lighter that lay beside his sleeping mat. It was imperative, he knew, that he let the opium guide him back into oblivion. He could not lie awake with nothing to do but remember while he waited for morning prayers. He needed to drift in lovely blackness, unhaunted, unpeopled, with no quivering images of bodies slamming into concrete. He lit the pipe and drew the burn into his lungs.

When he woke again from the same dream, light bled through the shutters making golden bands across his sleeping mat and the far wall. He felt agitated and unsure of where he was, and even who he was. This happened to him often—waking disturbed, only half remembering the dream and desperate to put it behind him as he began his day. Once his situation and identity became clear, he could tell from the color and strength of the light that he had missed morning prayers and the alms rounds to beg for food from the faithful. He had most likely missed breakfast as well, which meant he would eat only one meal today, at midday.

Lying on his back, he slid his head into one of those bands of light, feeling the pleasure of sunlight on his face, gazing at the striped wall, noticing the smell of wisteria sweetening the air. But the dream refused to dissolve. Those images lingered at the edge of his mind, and he knew it would be a grim day.

He rolled onto his stomach and reached for his lighter and pipe, only to find them missing. His agitation flared into anger.

He tried calling for aid, but his throat was raw from smoking, and no sound came. He managed a painful swallow and tried again. "Nop!" He swallowed once more. "Nop, where the hell is my pipe?"

As he waited for a reply, more images bombarded him. This part of the dream was different. The air, inundated with ash, turned everything—sky, buildings, people—gray. It was New York City, with its wide avenues and looming skyscrapers. He ran against a torrent of people, fighting through pandemonium, working his way toward the Towers. He felt a presence behind him but he had no idea who it was. It could be a person, or perhaps merely a voice close to him who understood better than he did the urgency, cajoling him to run faster, fight harder.

At the end of each dimly lit block he was tempted to turn and flee, but the voice behind him kept urging him on. Finally, he reached the square where the Towers had stood proudly only minutes before. He dropped to his knees, frozen, absorbing the shock, struggling to understand. The hole in his chest felt as large as the one in the skyline.

The dream changed again and everything dimmed. In the scant light, a dozen people wearing purple robes with hoods formed a circle around him. They all had their hoods drawn low, hiding their faces. One of them drew his hood back. Eddie Flores looked just as handsome as the last day he had stood on the earth. Eddie had been dead for ten years. Another person brushed her hood back, and he saw his wife, Gayle, moving toward him, holding out her arms. This was the first time she had appeared in his dreams. He was shocked that someone still living would appear. Both Eddie's and Gayle's faces were lit like Vermeer paintings. She did not speak but was clearly trying to communicate. The word that best described her facial expression was "imploring."

❖

He locked eyes with her. Her gaze conveyed panic, her mouth trying to cry out. She fiercely wanted something from him, something beyond her reach. *For the first time in ten years, she needs me. Could she finally have forgiven me? Doubtful. Or does this mean I have forgiven myself?* He couldn't understand what it was she wanted. As she reached to touch his forehead he woke with a cold fright, and realized he had nodded off into sleep again.

"Nop!" he called. "Nop, I need you."

He covered his face with his hands. She had been so vivid. He wished she had spoken. In the dream's aftermath, feelings of weariness and a gnawing sadness washed through him. He had an overwhelming need for more opium, anything to numb his memory of these people who were lost to him.

"Nop, Goddammit!"

The door leading to the hallway swung open and a man riding a motorized wheelchair glided in and stopped beside the only piece of furniture in the room, a desk that held a manual typewriter and a messy stack of papers. The walls were bare, except for shelves above the desk that were crammed with *National Geographics,* hardbound books frayed from many readings, and three statues of the Buddha, two sitting in meditation and one reclining. The top shelf held a framed photo of a young couple holding a year-old baby. Beside that sat a fireman's hat with a New York City emblem. The room was no more than a dark, damp cell. The fact that a long list of notable monks had inhabited this space as novices did not brighten it or lessen the humidity.

Annop tried to bring his unwieldy hands to his forehead as he bowed in the *wai* gesture. His body was the size of a twelve-year-old, dressed in the orange robes of a monk. His shaved head seemed too big for his body. It was a handsome head, but hard for him to control. It rolled to the side as his mouth spread into a smile. When he spoke, his words came haltingly and loud, but with the Thai singsong accent. It was not quite a man's voice, even though Annop was in his mid-twenties.

"Sleeping Beauty…is fin…ally awake," he said.

Annop always had difficulty making his hands go where he wanted them. They strayed every which way, the arms bending too much at the elbow and wrist, the fingers curling into impossible angles, making him look like those lovely Thai dancers.

"Fetch my pipe and my dope box."

Annop pushed a button on his control panel and the wheelchair crossed the room and stopped beside the sleeping mat. Annop's arm danced on the air before it came to rest on the man's shoulder. His grip was warm and convulsively strong.

"Philip," Annop said, "I…have…you in four…moves."

Annop swiveled his big head to focus on the chessboard sitting on a low wooden crate beside the sleeping mat. His hand jerked as he reached for a black bishop and moved it, placing the white king in check. Annop laughed, a loud strangling sound.

Philip Mann glanced at the board. Nine chessmen still stood in a star-like configuration near the center. He felt too weary and too overwhelmed to consider the move, even though the game had been going on for three days and he wanted to win.

"I concede. Now, the pipe?"

Annop drew Philip's head against him. He stroked Philip's cheek with as much tenderness as his uncoordinated fist would allow.

Annop said, "You…have a vis…itor. A *farang*."

Philip looked up into Annop's dark eyes without understanding. He had been at this monastery for ten years, and he had never once had a visitor, let alone a foreigner. But those eyes told him this caller was important. *It must be Gayle. Only she knows I'm here.*

"I'll get dressed."

Annop yawed his head in an unmeant parody of joy. His mouth opened wide, then settled into a smile.

Philip stood and opened the blinds, letting sunlight fill the room. The light made the small cell, in all its sparseness and its shadows, seem larger, more inviting. Even the faded blue blanket on the sleeping mat took on a new radiance. As Philip reached for his robes, Annop touched the button on his chair control. The chair spun around and whisked out the doorway as Annop waved a crooked hand above his head. Philip heard a hoarse snort of indragged laughter in the hallway.

❖

His hands shook so badly he could hardly manage to wrap the lower robe around his waist and secure it. The upper robe was easier to fold over his shoulder and wrap around his torso, but still his hands trembled. Was it the dreams, the drugs…Or fear? He knew it was all three, but predominantly fear, and as excited as he felt, he suddenly wished for an ordinary day where he could read over yesterday's sentences, spend a leisurely time making edits, and then delve into new paragraphs, new pages. He wished he could fill his afternoon with ordinary work while Annop attended to his needs.

He couldn't have refused to see his visitor, whoever it might be;

anyone who made that journey into Northern Thailand to see him meant it was significant, perhaps dire.

Annop glided back into the room and parked beside the desk. The teenaged boy who followed him to the doorway was lean-flanked, moving slowly and deliberately, his face solemn and his mouth marred by braces. He stood taking in the room's spartan décor before his eyes fixated on Philip. He did not, however, make any move to enter the room, as if he had no intention of treading on Philip's life.

Standing between the only window and the sleeping mat, Philip felt his knees liquefy. He held out an arm to brace him against the wall. He had expected Gayle, but the person before him was a carbon copy of himself twenty years ago—same build, same sharp facial features, same blue-black hair, and eyes the same color of gray—like rain—as his own. Even the braces were the same. Philip swallowed, but felt something hard lodge in his throat.

"Tru?"

The boy nodded.

Why did I ever agree to let Gayle name him Tru Mann? A ridiculous name. But then, he remembered, once she got a burr up her butt about anything, nothing short of a nuclear holocaust would change her mind.

Philip had the urge to rush to the boy and hug the life out of him. So many thousands of the hours spent in exile had he wondered about him. This morning, however, still haunted by his dream and woozy from the drug, he saw the boy more as an old memory, sharp in the pain it could summon but faded in its detail. Or perhaps it was merely shock. Whichever, it kept him from crossing that space between them. But that shock didn't stop Philip from remembering the boy of ten years ago. He had been such a social creature even at that young age. There was nothing Tru had loved better than being in a room filled with people. More than anything else, Philip remembered his laugh, its suddenness and its rich tone, the unique, touching, ringing sound of it. That boy of six or seven had been beautiful and clear-eyed and free of spirit, plunging through life like a colt in a springtime pasture. He had been an intelligent child, alert to the world around him, and deeply loved everyone. He was capable of colossal joy; he also harbored crippling sorrow, so that when his puppy died the world ended.

Judging by the expression on Tru's face, Philip realized that he was in shock too. Philip had a shaved head, dressed in orange monk robes, and ten years of scant diet and opium addiction had dissolved forty pounds of muscle from his body. His gaunt face and frame, he knew, made him look like an Auschwitz survivor. There was no way Tru could have anticipated such a drastic transformation. *I might as well complete the picture.* He brought his palms together in front of his forehead and bowed in the *wai* gesture. Tru didn't return it.

"Son, is your mother here too?"

"She died three months ago." Tru's voice was soft and beautiful and cold, and scarcely a whisper.

It took a silent minute for Philip to absorb those words. When understanding blossomed, he was taken back a dozen years when he was in his twenties. He and Gayle had lavished as much time and energy and affection as they could onto Tru. She had been fun then, full of happy life.

"How did you find me?" Philip asked when he had located his voice again.

"Mom saved your letters. After she died, I read them all."

Philip took hesitant steps toward Tru, and the next thing he knew he crushed Tru against him. "I'm so sorry, son." When it became clear that Tru made no effort to return his affection, his hands moved to Tru's shoulders and he held him at arm's length.

"Did you come all this way by yourself?"

Tru turned his head and stared at Annop with an unflinching brashness.

"Let's take a walk in the garden," Philip said. "We can talk more freely in private."

Question after question bombarded his mind as he led Tru along the hallway and down the steps. As they entered the garden he draped an arm over those narrow shoulder but Tru flinched and pulled away.

The morning had turned hot. They made a beeline toward the Bodhi tree that was the courtyard's centerpiece. A dozen temple dogs lay in the shade, sleeping. The only other people in the garden were tourists, all wearing bright shirts and shorts, snapping pictures.

Philip and Tru sat on stone benches three feet apart and facing each other. This was Philip's favorite spot on the temple grounds, which was an oasis from the chaos and squalor beyond the compound walls. He had come here with his ideas of freedom and equality and democracy, only to find that won him no friends. For ten years he had felt the deep sadness of exile. He was alone here with one exception, Annop. He was still the outsider, and too alert to the Thai ironies, niceties, and morals to be able to fully integrate.

Philip lifted the lid off a yellow plastic tub and scooped up a handful of birdseed. He scattered seeds over the pavement. A dozen pigeons flew out of the trees and began pecking at the ground. Their cooing sounds helped to relax him. He scooped up another handful and held out his arm, cupping his palm. A beautiful gray bird lighted on his hand and began to forage.

Tru's eyes narrowed. "Mom used to say pigeons carry diseases. They're feathered rats."

"She would say that, blithely overlooking the obvious fact that humans carry diseases too," Philip said, shaking his head. "My teacher would say that they are creatures no different than you or I. No more or less important."

"You talking about pigeons or rats?"

Venom tinged his words. This would not be a pleasant father-to-son chat. "Both, I suppose."

"Your teacher. Is he the funny-looking dwarf in the chair?"

"Tru, I can see you're upset with me, and I don't blame you," he said, trying to keep a sudden anger out of his voice, "but Annop is a noble man, a caring soul. I respect him deeply. You have no right to call him degrading names."

Tru's eyes blazed. "Like you just did about Mom? You lost that right the day you abandoned us."

There it is. She never told him why I left, never owned up to her part in this train wreck. "Yes, I abandoned you, but that wasn't all my decision. Look, Tru, I'm not an evil man, and if you can believe that, then that's a start." He shook the bird from his wrist, dropped the remaining seeds, and wiped his palm on his robes. "I'm betting you didn't come all this way just to spit in my face. What do you need from me?"

Tru's lips pressed together into a thin line. He sat silent, as if what he had to say was so momentous that he didn't know how to begin. In that muteness, Philip, for the first time, studied his son's appearance. Army green backpack that seemed larger than his body, running shoes with the laces untied, faded jeans drooping low over his ass, black shirt with a picture of Bob Marley on the front. *Do kids still listen to Marley?* His hair was cut short and uneven, a real hack job, making him look as mangy as the temple dogs. It was the fidgeting hands that now seized Philip's attention. They rested on his thighs, with long delicate fingers curved protectively over the palm. The nails were bitten to the quick, and so were the knuckles. *A nervous habit that lots of teens have.*

No big deal. Philip had done the same at that age. But then he saw a gray-pink vertical line extending up the inside of the left arm, above the palm. A three inch long, thin scar. A line on the right arm matched the left. *Horizontal cuts take longer for the blood to clot. He meant business.*

Philip searched for a way, some common ground, to get Tru talking. "Who butchered your hair?"

"I cut it myself when I was in a loony-bin lockdown."

"Looks like you cut more than your hair."

Tru moved his arms to hide his scars. His eyes shifted nervously about, as if looking for an escape route.

Philip leaned forward. Annop had taught him how to quietly fix his serene gray eyes on somebody to calm them, which made them realized, or so Annop claimed, that what they said next should be serious, that the time for casual play or evasion had come to an end.

"I can't go back home," Tru said.

Philip heard the depth of pain in that young voice. At that moment he could have devoured Tru, not ravenously but adoringly, infinitely gently, the way he used to hold him as a baby while he slept. Philip was brimming with a love so strong, so unambiguous, that it felt like an unquenchable appetite.

Tru told his story with a cold hostility. Philip searched his face for what it might unwittingly disclose, and he listened for nuances and clues into Tru's relationship with Gayle.

As Tru described Gayle's decline in sprit and health over the past few years, he smiled, as he had done as a child, but now there was anguish and a sort of bewilderment in his face. He brought the past into the garden with all its ugliness, and for Philip now, in these years after the death of his fellow firemen—his brothers—and now his wife, any reminder of that time carried a terrible and heavy melancholy. Time would not relent, and when he was young he had never imagined the pain living would bring, pain that only the opium quenched. He needed a hit of the pipe now.

Tru described how, after Gayle had leaped off their twenty-story balcony, in the absence of a father, Gayle's parents, Marilyn and Monty Lamb, became his legal guardians. Leading up to her death, Monty had had several significant real-estate investments collapse. The couple sold their condo in Brooklyn and moved themselves into Philip's Manhattan apartment where Tru lived with his great-grandfather. Marilyn and Monty placed the great-grandfather in a nursing home in upstate New York and were now living off the money from Tru's trust fund.

❖

Marilyn and Monty had always been stern and distant. By the time Philip had married Gayle, he thought of them as typical Republican assholes. Even Gayle had not been able to hold a civil conversation with either one.

Tru had come out to the family the day he turned sixteen, shortly after he met a man at the local Starbucks, Zack, and they became lovers. That's when Monty decided to take action. He placed Tru in a "get-straight" camp in New Jersey. Two weeks later, Tru cut his wrists. That landed him in a hospital under psychiatric care. Tru had stayed at the ward for two months, and then escaped with Zack's help. He broke into Monty and Marilyn's home and stole his passport, clothes, and enough money to get him to Thailand.

By the time Tru had finished explaining his situation, his voice and attitude had softened, showing Philip that he had changed little in ten years. The only real difference was that he had been abandoned by both of his parents and treated badly by Marilyn and Monty, which had left him dangerously fragile.

Philip was stunned that Tru was gay and out at so tender an age. But what really overwhelmed him was Tru's courage to cross half the world to track down his father. Philip smiled and patted Tru's shoulder, a comforting gesture more for himself than for Tru. "I hope someday you'll introduce me to your boyfriend," was all he could think to say.

The late morning light was liquid and silky in the courtyard. Philip sat in silence and listened until Tru's voice finally wound down and he sat with head bowed, staring at his chewed knuckles. He lifted his right hand to his mouth and began to nibble.

There were times when Philip didn't feel at all like a monk. This was one of those times. His gut burned with a peculiar sort of disgust with the world, with its injustice, with the fact that it poured tragedy onto those least able to cope with it. He was also reminded that although he had forsaken the world, it could still find him.

"Where will you go now," Philip asked. "What will you do?"

Tru's faced turned into a flawless poem of puzzlement. He remained silent while he lowered his hand to his lap. When he lifted his head, tears had pooled in his eyes. "Why did you leave?"

Philip knew that, above all, he must not give the answer that first popped into his head: that when Tru grew older he would come to realize how such decisions, matters of duty and resignation, were made. He quickly dismissed it and groped for something useful.

"What did your mother say about it?"

"She blamed Eddie Flores. She said he drove you away, but that doesn't make sense. He died in the Towers."

Tru caught his eye for a second, and it was as if a flash of light had paled the entire sky. Philip's memory reached back. Eddie had not died in the Towers. Philip had found him in the wreckage and pulled him to safety. At the hospital, Eddie had lain in a coma for nine days before dying, with Philip at his bedside the entire time. He had not talked about that incident when he came to the monastery, but he had not fooled the monks—especially Annop—who had watched his silent frown and the glance of his eyes, and somehow understood it all. They said nothing, of course, just as he was saying nothing now. It was merely a name, a memory that rang in his ears. A name that had once meant everything to him.

"It was a difficult time for your mother and me. Something had been brewing for some time, years, and the Towers falling threw it all in our faces. We were forced to make a blind leap into the darkness because neither of us knew what the hell we were doing. Making such a leap required us to be brave and determined. Such leaps take bravery, which we had, but being brave day after day to see it through proved too much for her, for us." Philip waved a hand to dismiss the subject. "That's a long, depressing story that I don't want to go into on an empty stomach. Let's talk about you. Look, I wish you could stay here at the monastery but that's impossible."

"Fuck that. Who wants to live in this shithole?" Tru turned his head, but didn't seem to be looking at anything in particular. "I lost my home, family, boyfriend. I thought you could help. My bad. I have about five hundred dollars left. When that's gone I'll either starve to death or die of loneliness. It'll be a coin flip between the two."

Philip's memories waged war on him, but he watched Tru carefully, weighing what the boy said while thinking of how best to help him. Tru was frightened, and Philip's sympathy grew stronger than the hold of his past.

Tru stood up to leave, and Philip accompanied him to the front gates. When he saw a tuk-tuk waiting, he wondered who was paying for it.

"Where are you staying?" Philip asked.

"A student hostel near Wat Bupparam."

"Good, I'll meet you there at five o'clock and take you to dinner. There's a noodle bar near by. We'll talk more."

Tru pursed his lips, about to say something, but clearly thought better of it. He reached out and grasped Philip's hand, interlacing their fingers as they walked toward the tuk-tuk. Tru didn't let go of his hand until he had climbed into the vehicle and it had begun to drive off. Philip stood there watching the back of Tru's head until the tuk-tuk lost itself in the traffic.

Eddie had been dead ten years, Gayle now lay in her grave, Gayle's parents had again crushed something he loved, and Tru had been too early cut adrift in the world. Philip glanced up at the monks' dormitory and saw Annop sitting in meditation on the balcony of his room. It was time to return. As Philip climbed the steps, there was a silence in the dorm, not a sound in the building except the low rumble, like a vague cry in the distance, of his own boundless solitude. The past had rushed to him with its arms outstretched, imploring, just like in the dream that had woken him that morning.

❖

When Philip entered his room, Annop was waiting beside the chessboard. The chessmen had been painstakingly set out. He tried to read in Annop's eyes—which were the only things not moving in his beautiful, tormented face—how important another game was.

"Let's pl…ay anoth…er."

"Is your ego so eager for a boost? You need to work on that."

Annop laughed. "Du…ly noted, Pot…zer."

Philip shook his head. "I need to write now. Let's play tonight after prayers."

Annop's face grew thoughtful. His eyes dropped to his lap, no doubt wondering why Tru's visit had changed their relationship. Philip wrapped an arm around his shoulders.

"Come on, Nop. Find another charity case to save for a few hours. We'll meet up at prayers and I'll whip your butt tonight." Philip guided Annop from the room, then stood staring at his typewriter.

Eddie Flores's name had never been voiced in the years that Philip had lived at the temple. His presence had been buried beneath the long hours of meditation, Dharma lessons, chores, writing, and, of course, opium stupors. Each night, however, he came back vividly in the dreams. And during the times that Philip worked on his memoirs, recalling his time at the New York City Fire Department Rescue Company 1, Eddie's name appeared often on the pages. Philip had begun work on the manuscript three years ago, but he only worked at it with fits and starts, and restarts. It often seemed sad to him that he had rendered so much of his private and public life into those pages, as well as the lives of his fellow fire fighters, and yet the thing he most needed to write had been left out. He had told himself that the manuscript would never be published, so it didn't matter. But he had never allowed himself to write those parts locked too deep in his heart. However, after hearing Tru's confession, seeing the courage of his offspring, he felt the need to write those skipped-over incidents now.

He sat at this desk and slipped a fresh sheet of paper into his typewriter. He closed his eyes and let the images come. It was hearing Tru say that name aloud that made the memories vividly present, within reach. That tone in Tru's voice now guided his words as he began to type.

He saw himself naked while standing in a shadowy niche at the firehouse gym, watching the shower room. The lights were bright, even though the locker room lay empty of people. He stared with tears pooling in his eyes, straining to see Eddie Flores under one of the showerheads lining the far wall. The sound of spraying water and the sucking drain grew loud in his head, eclipsed only by his own breathing. He inched closer with timid steps. Eddie, his member standing full and thick, began fisting it. Philip wanted to back away, to return to his locker, but he couldn't take his eyes off his friend. His gaze wandered over that smooth, copper-toned body until it found the patch of black brush above the swollen member and those hanging balls. The sheer size of that dick was inspiring—alarmingly big, its head a lovely plum color.

When Philip looked up at his face again, Eddie was staring back at him. His eyes flashed, and his scowl turned into a welcoming smile. He waved a hand, an offer to join him? Philip held his breath. He could neither retreat nor move closer.

Eddie's smile and wave were unambiguous; they made it clear what Eddie was offering. Philip knew, they both undoubtedly knew, that they were alone. Everyone else had already gone to the dining hall and would be chowing down for the next half hour. Philip wondered now if those minutes of craving were not the most genuine he had ever lived. The closest accurate comparison he could think of was the hushed flight to Thailand, that interlude suspended between heaven and earth, with no escape and nothing but the hopeful unknown waiting for him.

He had stood in that alcove, waiting for another wave of encouragement, not trusting the first, until he heard a door open back in the locker room, and knew they were no longer alone. The unthinkable had been snatched away.

Philip typed out the story of that first flirtation as the images came to him. He left out nothing. He even included the fact that he had rushed home and fucked Gayle with an intensity that surprised them both.

There were other such stories that he needed to write—stories of blossoming love, of adoration growing into worship—but not today. His hands were shaking too much to continue. He lay down on his sleeping mat and turned his face to the wall.

❖

When Philip walked from the airport terminal to the taxi line, he wondered what his first move should be. It was almost noon. The heaviness of the air and the absence of any wind made him understand that, whether he liked it or not, he was back home, or at least as close to home as he could get. He had spent three frenzied days in Chiang Mai giving away books, buying a new wardrobe, and saying good-bye to the people he cared for. He had contacted a Manhattan law firm and gotten the ball rolling on taking back the role of Tru's legal guardian. He had given no thought as to what he would do on his immediate arrival.

It had been ten years since he had seen Gayle's parents. They had driven him to JFK airport; their rage against him then was palpable, and they had complained bitterly all the way to the departure gates. Gayle never told them the whole story so, of course, they blamed him. To spite them, he had waved and flashed a huge smile. He had assumed he would never see them again but, he thought as he opened the passenger door of a cab, he had been wrong. He would be back absorbing their rage by the end of the day.

Once he and Tru settled in the backseat, which held a sour smell, he decided his first stop should be the law firm. He asked Tru if he could wait an hour before they had lunch and he nodded. Tru had been silent for most of the flight home. Now that they were back in New York City, he became even more so.

They entered Manhattan as the sun began to slant. He saw that neither tourism nor time had harmed the city's mixture of sadness and splendor. They made their way through Midtown along wide busy streets, swerving and twisting within traffic through the dimly recognized landmarks. That journey had attached a gravity to them, as through they were passengers being whisked theatrically to their doom.

Philip was overwhelmed by the hardness of the stone-and-steel buildings, and the creamy clouds moving across the sky as through with purpose. He could not stop asking himself what he wished for now, and the answer was always whatever Tru needed to help him grow into manhood. He didn't want the past back. He had learned not to ask for that. His dead would not return except in his dreams. Being back home and free of his wife's bullying gave him a strange contentment, the feeling that he could slowly rebuild his life according to his and Tru's needs.

They left the cab at Broadway and Maiden Lane, and entered a thirty-story building. He found the lobby opulent and bright, but the law firm's waiting room lacked personality, the furniture too modern to be comfortable. The lawyer, Juanita Carrillo, took them to Sherman's deli. While they waited for cheese sandwiches and potato salad to appear, she pulled a surprisingly thick file from her briefcase. She showed them photographs, affidavits, court orders, and miscellaneous documents she had gathered over the last three days. She spoke with exaggerated formality. Not much has changed, Philip thought, as she breezed through the case's status with the crisp efficiency of a seasoned professional. This was a country where everything was documented but little was understood. Everything had to be performed by the book without consideration for human feelings and unpredictable situations. The good news, she announced, was that a hearing was set for the following Friday, and it was a slam-dunk for Philip to be awarded custody of his son. The hearing itself would take less than an hour, a mere formality under New York state law. This, of course, would also mean that Philip would become executor of Tru's trust fund, which Marilyn and Monty had been dipping into since Gayle's suicide.

When the luncheon ended, Philip called his apartment. There was no answer. A wave of relief swept through him, letting him know how much he dreaded this confrontation. They decided to spend the night at the Hilton near Times Square.

The lobby was luxurious but their room seemed sterile. There was something about it that reminded him of the law firm's waiting room. Everything about it, including the bedclothes and curtains, gave off an aura of never having been used before. There was nothing homey or comfortable about it. He had never stayed in an American hotel before, and the impersonal feel of the room took him aback.

They had room service deliver veggie burgers and fries. They shared a bottle of sparkling water, which helped loosen their anxiety. Philip had not meant to talk about the temple and the years in Thailand, but once he began he found that he had summoned up too much emotion and he could not stop himself from talking more. He described his room with Annop with its own balcony, and how they would go out begging for food each morning and then come back to the temple for the main meal of the day, and the way the afternoon wind would make the temperatures bearable.

Tru interrupted to say that he disliked Thai food, it was too spicy, and how the hot, muggy weather had depressed him, and how he found the city shabby and his accommodations dingy.

Philip stared across the table, scrutinizing the delicate bone structure of Tru's face, its paleness, those lovely gray eyes, and the thin lips that always tried to hide his braces. He wanted to go on sharing his decade in the land of smiles, but he stopped himself and sipped his water. He knew that during the coming years, especially on the sweltering days of New York City summers, that he would miss the best years of his life in the place he had grown to love. He imagined himself sitting in meditation before a statue of the Buddha, the sound of temple dogs barking and the smell of curry cooking and Annop pondering his next chess move. That simplicity was all lost to him now, and it was hard not to feel that he was making a mistake of gigantic proportions by coming back to this place that held only pain.

After dinner, Tru stripped to take a shower. Removing his T-shirt, he exposed a tattoo etched over his shoulder—a treble clef and music notes, which started above his armpit and drooped toward his right nipple. Philip studied its detailed and artistic lines. "You must love music?"

"I sing. That's where I met Zack, he plays guitar at coffee shops and Central Park. I guess I love singing more than anything else."

"I'd like to hear you sometime. At the temple we chanted twice each day. I have a rotten voice, but I'll bet you're spectacular."

"Not as good as some others. At my school choir, I'm chorus, never a soloist. Whenever we performed, I would pretend you were in the audience. It's lame, I know, but it's the only thing I'm good at, and I wanted you to be proud of me."

Philip crossed the room and hugged him. He was shocked Tru

would voice something so personal after so many days of silence during their journey home.

In the stillness that deepened as the night wore on, a silence broken intermittently by gurgling pipes and noises in the corridor, he became thankful that this would only be for a single night. He didn't know if the gloom that had overtaken him was from the dismal atmosphere of the room, or from the anticipation of battling his in-laws the next day, or perhaps something as simple as jet-lag piled on top of opium withdrawal. On the other hand, it could have come from realizing the years of pain and loneliness he had caused Tru. Whatever it was, he only managed a very light sleep that was not at all restful.

That morning, once he had showered, put on fresh clothes, and eaten a plate of eggs with an onion bagel, he felt more courageous. He called the apartment, and again there was no answer. He decided to take action. They checked out of the hotel and took a cab uptown to his apartment building. As the driver weaved through the West Side, Philip realized that the attack on the Trade Centers no longer affected the mornings here; an army of men and women in dark suits marched the sidewalks, traffic buzzed in the grid-like streets, and shops were thriving. The place held the sense of old, stable wealth.

He tried not to conjure up memories deliberately, nor to compare the city of ten years ago to what he saw now. He refused to allow any nostalgia to dull the sweetness of sitting next to Tru. But seeing that the city had not changed, he tried to avoid the sadness at the knowledge that no new discoveries would be made, no new excitements felt, merely old ones revisited. He had loved these bustling streets, as though they were a poem or a novel by Capote, but he was no longer surprised and delighted. It was enough, however, to be sitting next to Tru as the taxi moved through the canyons steeped in shadows.

He began to notice that the men were dressed more formally than the jeans, polo shirt, and sandals that he wore. He must seem like a tourist from the Coast, and he wondered if Tru felt any embarrassment being seen with him. He would need to learn how to dress so as not to stand out. It would take time, he knew, and he hoped Tru would help him.

They collected their luggage from the taxi's trunk. Standing on the sidewalk, he felt the hard, bright heat of the morning. He knew he should have plunged directly into the building's lobby, but some force guided him to the corner where he stood looking up at the familiar stone and glass building. He knew exactly which window belonged to him, and that particular window had to have been the one Gayle had stepped out of. He stared down at the pavement in the alley, knowing the exact point of impact. He could not make himself move from that spot. He felt an urge to speak to her out loud, with a sense that her spirit, so restless and independent and audacious, would inhabit this alley for decades to come. She had not settled for an easy life, and she didn't make life easy for anyone around her, even in death. She could have taken pills or cut her wrists or shoved a gun barrel into her mouth if she had merely wanted to kill herself. Yet she chose falling through space as a last twist of the knife in his gut. She did it to make an unambiguous statement. And, of course, he could feel that blade turning now.

"Gayle," he whispered, "I'll do whatever I can." He stared at that pavement, imagining her beneath it, a place of no light and no love. She at last had become his equal. With that thought he could finally make his body turn and walk back with guarded steps, making no mistakes, until he reached Tru. Together they entered the building.

At the security desk, Tom Bolton, head security officer, who had been there for years before Philip left, simply said, "They're away for a few days."

"Where are they?"

"I'm sure that's none of my business, sir."

Tom seemed almost insolent. In the tense silence that lay between them, it struck Philip that Tom must know he and Tru had every right to enter that apartment. Hell, it was still in Philip's name and it was Tru's legal residence. He stood to his full height and stared down Tom, allowing his gaze to broadcast all the arrogance of entitlement that he could muster.

"They'll be back in a few days," he said again, although his voice seemed weaker, uncertain. He clearly, however, meant to keep them from passing to the elevators. Philip was tempted to taxi back to the hotel and wait for their return, but he had postponed things for a day already, and the idea of settling into the house without his in-laws there bolstered his courage. It would give him the upper hand when the confrontation hit the fan. They would be unwelcome guests living in his home.

"Then I'll need a key."

"Mr. Lamb gave me no authorization."

Philip didn't even blink. "Please don't make me call the police and the building manager to enter my own apartment."

A few minutes later he stood before his apartment door with Tru beside him and his luggage at his feet. He listened carefully, hearing the faint drone of a television or radio coming from inside. He suddenly felt nervous, and the sense of victory over Tom Bolton faded. He wanted the place to be empty, the rooms closed up and the curtains drawn, waiting for them to enter and bring new life back to his dark house. As he slipped the key into the deadbolt and turned the knob, he felt a surge of immense hostility toward anyone who might be waiting inside.

The apartment held the stale odor of old cooking. The first thing that struck him was that nothing had changed. The living room furniture, the original art hanging on the walls, the wide plank floors partially covered with Persian carpets were almost exactly the way he had left it, yet everything seemed smaller—the rooms, the couch and armchairs, the dining-room table and chairs. Somehow the place had shrunk, giving him a feeling of claustrophobia. The only changes were that his father-in-law sat on the couch wearing yellow-stained boxer shorts, watching a flat-screen TV mounted on the wall, and his all-white bulldog, Butch, slept at his feet. Monty was a big man, slow-spoken, slow-moving, level-eyed and dead-faced.

Butch awoke and lumbered to his feet, barking at Philip and slobbering over the carpet. Monty ordered him to stop but the dog seemed nearly rabid. Monty lifted a slipper from the floor and cuffed the dog's head. "I said shut the fuck up!" The dog yelped and retreated to a corner.

Philip noted the globs of slobber discoloring the fabric of the couch, the carpet, and walls.

As Philip dropped his bag in the entryway, Monty stood up. He had grown much heavier, now sporting a wattle of fat under his chin and a bulging belly.

"We weren't expecting you for a few more days. Your lawyer called to let us know you were coming back."

Marilyn walked in from the kitchen wearing a pink housedress with a red apron. "Welcome home. Tru, you had us worried sick." She moved as though to hug him, but he turned and hurried down the hallway to his bedroom, slamming the door closed behind him. Marilyn raised her fists to her hips. "Well, I've never seen such an ungrateful child."

"Where did he find you?" Monty asked.

"In a monastery on the dark side of the moon." Philip attempted a smile but neither of them responded. He stood his ground.

"You look good, Philip," she said, "although you've lost weight. I hardly recognize you with no hair. Coffee will be ready in a jiff. Have you two had breakfast?"

Philip nodded.

"Monty, put some clothes on, for God's sake," she said. "Philip, come to the kitchen and sit down while I pour you come coffee. We can talk better in here." She slipped back into the kitchen as silently as a cat.

Taking charge as usual, he thought. Like daughter like mother.

Philip followed her to the table. The kitchen, always the social center, had seldom been gay, but now it took on a gloomy, palpable decay. The lace curtains were ash gray, the floors, although swept, seemed sticky and dank, and the walls and windows were lacquered with a yellow film of grease. He realized with a bit of shock that the apartment had never been stylish or comfortable. It was a well-designed sanctuary for eating and sleeping, a grim shelter, unloved and unloving. It was no home, no place to long for or to come back to.

Before he could sit, music began blaring from Tru's bedroom. Philip assumed that was his way of shutting out the world, of not wanting to hear what needed to be said. The sound was chaotic noise, techno music, the kind of frenzied clamor that grated on Philip's nerves.

"Excuse me, dear. I'll just knock on his door and tell him to turn that down so we can talk."

Philip reached out and gripped her arm to stop her. "You're a guest in his house. He can play his music as loud as he likes."

She pressed her lips together so tightly they disappeared.

Monty walked into the room while still pulling on a long-sleeved dress shirt, but he still wore no pants, only his stained boxers. He pointed a thumb over his shoulder. "Makes me appreciate the last few months of peace and quiet."

Marilyn poured mugs of coffee and set them on the table. Monty leaned closer to Philip and asked, "So what are your plans? Are you back to stay?"

"I'm here for as long as Tru needs me."

A moment of nothing but techno music stretched into an uncomfortable tension. Philip watched Marilyn trying to think of some appropriate response, but, of course, she failed.

"We'll need to organize a room for you," Monty said. "Luckily, Grandpa Henry's old room hasn't changed. That should be plenty comfortable."

Philip dreaded the night ahead in these choky rooms. He was sure he wouldn't sleep well. Recovering himself, he opened his mouth to point out that they wouldn't be staying long enough for them to go through that effort, that he had no intention of sharing his home with them when Marilyn found her voice. "We've come to love living here. It makes us feel closer to her. And you're going need help managing Tru. Things are not like they used to be. He's become quite a handful and needs constant supervision."

Monty cleared his throat. "Your lawyer informed us that you're filing for custody. That's fine with us. Tru's been a constant source of worry, so you're welcome to him. Perhaps you can pound some sense into him."

Marilyn must have seen the anger heating Philip's face because she hurriedly added, "When we arrange Henry's bedroom, Monty and I will use it, of course. You should have the master bedroom. We want you to be comfortable."

He refrained from telling them at that moment that they should start looking for another place to live. They would realize that soon enough. He didn't relish sleeping in his old bed, the one he had shared with Gayle, and he felt no need to blatantly establish his authority, so he told them he would do just fine in the smaller bedroom.

"It's no bother," she said. "We can move our things out of the master in minutes. This is your apartment after all."

"I'm used to sleeping on a mat on the floor. I don't need much. No, you stay in the master for the time being."

"It's no trouble—"

"Put a lid on it, dear," Monty said. He seemed embarrassed by the topic.

"Well then, I'll just go tidy up the spare room and slip some clean sheets on the bed," she said as she hurried from the kitchen.

He sat at the table drinking coffee while she arranged the guest room and Monty took Butch out for his morning walk. When he finished his coffee, he carried the mugs to the sink where there were already several other plates and glasses. He took his time washing and drying them. He remembered exactly which drawers and cupboard to place them in. Nothing had changed.

The morning had gone smoother than he had anticipated, but there was still one issue he needed to explore before he asked them to leave. He needed to understand what had happened to Grandpa Henry Lamb, Gayle's grandfather, who had been living with Gayle and Tru. He decided that questions regarding Henry could wait for another day. He also knew he needed to get Tru back in school and begin hunting for a job. They could live off Tru's trust for a while, but he didn't want to deplete Tru's money.

❖

He woke early and stood at the window with a view of the Hudson River. He unlatched the lock and opened the windows fully. The sky was as blue as a sailor's eyes, yet softly whitened by the morning sun. In Chiang Mai the sky had often been like that after a night of rain, and it meant the day would be hot and oppressively humid, but here, he remembered, it could mean that the day would be fine. Even in high summer there could be a breeze rushing off the sea to cool the canyons of stone and glass. He knew that the day would be perfect, and the night would hold the day's heat.

Over breakfast with Marilyn, he asked why Grandpa Henry had been placed in an assisted living home.

"You'd better ask Monty," she said.

"I'm asking you."

Marilyn concentrated on her coffee mug as though something dangerous could crawl out of it at any moment.

"Sherman Yin, one of the neighbors, found Henry on the floor, having fallen out of bed. He had been there most the night, and God only knows where Tru had run off to. That's when we decided it was time to take charge."

"So you moved in here and put your father-in-law in a nursing home?"

"Monty thinks the old man is incapable of caring for himself. He wants the courts to award us his guardians and give us power of attorney."

He nodded. "Does this have anything to do with this building that Henry owns?"

She turned her head away, unable to look him in the eyes. "Lamb House is rent-controlled and barely makes a profit. Monty wants to convert all the apartments to condos and sell them."

"And Henry is against it?" Philip smiled, already knowing the answer.

"Henry has plenty of money already, but the damned fool put it all in Tru's trust fund, thinking that Gayle and Tru would take care of him. All the rent profits from the building go directly into the trust, and we can only withdraw a set monthly living allowance."

Which after the hearing on Friday I will control, he thought. As they sat in the silence that followed, he realized that Henry had foreseen all this, and had put all his holdings into a trust that Monty and Marilyn couldn't steal from him; that ensured that he, Gayle, and Tru would always be taken care of. *That doesn't sound like a man who's incapable of thinking for himself.*

She stood and grabbed the coffee pot, refilling both mugs. She finally looked him in the eye. "Don't gloat, dear. It's unbecoming."

He checked himself.

She shook her head. "This is the right thing to do, Philip. It makes sense to sell this wretched building. You have to strike at the right time, but Henry doesn't understand. He thinks that if he holds on to his property, he'll live forever."

The right thing to do for who? "I'm assuming that if you sell the building the profits won't go into Tru's trust fund. And what will you do if the courts don't grant you guardianship?"

"Then he'll have to sign over the deed for us to sell."

"I'll need the address. I want to talk with him."

❖

Rather than rent a car for the two-hour drive north to the assisted-care facility, Tru had suggested that Zack drive them. Philip sat in one of the living room armchairs, glancing at the wall clock for the hundredth time. An hour late without a phone call would have been rude even in Thailand. He had convinced himself that relying on Zack had been a mistake.

Tru made a rare appearance in the living room while still talking on his cell phone. "We'll be right down," he said, and slipped his phone into his pocket.

Philip stood. "He's not coming up?"

"He's smoking a cigarette."

"Perhaps when he's finished smoking he can come up for a proper introduction."

Tru's face darkened with contrition and something else—guilt, shame? "He's being considerate. He figures you won't want him smoking on the ride, so he's having a last one before we start."

A moment passed. Philip found himself standing on his favorite Persian carpet, full of parental disapproval, and rancid, wounded feelings, facing a son who despised him (he no doubt still did, didn't he?) for depriving him of a proper childhood. But why shouldn't Zack be held to a few social decencies?

"Let's go," Tru said. "He's double-parked." Tru produced an infuriatingly knowing smile, shook his head as he donned a backpack and headed out the front doorway.

Tru marched onto the sidewalk outside of their building with Philip in his wake. Zack stood by the curb, lighting a cigarette from the butt of his last one. Zack was close to Philip's age, covered with tats, and had a dozen rings in this lower lip, eyebrows, and ears. He looked stern and rigorous, shaved head beginning to show blond stubble, wearing salmon-colored jeans, a ragged white wife-beater, and tan combat boots. He moved with a heavy tread. As his arm wrapped around Tru's waist, his shrewd, suspicious looking eyes locked onto to Philip with a clear, unspoken challenge. Seeing them together in an awkward embrace, Philip thought of the time Tru dragged home a stray mongrel, all ribs and discolored teeth, who ostensibly needed a good home but whose brutal history made him too dangerous to tame.

"Nice to meet you, Zack," Philip said.

"Hey," he said, pumping Philip's hand. Zack's hand seemed surprisingly small and soft.

"Thanks for chauffeuring us. I appreciate it."

Zack shrugged. "No problemo, dude," he said, without masking the contempt in his voice.

Do people still talk like that?

Tru, seeming somewhat embarrassed by Zack's words, began to shepherd them into the fifteen-year-old, double-parked Jeep Wrangler. "On the way home," he said, "we can stop and buy you both something more fashionable to wear."

Zack flashed a smile at Philip. "I'm always gung-ho to bump heads with the homies or cops, but salesclerks scare the livin' crap out me. But Song-boy takes care of me, buys me whatever I need."

Philip realized, with some amusement, that Zack was making an effort to charm him. "Song-boy?"

"Tru's close friends call him that because he sings like an angel. Haven't you heard him?"

Philip shook his head, liking the sound of that pet name, but feeling jealous that this middle-aged mongrel knew more about Tru than he did.

Tru jumped into the passenger seat and Philip climbed onto the bench behind him. As Zack slid behind the steering wheel, he said, "It's all those choices. Showrooms filled with shit, all screaming at me to buy, buy, buy, and when some fashion geek with sculpted hair and tons of attitude comes up and says 'Can I help you,' I just want to punch his lights out and run."

Tru said, "Can we just shut up and drive?"

On the ride out of the city and deep into the northern green country, Philip had to remind himself of his Buddhist training. Zack was not his enemy. *He seems a man who lives on the edge of society and feels he has to break a few rules to get what he wants. It isn't his fault. He most likely can't impress anyone his own age, so he latches on to teenagers who don't know he's a sham.* Philip understood perfectly that Zack felt that it was better to be crude to the bone than a well-dressed queer with a respectable job. Still, Philip couldn't keep himself from wanting to grab Zack by the shirtfront and planting a fist in his face.

It's the nature of people who are hollow. They have to gussy up the outside to hide their smallish inside. Philip tried to stop this flow of judgment, knowing he was the smallish one at that moment, but he couldn't help wondering why an intelligent kid like Tru didn't see the obvious. Was Tru this desperate for a father figure? With the roar of the engine in his ear and the wind beating his face with velvet fists, he allowed himself to study Zack's strong back, the graceful lines of his neck meeting shoulder, the mounds of muscle in the thick arms. Philip slowly became overtaken by desire, and something else, a subtle and exquisitely burning nerve that wove through his longing. He finally realized that he too found Zack sexy, in a Stanley Kowalski kind of way.

❖

While holding Tru's hand, Zack steered the Jeep with his left hand through the iron gates of the Royal Gardens Assisted Living facility and followed a driveway through a garden that held a clear view of woodlands and a soft light beyond the river. It had several shade trees spreading over park benches, vast lawns clipped as even as a mortician's nails, and peonies crowding the flowerbeds. They stopped at the entrance of an unmarked brownstone building. Two large windows, one on each side of the front door, seemed like empty eyes staring out.

The three men didn't say a word as they strolled up the front steps and entered a vacant reception room swathed in earth tones of latte coffee and floor tiles the hue of red clay. The walls were lined with contemporary paintings of nebulous, non-assertive blotches. Not a sharp line in the bunch. The room held a stagnant silence Philip had only experienced at the temple—no tick of clocks, no whir of fans, no hum of machinery.

He heard approaching footsteps and felt a pressure on his shoulder. The facility director, Tom Bayard, stood beside him like a pallbearer in his impeccable blue suit, crisp mustache, and large eyes seen predominantly on nocturnal animals. He carried a clipboard that gave him an air of being in charge.

Introductions were made and Mr. Bayard led them into a lodge-like room with rows of tables all covered with linen and neat place settings. An imposing stone fireplace made up the far wall, and a small gas flame added no warmth to the room.

"This is where all our guests take their meals," Mr. Bayard said. "We call everyone who stays with us 'guests' because that's what they are."

Philip lifted a napkin from a table that was folded into a swan. He studied the room, which could easily seat two hundred people. There were several oldsters, men and women, all dressed in black and supporting themselves on canes and walkers. They were no doubt the last of the morning breakfast goers now shuffling out for the day's activities, whatever those could be. He looked up into Tru's distrustful eyes.

"Look, Song-boy," Zack said, "they all have their own seats with name tags and everything. The old fart's living in high cotton. I'll bet he's banging the nurses two at a time."

Tru winced.

Mr. Bayard took the napkin from Philip and replaced it on the plate. "This is a respectable establishment. Each guest is treated like royalty."

"Is that a good thing?" Tru asked, "that they are told where to sit, who to sit by? Mr. Bayard, how many people—"

"Guests."

"—guests do you house here?"

"We can accommodate up to seventy guests here at Royal Gardens."

"Then why do you have more than twice that many place settings?" Philip asked.

Mr. Bayard waved a hand at a hallway. "I'll take you to Mr. Lamb's room." As he led the way through a set of swinging doors he said, "All our guests here at Royal Gardens have private rooms, usually decorated by their family members."

It was a short walk requiring no less than five swipes of a staff card. It seemed every door required a staff card to open, and each of the staff wore their card on a retractable key ring hung round their neck.

They tiptoed into Grandfather Lamb's room—a cinder-block cell that had the basic furnishing of a vintage Holiday Inn. The walls were a lifeless beige hue, and the blankets and overstuffed chairs carried the mildewed scent that Philip assumed was identical to the cloakroom at a Greek Orthodox Church. They stood looking at the old man, who was asleep in the fetal position.

Tru's face blanched of color as he studied the room. "Oh, Grandpa-Henry." His voice had gone as soft as a heartbeat.

"He won't eat," Mr. Bayard said. "We have to force him."

"He ate like a horse at home," Tru said.

Mr. Bayard shrugged. "There's nothing actually wrong with him. We did a full blood-work, X-rays, exam, everything. I hope I'm as healthy at his age. Can't imagine why he won't eat. Pure stubbornness, I suppose."

"Could it be he hates it here?" Philip asked.

"Well, he's lucky someone found him," Mr. Bayard said, "and lucky to be here where he is well cared for. I'll leave you now. Can I have someone from the kitchen bring you some tea?"

"That's very thoughtful, yes."

Philip sat at Henry's bedside for forty minutes sipping tea while Tru and Zack waited in the recreation hall. There was a hush in this room, like death, of which he became acutely conscious of as he sat there. He had to admit the room had an impressive view of the wooded hills, but across the lawn a woman supporting herself with a walker picked sunflower seeds out of a bird feeder, one by one, and ate them. He did his best to stay cheerful, but he wanted to ask Mr. Bayard that if these "guests" were treated like royalty, why weren't they fed enough to keep them from raiding the bird food.

It occurred to him that he could take the boys for lunch and come back later when Henry was wake, but he resisted this impulse, knowing it was simply an urge to flee from this silent space that more and more felt like a crypt.

When Henry's eyes fluttered open and he saw Philip sitting beside the bed, he sat up in a hurry. "Nate, thank God you came."

"No, Henry, it's Philip Mann. How are you feeling?"

"Hand me my clothes from the closet, Nate. Let's get the hell out of this gulag."

"Hold on there," Philip said, standing and holding out his arm to keep Henry in bed. "I'm not your brother Nate. I'm Philip Mann, Gayle's husband."

In the room's dim light, Henry peered at him, no doubt trying to understand. Philip walked to the window and lifted the blinds higher, letting more light pour into the room. He pulled his chair closer to the bed and sat facing Henry. "I'm Philip. You remember?"

"Philip? What are you doing here?" Before Philip could answer he added, "It doesn't matter; just get me out of here. Did you come by car?"

"You're here for a reason. You fell out of bed and the doctors need to find out why."

"Bullshit. I was drunk, and they know it. This is all Monty's doing. That little chicken-shit is trying to rob me blind. Now get me my clothes and let's hit the road."

"I can't do that. Listen, the only way I can take you out of here is if you sign over power of attorney and grant me your legal guardian."

Henry stared into Philip's eyes without blinking. "You're in cahoots with them. That's why you want me to sign those papers."

Philip shook his head and looked away, searching for a way to convince Henry he wasn't trying to steal anything.

"Lord knows that little turd won't be satisfied until he steals everything I've built up," Henry said. "He isn't content with the life I gave him, or even the life he's made for himself. He had a good wife, a fine house, and a business to run. Why wasn't he beaming with joy? Why does he still live a life that stings with envy and greed? With all his blessings, he still wants a twelve-inch dick, a full head of hair, and money in his wallet to impress the whores. It's my fault, I'll grant you. I raised him wrong. Although what I should have done different is a mystery."

Henry's speech became slow, and his voice was so rich with grief that Philip felt himself moved. "The American myth: I am what I own...."

Henry nodded. "The fact is, he'd rather cheat you out of a dime than make an honest buck, because by cheating you, he not only gets your money, he proves to himself that he's smarter than you, and that's what he wants more than anything: to prove he's superior."

"He thinks now is the smart time to sell Lamb House. Maybe he's right?"

"Those families have been living there for thirty years. Most of them are living on pensions. They can't afford today's city rents. If I boot them out, I'd be forcing them into some filthy ghetto."

"I can help if you'll let me."

Henry turned to the wall. "Why should I trust you? You ran out on Gayle, killed her, that's what you did, as sure as if you put a gun to her head."

Philip's stomach did a slow cartwheel. "If you've got a better way to get your skinny ass out of here, then I'll say good-bye and good luck to you."

Henry turned back around. "What I want to know, is what would make you destroy a man who has done so much for Tru."

"You bet!" Philip said. "I can't wait to get that million-dollar check that's coming my way, once you're locked away for good. I'm going to buy me a fancy yacht, set sail, and travel the world. Boy, once you're locked away, life will be sweet."

Henry's face showed amazement. Suspicion. Then, more slowly, comprehension and a knowing smile. "You had me going, you little bastard. I sure do hope when you're my age and with one foot in the grave, that some smartass makes fun of you. Then you'll know."

Philip laughed for the first time in years. "Tell you what, I'll have my lawyer draw up the guardianship papers and deliver them here. Shouldn't take but a few days. If you sign them, the lawyer can bring you back into town. If you don't sign, then I can't help you."

Henry looked at him imploringly. "Don't leave me here."

Mr. Bayard led the way into a canary-yellow room where two dozen "guests" sat in wheelchairs scattered about, their spotted scalps visible through tufts of unkempt hair. One woman chattered incessantly at another women who sat staring blankly at the wall. Tru and Zack sat at a card table playing checkers, while a few feet away a man slept with an open book on his lap. The chatty woman shifted restlessly; her stringy hair shone the same muted yellow as her soiled blouse. A fifty-two-inch wall-mounted television blared out a soap opera that no one paid the least bit of attention to. Philip had the impression that he could change the channel to CNN covering a national disaster or to a Rocky and Bullwinkle cartoon and no one here would notice, not even the two Puerto Rican caretakers dressed in blue scrubs.

He watched a male nurse amble into the room and feed the woman who was talking incessantly a few pills and a paper cup of water to wash them down. Within a few moments, the woman grew perfectly quiet, her eyes glazing over like the others.

Philip walked to the card table and Tru flashed him a silent stare, and if looks could kill, he would have turned to salt on the spot. He cleared the emotion from his throat before saying, "I've seen enough. I'll wait for you in the Jeep."

Zack smirked. "Let's check out the discothèque and the bowling alley on our way out."

❖

On the drive back to the city, it began to rain. They stopped at a clothing outlet in Poughkeepsie. A men's store was sandwiched between other such stores on Church Street, a broad, bright half acre of colorful patterned shirts and denim jeans, ribbons of track lighting overhead, and loudspeakers thumping out hip-hop music.

The clothes were designed so different from what he had worn before he fled to Thailand. They all seemed tailor-made for rock stars. He examined the outfits on several mannequins, but felt he would need to somehow regress ten years to be able to pull off that look.

Tru and Zack followed Philip as he edged among a crowd of shoppers in rain-damp coats. He searched for a salesclerk who could help him select something more conservative than the racks of flashy clothing he saw in every direction. The clerks were all busy. In a far corner, however, he noticed one, a tall dark-skinned man, finishing a sale. The man took crumpled bills from a worried-looking Goth kid, punched the cash register, handed the kid his change and receipt, and gave the kid a smile. Dazzling.

Philip felt a tug of desire in his chest. The clerk was dressed in a severely cut gray shirt and black slacks. His penny loafers seemed so light they could have been slippers. He wore an elegant silver chain around his neck and a matching one on his right wrist. This man, Philip knew, would stand out in any crowd that Philip had ever run with. Too chic, exceedingly refined. But in New York, he seemed natural, and Philip was the one who felt out of place.

The clerk glanced at him over the heads of two other waiting customers. They locked eyes, and there seemed a sparkle of recognition in the man's stare. He had curious opaque eyes, like bright gems in a streambed. He pushed through the other customers until he stood before Philip.

"May I help you?"

"Zero for originality," Zack said.

Philip ignored the crack. "I'm looking for something conservative."

The start of a smile twitched on the clerk's full lips, but it didn't develop. He was already moving off. "I've got just what you want."

"I'll bet you do," Zack said, and barked a mirthless laugh.

The clerk glanced at Zack. "What, are we twelve?" he asked, making no effort to disguise his disdain.

Philip turned to Tru, who seemed mildly embarrassed. "Why don't you guys do your own thing. We'll meet at the front door in thirty."

He caught up with the clerk just as the man turned to him. "Is he by any chance your boyfriend?"

Philip shook his head. "I'd sooner be taken hostage by the Hizbollah."

The clerk chuckled as he waved an arm. "This is our over-thirty department. Tons of polo shirts and chinos. I've got racks of slacks and dress shirts as well."

"I didn't mean I wanted to dress like my father."

The clerk let his smile develop now. "Trust me, nobody will mistake you for anybody's father. I'll fix you up with some chichi accessories. These days, it's all about the accessories."

"You'll help pick them out?"

He pulled a cloth tape measure from his hip pocket and wrapped his arms around Philip's waist. "Just put yourself in my capable hands." He checked the measurement and then dropped to one knee to measure Philip's inseam. Looking down at the man, Philip held his breath until they were eye-to-eye once more. The man winked, and began gathering armfuls of shirts.

"So tell me," the clerk said as he held a shirt up to Philip's chest, "do you live alone?"

Philip looked away. The question sounded rehearsed.

"I live with my son, and for the time being, my in-laws."

"You're married?"

"Widowed," Philip said, trying his best to sound bored.

"I should mind my own business."

Philip reached up and touched his shoulder. "It's okay." He let his hand linger there, and the clerk didn't seem to mind.

In what seemed like only minutes, Philip stood nearly naked in a changing booth, trying on new duds. They were a bit snug on him, and not nearly as comfortable as his monk robes, but he realized that tight was fashionable these days. Clothes were a means of accentuating the physique, not hiding it under false modesty.

A soft knock sounded on the changing room door. "Are you decent?" the clerk asked.

"Sure I'm decent," Philip said, "and trustworthy, and devoted. An all-around great guy."

Silence.

An hour later, Philip stood dressed in new clothes and the clerk scanned the items into the computer register. He looked up, "Name? Address?" The man's smile was now in his eyes.

"Okay," Philip said, "but you tell me your name first."

The clerk's voice went soft. "Scotty. Scotty Harrison." He pulled a card from his shirt pocket and handed it to Philip. It had his name and address written on one side, and the name of a Manhattan nightclub on the other. "I tend bar at that club."

Philip didn't care that Tru and Zack were standing beside him and knew he was flirting. He couldn't have been happier.

❖

At supper, a strained silence hung over the table. Tru pushed his food around his plate, not really eating much. Philip told Marilyn and Monty he planned to stroll the neighborhood after dinner. He wanted to reacquaint himself with the city.

"Oh, we never go out walking after dark," Marilyn said. "It's become too dangerous. This is not the city you abandoned ten years ago."

Silence fell again, broken only by the sound of the television. Monty had left it on to hear the basketball game. Philip watched his in-laws and was tempted not to say anything about his plan to free Henry. But there was something about the gluttonous way they were both eating, something so self-satisfied, that he couldn't stop himself.

"I had a long talk with Henry today. He doesn't want to be there."

Monty sipped from a glass of beer. Marilyn stared at the wall.

"That place is a toilet," Tru said. "You've put him in a prison and he hates it."

Marilyn and Monty pretended that he had not spoken.

"Did you hear me?" Tru said. His voice rose, "It's worse than that fucking homophobic shithole you sent me to."

They didn't react.

Tru tried again. "Has all that fat clogged your eardrums?"

"Tru," Philip said, laying a hand on his arm.

Philip leveled his stare on Monty. "I want you to bring Henry back here, to live. Tru is right, Henry hates it there. If you do that, I'll see that you're taken care of."

Monty cocked his head. "If we're all going to live in this apartment peaceably, I suggest you stay the hell out of my business. He's my father, and I'm doing what's best for him."

"Monty, shut up," Marilyn said.

Monty waved a hand to silence her. "Because some of us can't afford to run away from our responsibilities. Some of us, I'm talking about real men, choose to stay and deal with problems. We can't dump our shit on someone else and sit in a cave staring at a wall."

"Monty!" Marilyn hissed.

Butch, who had lolled patiently waiting for scraps, lumbered to his feet and growled at Philip. Thick strands of saliva drooled to the floor.

"Go ahead, Monty," Philip said, "finish that thought. We're all adults here."

Tru clutched himself, shut his eyes, and shuddered with anger. It looked like a seizure. When he stopped, he had another look in his eye. It said: I'm outta here. He stood up and hurried to his room. A moment later, the walls began to shake to the beat of techno music.

"Gayle worked her fingers to the bone to keep Tru and Henry clothed and fed," Monty said. "It wasn't easy for her. It drove her over the edge, every day hoping that you'd come back. But you're a coward. You hid under a rock and let the world go to hell."

"Is that what she told you, that she wanted me back?"

"And you never phoned once," Marilyn said. "It broke her heart."

"Marilyn, she didn't have a heart."

Her stare could have frozen mercury. "And now you show up, after we've taken care of everything, just in time to unravel everything we've done."

Philip nodded. "Yes, just in time." He stood up. "That's exactly right." He left the apartment, couldn't stand to be in the same room with those people. All he could think of doing was walking the streets, no matter how dangerous they had become.

Broadway was more crowded that he had imagined. As he walked toward Times Square, passing pizza and doughnut dives, he heard firecracker—or gunshot—sounds in the distance, and also people shouting.

One thing Marilyn had said still disturbed him. He didn't mind the part about being a coward, of running away from his responsibilities. He knew that was untrue, simply more of Gayle's malicious lies. But Marilyn had wounded him with her comment about never phoning. That had been the only true statement they had made, and it had been a deep stab to the gut. He should have tried calling, talking things out. Perhaps he would have even talked to Tru if Gayle had been away from the apartment. He might have formed some kind of relationship with him. Regret burned as hot as a blowtorch. He picked up his pace, wanting to put that thought well behind him. He knew it was too late to feel sorry, but he did anyway, a deep, enduring regret. He had come back to set things right, to make up for being an absent dad, but he could not shake his anger at himself for not making more of an effort for so long a time.

After several blocks he noticed that he seemed to be the only one on the streets who was alone. There were numerous couples. Tourists wandered the sidewalks in groups. Young men roamed the pavement in packs of four or five. He didn't believe, as Marilyn had said, that he was in any danger, but he hated the idea of being the only man in New York City without someone to share the night. He thought about walking back to the apartment, but couldn't stomach that idea either.

He walked another three blocks before he remembered Scotty giving him the card of the nightclub he worked at. He pulled it from his wallet and checked the address in the light from a storefront window. He smiled as he stepped to the curb to hail a cab.

❖

As soon as he walked into the dim nightclub he saw Scotty huddling over a table with several other men. He thought if he simply walked by them on his way to the bar, Scotty might follow him and they could talk alone. As he walked by, Scotty recognized him, reached out and grabbed his arm, pulling him into the group. Introductions were made by shouting over the music. One of the men poured a glass of beer from a pitcher and set it in front of Philip.

Philip leaned close to Scotty's ear. "I thought you worked here?"

Scotty shook his head. "Off duty." He waved a hand at the group. "We're on a pub crawl. Join us."

Philip smelled the beer on Scotty's breath and it made him want to lean in for a kiss. Instead, he lifted his glass and took a long swallow. He hadn't drank tap beer since leaving the States, and the taste of Budweiser uncovered a limitless set of memories about going out on the town with his firefighting buddies. His head began to spin, and not from the alcohol.

"Drink up," Scotty said, "we're ready to blow this joint. Lots more places to carouse tonight."

Philip didn't ask where they were going; he didn't care. He welcomed the easy manner in which they included him into their number, assuming he would tag along. No one seemed interested in flirting with him, and he wondered if he was too unattractive or if Scotty had signaled something to make a claim on him. He closed his eyes, finished his drink in one swallow, and trailed the group through the crowd and onto the sidewalk.

Once they were away from the crush of bar people, he could get a better look at Scotty—slightly skinny and dressed like a rock star. Scotty looked cool, and his confident manner advertised that he knew it.

The air held a brisk scent. They ambled along the sidewalk, smiling at other pedestrians. Scotty pulled a joint from his pocket and lit up. Philip understood then why the group had such a mellow humor; they were all stoned.

As they strolled, the openness and nonchalance with which they smoked the joint surprised him. The passersby noticed, but none seemed to care. He understood that joining this crawl was an open invitation for Scott to make a move, and if he didn't want to spend the evening with this sexy man, or if he didn't want to get mixed up with drinking and drugs, he should walk away now. Scotty would know enough not to pursue him. He took a deep drag off the joint and passed it on. As he strolled along, he took a few more tokes and he began longing for the next cold beer to soothe his throat. He wasn't making an affirmative statement to have sex, only a determination to let things unfold naturally, to linger with Scotty, yet make no decisions. Let nature work it out, he thought. And if Scotty wanted to buy him drinks, stay close, and even nuzzle up to him, then what was the harm?

In the next bar they ordered tequila shots with their beers. The music was too loud for any conversation, so he and Scotty just hovered in each other's gravitational pull, swaying and smiling, with Scotty becoming even more mellow and cool. They moved closer, brushed against each other, and Scotty's arm curled around his waist and stayed there. That was a signal that unless he did something, they would be together all night. He felt his cheeks warm while chills ran up his legs and thighs. He did not move away.

This, he told himself, was how men of the world conducted themselves, those men he had withdrawn from, the men he had only fantasized about. This was how relationships began, with risk and excitement, stomach hollow, heart pounding, imagination ablaze with possibilities. How many years had he dreamed of this? And if they should end up in bed, triumphantly, how many more nights could they share? The nights to come would be softer and less inflamed, yet more intimate. He wished more than anything to see six hours into the future, to know the result of this adventure, adulation or cataclysm.

He felt a sudden and fierce desolation. He had hoped for too much, asking for the improbable. He forced himself to stay in the present, and let it play out minute by minute. He would wallow in Scotty's company for as long as it lasted. Come what may, he was ready to change his life, to put an end to the long, solitary days of his past. Scotty stood shining as the symbol of his future.

The next bar they stumbled into had softer music. They sprawled around a table and were joined by other revelers. Scotty didn't impose himself on Philip, but in his easy way he was attentive, going to the bar to get drinks, talking to others while making sure to bring Philip into the conversation. He made it clear he wasn't going anywhere without Philip.

A stocky redhead asked, "Philip, have you been in New York long?"

"No," he said. "I mean I haven't been here for ten years. I was abroad. Thailand."

"Wow, what are those Thai boys like? Did you see any sex shows?"

Everyone's head turned toward Philip. Since this was the first time the table was listening to a single conversation, he wished it was about something else. Anything else. "I wasn't into that scene. I lived as a monk."

The table lost interest and went back to multiple conversations, none of which included Philip. Under the table, Scotty took his hand and gave it a tender squeeze.

Last call came shortly before four a.m. He and Scotty waved good-bye to the others and walked toward the East River to watch the sunrise. The water was soft and beautiful in the morning light. He felt exhilarated by the night that was ending. He had an overwhelming urge to take Scotty home and make love to him, just to keep that feeling going for a few more hours.

In the cab back to the West Side, they brushed against each other fondly and remained silent. He knew everyone in the apartment would sleep for another few hours, so he had no worries about having to introduce Scotty to the in-laws or Tru. Nonetheless, he put his finger to his lips as he opened the front door and led Scotty to his bedroom as if they were thieves, not lovers.

Once the door was shut, Scotty produced another joint. Philip had to stifle a laugh as he opened the window to get some ventilation. He sat back on the bed and smoked while Scotty stripped down to his underwear. Then Scott dove onto the bed, making a loud clanking noise. They both laughed. Scotty took the joint from him, and between tokes, helped him out of his clothes. Philip couldn't stop snickering.

❖

Later, long after he stopped laughing and after making love, he woke to the sounds of movement in Tru's room. Scotty slept peacefully; one arm lay stretched out away from him and the other was curled around Philip's waist. Philip was ravenous. He slipped out of bed and tiptoed to the kitchen. He found crusty French bread on the counter and roast beef and sharp cheddar cheese in the fridge. He made two sandwiches and snatched a couple of cold beers. When he turned to sneak back to his bedroom, he found Tru standing at the kitchen doorway. Tru smiled in a disturbing, knowing sort of way. Philip opened his mouth to explain without a clue of what he would say, but Tru simply turned and hurried back to his room. Burning with embarrassment, he sank down on a chair, dropped the food on the table, bent over, and put his face in his hands. Should he go after Tru now and explain, or let him come to grips with this new wrinkle before they talked?

As he wrestled with his shame, he realized that Scotty's joint must have been laced with something more powerful than mere grass, because it had lasted through their long bout of sex, and he was still flying in the stratosphere. Better to wait on that talk, he realized.

Scotty, when he woke, wolfed down his sandwich and beer in the same gluttonous way he had made love. Philip sat back on the bed, loving the way he attacked his food, savoring every bite. Philip wanted to see him again, to make love again, to see how far this sensual thing between them could go, but he had no idea if Scotty felt the same. He saw all his vulnerability laid bare. *Was I simply low-hanging fruit— easy pickings? Will he want another taste?*

They slipped back into their clothes when sounds from the kitchen made it clear the in-laws were making their breakfast. They promised to have coffee the next evening at a café in the Village, and Scotty wrote down Philip's phone number and address and slipped it into his wallet. Philip was able to sneak Scotty out of the apartment without the in-laws seeing.

Once he entered the kitchen, however, Marilyn shot him a glacial stare.

"There is something evil going on here," she said. She stood at the stove while the edges of four eggs frizzed to brown ruffles in bacon grease.

Philip felt his stomach knot as he sat across the table from Monty.

Monty glanced up from his newspaper. "What do you mean, dear?"

"The story is right there on the back page," she said, flipping eggs, "two men going door to door, posing as FBI agents to swindle seniors out of their pensions. What is the world coming to? Tell Tru not to open the door to any strangers."

Philip relaxed and gave a little chuckle.

"What are you up to today," Monty asked.

"Tru and I plan to visit Gayle's grave." The humor of a moment ago left him as he realized he and Tru would be alone at the gravesite, and he would need to explain everything. In the silence broken only by popping grease, he knew this would be an awkward day.

He dreaded having that conversation with Tru, but for as long as he could remember, he had felt a longing inside for something he refused to indulge. That longing had created an empty space in his chest. He had shoveled everything into that space—books, meditation, prayers, helping the needy—but nothing filled it, until now.

Suddenly, he wanted to tell Tru everything. He began to laugh. For the second time that morning, he couldn't stop himself. He watched as

Marilyn and Monty shot each other nervous stares, and still he couldn't control his laughter.

❖

The gray morning turned wet with a thick mist, and it held all the promise of a hard rain by noon. Philip and Tru dressed warmly and wore windbreakers. Zack picked them up in his Jeep and they sped out of Manhattan and into New Jersey just as the commuter traffic began to dwindle. As before, Zack was as reckless with his driving as he seemed with every other facet of his life. Philip sat in the backseat, braving the spray of mist. He was on the verge of suggesting that Zack slow down, that there was no hurry, but the determined look on Zack's face and the way he handled the Jeep made Philip hesitate. He realized that Zack's behavior, which was gruff, masculine and competent, was utterly American—a product of a supercilious culture—and Zack would consider him a pussy for insisting he drive responsibly. Zack, in his flip-flops, torn jeans, NRA T-shirt, and uncombed hair, seemed a modern-day renegade.

Zack pulled the Jeep off the highway west of Newark and they climbed a hill. When they topped the rise and wound down toward affluent estates, it seemed the day would blossom into something wet and utterly forgettable. Below, the valley had a thin coating of water and the mist grew heavier. Philip was hopeful that he would reach the cemetery before the rains came.

The steep and winding road was slick, and there were no guardrails. Zack drove more slowly, but still too fast for Philip's liking.

Why, he wondered with a sour smile, did she kill herself? His mouth tightened. Several times under a drug veil, he had harbored those same urges, but that was finished. He'd made up his mind to live. Hadn't he? Live and do what was needed, whatever the hell that was. As for dealing with Gayle's death, he knew that would take time. Enough time for him to overcome all the pain seemed impossible, but all the books said it would happen eventually. The sum of human wisdom. Meantime, he had a decision to make.

As the Jeep found the valley floor and began to pass the pristine houses, Zack jerked out of his silence.

"Welcome to New Jersey's upper crust." His tone was jovial, but he couldn't hide his jealousy, or was it contempt?

Even though the sky threatened rain, sprinklers revolved over manicured lawns and the water made a swishing sound as it licked at the grass. Nothing but gardeners' trucks were parked in the driveways. They soon left the estates behind. Zack slowed and turned off the main road, swinging through the cemetery's gateposts and driving along a narrow road to a secluded area.

When Zack parked, Philip crawled from the backseat. Cold. He shivered and hunched his shoulders. He pulled a box from the back and followed Tru over the verdant lawn searching for Gayle's marker. The mist laid a slick, eager surface on the grass. His shoes were soaked after only a dozen yards.

They easily found her gravesite. It lay beside a line of towering cypresses. Behind them, white violets ran wild up a slope that was glossed by moisture. He walked those last ten steps like an ox to the knife.

A cold wind blew over the hillside and rose to a keening whine only moments after he placed the box beside a gravestone on which the name Gayle Mann, two dates, and the words NEVER FORGOTTEN were carved. He shoved his hands into the pockets of his windbreaker and stood staring at the stone for a long time.

He crouched on his knees, pulled a bouquet of lilies from the box, and placed them in a marble holder. He folded his hands over his chest, as if in prayer, and went utterly still, staring through space in a trance.

His focus lifted slightly higher than the line of trees at the edge of the road, and he watched the smooth flight of geese, a great wedge flying south. He studied their sleek contours like da Vinci would have done, and that pulled him into a deeper state of calm.

Minutes later, kneeling amid rows of headstones on a drizzly morning, gazing at nothing in particular, as if staring through a window into another dimension, he opened himself up to all that is, offering himself to the energy that binds the universe. He felt himself become weightless, floating.

Tru and Zack must have presumed he was steeped in prayer, but Philip was merely trying to stop all conscious thought, to open his mind and merge with the cosmos so it would send him a message or nudge him in the right direction. And just then, what he hoped for most was a sign—move forward or retreat.

He felt like a surfer balanced on the arch of a wave, caught between two worlds, two different cultures, trying to snatch a few perilous minutes of bliss before the wall of water came crashing over his head. The larger part of him yearned to fly back to the simple life at

Wat Phra Shing, but then Tru dropped to his knees beside him, staring at the sky and mimicking him. He could feel the energy radiating from that slender body—a lustrous warmth. The binding threads of his love for Tru uncoiled, and he knew Thailand was out of his reach, for good.

As he sat there, feeling the wind press against his face, a vision came to him of her inert body lying in the coffin, consigned to darkness, closed away for all time. It was an unbearable idea, even though he felt no love for her. From that box six feet below, he still felt the will of her wrath pulling at him, manipulating him.

He realized that his mind had wandered. His memories had made him angry and deepened his breathing. With effort, he released his thoughts and opened himself to the universe once more, now hoping for some form of forgiveness.

Minutes spanned into a half hour. A light rain began to blow on the wind although the sky was not entirely covered with clouds. The wet breeze kept a steady pulse against this face, pressing against him like a living force. He glanced up to see a windblown plastic bag billowing against a dark sky. It rippled like jellyfish tumbling through the surf. He became transfixed, unconsciously imagining his own life being tossed around on the whim of unseen forces.

"Hey, you two," Zack said, "I hate to disrupt your Zen fest, but getting soaked is not going to bring her back."

A flash of anger sizzled Philip's nerve endings. Much as he didn't want to admit it, he truly detested Zack. He pulled an empty coffee can from the box and placed it near her gravestone. Tru drew several letters, still in their envelopes, from the box. He struck a lighter and held the flame to the letters until they caught, and placed the burning paper in the coffee can.

The box was half full of letters, the ones from her he had carried from Thailand and the ones he sent her that Tru had saved. He grabbed a handful and, by ones and twos, fed the flame.

It struck him forcefully as he burned his past how calm his life had become while living at the temple. These last several days had smashed the equilibrium he had achieved with Annop. Jet-lag and morphine withdraw had much to do with that, but coming home had turned his emotions to shambles. He began to feel that with each letter he fed to the flame something palpable from his past would fly out, and he tried to reassure himself that he was being a drama queen.

For the first time the letters seemed so flimsy. Raindrops falling on them blurred the ink, making the handwriting illegible. Nonetheless, they were from and to her, and as long as they existed they would remain part of his past, locked in his being. He fed the can until the flames rose well above the lip.

When the last letter took flame, he knelt with his head in his hands. He looked up and gazed at the flower-covered hillside. He felt, for the first time, that he could leave her behind, to follow his own nature, his own path. But even as the flames died down, he was overcome with sorrow and guilt. His mind now battled with his sense of his own ruthlessness, his own will to survive. Finally he turned to Tru, feeling a sharp and unbearable idea staring at him, like some predatory animal whispering to him that he preferred her dead rather than alive. He tried to bury these thoughts out of fear Tru might be able to read his mind, but they glided back to the surface on their own.

He was horrified by his sheer callousness, and it made him feel vulgar and ugly, yet he couldn't deny it.

He saw something in Tru's eyes, and he thought, this is what I have now. He would embrace this new life, hold on to Tru, and let their relationship improve with time, become more complex and less vulgar, less ugly, more resonant. Yes, that was his future now.

He and Tru stood at the same time. They all walked toward the Jeep.

"So Song-boy tells me you're fucking some dude?" Zack said. "Maybe we can double-date some time. You know, get an orgy thing going."

Blood began to pound at Philip's temples. His throat suddenly felt scratchy. "Do me a favor, Zack. Try not to be such a prick."

Zack jumped in front of him and stopped Philip with an arm to the chest. "You're the prick, dude."

Philip glanced at Tru, who was backing away and seemed to be searching for a rock to crawl under. He looked back into Zack's eyes with a cold, wary stare.

"Hey you guys—" Tru said.

Zack puffed out his chest. "I fucking hate you ass-bandits who hide in the closet and don't have the guts to be yourselves. You're a fucking coward."

Something exploded in Philip's head. The line of green cypresses, the field of gravestones, the lush lawns all dissolved into broken bits of color, heading swiftly toward him as he slammed his fist against that sneering face. As Zack hit the ground, a sweet rush of mindless ecstasy washed through Philip, becoming a perfect release of everything he had been holding in.

Zack jumped to his feet and grabbed Philip's jacket. They pushed and shoved each other until they both went down, sprawling on the wet grass. Zack had him in a headlock, punching his face. Philip didn't try to fight back; he simply struggled to get free.

"Goddam you, Zack!" Tru screamed. He pulled Zack off Philip.

Zack took a few steps back and then leaped toward Philip and kicked him in the gut. An explosion in the pit of Philip's stomach turned into a solid wall of pain that pushed up into his lungs. There was no room for air. He gasped but he couldn't suck air past the blockage in his throat. Everything became bathed in yellow light, like an overexposed photograph.

"Let's go," Zack said, turning to Tru.

"Fuck off, you animal."

"He started it. Are you coming or not?"

Tru crouched and pulled Philip to a sitting position.

"You okay?"

Tru helped him to his feet. He straightened slowly, still gasping for breath. Blood poured from his nose. The yellow light began to recede.

"I guess I had that coming," he said. His knees trembled, and his gut felt loose and watery. He held up the hand that had thrown the first punch. The knuckles were scraped raw. He flexed them, trying to ease the pain.

The Jeep sped away. Philip realized he and Tru had lost the opportunity for the reconciliation he had hoped coming here would nurture. He had envisioned them hugging, perhaps a purgative cry, and a promise for a new relationship. All vanished.

"I'm sorry, Tru, but that man has a stripe of crudeness running down his back as wide as a skunk's."

"What do we do now?" Tru asked.

"Unless you've got a better idea, I think we should walk to the funeral chapel and call a cab to take us to the nearest train that will get us home."

They began to walk. Philip asked about Gayle, about her condition these last few years, and why she might have committed suicide.

Tru found the strength to overcome his anger and told how she lived after Philip abandoned them, how she never recovered from the shock and sorrow and humiliation. She spent most of the last two years in bed with Tru waiting on her as best he could. The doctors could find nothing physically wrong with her and said her suffering seemed almost willed, a form of self-abuse. The nearest they could come to naming a malady turned out to be chronic depression. They prescribed pills, which she seldom took. Her illness was incurable, Tru explained, because she clung to it. It became her lover.

His voice grew angry, but oddly distant and low. Philip knew how difficult it was for him to speak like this, and he knew also that what he said was true. Philip saw the image of an empty seedpod shriveling away because it was now useless.

Tru explained how, once her health diminished, she became so dependent on him that she couldn't stand for him to be out of her sight. She made him miss many days of school, and he lost contact with his friends. He had become, however, devoted to her, so he didn't have time or the energy for companions. Philip knew she no doubt fed on that devotion, a young boy's love, like a vampire feeds on its prey, but over time it was not enough. Rather than find a new husband, she chose to punish the unfaithful one in the only way she had left.

He felt rather sorry for Gayle, but he felt much more sorry for Tru. She had brought it on herself. Tru was a victim.

By the time they reached the road that led to the chapel, Tru had wound down his narrative and Philip didn't want to hear any more.

Tru said, "Now that I know you're gay, that explains a lot. But then, why did you marry her?"

"I was nineteen. I met her before I realized I was gay. She was older and hot for me, and I was hot to get away from my family. We hung out at the same coffee shop. Before I knew it, I was living with her and Grandpa Henry in Lamb House. One thing just led to another."

"Then you realized you were gay and you left us?"

"Not exactly."

"Were you fucking Eddy Flores? Is that why?"

Philip felt time snap backward. He turned to ensure he had Tru's full attention. "Before the Towers fell, I loved Eddy, only him, but we never had sex. How could we, we both had wives and kids. We couldn't screw that up on something we were both unsure about. Once the Trade Towers fell I felt like I was underwater, seeing things only in vague outlines, desperately trying to come up for air. That's what it felt like every minute of the day."

"Was that from shock of the attack or from losing Eddy? Mom said you were brave that day, that you ran into the rubble to save lives. She made it sound like you were a hero."

"I don't know what the attack did to me, save that I survived while the men I cared about didn't. I do know that words like 'brave' and 'hero' and 'shock' are merely words. They don't tell us anything—nothing can—about what you experience during the moments it's happening. All I can say is, that day I lost a huge part of myself, and I've never gotten it back. For a long time my soul was paralyzed. Normal feelings dried up in me, and I compensated by trying to live a spiritual life. All this time I've been searching for an answer, and the question was how to become involved again, to drink up the life around me. That's where you came in. You're helping me find that, and I'm grateful."

Tru looked like he was about to say something, but he pulled back. If he had his own confession to make, he was not yet ready to share it.

"So you ran off to Thailand to be gay?"

Philip felt the sharp deliberation of Tru's tone, the raw cruelty of it. He was, he thought, being questioned and judged without any sympathy or affection.

"It was not my idea to leave home. She chased me away and threatened me with a court order. And here's the irony, she claimed she wanted me gone so I couldn't turn you gay."

"I don't understand."

"Neither do I. Women are emotionally incoherent. It's one of their defining characteristics."

Tru smiled. "I thought you ran away because you had something to do with 9/11. All this time I assumed you were a terrorist."

They both grew silent. That last statement had Philip kicking himself once again for not making more of an effort to contact Tru, to explain.

Philip glanced over his shoulder at a thunderhead riding over the hills on a galloping wind. It ballooned in dark rolls above, and beneath it drew a long trailing skirt of rain. The cloud rumbled and flashed. "Oh shit, we're about to get soaked."

Tru turned to look. They began to run, and the cloud boomed at their backs and lightning shattered the air. The rain caught them halfway to the chapel, with the first stout drops plopping the pavement around them. Philip could smell the sweet odor of ozone.

They raced as hard as they could. Rain fell in sheets, soaking them through and streaming into their eyes. By the time they reached the chapel, they were drenched, and there was no longer any need to run. Under the covered porch, they looked at each other and began to laugh.

❖

It was after six p.m. when they arrived at their apartment, which was dim and quiet. The kitchen table was set up in the middle of the living room, and there sat Marilyn and Monty with their hands joined with a strange-looking woman dressed like a gypsy. They all had such serious expressions on their faces that had they mentioned another death in the family, Philip would not have been surprised.

Tru rolled his eyes and tromped off to his bedroom.

"Mrs. Polk is a medium," Marilyn whispered, "and we are talking to Gayle through her."

Philip suppressed the urge to smile. "Have you done this before?"

"Several times."

Their tone made it clear that they firmly believed what they were saying. And from their defensive reaction to his expression, he was sure that his face publicized his contempt for mediums and his belief that séances were pure nonsense. This dabbling in the occult was, for him, the grossest sort of idolatry. On the other hand, he held no wish to mock them.

"Is she at rest?" Philip asked.

"She is at rest, Philip," Monty said in a normal voice. "She is watching over us all from that mysterious realm that lies beyond. But she is disturbed by your presence here."

Lies beyond is exactly right. Lies beyond anything plausible. "Well, be sure and give her my love." He turned to leave the room.

"Wait," Marilyn said. "She wants to know your intentions." She stared at him gravely as he took this in without speaking.

"She described you and Tru at the gravesite today," Monty added, "even the clothes you're wearing."

It was on his lips to asked if she described him pissing on her grave, but he bit it back.

Mrs. Polk began to speak. "I want you to leave this house. Go back to your temple and finish your memoirs. Leave us alone."

Monty folded his hands over his chest and closed his eyes, his face expressing some sort of agony.

Philip excused himself and began to walk from the room, again. He had assumed his silence on the matter was enough to covey his disbelief. *But how did she know about writing my memoirs?*

Marilyn's voice stopped him. "Have you no respect for the dead? For your own wife?"

"I don't want this sort of thing around Tru. He's young and too impressionable. Do not bring this into my home again."

He walked down the hall to his bedroom and shut the door behind him.

❖

When Philip returned to the nursing home the following Saturday, he brought Tru and his lawyer with him. He found Henry in his room, dressed in a sport coat over a white dress shirt, green bowtie, and black slacks. He sat on his bed next to a packed suitcase, waiting.

"Good to see you looking so well," Philip said.

"Take me out of here," Henry said.

"First you need to sign some papers granting me power of attorney. This is Mrs. Evens. She's the lawyer who drew up the paperwork, and this is Mr. Grimes, the notary."

She took the forms and a gold pen out of her briefcase and handed them to Philip.

"I need you to sign these forms for the courts," Philip said. "I have a pen here."

Henry shot him a look that seemed to alternate between childish helplessness and a weary resignation.

"What are they for?"

Philip said, "This one moves ownership of Lamb House into Tru's trust, so that nobody can sell it. This one allows me to make personal and financial decisions for you. Most importantly, they grant me the right to take you home."

Henry pretended not to hear. "I don't understand and I don't want to sign anything. Why did you bring a lawyer?"

Philip knew Henry had absorbed every word and understood perfectly. Rather than try to explain again, he simply handed Henry the forms and pen, and pointed to the lines he needed to sign on. "Here and here. I'll add the dates and anything else we need."

Sadness and distrust lay heavy in Henry's eyes. He shook his head. "Getting old is being robbed of the things that you love, one by one, until there is nothing left but your dignity. When you take away my right to make my own decision, then you take that too." He looked up into Philip's eyes, his expression was cold and hard and wounded.

Philip gave him nothing back, no pity, no reassuring smile. He merely waited.

"I don't trust you," Henry said. "You're worse than Monty."

Tru crossed the room and stood beside him. "He put the trust in my name, Gramps. I'm the sole executor. Nobody can touch it but me." He held the papers steady on the bed. Slowly, Henry bent over the forms and scrawled his signature on both lines, and then he pushed the sheets of paper away.

Henry's mood brightened considerably as Mrs. Evens drove them all back to Manhattan. When they pulled up to the curb in front of Lamb House, his eyes were bright with tears. Philip suggested that Tru and Mrs. Evens take Henry to the corner deli for lunch while Philip broke the news to Marilyn and Monty.

Hurrying from the backseat of the car, Henry said that was fine with him. He could eat an elephant.

Entering the apartment, Philip found Marilyn and Monty, Butch, and a Catholic priest waiting for him in the kitchen. Marilyn stood at the sink peeling potatoes. Monty hovered over the cutting board with a knife in hand, slicing broccoli and placing them in a steam cooker. The priest, a grumpy-looking elderly man, was badly shaved and had dandruff speckling his black shoulders, and bushy eyebrows that made his face look like an owl. He sat at the table sipping coffee.

The priest stood and introduced himself as Father Horan. He shook Philip's hand. "The Lambs tell me that you are planning to enroll your son in school again."

Philip flinched. He had told them nothing.

As if reading his mind, Marilyn said, "The school called while you were out to confirm your appointment." She turned her head slightly away from him. She wore her hair differently today; a sharp white line parted the top of her scalp, wings of hair swept back and clipped to the back of her head in a tight knot.

Philip nodded. "He has two years of high school to finish, and then we'll see about NYU. Is that a problem?"

"The problem is his sexuality," Father Horan said with a hostile voice. "The sooner we place him in a conversion therapy clinic, the better our chances of turning him into a normal, God-fearing Christian."

"Is this a joke?"

Monty held up his hands in an attempt to calm everyone. "Philip, we know things didn't work out the first time, but we must try again. It's for the boy's own good, can't you see. We mustn't let him go through life as one of them."

Philip stepped back, leveling his stare from one face to the other. He felt the sudden urge to kick Butch in that fat belly, and he checked himself. He took several deep breaths.

"You bring this homophobic bullshit into my home?" Philip said, his voice surprisingly calm. "I will not let you subject Tru to your ignorant bigotry."

"He could be back in school by the next semester," Marilyn offered.

"No!"

They all stood silent for a moment.

"Why don't we ask Tru if he wants to go?" Father Horan said. "I think he will. Why wouldn't he? Surly he doesn't want to go through life living as a deviate."

Philip rapped his fist against the wall, making a sound so loud that everyone jumped.

"Philip, calm down," Monty said. "No one is casting any blame in your direction. We just want to help him. God knows nobody wants him making the same mistakes that you've suffered."

Philip shook his head. "This is not about blame and not about what happened between me and Gayle. There is nothing wrong with Tru. He's a fine boy, and I'm proud of him."

Monty dropped his knife and slapped the lid on the steam cooker. He placed it on the stove with a clanging sound, and turned on a burner. "Then you expect us to go on sharing a house with a homosexual? God only knows who he'll drag in next."

"No. I don't expect you to go on living with Tru or me. Tru is down at the deli having lunch with Grandpa Henry. I want you to pack up and leave to make room for Henry."

Monty took a step forward, his cheeks going red. "You took Henry out of the clinic?"

"He signed over power of attorney and guardianship to me. There was a lawyer and a witness present."

Visibly stunned, Marilyn tried to speak but couldn't. Monty looked as if the floor had opened up and swallowed him into pitch darkness. Philip became calm with righteousness. The pot on the stove had begun to simmer. A rolling boil was only seconds away.

Marilyn found her voice. "You can't mean leave today?"

"Not today, right now. Go into the bedroom, pack your clothes, then take yourselves, your priest, and your fucking dog out that door for the last time."

"And just where do you suggest we go at this hour on a Saturday afternoon?"

"I recommend checking yourselves into a clinic that will cure your homophobia. There must be dozens across the river in Queens."

❖

Philip woke in the night, dreaming of falling bodies, tumbling through silent space with only one place to land. He shot upright, trembling.

Bright air slipped in from the outside through the single window that was like an afterthought, and it washed against the dimness and the smell of stale bedclothes. It touched his body like cool fingers. The sensation brought on that old wild surge, hardening his belly and bringing sweat to his palms.

He was about to lie back down when he heard a muffled cry and knew it must be Tru. For the length of a breath he could have been a teenager again, leaping from his room to Tru's bedroom. It seemed a flash, but it was real, and when he scooped Tru into his protective arms, it became perfect. Tru, now awake, hugged back, surprising Philip at how natural the connection felt.

He sat on the bed, holding him to his chest, running a calming hand through Tru's hair. Tru obviously had terrifying dreams as well, and Philip wondered if they were the same as his, of bodies falling, smashing into concrete. He had come to know his son as an intense young soul who wore his sense of failure on his bosom. Like himself, Tru felt that he had been rejected by God and by those who loved him, and for cause.

Tru pulled back. Their eyes locked on each other in the dim light. "Tell me about her."

Philip knew then what dream Tru had been fighting, and he felt the need to comfort him. His Buddhist vows made him incapable of lying, yet how could he tell Tru his mother was a monster?

Monsters are sometimes born to human parents. Some are horribly misshapen, with huge heads or no arms or legs, or three breasts and no mouth. Unavoidable accidents. But there is another kind of monster, ones who are mentally deformed. In Gayle's case, her face and body were perfect, yet some twisted gene or malformed egg caused her to have a deformed soul.

Monsters are variations from the accepted normal to a greater or lesser degree. As a child may be born with a cleft lip, so one may be born without kindness or the potential of a conscience. A person with no arm or leg eventually will adjust himself to his lack, but having never developed a conscience or the ability to love, he can't miss them or even know there is anything amiss. The inner monster has no visible thing to compare with others. They must, surely, assume everyone is as heartless as themselves. To a woman without a conscience, any soul-stricken man must seem as foolish and ridiculous as honesty seems to the criminal. To a monster, what is normal to most human beings is monstrous.

He knew it was true in Gayle's case, yet what to tell a frightened and disturbed son?

"She was a strong and independent woman who didn't take shit from anybody."

"I read your letters. She saved them all. I don't think she loved you much. I know you wanted to be here but she kept you from coming home."

He hugged Tru, a long meaningful embrace. "The important thing to remember," he whispered in Tru's ear, "is that she did love you. More than anything else in the world. We both did."

"But why did she—"

"Only she could answer that. I'm sure it wasn't because of you or the fact that you're gay. In all her letters to me, you were the shining star of her life. It could have been because of me. She might have grown tired of hating me and realized she's made a mess of things. Who knows?"

Tru pulled back and laid his head on his pillow. "I'll be okay."

Philip patted his shoulder. "I know, son."

He walked back to his bed but he couldn't sleep. Had he lied? Did she love anybody but herself? He wanted to believe that she did love the seed of her body, if only because it sprang from her.

An hour later he gave up trying to sleep. He slipped into his clothes and tiptoed through the apartment and out the door. Once on the street, he walked fast, heading downtown.

As he neared the site, a hint of dawn came up in the eastern sky. He saw chinks of vague light between the dark buildings and the star-laden firmament. It was four-thirty; he had forgot that the sunrise began so early. He watched for a long time but it didn't appear to get any brighter, as if time were somehow stuck. He felt alone, isolated from everything he cared for, and so tired he could not summon up the strength to care.

The air was cold and a sharp, thin breeze came from the east. As he reached the site, that last day he had been there came rushing back to him. He had called in sick to work that day because Gayle had demanded that he take Tru to a doctor's appointment. He had hated the idea of missing a day at the firehouse. If there was an emergency or high-rise fire, his buddies would need him. But Gayle could never swallow a "no."

He had sat reading a *Sports Illustrated* magazine in the waiting room, ten blocks from the World Trade Center, when he heard the roar one hears at the end of a runway while jets fly low overhead. He felt his heart sink. A tremendous crash followed, making him leap to the windows. On the street, people were immobile, gazing up at the southern skyline. He turned to look in that direction and saw sheets of paper floating on the air like confetti, and smoke pouring from the North Tower. He leaped out the door and took the stairs, knowing there was no time to wait for an elevator.

Before he made the street, he heard another boom. Running out of the building, through the papers and smoke and dust, he saw that both Towers were in flames.

Sirens from fire trucks echoed off the buildings. People gathered on the sidewalks in shock; some were obviously fearful. He cursed Gayle for taking him away from the station as he ran toward the Towers. He realized that there must be several hundred people trapped on floors above the flames. He made a silent prayer that the fire stairwells were passable, but then he saw bodies plunging through space and knew they had no chance at all. He pushed himself to haul ass faster, but that didn't stop more bodies from falling.

Halfway there, the South Tower collapsed. People who had stood on the pavement in shock began to run north, away from the Trade Center. Racing against the current, he could feel their panic, but his emotions and his mind had switched off. He ran on pure adrenaline.

The stench of burnt plastic was everywhere. The air became laden with white dust and suspended debris. He pulled a handkerchief from his back pocket and held it over his face as he charged into the now-dark sky. Through the veil of dust, he saw the North Tower crumble.

As he neared the site, he saw people lying on the street, some still alive, most dead.

Some survivors wept, others cursed. White dust covered everything except the blood, which appeared dark and wet. Sirens howled around him. He helped carry the survivors to the ambulances. After thirty minutes, he found Eddy Flores in the rubble, and his heart shattered.

Afterward, everything made him ill. Food and the sound of people eating, crushing breaking slurping food. And smells, he would lift a glass of juice to his mouth and gag from the acrid odor of dust, blood, and burnt bodies. He could neither eat nor sleep, but kept living in a hopeless rerun of that day. That became his hell, unchangeable and forever, until that future time when he joined his lost buddies.

But being at the site again was not as emotional as he thought it would be. It was something he had feared, hiding from it for a decade. But in such tragedies time works like a damp brush on watercolors. The edges blur, the colors blend together, and separated lines begin to form a solid gray. He realized that he couldn't remember the feel of horror, pain, or choking emotion. No one can. A person only remembers having had them. *In another few weeks, I might have another date with Scotty, in a year the dreams might fade, in some vague future I might well become a happy man.*

Still, he felt a blackness on this hallowed ground, as if even on a blinding white day this place would cut off the sun and suck the light out of the air. It had been restored with new buildings and glorious fountains, yet he felt the violence of this hole that nothing could expunge. He felt it not only in the ground and air, but also in the people gathered at that particular sunrise.

As he watched the gray rim of dawn, he was overcome by a feeling that he was being watched, studied. The feeling grew until he spun around to find Tru standing only steps away. His eyes seemed magnified, unguarded, vulnerable, nervously watching him, and his stubbly hair reflecting the starlight.

Tru swallowed several times, and he spoke with a dry voice out of a pinched-up throat. "I followed you."

Philip was too shocked to speak.

Tru tried again. "About bringing Grandpa Henry home and tossing Marilyn and Monty out, I think you did a good thing."

"Well, maybe so. But I'm not sure it was the right thing."

"Comes close."

"What about chasing Zack away? You still mad?"

"He's kind of stupid and reckless."

"In my day they would have called him a knuckle scraper."

"They still do," Tru said. "Only now they put 'fucking' in front of it."

Philip grinned. "I guess we haven't evolved very far, then."

Tru smiled, but it was a painful-looking slash across his face. "You're going back to Thailand, aren't you? To be with Nop? You love him as much as he loves you. I got that the moment I saw you together."

He thought about Annop—easygoing and unfailing, modest and decent and caring. He realized that Tru was spot-on. Annop did love him, and he wondered why, why Annop had needed someone who had none of his virtues? Could it be that Annop needed to care for him, nurture him, as he had done with Tru these last few weeks? Is it only by caring for others that one comes to find love? He had never let Annop know the constant daily urge for intimacy Philip felt for him. He had kept his feelings at bay by fear and will. Did Annop struggle with those same urges? Suddenly, he hated the distance between them, and he knew he would, he must, return to the temple.

"Will you write to me, like you did Mom? Can I come visit you?"

"Visit? I thought you said it was a shithole."

"That was before I got to know you."

"I would be grateful if you'd visit, and yes, I'll write every week, just like with Mom."

Tru grinned up at him, his brows hooking up his forehead. Philip always remembered it, later, as having been a look of secret understanding, a glance that swept aside the tourists, the construction workers, the commuters, and the buildings, leaving only the two pairs of eyes that recognized each other as reluctant survivors. Neither one had wanted to live while their loved ones perished, but now both had a new world to explore. That was the bond they now shared, the foundation of a new beginning.

"You never heard me sing."

Philip remembered the tattoo of treble cleft and musical notes on Tru's chest, and that he loved to sing in the choir. "Sing for me now, son. Sing something from your heart, something I can take with me."

Tru looked around at all the tourists and construction workers and business people scurrying to work.

"It's okay. They'll think we're singing for handouts."

Tru began to sing, his voice nasal and thin, but also sweet and clear. His eyes were closed. A few tourists stopped to listen.

Of course, Philip thought, "Empty Chairs at Empty Tables" from *Les Miserables.* The perfect song to honor our dead.

Tru kept his eyes closed, as if he sang from a dark hole where eyes were useless and everything was seen with nerve endings. He sang softly at first, and his voice grew louder as the emotion built.

Philip tried pretending that this was merely a song, that once Tru stopped everything would be fine again and the hole in his chest would shrink to nearly nothing. But then he understood that he shared that hole with Tru; they both were afraid of it and they both suffered from it. And because it was something they shared, Philip finally embraced it, the depth of his sorrow, wholly, and it began to fill with gratitude for his son.

As he listened, Tru's voice soared in the last verses of the song. He clearly loved the sounds of the words and the depth of their meaning.

Tru laid bare his soul—his art—in the way Philip had always covered his, those raw nerve endings in him that were unsettled and untrusted. The only response he could give his son was tears. Those drops of moisture held all his grief and all his joy. He let them fall in a steady stream.

He thought of his life as a kind of music, not always a melodic or even happy tune, but always having form and cadence. And his life had not been a full orchestra for a long time now. A single note only from a lone instrument—a rusty squeezebox—stretched out into the future for as far as he could see. Tru, however, had brought new music to his soul, like a bird's song in the night.

Philip dried his eyes as Tru finished his song. They hugged for a long minute. After, they strolled to a nearby coffee shop wedged between a deli and a camera shop that also processed film. They ordered blueberry muffins and coffee with extra cream. They sat at a table by the window to watch the flow of morning commuters hurry by.

Sipping his coffee, he knew he would fly back to Chiang Mai as soon as he could get his affairs in order and sign over guardianship of Grandpa Henry to Tru. That might take years, or perhaps a few months. He would let the lawyers make that determination. He knew the temple would take him back however long it took to return, and he looked forward to wearing the robes once again, of morning prayers and walking the streets for alms. He thought of the temple at Wat Phra Singh with its graceful lines and peaceful ambience. He could almost hear the sonorous voices of chanting monks. And he imagined Annop, waiting beside the chessboard with the chessmen painstakingly set in rows, and Annop's eyes sparkling in that loving face. More than anything he wanted to lift that man out of that wheelchair and hold him, simply hold him to his breast, and then perhaps sleep beside him on the mat on the floor.

All around him in the coffee shop, people chattered in foreign voices—English, French, Chinese. He longed for the singsong cadence of people speaking Thai. The first thing he would do when he arrived at the temple would be to bow before the statue of the Buddha and give thanks. In the meantime, he would sip his coffee and enjoy his time with Tru, and he would have a good sleep, alone, in peace. He would always be grateful for Scotty, but he would not call him again. As he lifted his coffee cup to his lips and blew over the rim, he felt a contentment that he had never expected, and an ease he had never believed would come his way.

ALMOST ENOUGH

A week after Master Satchapalo died in Yangon, we set off for Ayutthaya, the capital of Siam, a tortuous two-month pilgrimage on elephant back. From there we continued our journey to Sukhothai to visit the sacred sites of the kings and scholars who brought Buddhism to Siam in the thirteenth century. My new master, Master Chamathevi, was the emanation of several holy men of Eastern traditions, and his reputation afforded us an unbridled reception everywhere we went. For me that journey became life changing, and has remained full of breathtaking memories.

I closed my book and glanced at the clock on the nightstand. The alarm would sound in another two minutes. It was a Tuesday, a work day in January, that disheartening time of year when I arrived at my cubicle before sunrise and left for home after sunset. I switched off the alarm button and picked up my book again. I checked the cover page, *The Thai Philosophy of Living Through Karma* by Gho Tuad, turned to the last page I had read, and began the next one. I was trying to lose myself in a stimulating parallel universe for as long as possible.

Indeed, while reading, the air seemed heavily scented with incense and more densely palpable because of all the possibilities that Gho Tuad offered up on a gleaming platter. His words were unpretentious, profound, and presented in a spirit of benevolence.

When I looked up again, it was well past seven. I would arrive at the office late, again, but would anyone notice? I laid the book face down on the bedspread and slipped my feet from under the covers. As they touched the cold tile floor, my left hand caressed the book. I craved more, just five more pages before sloshing through my morning routine. I knew, however, it wouldn't be enough. I wanted to hole up in my bedroom (no, our bedroom) all day and read, be challenged by one of the most revered spiritual masters of the last century.

And why not? It was my birthday, after all. Shouldn't I be allowed a day off on this special occasion? But, of course, it being *our* bedroom, she would eventually barge in to see what was keeping me.

I pulled my hand from the book. I should not permit myself to read in the mornings, not even on my birthday. It only spoiled my mood for the rest of the morning.

By now I should have been showered, deodorized, dressed, and eating breakfast with Julie and Hunter. I imagined her downstairs, cooking pancakes and ministering to Hunter. I should be at the table, dressed in my gray suit and power-red tie, full of simple, encouraging banter. But that was exactly what I didn't want. It wasn't that I felt no love for my wife and son, but more and more I found my life with them to be, well…like a low salt, low fat, no alcohol, gluten free diet. It was impossible to get excited about it. More and more I sought to be alone in this confusing world, searching for answers to questions that seemed beyond me.

That, I knew, was impossible. I had, after all, obligations. I must provide the roof over their heads, feed them, pay the utilities, and dump money into Hunter's college fund. Still, I felt there should be more to life beyond sleep, meeting obligations, and an occasional dinner party.

I decided to read one more page, just one, to motivate myself to abandon the bed.

We were a large caravan of about thirty elephants in all. During the day I rode on my master's elephant, acting as his mahout, with my master riding directly behind me. While we rode he gave lessons, told stories, and created a number of practices for me. One afternoon, as we came to the sleepy town of Lamphun and caught sight of the golden radiance of its Wat Phra That Harinpunjai, another monk in our party, Master Mahawan, began to die.

Mahawan's death became another powerful lesson for me. He was the tutor to my new master, and was regarded by many as South East Asia's foremost holy person, a humble monk who for me was an embodiment of devotion, and teaching through the simplicity of his loving presence.

I inhaled deeply. The idea of having a teacher, a master, seemed so beautiful; in another life I might have sat at a master's feet, listening to sagacious stories and reading the scriptures through the cool hours of the morning. But this current life, this post-9/11 world, had no time for sage wisdom and no patience for idleness. Long wars were being fought, much had been lost on both sides, and many had died. I had died twice on the field hospital's surgical table in Afghanistan, but enough voltage from the defibrillator resurrected me both times. Later, the surgeon joked that I was one up on Christ.

I had returned from the realm of the dead to receive a Purple Heart and a medical discharge. I now walked with the aid of a metal cane. Julie and Hunter considered me a true American hero. Imagine that: Palmer Warren a hero. It was nonsense, I knew. It took stupidity, not courage, to leave myself exposed in a firefight. Had I not been stoned on patrol, I might still be there with my buddies, instead of here dreading the moment I would need to leave my (our) bed.

Just one more page, I thought, before I would drag myself to the shower. The day that lay ahead still seemed too thin, too tenuous. Another page would shore up my resolve.

We raised our tents in a clearing outside the walls of the golden temple. I was tending Master Mahawan. He and I were the only two people in his tent when he suddenly called me over. He had an endearing way of calling me "A-mi," meaning "my child" in his local dialect. "A-mi," he said tenderly, "it's happening now. Remember, you are fine as you are: I am well pleased with you. Serve your master as best you can."

I turned to run out of the tent but he caught my sleeve. "Where are you going?" he asked.

"To bring Master Chamathevi," I said.

"There's no need," he said, and smiled. "With a master to his student, there's no such thing as distance." And then he gazed up to the top of the tent and passed away. I sat there, unable to move.

A sea swell of feelings rushed through me, rising from under my chest and buoying me up and out of bed. It took courage to face death as Master Mahawan had, and the beauty of it affected me deeply. I held a profound respect for holy men, those mysterious souls who wander the earth in search of truth. I considered myself a spiritual being, a seeker of truth. It was one of my most cherished secrets. Spirituality had come to me slowly, during the long hours of lying in that hospital bed, hopped up on painkillers with nothing to do but wonder about how I fit into the grand pattern of the universe.

As I stepped into the chilly spray under the showerhead, I focused on the here and now, and that meant sharing a half hour with my family before driving to work. I summoned my resolve. I would dress and march downstairs. I would be cheerful and loving. After all, I didn't dislike my family. They were a perfect part—much like my mid-century modern house and hybrid car—of the Southern California lifestyle. For me the war was over; life on the razor's edge was a memory. I had survived the horrors of battle, and now the rest of my life would be air-conditioned rooms, heated swimming pools, china plates and cloth napkins. My purpose in life had shifted from keeping my buddies alive to providing for my family. I was safe (if not happy) and comfortable and working toward affluence. If my buddies could only see me now. Still, even from the shower, I could feel the gravitational pull of that book still lying face down on the bedspread. If only....

I showered, brushed my teeth, dressed, and limped downstairs into a cool winter morning. I had decided on a salmon-colored tie, which was what I wore when feeling a bit rebellious. I paused at the landing, holding my breath as if waiting to go onstage before a packed house, which, of course, was ridiculous. My home was no theater and I didn't need to play a part. The only thing required of me was being myself. Simple. Too simple. Yet I had to will myself across the dining room and into the kitchen.

My metal cane tapped out a cadence on the pine-planked floor. I thought perhaps my limp wasn't as noticeable as the month before.

The kitchen was not my territory. It was full of foreign smells, pearl-colored dishes stacked like holy implements behind glassed cupboard doors, and KitchenAid gadgets poised for use on the granite countertops. I could remember Julie's anxiety about every purchase. For her, it had to be the best value, which meant best quality. For me they were simply choices that didn't matter. I would have been just as happy ordering Chinese takeout every night and eating out of cartons with wooden chopsticks.

I sometimes thought that my negative mood swings stemmed from pretending that this stuff, this scaffolding that supported my lifestyle, meant something. Under the influence of that depression, I occasionally thought about escape. And if I walked away from the pearl-colored dishes and KitchenAid gadgets and hybrid car, what would I have left?

But, of course, that was depression talking. This scaffolding *was* my life. I wanted no other.

Julie looked up from her griddle. "Looks like the birthday boy has finally joined the living."

I smiled, yet I found the whine in her voice somewhat irritating. Hunter looked up from his pancakes, his Bambi eyes wide and glistening. I sat at the head of the table and ran a hand through his thatch of hair.

"Good morning, sport."

A vase bursting with irises stood in the center of the table. The deep violet color and sensual beauty made them my favorite flower.

She placed a mug of coffee before me and kissed my forehead. "I was beginning to worry."

That whine again. I tried to ignore it.

She set a plate of scrambled eggs, bacon, and pancakes before me. I lifted my face for the obligatory peck on the lips while I placed a napkin in my lap. "This looks wonderful," I said, raising my eyebrows as if I were surprised and delighted.

"Do you like the flowers?"

"You know I do, sweetheart. They're as beautiful as you are."

"Guess who helped me pick them out yesterday."

I glanced at Hunter, letting my eyebrows lift another centimeter. "You helped?"

Hunter—three years old and dressed in blue pajamas with embroidered galaxies behind Luke Skywalker, Obi-Wan, Han Solo, Chewbacca, C-3PO, and R2-D2—nodded shyly.

"I'm so proud of you," I said, patting his shoulder. "Thank you, sport." He glowed, visibly transported by love for both his parents. He was a joyful child, full of cheer even as an infant. He laughed out loud long before he said his first word. He, much like his mother and the new baby on the way and the house and the car, was practically everything I could hope for. They were almost perfect, almost enough.

I drained half my coffee. She refilled my mug. I patted her belly. "Nothing showing yet, but it won't be long." She had wanted another, quickly. I had given up our twenties defending our country in some Middle East sandbox. Now there was no time to lose.

"Don't let your eggs get cold," she said.

I began to shovel food. "How are you feeling this morning?" I asked through a full mouth, wondering if she was still having morning cramps.

"About the same as yesterday."

"When do you see the doctor next?"

"Monday. Really, it's not as bad as last week. I'm just being a baby. Don't worry."

I shoveled more pancakes and my jaw creaked as I chewed.

She poured herself a mug of coffee and sat across from me so that she could watch me eat. Her love was as transparent as Hunter's. She asked a question but I didn't hear. I was already thinking about my commute, which would be worse now that I was running late, and about the presentation I would give to the board of directors at the end of the week. I wanted to linger here, but I shoveled even faster. Every minute I delayed meant another ten minutes sitting on the 110, breathing exhaust fumes. Every minute here was ten minutes less time to get caught up on paperwork before the phones started ringing and the meetings began.

I glanced at my watch, even knowing perfectly well what time it was. "Sorry, sweetheart, gotta run."

"Have a good one," she said.

I stood and kissed Hunter on the head. She also rose, absorbed in the ritual of getting me out the door: handing me my coat and briefcase, a peck on the cheek, a wave at the doorway. She and Hunter stood on the porch like spectators at a parade as I backed my moss-green Prius into the street and pulled away. At the curb the gardener, Jose, wrestling his lawnmower from his pickup, also stopped to wave.

I focused on maneuvering through traffic. My mind made the transition from family man to businessman with no conscious effort. Neither my book nor my family would enter my thoughts until I left work.

Indeed, I felt a sense of relief being alone in the car, that time between home and office where I could be entirely myself. At home I often felt unmoored; at the office I felt under pressure. But behind the wheel I felt a silent contentment, much like reading, where I was not onstage, not playing a part. The only demand on me was that I negotiate the drive downtown. I could manage that, even make a game of it.

I swung onto to the 110 on-ramp, hitting the light perfectly. As I sped and then slowed, I felt exhausted. I had stayed up until after one, reading. I knew I'd be dragging ass by midafternoon, but I also knew the local Starbucks would get me through it. I promised myself that I would not read tonight. I would take her out for an early birthday dinner, and we would come home to pay the babysitter and put Hunter to bed. Then I would make love to her. The book would be there the night after, but tonight belonged to her, and I would be asleep by eleven.

I was proud of my decision, knowing I had learned what was required to maintain my relationship. As always, I would do whatever was necessary.

❖

An hour and twenty minutes later I limped through a maze of cubicles, dropped my briefcase on my desk, and switched on my computer. I stood for a moment, staring over the tops of the other cubicles. The place looked forsaken, like the realm of the dead, yet I knew people were hunched over their keyboards. And besides, the realm of the dead at least promised release and slumber. This office offered neither.

The other IT people on this floor were much like myself, oftentimes disillusioned geeks of thirty-something years, going flabby around the waist, overworked, underpaid, and giving everything to the nine-to-nine—often ten, occasionally eleven—office life. I knew of a dozen or more Chinese and Indians who were a decade younger and who owned their own firms in Silicon Valley. But I had been passed by. Rather than becoming a successful venture capitalist, I became a screenbound slave of the digital age. I spent my days staring at a computer screen, searching for patterns in rows and columns of numbers that represented cable television viewer ratings. My job was to recognize patterns that could predict where future viewing would occur, based on a number of random factors. My analysis informed the bigwigs how much to charge our advertisers. I told friends and family that my job was gazing into a crystal ball to see the future. I was also developing a mobile application that would do the same analysis hour by hour from anyone's smartphone, so that television executives could access the same information anytime, anywhere.

Out a wall of windows lay an interlude of grass and trees separating my building from the next. I could see birds flurrying over the tops of the palm trees, which made me briefly, yet deeply gratified.

I sat and surveyed my desk. It was exactly as I left it. Not a sheet of paper out of place, Hunter's drawing of our house on my pin board, the computer waiting for me.

I signed on and checked my meeting schedule. Thankfully, I still had an hour before my first meeting. I pulled up a spreadsheet and began checking columns of numbers.

A soft knock on the wall lifted my head, and there stood Scotty Baldrich, the recently hired intern, holding out a cup of Starbucks.

"Hi, Palmer. I made a coffee run and thought you could use one."

I tried to swallow but my throat had suddenly gone dry. Scotty had the pale skin and fair hair that one expects to see in Iceland or Finland, but rarely in L.A. His wiry build and thick glasses never failed to remind me of my college roommate, Clifford. The likeness was uncanny.

"You take it black, right?" Scotty asked.

I forced a smile. "I take it any way I can get it." I felt my cheeks warm. *Christ, I can't believe I'm I flirting.*

Scotty leaned into the cube to set the cup on my desk, but managed to spill some on the brown carpet. He looked at me in alarm.

"Oh shit," he said.

I sighed. Clifford had been the same way, delicate and prone to fits of nervousness whenever we were alone together. I had to be careful around Scotty, to harness my emotions, because he and Clifford were such twin spirits. For a moment, Scotty's face, his whole being, subtly altered, becoming more defined, livelier. A soft golden glow seemed to surround him. In that moment, I had the urge to push him out of the way and dash out of the office. I wanted to soar down the block like the birds flittering from tree to tree. I had no desire to harm him, just like I had never meant to harm Clifford so long ago. I simply wanted to be free, blameless, unaccountable. Most of all, I longed to go back to that time with Clifford and make things right.

"Not a problem," I said. "That's why we employ janitors."

Scotty smiled, almost insanely relieved. He hovered, as if waiting for something more. But what could he need? More kind words? A bit of reassurance? Small talk?

I lifted the cup and sipped, mostly to moisten my throat. "So how are you getting alone with the new job? Do you like working here?"

He nodded with such guileless, unguarded enthusiasm that my throat constricted in a spasm of emotion. It suddenly seemed easy to leave this job, this life, and start fresh with someone so innocent and so ingenuous. But that, of course, was ludicrous. I loved my wife and son.

I didn't resent married life, had no wish to abandon it. Not really. It felt like Scotty was pushing me across some invisible boundary, that line in the sand that had always (except with Clifford) separated me from what I preferred. But, of course, it was not possible for me to undergo that kind of profound transformation in this familiar cubicle on this ordinary Tuesday. It was that damned book that had me all muddled. I had worked so hard for so many years, first in Afghanistan and now here, and in such good faith to create this amazing life. I had learned the knack of living happily, the way a child learns to balance on a two-wheel bicycle, with my share of falls along the way. This was no time to lose hope or to mourn all those lost possibilities.

I set the cup down and turned my back on him. At some point during the day, when he was not so excitable, I would speak to him about the inappropriateness of that mustard-colored tie and matching socks. I began to study those columns of numbers, again, but they no longer made sense.

The presentation charts and handouts arrived by interoffice messenger, the ones I ordered from the art department to accompany my presentation on Friday. They were less that I'd hoped for. *It's only the visuals,* I told myself. *It's the information they exhibit that's important. The data will wow them, who cares what the pie charts look like.* Still, they were not what I had pictured. There was nothing exactly wrong with them, but I had imagined something with more pop. These charts felt small, ordinary, almost amateurish. "They're fine," I said to myself, but I could detect the lie in my voice.

I turned back to my computer screen, but I couldn't push the charts out of my head. I knew I'd be agonizing over them for the rest of the week.

Mr. Arnold stepped into my cube. "Palmer, can I have a word. Meet me in conference room A, quick as you can."

Mr. Arnold, Division Vice President, was not a man you kept waiting. I whirled around, jumped to my feet, and grabbed my cane. I followed him to the largest conference room. When I ambled in, the entire IT staff was crammed in there. They all yelled, "Happy Birthday!"

A white cake sprinkled with coconut sat in the center of the conference table. It was obviously homemade, with a scattering of crumbs caught in the icing and barely legible lettering. It seemed as disappointing as the storyboards had been. A gift-wrapped box sat next to it.

I raised my arms to say thank you before they could all break out in an off-key rendition of the birthday song. "Wow, what a surprise," was all I could think to say. "You guys got me this time."

Mr. Arnold handed me the wrapped box. I tore the paper open to find a leather traveling case containing a bristle brush, nail clippers and file, tweezers, comb, and small mirror. I wondered if this was a message that my job would require more traveling in the future.

"This is awesome," I said with as much enthusiasm as I could muster. "It's really too nice. You shouldn't have." They could have given me a nine-hundred-pound purple elephant, and I would have given them the same reaction. It is intentions one appreciates, I thought. We live in a society where we want whatever we receive.

Miss West lifted a knife and began cutting the cake into squares, doling them out on paper plates with plastic forks. This party had all the makings of a speedy affair. Nothing more than a quick sugar fix, a few slaps on the shoulder, and back to work. And why? Because nobody really cared. Tradition dictates that no one is left out. Still, I wanted to fit in, wanted appreciation for my contributions. I would have been offended had they not done something, although I wished they'd have at least sprung for a store-bought cake.

I knew, however, that I was kidding myself. The party was a failure. My fake enthusiasm mirrored their fake smiles. My nonexistent gratitude echoed their lack of interest in me.

I would not let myself be disappointed. I would eat my allotted piece of coconut cube, return to my spreadsheets, and then come back here for the first meeting of the day. I would give my presentation on Friday with those crappy storyboards, and then pick up my paystub at the end of the month and tap dance all the way to the bank.

I glanced up to find Archer Jackson standing in front of me. My heartbeat accelerated, and I realized I'd have been brutally disappointed had Archer failed to attend this party.

Archer was striking, robust, seemingly carefree, and several years younger than me in an office where almost everyone was older. Archer had an exceptional physique, the type that showed true commitment to fitness without the unenlightened pursuit of mere size and shape. Archer's well-balanced contours spoke not of the gym, but of basketball games, grueling tennis matches, and rock-climbing peaks. His most important attribute, however, was that he had become one of this network's biggest primetime stars. He was beyond famous, recently becoming a household name from coast to coast. Half the country merely watched his comedy show, the other half thoroughly loved him.

Our bond came from what we had in common—both of us were heroes. I on the battlefield, he in the nation's living rooms. Neither of us quite fit in with this staunch business landscape. Archer had voiced it once: "It's lonely, isn't it, not thinking the way everyone else does?"

To say I was star-struck would be an understatement. I had memorized tiny details about my friend, like the fact that he always asked after Julie and Hunter, he covered his mouth with his fingers when he laughed, his eyes sparkled whenever he talked about people outside the network, and he never gossiped about people at the network.

Archer shook my hand, carefully, like a medic feeling for broken bones. A silence hung between us as I studied his thin, easy, curving lips and eyes that resembled Zen brush strokes. His clothes showed he took a utilitarian approach to dressing rather than a desire to impress. And judging by the precision Omega watch strapped to his wrist with an inexpensive leather band, he was someone who had money and power but preferred not to flaunt it.

I felt myself blush as the silence grew uncomfortable.

"These things are such a pain in the ass," Archer said. "How are you holding up?"

"I wish I could click my heels three times and be home reading my book, but I'm fine. I'm okay, really." But I realized I was still caught in the grip of despair, that stage where you're functioning and everything seems so familiar that you believe your life hasn't changed.

Archer displayed a cool nonchalance I associated with the worldly, private-school set. Or maybe it was his unsettling looks. He stroked his chin, smoothing down his fashionable stubble.

"Did you get a piece of cake?" I asked.

"I'm generally a sugar avoider."

Archer leaned closer, and for an instant, I thought he meant to kiss me. I was startled, but I didn't pull away.

"Can we talk in private?" He asked in a low voice. "We can use conference room C."

I stood motionless, holding my breath. I felt a spike of panic at the drop in his voice. It's only Archer, I told myself. It's only my friend from two floors up, and this, of course, was what people do. They have private conferences all the time. Suddenly the crappy cake, the travel kit, and the failed party were forgotten.

"Lead the way."

When we entered the small conference room, I was somewhat disappointed that it had a glass wall with no shades so that we were in full view of all the cubicles. *There is no such thing as privacy in this world unless you occupy the top-floor corner office or are rich enough to own your own yacht. Better yet, your own island.*

"I need a favor," he said, making no move to sit in any of the chairs around the table.

"Name it, buddy."

He gave a friendly, slightly flippant thanks as he plopped into the nearest chair.

I noticed that someone had made a fresh pot of coffee, no doubt for the meeting that would start here within the next ten minutes. "There's coffee. Want a cup?"

"Sure."

I poured two paper cups, leaving room for cream and sugar. Archer lifted out of his chair and stood beside me. He wore a virgin white shirt with the sleeves rolled to his elbows, open at the collar, no tie, with tan slacks, and shoes that made a crisp sound when he walked. It had taken me years to realize he had four personalities, depending on which color shirt he wore. Blue, which he most often wore: compliant, eager to please, sunny. Green: confident to the point of being cocksure, outgoing, often funny, and a bit conceited. Red: bold, demanding, unyielding, and prone to ill temper. White, which he seldom wore but he wore this day: reserved, introspective, brooding, introverted. Knowing his color moods gave me the illusion of knowing what to expect from him.

I looked at my own suit, and wished like hell I'd not dressed so formally. When around him, I tried to project an image of casual, debonair, charmingly unconcerned. At least I wore my salmon-colored tie, but I felt the urge to rip it from my neck and throw it in the trash can.

I lifted a cup and sipped. "God, I hate office coffee. But what can you do?"

"Goes with the territory."

Archer took his cup and returned to his chair. I sat to his left, facing the glass wall and the cubicles beyond.

What always surprised me was how much I reveled in this friendship. Archer gave off an air that seemed to enlarge any room, like the most dynamic movie stars. He reminded me of James Dean with that flawed and idiosyncratic beauty that seemed both common and amplified. He was the kind of person who was wildly popular in any crowd, and impossible not to notice.

"How's Julie and Hunter?" he asked.

"Always the same." I would have liked to ask after someone in his life, but Archer was spouseless and childless (people at the network were starting to talk), and he never mentioned a girlfriend or flirted with the available women in the office.

"It must be amazing, being married, I mean," he said.

Amazing? Why did I marry her. Out of love? Guilt? Fear of being alone? Fear of discrimination? She had been, I knew, simply too kind, to earnest, and too needful to turn down. She, not I, had popped the question. I glanced at my wedding ring. "You have no idea."

I wanted to ask him about the flipside of that coin: what it's like to be free, rich, famous? I imagined that combination as a powerful drug, allowing one to occasionally act unhinged, infantile, selfish, full of passion or full-on rage. Weekends in Mexico without drawing a sober breath the whole time. The opportunity to fall in love, a new one each month if you wanted. Most importantly, have the time to wander that spiritual path I'd read about, time to search for truth that would give meaning to life.

"You know," he said, "this coffee's not so bad. Maybe they switched brands." He studied his cup with elaborate false absorption.

I glanced up to see Mr. Arnold walking by—fifty-five, corpulent, leathery face, and a seemingly hollow interior. That, I thought, is me in twenty years. A tremor ran up my spine.

"So," I said to shake Arnold's image from my mind, "what can I do for you?"

Archer sat motionless, looking neither at me nor away. He visibly gathered himself. "I need to go into the hospital for a few days."

"Nothing serious, I trust."

"They think I have some sort of growth in my head. They want to take biopsies, brain scans, and do a lot of motor-skills tests."

"Christ. When?"

"I check in this afternoon, surgery is in the morning. I was wondering if you could drop me at the hospital on your way home?"

"How long have you known about this?"

"Dr. Allen called an hour ago."

"What's the rush? I mean, what did he say, exactly?"

"Just that there's no point in worrying until they know the results of the biopsy."

I felt myself go as numb as Archer suddenly looked—a combination of sorrow and tenderness.

He stared at his coffee. He didn't move, didn't cry. "I'm not worried. What's the point, right?" he said with a voice that sounded not his own and far away.

I knew, or thought I knew, that there was much to worry about. Here was a man, James Dean, who had everything I craved, and whose life was unraveling before it could bloom. The knowledge of it, the understanding that we would not watch each other turn into Mr. Arnold, made a fire rage in my gut. It seemed as much sorrow as I'd witnessed on the battlefield and in the hospitals during my convalesce. It was too immense to swallow.

I stood and took Archer's hands in mine. "Come here." I pulled him out of his chair, as if he were Hunter, and embraced him. He stiffened, then let himself be held, surrendering with a sigh. He didn't cry, didn't say a word. I could sense the relinquishment. I had never been so close to him except in my dreams. I'm sure he felt my heart thumping. He had that kid-brother smell under the faint odor of lavender soap and talcum powder, and again, I was reminded of hugging my own son, of comforting my beloved family. I felt his calm, courageous heart beating beneath that snowy-white shirt. For a moment, I thought I felt that untouchable manly essence that I had many times dreamed of, yearned toward, searched for in Julie without success.

I pulled back. Archer lowered his head so I couldn't look him in the eye. I kissed his forehead. It was a long, meaningful kiss that he allowed.

"I'm fine, really."

"I'll help you get through this," I said, becoming drunk on being so close to him.

"I just need a ride."

I pressed my forehead against his and nodded. I had offered up everything, and was rejected. I unwound my arms from his waist and placed my hands on either side of his face, lifting until we were eye-to-eye. He brought his lips to my mouth, a warm conciliatory brush of our lips. I didn't pull away. I had taken an enormous risk, and now felt blessed. We both knew the score. We both needed something more at that moment.

I leaned into him and pressed my lips to his. Arms wrapped around me, I felt the blood drain from my head as he kissed back. He seemed surprised at how famished my kisses were, how desperate. My knees liquefied, and for a moment, we had to hold each other up. Then he released his grip and stepped back.

We stared at each other, breathing loud. We had gone too far, yet I felt a stab of disappointment because his kisses lacked the zeal I now craved. I noticed movement out of the corner of my eye and I turned to see Scotty on the other side of the glass wall with his mouth hanging open. He stared nervously, adoringly.

"So can I count on you?" Archer asked.

I turned back to my friend and nodded. I had no idea where all this was leading, but I had already surrendered to him. I would do anything, and he must have realized it.

"What time can you be ready?" he asked.

"Let's blow this joint now."

Archer glanced around the room with an expression of weary approval. "Meet you in the lobby in ten."

More than anything, I wished I would have followed my first impressions of the day and stayed in bed to read my book, but now I was caught in some sort of vortex. I followed Archer from the conference room and navigated the maze of cubicles to my desk, forgetting about the coconut cake and travel-case gift still waiting in conference room A. Glancing at the stack of presentation charts, I grabbed them all, muscled them into one fold and then another, and crammed them into the trash can. I felt better, as if a boulder had been lifted off my chest. Now I could start over and make it the way I wanted in the first place.

❖

As I navigated my Prius along the Pasadena Freeway, everything seemed dreamlike—the hazy, blue-white sky; the traffic that was heavy even at this time of the day; my silent, immovable passenger. I felt as though Archer was stuck to the seat as if he was a giant butterfly pinned to a Styrofoam board. I drove with care, not too fast or too slow, periodically checking the rearview mirror. I couldn't think of a single thing to say. The fact was, I didn't want small talk, serious talk, shop talk, any of it. I wanted him and the open road, the sea breeze, and the smell of him near.

I had left all thoughts of my job and family behind and stepped into a new dimension where everything was new and unfamiliar. My only goal was to somehow help Archer through a difficult time. I felt more unnerved than what Archer was showing. Indeed, Archer seemed to express no emotion at all. If we could only find a comfortable place to be alone, perhaps lie down for an hour, then we could shut out the rest of the world, and the panic I felt (I was convinced we both felt) could somehow ease.

Archer's calm baffled me. I was keyed up by the birthday party, Archer's confession, and the kiss in conference room C. It all boiled down to those three elements as I sped along the slow lane. Feeling his peace, I wondered if this was what it was like to go crazy. I had always imagined shrieks and wails and pulling of hair. But his mood was serene, as if he were numb with hopelessness. Right then, all I could think of was to get him somewhere safe, away from the office, away from the hospital, away from life for a few hours so that he could reconnect with the reality of his situation. I felt faintly, foolishly, in charge of him.

Later, I would drop Archer at the hospital, and then drive home for that birthday dinner with Julie, but for the next few hours, I would find us a sanctuary. I wished that I could take him home, and we could both take the book I'd been reading and somehow enter that adventure of searching for truth.

I touched my lips, remembering his kiss. I didn't care what it did or did not imply. I no longer had any pretense of not craving my friend. I desired his force, his youth, and yes, his body. I still desired Julie as well, but more in a devoted, dutiful way. This yearning with Archer was darker, more immediate. I tried to imagine Archer and myself lying naked within the folds of sheets on a bright Saturday morning, laughing softly so as not wake Hunter, both aroused, hopelessly in love with our own recklessness.

What I couldn't bear the thought of was that after savoring these images of us together, after tasting his lips, I had to go back to Julie and Hunter tonight and be back at my desk tomorrow morning. I was so close to freedom I could reach across the seat and touch it, yet it was a false promise.

I'm a failure. My life has come down to this failed prison I live in. I knew I was not alone, that most people shared this same failure. I wished I didn't mind so much. There was something wrong, not only with me but with all of society. Something so wrong it killed rather than uplifted.

I glided the car to the left-hand lane and pressed the accelerator. Once I dropped Archer at the hospital, I would go back to my life, but for the next few hours I would be anyone I wished. I had a near-full tank of gas and plenty of cash. I could drive anywhere, be anybody.

After that, it was back to the salt mines, but I didn't want to think about that just yet. Ahead lay freedom.

The question was where to go, what to do. When you had all these possibilities, it was difficult to zero in on one. *Someplace in West Hollywood? Beverly Hills? The beach at Santa Monica?* I couldn't think of a single place to be alone with someone famous. If we went to a restaurant we'd have to perform, pretend to need something, act like everyone else, lest we stand out and be recognized. If I simply parked the car somewhere and we sat there, two men seated in a parked car would call attention to themselves. Even a park or the library would be too public.

An idea bubbled up as if from a tar pool. I would check us into a hotel I knew of in West Hollywood where, if I said we were staying the night, no questions would be asked. *What's the harm if we only stay a few hours? Sure it will cost, but we need privacy. It'll be worth it. And why else do I slave away at that job if I can't spend a few bucks from time to time?*

I knew there were safer places to go, motels out by the beach or on the outskirts of downtown, but I couldn't bring myself to consider those places. A motel seemed a bit sordid, and I would not subject Archer to less than he deserved.

Thirty minutes later, I pulled into the parking lot of the Wilshire Crest Hotel. The building was large, and the grounds were clean and as unremarkable as most three-star hotels in the area. We left the car and walked through a sliding-glass doorway into a cool, white lobby. He dropped back and tried to look inconspicuous while I hobbled across a marble floor to the front desk. I knew immediately that the place was a textbook hideout—a total lack of personality, smells, and people, yet it had an air of sanitized respectability.

I felt giddy with the possibilities waiting for us here.

A redheaded clerk young enough to still have acne appeared competent and unconcerned. I offered no explanation for why we needed a room or why we had no luggage, and he didn't ask. I hated lying and hoped I could transact this business without doing so.

It proved surprisingly easy. I asked for a room with a double bed for one night. He consulted his computer screen. My face burned but I wouldn't back down.

"I only have rooms available on the lower floors," he said.

I didn't flinch. I nodded, removed my wallet, and produced a credit card. It crossed my mind to give a false name on the registry form, but my credit card had my real name.

"Room five-twelve," he said, passing me a small envelope with the card key.

I walked Archer past various arrangements of sofas and chairs and potted palms with a sense of relief, like a spy crossing Checkpoint Charlie with no provocation. To one side of the lobby stood a convenience store and coffee shop. At the far end stood the hammered metal doors of four elevators. We rode to the fifth floor and found the room. I fitted the cardkey into the lock and opened the door.

We entered a new, private domain. Leaving the old world behind felt like a shot of morphine to a burn victim, not eradicating the pain but simply making it cease to matter. In this new space we could mutate into new roles. I could become the caregiver, ministering to the indignation and recriminations of my friend.

I ushered him into a turquoise-wallpapered room with a similar colored bedspread. The blond wood furniture was several years old, and the room smelled of a place that had been used time after time, and had become tired. Not even the scented soap smell of the bathroom could mask that heavy used odor. I had expected the room to be brighter and grander. This color seemed too gay. I was not, however, disappointed. The room was private, safe. We could do anything we wanted.

Archer drew the bedspread back and sprawled on the bed fully clothed while I limped to the window and parted the filmy white curtains. West Hollywood spread beneath me. That view, those people below, however, belonged to that other world, the sad place Archer and I had abandoned. This new turquoise and blond universe was filled with that particular silence that prevails deep space, utterly unworldly, layered over a substratum of creaks and quick steps on plush carpet.

I thought of how frail men were, how full of terror. It seemed that I straddled an invisible line, one foot in this room and the other still in that world spread below me. One side where Julie waited impatiently, almost gleefully, for my return. The other was this opportunity sprawled on the bed. If I crossed that line altogether, would I ever find my way back again? Would I even want to?

Leaving my cane, jacket, and salmon-colored tie on the chair by the window, I slipped off my shoes and crawled onto the bed. I lay next to him in that deep-space hush, feeling like a newlywed waiting for something. Not waiting for a man, not Archer, but rather, waiting for myself to flower.

I rolled to my side and draped an arm over him, pulling myself closer. With a sensation of buoyant release, I began to breath in cadence with his rising and falling chest. He didn't push me away. No doubt he needed this human contact as badly as I needed to give it.

Is it possible that he will die here, suddenly? If he does, should I go with him, commit suicide? The thought made me feel reckless. *I could decide to die, and wouldn't that be a beautiful ending, going with Archer, my new love. A shimmering notion, not at all morose. My last act on earth could be ushering this beautiful soul into whatever is beyond death, and then following him like a puppy.* We had already left that other world behind. Now we hovered in the aloneness of this turquoise room that, for the moment, belonged only to us. This room could be purgatory, that steppingstone between life and the afterlife. Here, hunkered within these smooth walls and blond furniture, the idea of death felt positively comforting.

The cool silence began to feel like an Antarctic ice field awaiting a lovely sunrise after a season of darkness. I could hear Julie telling her parents: I had no idea; I though his mood swings were ordinary sorrows and disappointments; he never let on.

I began to stroke Archer's belly.

"I would never do that," I said to myself.

Archer turned his head to stare. "What?"

"I was thinking, I've never done this before. You know, go to a hotel room with another man. Or woman, for that matter."

"I'm glad we're here," he said. "I was climbing the walls back at the office."

I kept stroking his belly, and he didn't seem to mind. I began to unbutton his shirt. "Let's get more comfortable."

He nodded, as if not trusting himself to speak.

I spread the shirt open and caressed bare skin. That smooth heat seemed like a form of sympathy, the illustration of generosity and goodness. I ran my fingertips over every inch of his strong torso, memorizing each contour. He lifted to allow me to pull his shirt completely off. When he lay back down, I reached for his belt buckle.

I disrobed him with tantalizing slowness, until he lay with only this virgin-white briefs showing that attractive three-knuckle mound of bleached heaven. I could not pull my eyes away from that tanned flesh as I removed my own clothes. Wearing only boxers, I crawled onto the bed again. My own skin looked pathetically pale next to his amber flesh. I drew the bedspread over us to hide my embarrassment. I took him in my arms, cradling his head on my breast. I thought of Rodin's *The Kiss,* lovers being covered to the neck in a turquoise blanket.

Our lips touched, and the combination of his scent and warmth made the room lurch off balance, or was it simply the newness of the experience, this being near naked with another person other than Julie?

This was a new beginning. Year after year of marital fidelity had finally become too much of a sacrifice. It had been a cowardly mistake. It was now futile to pretend otherwise. There was no point in comparing Julie's round soft curves and hot wetness to this display of rangy male hardness and angular lines. They were two different types of beauty, he being a rigid marble statue, she being a fluid wave rolling onto a beach.

He turned on his side. "Just hold me?"

I snuggled to his back, hard-on pressing ass, lips pressing neck. *Is he a romantic who loves me in some humble way and wants to take things slow? Or does he not want to do anything that would disturb my marriage? He's let it go this far, and now he pulled back. Perhaps he only wants to not be alone?*

That's okay, I thought, my mind racing now. *Being married, I have every reason to keep this simple until I know the score. Right now, in this room, there is no past, no future, only an absolute and abundant present. Let's enjoy it regardless of what he has in mind.* I felt like I was treading water, trying neither to drown nor to swim to safety. But was it possible to just stay in place and keep my head above water? Yes, I told myself, I would stay here for as long as possible, because this was the closest to truth that I'd allowed myself in many years, the kind of truth I couldn't share with Julie or the people at the office.

"I keep flashing back," he said, "to a time when I was the most happy."

"When was that?"

"I was in Chiang Mai, Thailand, with both my dads. We were all living as monks at the main temple there."

"You, a monk?"

"A novice. Can you believe it? My dads were on some kind of pilgrimage that I didn't understand until recently. For me, it was the adventure of roaming around in robes, playing in a totally exotic culture."

"How long were you there?"

"We were supposed to stay a month. That was the name of the

program, Monk for a Month, but a man drowned in the river, and my father fell apart over it. We ended up staying four years in all. I hated coming back to this country."

"Readjusting must have been hard."

"I'm not sure I ever did. I've gone back several times, but only as a tourist. If my diagnosis is terminal, I want to go back and take up the robes again."

I wanted, at that moment, to be him; not to be with him, but to be him, an unhappy person, faithless, loose on the world, and have a plan for the future. *He knows exactly what he will do, perhaps for the rest of his, albeit short, life.*

"Yes," I said, "I think that's a great solution."

I inhaled that smell—the essence of him mixed with crisp sheets—of profound cleanliness that felt like home. As rousing as holding him felt, I eventually fell asleep, and then woke up shortly before six that evening, dry mouthed. I lay alone on the bed. Through the window I could see the sun had set. A note lay on the nightstand:

Palmer,
   This was exactly what I needed. Thank you. You're the best. No need to wake you. I'll grab a cab to the hospital. If the news is bad, I'm flying to Chiang Mai. Come with.

I stayed pressed to the pillow for several minutes, inhaling that lovely man-scent where his head had rested. I knew it would be difficult to go back to my own bed (our bed) and Julie. I felt a deep hunger, having skipped lunch, but there was no time to eat. I showered and dressed. I considered going to the hospital to find out what the doctors had said, but I remembered that the surgery was scheduled for the next morning. Besides, had he wanted to share that, he would have stayed with me.

I left the hotel as quickly as I could, shambling to my car at a pace that was almost a jog. On the drive home, I thought about picking up a gift for Julie, but I couldn't imagine what to get her. She had already bought flowers for my birthday, and she claimed to dislike chocolates. I decided I would take her in my arms, hold her like I had held Archer, and tell her I loved her. That would be easy enough, and she would appreciate it. We had never been stingy with our affections, so this act would not arouse any suspicions. But at the same time I thought this was too easy, that I wanted to say more, something that extended beyond comforting and reached right to the heart of passion itself.

And then, of course, it dawned on me that my passion was for Archer, not Julie. Some titanic event had happened during that simple act of undressing him and holding his nakedness, or perhaps it started with that kiss in conference room C. In the crosshairs of pity and lust, something had bloomed that couldn't be taken back. I wanted to whisper these loving comforts in his ear, not hers, as a way to assuage him in the face of imminent, devastating loss. And the loss would be mine. If something happened to him, I would go on living with my family, but I would not, exactly, survive. My heart would beat, my lungs would fill and deflate, but I would forever remain empty inside. I could bear the thought of losing my family, even the thought of my own death, but I couldn't bear the thought of Archer's passing. This budding love of ours was permanent, a yoke I would carry from that day forward.

I drove the 110 east in slow stop-and-go traffic and pulled off the highway to stop at a Korean market on the corner across from the off-ramp. I knew they stocked flowers in a cooler on the back wall. *Fuck it, I'll get her flowers anyway.* That somehow seemed more honest than anything I could tell her.

The usual array of mums, freesias, and a scattering of haggard lilies stood in plastic buckets behind the glass doors. Bunches of hothouse tulips with white, yellow, and red pedals looked inviting, but I gravitated to the single bunch of white roses. They were just beginning to open. The petals held a deep polar storm, so profoundly white they almost glowed silver. I opened the door and snatched them up because I couldn't bear the sight of them clustered with all the other flowers that were drab by comparison.

I drove the rest of the way home with the roses on the passenger seat, feeling exultant as I watched the evening sky parade its lavender depths. When I entered the house I was aroused and felt the need for sex, rough sex. How long had it been?

The house was drenched with a rich brown smell, some sort of meat roasting (weren't we planning to eat out?), and was so silent I could hear the clock on the mantel, ticking out a steady cadence. It reminded me that I was later than usual, but not so late as to need an explanation. I thought of the book waiting upstairs, but for the first time since purchasing it, it held no special interest. I wanted to stay in the moment, to be in this reality, to feel everything that was surging through my heart and head.

Hunter came running. He threw his arms around my waist and hugged me hard. "Happy birthday, Daddy."

"Hey there, sport. Were you good today?"

He nodded.

"Did you miss me?"

He nodded again, and his face lit up with an aura of adoration and relief. "I love you, Daddy," he said, louder than normal. His tone was somewhat chilling. He would not let go of my waist, clinging while rocking gently back and forth.

I ruffled his hair, and his cowlick bent into a dark question mark. I was overtaken by the feeling of being in the Twilight Zone. There was no other way to describe it. Going to that hotel had somehow slipped me out of my life. This room, this boy, felt utterly bizarre. I told myself it's just the strangeness of what's happened, and that there was no real harm done. We didn't have sex. It was not some cheap office romance. I merely comforted a friend from work, and then fell asleep. I had nothing to hide, yet I knew I would keep it to myself because I couldn't think of any way to explain, well, any of it—the hotel, the kiss, the note with the invitation to join him in Thailand.

Julie walked into the room, and her smile turned down. She could tell something was wrong. I knew all her moods, all her facial expressions. This one meant she was very concerned. The scene took on the feel of those little ambushes in life that always take you by surprise, but shouldn't have because there were plenty of warning signs along the way.

With some effort, I drew a breath and flourished the roses. "I thought you deserved something special, sweetheart." I could see the flowers were not enough to conquer her suspicions, so I added, "And I've got something else I'll give you later." I patted my crotch.

She crossed the room and took the roses at the same time she leaned into me for a kiss. We held that kiss for a time, long enough to cross an invisible boundary into a joyful moment. Yes, right then, with the three of us clinging to each other, we were as happy as we had ever been. We loved each other. Julie and I love our child and our home and our life together. It was, nevertheless, not enough. For the first time, our love was not enough.

Later, after the leftovers were put away, the song sung, the candles blown out, and Julie and Hunter had given their applause, a spasm of fury arose from my chest and lodged in my throat. I sat staring at the few drops of spittle I sprayed on the icing. The whole celebration seemed a means to tie me down, spin a tighter web to keep me there forever, posing as the happy husband, the loving father. But there was nothing to do but wait for word from Archer. I would eat my cake, and then watch TV snuggled next to Julie with Hunter sprawled on the floor. Once he was in bed, I would make love to her while remembering the feel of hard muscle and the clean smell of crisp sheets.

As Julie removed the burnt-out candles, my anger passed. It's fine, I told myself. They love me.

Julie cut the cake and doled out meager slices.

I ate a bit of lemon cake, my favorite. "This is wonderful. Perfect."

She stroked the back of my neck.

"Did you make a wish?" Hunter asked.

I shook my head. "I already have everything I want, sport." At that moment, however, all I could think about was Archer lying in a recovery room waiting to hear the verdict. I felt both saddened and hopeful.

Julie carried the dessert plates to the sink. I pulled Hunter onto my back and carried him to the living room to watch TV until bedtime. I heard the rattle of dishes and the spray of water, and I told her to let the cleanup wait until tomorrow.

She joined me on the couch, nestling close. I draped an arm over her shoulder and kissed her forehead. The TV vomited images one after another that I could not keep up with. I still held that vision of Archer stretched out in a bed, waiting.

An hour later she announced bedtime. Hunter turned to face us with a frown. I smiled at him, serenely, from what seemed a great distance, and we all rose. The TV went dark. We rambled upstairs together, a loving family with multitudes of breakfasts and dinners and victories and setbacks all waiting for us tomorrow, and the day after, and the day after that.

I saw the next few minutes with absolute clarity as I climbed the steps. I would brush my teeth and spit in the sink while she drew the bedcovers. When I came out of the bathroom, she would be on her side of the bed, my book would be on the nightstand on my side of the bed. She would ask if I'd had a nice birthday. I would tell her, "You have no idea."

Then I would turn the lights out, and that would be that—the loss of a dream.

❖

I wanted to make sure Archer had a comfortable flight, so we left LAX on Singapore Airlines, riding first class. Julie and Hunter had come to see us off. Julie, elegant and correct in her black Chanel suit, seemed to heartily approve of me accompanying my terminally ill TV star on his final journey. What she didn't understand, because I was keeping my intentions secret, was just how long I would be away from home.

We had arrived at the airport three hours early, knowing the post-9/11 security measures were an arduous obstacle course. Check-in had gone surprisingly smoothly; now we had time to spare, but I was anxious to get the good-byes behind me.

Julie suggested we grab a cup of coffee at Starbucks so she could get to know Archer a little before we dashed off. "Besides," she said, "This might be your last chance for a good cup of coffee for a while."

"Julie, I'm sure they have coffee shops in Chiang Mai," I said. "Probably even Starbucks." But I allowed her to lead us to the counter, order three lattes, and we crowded around a table.

Archer was unshaven, pale, and dressed in a T-shirt, threadbare jeans, and flip-flops. He somewhat resembled the aging street hustlers one often sees in Hollywood. As we chatted about the long flight ahead, with the three-hour stopover in Singapore, I could see the disapproving glances from Julie, which said as clear as words she didn't want me spending time with someone who looked so disreputable in public, even if he was a huge television personality, and even if this was a mission of mercy. Julie asked no questions about Archer's medical condition, trying to keep the conversation light. I had told her Archer had brain cancer, but I was making assumptions, as Archer had not filled me in on the specifics of the diagnosis.

Julie glanced at her watch and announced it was time to get moving. We all rambled to the entrance of the international security check area.

I knelt in the dim filtered light of the airport terminal and gave Hunter a loving hug. He, of course, cried while trying to be brave. He acted as though he would never see me again, and much as I tried to reassure him, I wasn't altogether sure either. I took Julie's hands and brought them to my face. I pressed dry lips to her fingers, forehead, and lips as I took her in my arms. She looked on the verge of tears herself.

"I'll be back as soon as I can," I said.

She pulled a two-pound box of See's Candies from her purse

and handed it to me. I smiled, knowing that it was all chewy nougat. I hugged her again, with less formality this time.

She made me verify again that I had my passport and other travel documents. I also checked my backpack for the traveler's checks, and I touched my belt with the secret compartment holding emergency cash in U.S. dollars and also some Thai baht. It was enough money for a return ticket home.

"Wear the belt even when you sleep," she said. "I don't want you stuck over there any longer than is necessary."

Archer took a family photo using my phone.

I tousled Hunter's hair, and then it was time to tackle the security lines. Archer allowed me to take his arm and steer him through the security doors. We stopped at the entrance for a final wave. At that point, seeing my family being brave, I considered abandoning the idea of this pilgrimage. I suddenly felt like a selfish bastard, knowing that neither Julie nor Hunter would understand. For a heartbeat, it seemed inconceivable that I could wish to be anywhere except our comfortable midcentury-modern home. What the hell was I thinking running off with this TV star who I knew so little about, flying to a country of which I knew nothing? My only knowledge of Thai culture came from the book I now carried in my backpack.

Archer tugged on my arm, pulling me into the security area. Waving again, I cocked my chin, raised my eyebrows, knowing they would never comprehend. I wondered if I understood any more than they did.

A moment later, I stood with Archer while jammed into a line with a thousand other travelers. I told myself if my guilt didn't diminish, I could always follow the plan I had given Julie, that I would install Archer at the monastery and then fly right back home. That made it a bit easier to navigate customs without feeling like such a cad.

For me, it was a waste of money flying first class, because as soon as I buckled my seat belt, I swallowed a sleeping pill, and the next thing I knew, Archer was shaking me awake for landing at Singapore. I was groggy during the layover, and almost missed the connecting flight. Several cups of coffee on the four-hour plane ride into Chiang Mai revived me to the point I took charge at our destination. I propelled us through customs, baggage claim, currency exchange, and into a taxi. An hour later, we had both signed the necessary paperwork for us to become acolyte monks, and were shown to our room by a boy not much older than Hunter. On arrival at the temple, Archer had explained to the venerable abbot that he had worshiped here as a boy, and wondered if we could share the same room he had shared with his two fathers. The abbot's face, cracked like the glaze on ancient potter, lifted in surprise as he remembered Archer. He seemed delighted and agreed to give us the same room.

The boy led us to the dormitories and up three flights of stairs. He didn't bother to knock when he reached the last door on the left wing; he simply pushed the door open and entered the room. Archer followed. I, carrying my backpack and two suitcases, entered last. A warm breeze from the open windows quarreled with the cooler air of the tiny room. I smelled frying oil, being carried on the wind from the street vendors on the other side of the monastery walls.

I laid the suitcases and backpack near the door and studied our new home. Sleeping cushions stretched almost the full length of the far wall, with light cotton blankets and pillows nestling between the wall and the wardrobe in a secure, inviting way. *This is where we will lie, our cocoon.*

The only piece of furniture in the room was a desk that held an electric fan and several books frayed from many readings—Sartre, Camus, Graham Greene, Isherwood, Maugham, and Mary Renault's *The Persian Boy.* The walls were bare except for the shelves above the desk that were crammed with *National Geographics* and three statues of the Buddha, two sitting and one reclining. The top shelf held a framed photo of a couple holding a year-old baby, and a fireman's hat with a New York City emblem.

I was curious to know what the hell the NYC fireman's hat was doing there.

"Oh my God," Archer said, while also staring at the shelves. "These are the same books that were here when I was a boy. I'm sure of it."

I was immediately surrounded by him, Archer. The gravity that had once held his family together now seemed to link the two of us. But at the same time I noticed there was an additional sleeping cushion and blanket on the floor. Would we need to share the room? Would someone invade our space with the intention of staying?

I opened the wardrobe and pressed my face against the folded orange robes, no doubt our roommate's, searching for his smell. I found an indecipherable scent, like raw cinnamon combined with something spicier, something beyond my knowledge. I held that fragrance in my chest for a long minute before exhaling.

As Archer thumbed through the copy of *The Persian Boy*, I knelt and tested the firmness of the pillows and sleeping mats, and I knew that sleep would not be a comfortable affair. I glanced up to see the boy closing the door behind him on his way out.

I stepped onto the balcony that overlooked Wat Phra Singh complex. Three large temples, a bell tower, and an impressive stupa sat at the center, with the main temple situated closer to the front gate, near the main road with its traffic clamor.

Archer joined me and we both leaned our elbows on the railing and looked down at the compound. He pointed to the smallest temple, beside the enormous white stupa. "That's the oldest place of worship in the town, and is where the principal Buddha image is enshrined. Surrounding these main buildings are dormitories where monks live." He pointed across the complex. "Those smaller houses are called *kutis*, and the senior monks reside in them."

I noticed an open-air pavilion where dozens of brown men in orange robes were now gathered. "What's going on there?"

"They're probably hearing dharma instructions on the Lord Buddha's teaching." He stretched his hand in the other direction. "And that is a large Bodhi tree, the kind under which the Lord Buddha had sat in meditation when he achieved enlightenment. Every monastery has one. It's a favorite gathering place for monks and temple dogs on hot afternoons."

"This place is just how I pictured it," I said, and it was. The grounds had the slow, peaceful vibe of lovers cuddled together after making love. My heartbeat slowed to match this new cadence.

He patted my shoulder. "I'm in need of a shower. Good thing I packed a towel." He walked back into our room, leaving me at the railing.

I felt lightheaded from the twenty-three-hour journey, but stood there drinking it all in, studying the tourists and brown men in robes walking along the concrete pathways that meandered through the complex. It was as if I felt, by scrutinizing these people, I could comprehend what was expected of me. This monastery had a different set of rules, different expectations. I was a child who needed to learn everything anew.

I stayed on the balcony until long after the monks at the open-air pavilion dispersed, moving back to the dormitories to escape the afternoon heat. Only then did I realize I was dripping in sweat. I turned to move back into my new bedroom, and I saw climbing roses, growing from a pot and clinging to the side of the balcony. The blossoms were blood red and fully open. That was the last flower I expected to find in this tropical landscape. I bent, snipped off a bloom, and brought it to my nose. The scent almost lifted me off the floor.

I stepped into the room and pulled the door closed, shutting out the heat, but the room was only marginally cooler. In the dim light, I saw Archer's suitcase lying open and propped against my own luggage. His traveling clothes were piled in the middle of the floor, and a damp towel hung on the doorknob.

He lay on his back on one of the sleeping mats, one arm thrown across his face to shade his eyes. His hair was still damp, letting me know he had bathed, but he had not shaved. He was naked. I had served in the military, so it was no revelation to see a naked man. Yet there was something about those lovely lines defining each muscle group, the tufts of hair under his arms and above his organ, the narrow band of milky, untanned skin from pelvis to thighs. I could not keep from staring.

I focused on his uncircumcised member, made more lurid by that livid white scar left by his bathing suit and the brush of black pubic hair. The rest of his body was deeply tanned and hairless, like a boy at the end of summer. But he was no boy. He had a man's body, fully fleshed and powerful. It seemed impossible that a few million cells going crazy in his brain would soon destroy such a formidable physique.

My head wagged side to side. I felt half confused, half angry. I stood like that for long minutes, a chasm of silence between us.

I crushed the rose blossom in my fist as I stepped to the sleeping mats. Raising my arm, I let the petals trickle from my fingers, one at a time. They fluttered down and landed on his sternum, the declivity between his abdominal muscles, and finally his groin. The petals were slightly redder than his nipples, and stood out against his skin.

Before I could stop myself, I cleared my throat and whispered his name.

He shuddered and abruptly swung his arm away from his eyes. He looked startled, with eyes wide and confused. He lifted his head and saw the trail of red paw-prints walking down to this crotch. "Jesus, Palmer, I'm not dead yet."

Embarrassed, I groped for something to say. "I'm starving, and

I thought you might need some food. Let's walk into town and grab some chow."

His face relaxed, looking sleepy. "We're not supposed to eat after the noon meal."

"Sure, but that starts when they shave our heads and give us our robes. We're not monks yet, right?" In truth, I didn't want to stay in the room gawking at his nakedness, and I also didn't want to negotiate the town alone. I refused to beg, so I pleaded with my eyes, letting the silence in the room encourage him.

He yawned and stretched, clenching his fists over warm air as if trying to grasp whatever he had been dreaming about before it vanished. He stood and reached for the pile of clothes on the floor, but then changed his mind and leaned over his open suitcase. The petals I had bejeweled his body with fluttered to the sleeping mat, making it resemble a bridal bed, or perhaps drops of blood to prove the bride's innocence.

As I opened the door and stepped into the hallway, I glanced back over my shoulder and was rewarded with an eyeful of pale buttocks and dangling genitals as he stepped into a pair of sherbet-colored boardies.

The sun hung high in a cloudless dome, and hammered the pavement and anything that moved. Archer already looked like a local in his sandals, boardies, and white tank top. Every inch of his skin glistened with perpetration. Under that heavy heat and the stench of car exhaust, I cursed my stupidity for not changing clothes before leaving the temple grounds. My shirt and pants were damp by the time we passed the front gates and began to wander down Thanon Ratchamankha Road.

He took the lead on the narrow sidewalk. "I know a good bar by the Tha Phae Gate," he said over his shoulder. "We can get something cold to drink. Since you're hungry, we can grab some street food on the way, but I can't see how you can eat in this heat."

I had trouble keeping up with him; now that he was roaming the town he became excited, wanting to see it all at once. My cane tapped out an irregular cadence as I hurried to keep up. The buildings in this old part of town were shoddy two-story structures, with storefronts on street level and living spaces upstairs.

The sidewalks were crowded with tourists, clusters and couples and knots of families pushing baby carriages, and edgy groups of the same nationality clogging the pavement. I heard snippets of Italian,

French, German, Chinese, Russian, and the Thai singsong clip that I was already beginning to adore. I heard very little English, and most of that was heavily accented Australian or British. I felt cut adrift on a peculiar sea, and I was grateful that Archer guided me along.

We passed a number of western-looking restaurants where tourist huddled around tables on covered verandas. Street vendors sold everything from fried chicken to fresh mangos to dried crickets. We stopped to buy steamed dumplings from a wizened man who wore only baggy shorts and sandals, and weighed no more than a pocket full of feathers.

I wolfed the dumplings as we passed a number of temples along the way, seeming one each block, and then strolled under the toothy, carious remnants of the old city walls. We crossed a wide square and darted through traffic on the next street. Three doors down from the corner lay an open-air bar. The interior was dim, even in the intensely bright afternoon sunlight.

I settled into a chair at the end of the bar, which was nearly on the sidewalk. Archer ordered drinks in Thai. A jukebox beside the bar played '60s rock music.

The traffic noise was almost as obnoxious as the exhaust fumes, but I wanted to watch the people stream by. I had hoped that walking the streets would allow me to feel more relaxed, more at home, but it had had the opposite effect.

"Hope you like Thai brew," Archer said as he pressed a sweating bottle against my upper arm.

A chill penetrated the thin fabric of my shirt. I accepted the beer and examined the bottle, Chang beer. I had expected Singha, which was the beer served in Thai restaurants back home. "I thought—"

As if reading his mind, he said, "Only tourists guzzle Singha. Locals drink this or Tiger beer. It's cheaper and has more bite."

I took a deep swallow. The cold felt glorious. We sat in silence for a few minutes, taking in the rhythms of the street life. Locals idled by on the sun-washed sidewalks while tourists whizzed by in the backs of tuk-tuks—little three-wheel vehicles with open-air backseats.

The alcohol hammered my jet-lagged brain, and I was thankful that we had stopped to eat those dumplings.

"Feeling homesick?" he asked.

From his expression, more quizzical than concerned, I could see his sympathy was polite chitchat rather than worry. I shrugged. It felt like I had not yet arrived, but rather was afloat between one continent and another. I did feel a positive thrill of being in Asia, yet fatigue and regret were draining my enthusiasm. "I'm just feeling out of sorts." I held up my beer. "This should help."

"Drink up. I'll get us two more."

He waved at the barkeep, held up two fingers, and said something in Thai.

The bartender's look of boredom turned to disgust, yet he remained courteous as he busied himself with our drinks. He was somewhere in his fifties, and had a smoking-induced cough.

As Archer laid a wad of bills on the bar, I asked him what he said that put off the bartender.

"I told him: 'Two more Changs and two shots of Thai whiskey. This is our last day of freedom before becoming monks, so we're in full party mode.'"

I wondered what annoyed the barkeep, the fact that two Caucasians were going into the monkhood, or the fact we were drinking to celebrate it, or perhaps he assumed we were lovers and didn't like the idea of queer monks. Hell, it might have been all of the above. I could read nothing specific in his expression.

The barkeep placed the beers and shots before us. I lifted my shot in a toast to freedom, and knocked my head back, taking the drink in one hot swallow. Archer stared at me in obvious surprise.

"I assumed you would sip it. I didn't think you liked hard stuff."

"This is a celebration, right? Why hold back?"

Archer lifted his glass and sipped. "Truth is, we don't have much to celebrate. The next few weeks, or maybe months, won't be a picnic. But whatever comes, let's agree now, no regrets."

I lifted my beer bottle. "No regrets."

We fell into a quiet, good-humored stupor, finishing our beers yet not ordering more. I wanted to go on drinking, but I let him call the shots.

My curiosity would not be put down. "Will it hurt?"

"At the temple, you'll learn that all life is suffering. There are only two ways to anesthetize the pain, drugs or attaining enlightenment."

So that was his plan? He thought he could become enlightened before the suffering became overwhelming? "Are you afraid?"

He stared at me oddly, and I had the uncomfortable feeling he was hiding something, something big.

"Comes and goes," he said. "The other thing you'll learn is that life is a series of moments. You have to give up all the ones that have come before in order to truly appreciate this one. If you don't, they pile up on your shoulders and eventually crush the life out of you by their combined dead weight."

By then I was drunk enough for that to make perfect sense.

The bartender brought us two more beers and two more shots, even though there was no more money on the bar. He told us to have this last drink on him, and then not to come back once we shaved our heads and donned the robes. "Monk drinking in bars give the town a bad name," he scolded, "so drink up and make it your last."

I downed the whiskey, which burned all the way to my belly. I felt my courage rising as my head went numb, enough pluck to ask the one question I was desperate to know. "What do you want from me?"

He stared at his drink for minutes, which I gathered was a very bad sign.

"I want you to hold me in the dark."

I was already too numb to feel the weight of that answer. "What if that's not enough? What if I'm not enough?"

He patted my head like I was his dog. "Only one way to find out."

His reminiscences rambled around monastery life as the afternoon declined. He spoke nothing of life back in America, nothing of his illness. He had seemingly moved into the present moment with no baggage. Trying to mimic him, I had nothing to discuss, so he carried the conversation as we grew drunker.

At one point I glanced out at the street to watch the stream of tourists jostling by, and there stood the abbot who had welcomed us to the monastery. He obviously had been leading the group of four other monks somewhere in the town, and happened to see us at the end of the bar, swilling our drinks. He stood as still as stone with an unreadable expression. We made eye contact, and I bowed my head. He moved on without so much as a raised eyebrow, and the others followed.

We fell into a quiet, good-humored stupor, finishing our beers. Archer yawned and asked if I felt sound enough for the walk back to our room.

At the mention of the room, I pictured him stretched out naked, as he was earlier, with those molten rose petals burning into his skin. Feeling drunkenly tender of him, I nodded.

We gathered ourselves, slid off the bar stools, and I flowed him back by the same route we had taken, my cane tapping out a wobbly rhythm.

Once we reached our room, he collapsed with a groan onto a sleeping mat, turned his face to the wall, and mumbled something I didn't catch.

I had to laugh, because I had matched him drink for drink, and felt only mildly drunk, yet he was passed out cold. Then I realized that I had probably sweated the alcohol out of my system on the (for me) arduous walk back. My clothes were damp and smelled like the bar we had spent the afternoon in.

I walked out onto the balcony and leaned over the railing to catch the last rays of the sun as it dipped below the hills. The pink haze over the town was quickly turning red, and the smell of roasting meats permeated the air. The monks had gathered in the main temple and had begun to chant. Their voiced combined to create a buzzing melody that enriched the evening. In my mellow condition, I wanted more than anything to join them, even though I didn't understand the words. The idea of sitting within their midst, watching the words roll from their mouths, seemed erotic. I was, in fact, too shy to barge in on them uninvited, mostly because I didn't know if I'd be welcome.

It occurred to me that all the monks of the monastery must be at this evening chant, allowing me the opportunity to bathe at the communal washroom without anyone seeing me.

I slipped back into our room with the intention of retrieving a towel, clean underwear, and shorts from my suitcase. Archer still lay asleep, but he had attempted to take off his clothes, and his shorts were now bunched around his ankles. His nude body had those same lovely curves as before, but now he sported an impressive hard-on. It reared up, unsupported, and curved away from his belly, dipping and rising with each breath. Around his body lay the rose petals I had scattered over him earlier, and they were the same color as the head of his cock, half covered by that lovely foreskin. He could not have been more beautiful or more desirable. That rigid member seemed to call to me, begging me to gather it in my mouth to keep it warm and safe. Without thinking about it I moved to the edge of the bed and crouched down for a closer inspection.

The air in the room seemed to change density, and I heard the whisper of the door leading to the hallway swing open. A monk riding a motorized wheelchair glided in and stopped beside the desk.

The monk tried to bring his unwieldy hands to his forehead as he bowed in the *wai* gesture. His body was the size of an adolescent, dressed in the orange robes. His shaved head seemed too big for his body. It was a handsome head, but it seemed hard for him to control.

I rushed to my backpack and pulled out my phrasebook. I flipped through the first few pages and tried to read the word for greeting—*sa-wut dee krup*. He pretended surprise that I would attempt to speak his language.

When he spoke, his words were English, and came haltingly and loud, but with the Thai accent. His was not quite a man's voice, even though he was in his mid-twenties.

"Sleeping Beauty...needs...a kiss," he said, flinging an arm toward Archer. "I'm...Annop."

I felt a wave of gratitude move through my head that we could converse in English.

It wasn't easy for Annop to make his hands go where he wanted them. They strayed every which way, the arms bending too much at the elbow and wrist, the fingers curling into impossible angles.

I brought a finger to my lips as a gesture that he should whisper so as not to wake Archer. "I'm Palmer, and this is Archer."

Annop pushed a button on his control panel. The wheelchair crossed the room and stopped beside the sleeping mat. Annop's arm danced on the air before it came to rest on my shoulder. His grip was warm and strong.

"Palmer," Annop said, just as loud as before. "He...your man?"

Archer didn't stir as I lifted my hands in a gesture that meant I didn't really know.

He found my answer hilarious, and could not stop laughing until he began to hiccup. I pounded him between the shoulders, at the base of that lovely long neck. I wanted to tell him it was not funny, this loneliness I felt, this not knowing if I belonged to anyone or anything, and in my staggering mind all this longing to be attached to something was all embodied in that sleeping figure with its penis lifting off his belly of its own accord.

Annop's big head nodded up and down, and he pointed to the picture on the shelf, the one of the couple holding an infant. "He... my...man."

"Does he share this room with you?"

"He...went America...When come back...he go Burma." An

expression of sadness transformed that happy face into a mask of aching. "Now he…prison…three months. He need…help."

I wanted to know more about this mysterious lover, about how long they were together and how long they'd been separated. Mostly I was surprised that this monk might be gay, and wondered if that was acceptable at this monastery.

His hand bobbed around until it touched my cane, then he patted his chair. "You…me…samesame…I think."

I nodded, feeling an immediate and powerful connection with this lovely bald monk. I asked him why he lived on the third floor of the dorm, considering he was bound to the chair and there were no, as far as I knew, elevators. He told me he spent a lot of time in his (our) room, and that he enjoyed a balcony where he could look out over the compound. From up here he could see everything. It was never a problem finding someone to help him up or down the staircase. Then he took my hand in his and said, "Come…you bathe."

I didn't know if he thought I smelled, which I certainly did, or if he thought the cool water would sober me. Either way, I pushed his chair along the corridor and maneuvered him down the three fights of steps. His arms directed me to the washroom where several monks were in the process of bathing. The steamy twilight was pierced by reedy, frail shafts of light from the low-watt lamps attached to the walls.

There were no bathtubs or showers. Monks scooped water from a large wooden tub filled with rainwater, and poured it over their heads, then scrubbed themselves with soap and rinsed by scooping more water over themselves. It was exactly as I had pictured an Istanbul hamam, with each monk being both customer and bath boy—scrubbing and dousing and massaging each other.

None of the monks were nude. Some wore their bottom robe while others wore shorts. Each had a slim, hairless, nutmeg-brown body that glistened with water. Every one was lovely, but all together in that sweaty little room, they were a vision of heaven. I stood watching, leaning on the back of Annop's chair. "Beautiful," I said, excited with drunkenness, with confusion, with hilarity, all mixed up but still clear in my mind.

Annop pulled his upper robe off and handed it to me, pointing to a hook on the wall. I hung it up while he shimmed out of his lower robe to expose his cream-colored panties. He had undressed rather matter-of-factly—not coy, not immodest: as if he were undressing for bed—and seemed to have none of the shyness of the others. He finally shucked off his panties. His body was bent at awkward angles, impossibly thin, and the same rich color as his fellow monks.

His eyes never left mine as I pulled my shirt over my head and stepped out of my pants. I didn't know if I should leave my underwear, but I dropped them as well. I figured if he could go nude, so would I. There were nervous giggles from the others, but Annop only smiled and pointed to a plastic stool beside the water tank.

I stooped, ran one arm behind his back and the other under his legs, and lifted him off his chair. I was a bit unsteady on my feet because I was standing without the aid of my cane, which I'd left on a hook with my clothes. He weighed little more than a toddler, and he gave off a pleasant warmth. I stood there not moving, simply holding him, because that human contact felt so comforting, and because I thought my knee might buckle if I tried to carry him.

"You're...drunk," he said, but with amusement. Then he kissed me, a soft brush of lips full on the mouth. It was a compassionate kiss, more so than even Archer's kiss in the hotel room.

I stared into his black eyes and found only humor. He was clearly enjoying this moment as much as I. His arms tightened around my neck. His breath was spicy sweet.

"And you're lonely," I said, understanding without thinking about it just how much he missed that man who now sat rotting in a Burmese prison. I felt that loneliness all the way to my soles. I kissed him, and opened his mouth with my tongue, exploring that warm goodness. We stayed like that, our mouths locked together, as I shuffled across the room on my bad leg and lowered him onto the plastic stool. The other monks were laughing now, throwing pleasant gibes at us in Thai. I didn't comprehend a word, but there was no misunderstanding their tone.

When I kneeled beside Annop, he used a bamboo dipper to pour rainwater over my head. I groaned. The cool sensation felt erotic. For the moment, I forgot about Archer and everything else. I took a bar of English soap, Yardley's, and lathered my chest. The soap smelled like lavender. It overwhelmed me that, in this place and after all I had endured in the last twenty-four hours, I could remember what lavender smelled like. I meticulously scoured my body from crown to toenails. It felt like a baptism, letting all traces of my past life gurgle down the drain.

Annop rinsed me off with more rainwater.

We splashed each other and kissed again while pressing together.

Not sexual, but rather, kisses from men who had discovered that we were bound by loneliness, out of need, in a way that surpassed even love. We were two halves of the same mourning: yin and yang.

After my rinse, Annop leaned back to inspect me, tilting his head to the left while admiring my black hair, sculpted chest, and narrow hips. He bobbed his head forward and back as he nodded his approval.

I took the dipper and poured water over his head. I took the bar of Yardley soap and scrubbed the hollow of his chest. We shared a smile and I washed under the socket of his left underarm, up over the shoulder blades, into the right socket, and down his torso to his crotch. I occasionally poured another dipper over him. The only sounds were the splattering of water, the slapping of flip-flops on the tile floor, and the gentle drag of my palm over his wet skin.

He was already hard when I soaped his genitals. He pushed my hand away. I assumed it was modesty, but he told me with an amused voice that he was too close, and any more touching would send him over the edge. I scoured down both legs and even cleaned the crevices between his toes. I scrubbed his back, scalp, and finished by scouring behind his ears and then his face. I poured dippers of water over that thin body until he was free of suds. I wanted to lift him up and lower ourselves up to our chins in the tub of delicious rainwater, but I knew the other monks would riot.

We lounged naked, sharing a bench on the WC patio while our bodies dried in the warm night air. It was fully dark now, and only a little moonlight leaked through the thatched covering over the enclosure. I felt his heat, his silky skin against mine. We were alone now, and it would have been easy to bring him off, just to help quell the loneliness I knew he felt. I pulled him closer, held him tight, and reached for his prick. Again, he pushed my hand away.

"You're not...Philip."

And you're not Archer, I thought, through my disappointment. But, of course, he was right. What we could do together was not a substitute for what either of us really desired. I wanted to help Annop deal with his loneliness, but I would have to find a different way. He must have had the same thought about me because he kissed me once more and then pushed me away, telling me to go back to the room, without him.

I walked back into the WC and dressed.

When I entered our room, the lights were on and Archer was

lounging naked on the sleeping mats. He leered at me, complicit and sarcastic. Beside him lay the box of See's candies Julie had given me, its lid open and its contents rifled. I saw that most of the nougats were missing. The whiskey taste still in my mouth turned sour. He lifted another candy and popped it into his mouth. He gazed up benignly at me, waiting, no doubt reading my disapproval, not at the loss of the nougats, but of his lack of shame in pillaging Julie's parting gift to me.

He mumbled through a full mouth, "I got hungry." He spread his legs, giving me a view of his crotch, and patted the mat beside him. It was an invitation, the kind I'd been hoping for but was now not sure of.

With painstaking slowness I began to disrobe. My jeans and underwear bunched around my ankles, and I stood naked before him.

As he scrutinized me, his dick lifted off his belly. His voice held a teasing quality as he said, "You don't look so needy now. That cripple give you some good head? Did he let you fuck him?"

Shocked, I crouched to retrieve my pants and pulled them back on. "You have no right to talk about him, or me, like that."

"Don't be such a prude. We both know why you came here, what you want from me." He plucked another candy from the box. "Just remember, you can give that cripple all the dick he can swallow, but your ass belongs to me."

I bit my tongue as I bent to reach for my shirt. Before I could retrieve it, he leaned toward me and grabbed a belt loop, pulling me onto the sleeping mat. I struggled to rise but he pinned to me under him.

"Just relax," he said. The sweetness in his mouth from the stolen candy seemed rancid. "You've wanted my cock, now you'll have it. Every inch."

I wasn't sure what to do. Yes, I was pissed that he had suddenly turn so crass, but he was right. I wanted him, wanted his cock. He held my wrists so I couldn't strike him, but then he let go. I didn't pull away. We stared eye-to-eye, and he grinned. That grin said clearer than words, "I own you." He grabbed my jeans and yanked them to my knees. He whirled me around, face down. I didn't struggle. He'd made me his bitch; I let him take. My ass became another box of candy.

I knew from my reading that all the evils of the world arise from people wishing to be something other than what they are, and that desire gives birth to despair, covetousness, and sickness. It is the vilest sin, perhaps the only one. So I fought back the urge to wish for something different. I was now his property. *When we accept our truth, our nature, as I have, we accept a boundless gift.* I knew I was about to pay a price for that gift.

He grabbed me by the hair and mashed my face into the sweaty sleeping mat. I felt a searing pain rip into my bum. He hadn't even bothered to use spit; he took me dry. I groaned a muffled cry. The room spun about me. I focused all my attention on relaxing my body as he worked me over, roughly and clumsily.

Details of what was occurring filtered through my numb consciousness: the taste of whiskey in my mouth, the stink of candy on his breath, the labored panting, the animal-like grunts, and the pain shooting up my spine to explode in my head. My mind drowned in a sea of flames.

An eternity seemed to pass before he began to slap my buttocks and pumped his hips like a jackhammer. He savagely moaned in my ear and I knew it would soon be over. But I also knew that it would never be over. I would suffer this humiliation every minute of my life. I whimpered as he pulled free of me.

I felt used in a way I'd never imagined, and never wanted again. My first concern after coming to this godless country was that I would not be enough to satisfy Archer. Now I realized the ludicrous nature of that fear. The idea of enough of what, of anything, floated in my numb head. I tried to grasp it, to fathom the concept, but understanding slipped though my fingers like soft butter. The harder I clenched my thoughts around it, the more it slipped away.

I could feel a difference in him, a pulling back. I sensed his confusion…and could it be shame? He climbed to his feet and staggered onto the balcony. Was it for fresh air or, even in his drunken state, could he not look me in the eye? Even though at that moment I hated him, I wanted him to hold me. I needed some amount of tenderness to counterbalance the brutality. He, obviously, wanted to put distance between himself and his bitch, who was now used goods. Or was it the act itself that he wanted to distance himself from? Did he need to flee his ruthless nature, the ugliness that burned in his gut?

I pulled a blanket over me, wrapping myself in it cocoon-like, and turned my face to the wall. I curled into a fetal position and cursed my stupidity until I no longer cared about anything. Then, mercifully, I drifted into unconsciousness.

❖

When I awoke the room was shadowed in humid darkness, but I could see a watery orange light paling the window and pushing back the gloom. The air felt somewhat cooler, but I was sweating under the blanket. The day was already growing warm. I kept my eyes closed and my breathing deep, trying to go back to sleep. As the room grew lighter, I opened my eyes and scanned the surroundings. I was alone. Had Archer spent the night on the balcony? Had he slept with someone else? I closed my eyes again, trying to remember all that had happened during our drunken adventure.

My mouth tasted faintly of foul whiskey, and I realized I had not brushed my teeth since leaving the States.

Voices in the hall became loud as the other monks began migrating toward what I assumed were morning prayers. *Should I join them, or go looking for Archer?*

My pulse quickened; my head throbbed with a gnawing pain. Gingerly, I reached up and touched my scalp, pressing to help alleviate the hangover ache that suddenly felt like I'd been kicked in the head.

The door opened and the abbot stood staring down at me.

"Where's Archer?" I asked.

He shuffled nearer and held out a piece of paper. I froze, not wanting to read it. It could only be bad news.

"It's okay," he said.

I took the note and began to read Archer's fine script in that dim light.

Palmer,

> *What I did is unforgivable—a combination of jealousy and rage, rage at my medical condition. I've been holding in that rage, and the whiskey let it fly. I hope you can find the compassion to understand. Please know I am appallingly sorry.*

> *I'm leaving tonight, not because I can't face you, but because I realized once we got here that this was not what I'm searching for. With the little time I have left, I don't want to hide in a monastery wallowing on the pity-pot; I need to make a difference in this world before I leave it, make a statement about my life and what I believe. After talking to Annop, I have an idea where that quest will take me, and it's a dangerous place. I have no right to drag you along.*

I know you will land on your feet. Please don't be concerned about me.
Give my love to Julie and Hunter.
Archer

"I think I'm going to be sick," I said.

The abbot bobbed his head, kindly, before he helped me up and pushed me toward the balcony. I leaned well out over the edge and vomited into the garden below. The next thing I knew he walked up behind me, stroked my neck and my shoulders, and murmured endearments in Thai.

When my stomach was purged, he led me back to the sleeping mats. He called into the hallway, giving instructions to someone in Thai. Moments later a boy hurried into our room and gave me a glass of water and also handed the abbot a wet towel. I lay back on the mat, and the abbot pressed the cool towel to my forehead.

"Feel better?" he said in excellent English.

I felt like I was falling through space.

"Where did he go?"

"No matter."

"It matters to me, dammit."

But then I realized he was right. I would never see him again, because he didn't want me; I was not enough. He searched for something I couldn't give. I would be forced to go back home or go on alone. The loss seemed appalling. But I knew about loss, how it worked. I had lost Clifford at college; I had lost buddies in the Middle East. I would ache and grieve for Archer, and then wake up a year from now feeling normal. I would pull myself together, whatever was left of me, and move on. This friend I'd mourn so deeply now would have vanished from my thoughts, and I wouldn't remember what he looks like. And of all the truths that loss had to teach, that seemed the cruelest one of all.

"Archer and Brother Annop left together. I don't know where."

I was too stunned to respond. Another wave of nausea washed through me. Archer had chosen Annop over me.

The abbot told me to dress and come to the washroom to clean myself before my induction ceremony. I froze, knowing now I should catch the next flight home. Going back to Julie, my home (our home), seemed better than the loneliness that lay ahead if I stayed.

He took my hand. "Fear not. I will teach you."

The compassion in his voice mirrored the kindness in his

expression. *Yes, I'm not alone.* My mind flashed on the cozy feeling I'd had while holding Annop the night before, before my world turned on its head. *Perhaps I could find that feeling with one of the other monks? Perhaps even with this aged abbot?*

I climbed into my jeans and donned a T-shirt. Still barefoot, I followed the abbot down the hall and we descended the stairs. He watched as I stripped again and then washed beside the wooden tub in the WC room. As I soaped and rinsed, he began his first lesson.

"When you least expect it, nature has cunning ways of finding our weakest spot to humble us. Remember: I am here. Right now you feel numb, afraid. Perhaps it's not with me that you'll want to speak about these things, but feel something glorious you did. Treasure that."

I stared at him. This was the moment when I should walk away, catch a tuk-tuk to the airport and begin the journey home.

"You had a beautiful friendship," he said in the same soothing voice. "Maybe more than a friendship. I envy you. If there is pain, nurse it. If there is a flame, encourage it to give you light. Don't be brutal with yourself or with him. He gave you a gift. Take it gratefully."

I dressed again and we walked to the temple. We made a dreamlike entrance upon a scene of monks sitting on the floor of a massive hall, chanting in guttural voices. They were all dressed in the minimal concessions of a monk, and all were bronzed and superbly physical. At one end of the hall sat a dais, and behind that stood a golden statue of the Lord Buddha.

Incense sticks sweetened the air, sending spirals of perfumed smoke toward the ceiling. We strolled to the dais and he turned to face the gathering. He wore a voluminous saffron cassock, looking beautiful in his quiet dignity. He sat in a chair. A young acolyte ran up with a virgin white towel, laid it across his lap, and then handed him a straight razor. The acolyte sat in the lotus position beside the abbot. Another acolyte, a year or two younger than the first, join used, sitting on the other side of the chair. He held the orange robes of a monk in his arms, and I understood that they were for me. Once my head was shaved, I would don these robes, become an acolyte, and the abbot would be my teacher. I could finally throw my books away and make my own story.

In that musty room lit by candles and overhead fluorescent lighting, the abbot seemed to exude a faint light from his black eyes, shaved head, pursed lips, and the delicate curve of his neck. We made eye contact, the abbot and I, and I felt my soul exposed. I dropped to my knees and placed my face to the towel on his lap—not out of spite for being abandoned by Archer, not out of reluctance to return to my family, but rather with clearheaded recognition of a new existence and with a resolve to face the inevitable.

As I turned my head to the side, I saw gilded light pouring through the windows like melted butter. The autumn breeze drifted in via the open doors to mingle with the voices of the chanting monks. What a thrill to witness a sunrise, my own rebirth, being aided by this lovely, bald, saffron-robed abbot in a temple of piety.

The volume of chanting grew faint and ripened into silence. Above the stillness was a tranquil singing of the wind accompanied by the measured booms of the temple bell.

"Are you…ready?" the abbot croaked.

My body shivered. "Yes."

The abbot made a slow, graceful sweep up my neck with the razor. I could feel my hair falling away. I closed my eyes and followed the blade's progress with my mind's eye.

"We gather your hair so you can send it to a loved one."

As I tracked the razor's path in my head, I thought that sending Julie my hair would surely be enough of an explanation. No need for a long, descriptive letter. A few ounces of hair would say everything, be a symbol of everything I'd given up.

The abbot appeared cool and relaxed as his hands hovered above my scalp. Ever so slowly, he scraped away my hair to reveal the raw, animated contour of my naked head. It seemed to take an eternity for my newborn head to emerge. I saw it in my mind's eye, looking clean and fresh as a sunrise.

WHITE MONKEY

Martin Braxton climbed the steps of a four-room dormitory that stood across a courtyard from a modest Buddhist temple. He followed a wizened abbot dressed in simple carrot-colored robes and a yellow woolen stocking cap with a label that said "Aspire" in English. Tich mounted the steps behind Martin, and he also wore the shaved head and orange garb of Thai monks. His wool cap, however, had no label.

Martin tried to look humble but also alert as the abbot, without looking at him, spoke with a voice that had a melodic quality. He spoke Thai, which Martin didn't understand, but Tich proved a competent, albeit reluctant, translator.

As both men chatted, Martin learned that he was being allowed to stay at the *wat* (monastery) as a temple helper, and would not wear the robes of a novice or monk, but must dress in all white, like the Buddhist nuns, who also stayed in a separate dormitory within the *wat* compound. His duties would be to sweep the temple and monk's dormitory, rake leaves in the grounds, help gather alms in the mornings, and serve the monks and novices their meals. He would have afternoons free to walk into town for recreation, but was expected back at the temple for evening prayers. Each time Tich named a task, Martin nodded and stayed attentive, to let the abbot know he understood and agreed to the terms. He wanted to present an image of being willing and grateful, not only to the abbot but also to the other monks lounging in the rooms they were passing through.

Although the abbot's disarming smile projected empathetic warmth, Tich remained curt and his frown deepened. When Tich had met him at the bus station in Huay Sa Tao a few hours earlier, he had not even said hello. His first words were, "Don't touch me."

"Would the word 'why' be utterly absurd?" Martin had asked. Martin hailed from the British Isles, and although he had lived in California long enough to lose his British lilt, he still spoke using very proper English.

Tich sighed, a sweet oboe-like sound, and explained that in Thailand, non-monks were forbidden to touch disciples of the Buddha. For Martin, that had been both a shock and a struggle. With his shaved head and eyebrows, and wearing those robes that bared his slender neck, right shoulder, and one pink nipple, Tich had never before looked so ravishing. Tich's gaunt face showed that his thirty-one-year-old body had lost a substantial amount of weight and had recaptured that slender, effortless muscularity of youth. Martin had felt compelled to take him in his arms for a caring hug. He tried to explain how ridiculous this not-touching rule sounded, seeing as how he and Tich had been lovers for six years back on Martin's Northern California mushroom farm, but Tich had not been swayed. A silence caught and held, and then blossomed into a decisiveness, like the interlude during a date where it becomes apparent things are not going well and nothing promising will happen. Tich turned and walked away, having brusquely indicated that Martin should follow him. Martin glanced at Tich's ratty leather sandals, and then at his own Prada loafers, wondering how far they would have to walk. He shouldered his backpack, lifted his suitcase, and did his best to keep up with Tich's impatient pace. They had marched deeper and deeper into the rainforest. It had grown greener, darker, denser—reaching over the unsurfaced track. At times it would thin out again, allowing light to play with the shadows.

As they walked along a four-mile trail winding through the foothills beyond the town, Tich explained that he had abruptly left America because his parents had demanded that he come home to fulfill his requirement as a Thai citizen, which meant spending time in either the army or the monkhood. The army was a two-year commitment; being a novice monk could span anywhere from two weeks to several years, depending on the abbot's judgment of how much the novice had to learn. Tich, being a loving and gentle soul, obviously chose the monkhood, but there was another, more important reason. Tich claimed that by becoming a monk, he gave his parents merit for their transition into heaven.

Regardless of the reason for his return to Thailand, Tich was obviously living his new role earnestly. He said this was a turning point in his life, which gave Martin the impression he was considering the monkhood as a permanent calling. Martin was struck dumb. A mere two-month separation and Tich was thinking of throwing everything they'd built away. It dawned on Martin that the reason Tich had simply vanished without so much as a good-bye was that even then, he had no intention of returning to California, and he didn't have the guts to say good-bye for good.

Martin didn't know what to do. A twenty-two-hour journey from San Francisco to Bangkok, another two-hour flight to Chiang Mai, and a six-hour bus ride to this remote town near the Burmese border had left him too exhausted to consider his options. Even through his fatigue, however, he could feel his fear rising by the accelerated heartbeat pumping in his ears.

At the end of the road stood tall, sunbaked walls the color of dried bones, which had sitting-Buddha statues placed in niches about every dozen feet. He and Tich had marched though an open gateway into a courtyard surrounded by several buildings, a traditional Thai temple, and a smallish white stupa, all enclosed within the thick compound walls. The temple—an arresting gold-trimmed, deep-red building with a high triple-tiered pagoda roof—occupied the center of the courtyard. The temple's stone steps were set between two serpent Nagas and littered with sandals and running shoes. Martin found the grounds dark and frightening, yet he realized it was an oasis set in the rainforest miles away from any civilization. Monks sweeping the stone paths that wound through the buildings stopped to stare, as did a half dozen temple dogs who were lounging in the shade of a banyan tree. Tich had come to a halt before the abbot, placed his palms together in front of his face, and bowed in the traditional *wai* gesture. Martin had followed his example.

Now, as Martin came into the room he would share with Tich, his heart sank to new depths. There were six sleeping mats on the floor with mosquito netting hanging from the rafters, and two of them were occupied by a pair of monks reading from what looked like religious texts. Martin struggled to accept that he and Tich would share the room with four other novices, and they would have no privacy. For a moment, he wondered what the hell he was doing there, especially since Tich seemed so unwelcoming. This long journey seemed a total waste of time and money, chasing after something he could never recover.

"Don't panic," said the voice in his head. He took stock of the room, which smelled dank and musty. Its orange-red plaster walls hadn't seen a coat of paint in years. That didn't surprise him, as it was obvious the whole *wat* had fallen into a shabby condition. In addition to the sleeping mats that were lined against one wall, three tables stood against the far wall. Two of them held oil lamps. The center one bore an assortment of Buddha statues, ranging in size from a few inches tall to the largest one being two feet tall. The large one was embossed in tiny squares of gold leaf. The only picture on the walls was a photograph of Bhumibol Adulyadej, the reigning king of Thailand.

Tich told him to place his bags in the corner, next to the sleeping mat he would use. As Martin dropped his suitcase and swung his backpack to the floor, the old abbot placed his hands together and bowed, and then left the room.

Tich turned on Martin. "How did you find me?"

"If you didn't want me to know, you shouldn't have told Pic where the hell you were going. One double Cosmo and that blabbermouth broadcast to the world everything secret he knew."

Tich looked away. "So much for best friends."

"Tich," Martin said, "tell me what the hell is going on? What's all this about me being a helper?"

"You came here to see me, to see my new life? Well, I've arranged for you to stay here so you can."

"How long can I stay?"

Tich's lips pressed together primly. "For as long as you can stand it. I'm betting you're on tomorrow's bus back to Bangkok. While you're here, you must work. Did you bring any loose-fitting white clothing?"

Martin nodded, but was astonished that Tich didn't respond to the exasperation in his voice. How could they know each other so little, after all these years?

"Good. Change clothes and meet me in the temple. We eat one meal per day, and you missed that, so you'll eat nothing until tomorrow morning." Tich said something in Thai as he left the room, which made the other two novices chuckle.

Martin stared at his luggage. It would be relativity easy to walk back into town. He wasn't sure if there were any tourist accommodations, but there would surely be a place to grab a meal before he caught the next bus to anywhere. He knelt beside his suitcase, opened it, and pulled out his white linen shirt and chino pants. Much as his better sense railed against the idea, he changed clothes and walked to the temple.

He left his loafers on the steps and walked into the temple barefoot, as custom demanded. The temple was small by Thai standards, built of stone and teak. The altar was a wondrous thing, decorated in part with statues covered in gold foil and festooned with red paper chains; gauzy orange scarves partly covered other statues; several peacock feathers; cut flowers; more than two dozen Buddha images; incense burners and oil lamps and offering bowls. A photograph of their beloved king hung on a wall beside the altar.

Tich handed him a broom with a two-foot-long handle. He had to stoop over to sweep, which he did, starting behind the altar where a massive Buddha statue sat in meditation, and worked his way through the temple. As he swept his stomach began to growl, reminding him that he had not had any lunch. He thought about the hardship of not eating until the following morning, and after that, existing on one meal per day. He tried to focus on a silver lining, that at age forty, the last decade of good living had expanded his waist by an extra twenty— okay, thirty—pounds. He was a tall man with a handsome face, and all through his teens, twenties, and well into his thirties he had enjoyed an athletic build. Perhaps a week or so of living on a monk's diet would slim him down, and that would make him more attractive to Tich, wouldn't it? Bottom line, he figured, was that being back with Tich was worth the privation and would bring some health benefits along with peace of mind. He kept sweeping until he had cleaned the entire floor and swept the debris and dust out the front door and down the steps.

He moved back to the temple doorway and stood gazing at the beautifully painted hall. Several murals adorned the walls, each portraying an important scene from the Buddha's life. He wondered if he should do something else, and tried to look busy, even though it must be obvious that he had nothing to do.

Inside the temple, the abbot stood beside a glass display counter of religious items, ceremonial trinkets, and small statues of the Buddha where visitors and tourists could buy keepsakes. There had apparently been customers earlier in the day because the old man was counting bills, Thai baht, which Martin assumed was the day's take. When the old man finished counting, he put the notes into his shoulder bag and left the coins in the drawer. Then he walked out of the temple without speaking.

The atmosphere changed as soon as the abbot departed. Two of the novices, young boys, who were sitting on pillows before the dais, began playing a game by slapping their palms together. He wondered if some of the disciples begrudged him being there, resented his sullenness and his silence, his not understanding their language. Indeed, there were many glances his way, then much chatter and giggling. He wondered how much they knew, and how much they had already guessed.

Martin could feel his energy level sinking below the critical level, and he wanted to sit and close his eyes for a time, but he worried that the abbot would return and find him napping. He walked back outside where there were still two monks raking leaves. The others sat in the shade of the banyan tree. It looked like one old monk was giving a lesson of some sort.

Martin decided to walk around the grounds. Behind the stupa he found a small altar of murky spiritual origins set into a niche in the monastery wall. Someone had placed jungle flowers in a vase on the narrow shelf beside the ubiquitous brass bowls. Between the two dormitory buildings, one for monks and one for nuns, he found a whitewashed stone washroom with a large tub of rainwater collected from the runoff of the roofs. Inside, a bald monk with arthritic hands rinsed out lengths of cloth, then spread them over warm courtyard stones to dry. The kitchen and dining hall lay opposite the courtyard. The nuns cooked on a stove made of stone and fueled by a wood fire. There was no running water in the kitchen, the washroom, or the row of toilets. The scene became a perfect illustration of Thai Buddhism's approach to religious sites.

Martin did not move beyond the compound walls, but from the front gate, he saw a Caucasian monk in his mid-forties leading two elephants. The animals were dripping wet, and Martin assumed the monk was leading the beasts back from a forest stream where the three had been for an afternoon bath. They seemed to share a great affection for each other. Martin was not quite sure which surprised him more, the bald Caucasian wearing the saffron robes, the bull elephants, or the love they visibly shared. He watched the monk guide the beasts to a corral and shed a stone's throw from the front gate.

Martin turned back to the compound and began wandering again. He liked how, gradually, he was becoming known to the monks as he strolled the grounds. He enjoyed being greeted and saluted. Now that the newness had worn off, they were obviously trying to make him feel welcome. He felt comfortable that although his suitcase held all his valuables, there was no need to lock it. He was sure nobody in this remote outpost would touch it, not even the Caucasian elephant handler. Indeed, his impression was that he had nothing these people valued.

He sat on the steps to the dorm, watching the activity in the courtyard. He sat there until the sky reddened. The jungle became exquisite: thicker, deeper, more mysterious. The last light turned the sky purple. As the compound slowly surrendered to the night, all the monks gathered in the temple, leaving their sandals on the steps and going barefoot into the hall. Tich climbed the temple steps, and he motioned for Martin to join the monks. Martin crossed the courtyard, slipped off his loafers, and entered the sanctuary.

The monks had gathered around the altar in rows, elders and fidgety novices knelt on the floor with their butts resting on their heels, chanting words from their hand-lettered, wood-bound, Pali-Sanskrit texts, each page a work of calligraphic art. Martin sat beside the elephant handler in the last row. Rather than chanting with the others, the handler held a carving knife in one hand and a block of wood in his lap, meticulously carving what appeared to be an elephant statue. Martin was about to introduce himself, but then the low, dull cacophony of chants took over his senses.

As the monks intoned, "Buddhang saranang gacchami..." the handler whispered the translation to Martin, "I take refuge in the Buddha. I take refuge in the Dharma. I take refuge in the Sangha."

Although there were fewer than a dozen monks, it sounded like a hundred simultaneous orchestrated recitations. Martin had never heard a sound quite like this hum of *wat* inhabitants chanting their daily prayers. It had an unearthly pitch and intonation, and a delightfully hypnotic cadence that produced an unusual clarity that seemed to empty the atmosphere of distractions and expose the soul. Still, at that moment, the only sound Martin wanted to hear was the comforting clink of ice cubes falling into a martini shaker.

The altar was cluttered with offerings and ritual objects; the air became hot and pungent from the breeze blowing in through massive open windows. Martin had to fight to keep his eyes open as the hypnotic sounds lulled him toward sleep. It was only the hunger in his belly and his craving a drink that kept him awake.

He didn't know how long the prayers lasted, or who had helped him to his sleeping mat. All he knew was the great relief he felt when he finally stretched out and closed his eyes. Not even his noisy belly could keep him from plunging into sleep.

❖

Hunger pangs woke Martin in the darkest stretch of the long night. He lay awake on his mat, in the grip of a hunger-driven insomnia. The others were sleeping peacefully, under light blankets that did little to battle the cold mountain air. A foul smell infused the room, from sticks of incense to keep the mosquitoes and other biting insects away.

He crawled out from under his mosquito netting, and then reached up and pulled open the curtains of the window above his mat. He looked out at an acrylic-black sky bejeweled with a million brilliant stars. The jumbo specks of light, which seemed to pulsate and flare, mesmerized him. The moon shone on the temple and surrounding walls, illuminating this oasis set within a backdrop of nothingness. He lay back on his mat listening to soft breathing of the five monks. Tich lay on the next mat, and Martin needed, even more than food, to reach across that empty space between them and caress that russet-colored skin. But rather than risk Tich's anger, he stopped short, fingering his lover's saffron robe instead.

After hours of torturous hunger, the others began to stir. When Tich woke, it was clear he had no wish to speak to Martin. He gathered his robes and left the room.

Martin joined the others in a cold bath, taken by pouring buckets of water over his head and then letting the cool morning air dry him, and then back to the temple for more chanting. As the sky in the east blushed a beautiful rose color, all the monks piled into the back of a white Toyota truck parked just outside the main gate. Three nuns sat in the cab with the engine idling. Martin sat sandwiched between Tich and the elephant handler. Both were careful not to touch Martin.

The Caucasian gave Martin the wai gesture and said, "I'm Corbin Edwards, but everyone calls me Mahout."

"Is that your Thai name?" Martin asked, returning the wai.

"It means elephant handler. They call me that because I care for and feed Soapsuds and Padre, the elephants we rescued from some unsavory characters preying on tourists. Hold on tight, the checkered flag is about to drop."

A moment later, with the covered truck bed crammed with monks, three standing on the back bumper, and two on the roof holding on for life and limb, the truck took off at a gallop with tires spewing dirt and leaves. They raced down the road heading to town. Martin was sure the beat-up old truck couldn't have gone any faster, and he was convinced that the nuns were as hungry as him and wanted to get to the food handouts as quickly as possible. The younger monks began to whoop and holler like cowboys riding bucking broncos. It seemed like a joyous carnival ride to all but the older, solemn monks.

Corbin leaned close and shouted over the boys' yells, "The nuns drive because monks are forbidden. We call these girls the Flying Nuns, for obvious reasons."

The truck sometimes struggled in the sand or on the dry but steep creek banks. As they passed through the town gate, the driver slammed on the brakes and the truck skidded to a halt before a restaurant/bar just inside the wall. The monks piled out and formed a line from oldest to youngest, and began walking toward the center of town. Each had a begging bowl, with the exception of Martin and Corbin. The nuns stayed in the truck, waiting.

Corbin handed Martin a large shoulder bag. "Follow the monks. As their begging bowls fill up, they'll transfer food to your bag. Don't talk and don't look the townsfolk in the eye, just carry whatever they put in your bag and keep your head down."

Martin nodded. "Where's your bowl?"

"People are too shy to give a white monk food, so I go into this bar and wait. The owner and I have an arrangement. He gives me a beer to nurse, and sometimes a shot of whiskey. That stuff on an empty stomach moves me that much closer to nirvana."

Martin trailed the line of monk and he tried to keep his eyes on the patch of road in front of him. Like the monks, he walked barefoot and without talking. They followed a route up the main street for three blocks and then turned onto a *soi,* or alley, with numerous shop houses on either side and parked cars and motorbikes crowding the side of the pavement. The street was lined with the Buddhist faithful, mostly women with their children who knelt waiting to give alms.

The abbot stopped before the first believer. She offered a *wai* of respect and dropped two rice balls into his bowl, being careful not to touch him. He offered her the customary blessing, and moved on. The process repeated itself as the line of monks worked their way back toward the town gate.

As each monk's bowl filled, he would empty his food into Martin's bag. Martin's hunger had grown to painful extremes, and now he snatched rice balls from his bag and wolfed them down. After several mouthfuls, his hunger headache began to lessen.

A motorcycle screeched to a halt beside him. The rider, a good-looking girl perhaps twenty years old, sat teetering off balance. Her dark cheeks were decorated with *thanaka,* a yellow powder used to keep the skin young, and her wide eyes were fixed on Martin as if he were a trained seal doing tricks. The girl revved her engine and sped away, and as she raced up the street she began yelling in Thai. Shortly after that, more people rushed out of their houses. They knelt at the side of the road waiting for the monks to take their offering and bestow a blessing.

The coming dawn had lightened the sky. The monks snaked to the end of the *soi* and turned onto a street. More people rushed out of their houses with offerings—fruits, vegetables, eggs, baked goods, canned goods, bags of rice, flowers, fuel for lamps, knitted caps, and sandals; everything but meat and money. The most important offering for Martin was bottled water. He would need that to stave off diarrhea. Martin avoided eye contact with the faithful, but he could not help but notice that they all snatched glances at him; the children openly stared. He became uncomfortable, but there was nothing to do but try his best to look invisible.

Martin struggled to keep his focus on Tich, watching his lover move with dignity and grace. Martin grew intrigued at how single-mindedly Tich went about his business, how determined he was to give blessings, to act his part with all the gravity of the Buddha himself. Martin had never seen this serious side of his lover before now, and he was both impressed and worried.

It took more than two hours to loop through the town and make their way back to the town gate. The sun hovered above the horizon and the sky had turned a shimmering blue. Martin's shoulder bag had begun to feel like a load of bricks. The strap dug into his shoulder. He knew it must weigh eighty or ninety pounds.

Corbin and the nuns were waiting.

As the truck raced back to the temple, all the monks were chattering. Corbin leaned over to tell Martin that he had become a rock star in the village. They had never before had so many people come out to give alms, and the take was four times its normal volume. Martin could easily believe it, for he had to lug that heavy bag through miles of backstreets. Word had spread from home to home that a Caucasian helper had joined the *wat*, and everyone wanted to get an eyeful.

They unloaded half of the food back at the kitchen, and while Martin and two nuns prepared breakfast, the third nun, Nook (everyone called her Nookie), drove off in a cloud of dust to deliver the rest of the alms to an NGO (non-governmental organization) engaged in supplying food to the exiles fleeing the military regime in Myanmar. The NGO was run by Christian and Buddhist aide organizations, and operated three refuge camps inside Thailand. They also, whenever possible, ran supplies to rebel camps inside Myanmar.

Martin washed and sliced fruit while the nuns prepared Khao Tom (a spicy rice porridge), green papaya salad, Pad Thai, sliced mangos with sticky rice, and large platters of bananas and guava and jackfruit and pineapple and pomelo. The nuns laughed to themselves watching Martin eat nearly as much as he sliced. He felt deeply embarrassed, but his profound hunger overrode his shame and he kept nibbling as he worked.

One nun, who came from Myanmar and spoke pidgin English, introduced herself as Ko Min Aung. She told Martin to eat up. "*Ahmanabarne.*"

"Aban mar nah nay?" Martin repeated.

The other nun laughed.

"It mean, no be shy," Ko Min Aung said kindly.

"I don't mean to be a pig," Martin said. "My stomach is cramping. I'm not used to eating only one meal per day."

"Is good you eat lots to stay healthy. If get sick, no doctor."

Martin nodded, appreciating her kindness.

She wrapped some bananas, rice balls, and three hard-boiled eggs in a cloth shoulder bag and hid it in a rough-wood cupboard. "For later, you eat."

Martin bowed to her, wanting to lean over and kiss her beautiful shaved head. Both nuns laughed at him, but he felt no shame, only gratitude.

At last Martin carried huge platters of food and bowls of soup to the waiting monks. By Thai standards it was a banquet, and the monks seemed overjoyed. Even though Martin had eaten his fill, however, he knew that within a few hours he would be hungry again, and have nothing but Ko Min Aung's stash to see him through the afternoon and long night. In the midst of the monks' delight, he felt disheartened.

❖

Martin kept busy well into the afternoon, washing dishes, sweeping the temple and the monks' dorm, washing his underwear and spreading them to dry. The whole time Tich had ignored him. His chores done, he decided to walk into town and get a better look at what was available. He was especially interested to find something to eat so he could save Ko Min Aung's stash for bedtime, thinking that would help him sleep.

He walked to his room inside the dorm and pulled a few hundred-baht bills from his suitcase, then left the compound. As he passed the elephant pen, Corbin sat on a stump between Soapsuds and Padre, carving his elephant statue.

"Stay in the main market area, Slick," Corbin said. "There's a few tourist restaurants there and guest houses that serve food. The police don't like *farangs* wandering around the town. They could mistake you for a do-gooder."

"Do-gooder?"

"People here are sick of foreigners who regard themselves as all-important angels of deliverance come to save the blighted poor folk," Corbin said, and his tone meant business. "Foreigners are full of grand words and deepest sympathy, then they retire to their air-conditioned hotel for a huge meaty meal before catching the next bus back to Bangkok. The police don't much like tourists either, but they put up with them because they bring money to the town without expecting the locals to kiss their feet." Corbin gave Martin his shoulder bag. "Take this, and bring back some bottles of Tiger beer," Corbin said with a wink.

By the time Martin had trudged into town, he was famished again. He had passed several farms along the way, and realized that, in addition to rice, the locals grew lettuces, cabbages, cucumbers, spinach, long beans, and even tomatoes. Animal life was prolific. There were cats and dogs everywhere, wandering wherever they liked. He saw ducks, chickens, bantams, and dove-colored peacock-type birds with no tail. He also found an abundance of cows and oxen and pigs and goats. For a people who seemed predominantly vegetarian, there was no shortage of available meat.

He followed the main road to the center of town. There were several tourist guesthouses and restaurants, but not many travelers made the trek this close to the Myanmar border. There were enough service industries to give rise to a comfortable middle class. A handful of land-rich families lived well, though not in mansions. Most luxurious homes Martin passed had wide-open windows, and he could see from the street that they had perhaps five or six modest rooms, plus a simple kitchen and bath. Pieces of handcrafted teak furniture, including some fine antiques, were crammed into their parlors and dining rooms, each not much more than ten or twelve feet square. Near the town center, he checked out several restaurants and found that the measly two hundred baht he had brought wouldn't buy him more than a toothpick in any of the tourist places. He wandered to the south side of town where the morning market vendors were packing up their produce to march back to their farms.

The bazaar was a somnolent, relatively open space with some shade trees. At one end, a bust of the king was mounted on a tasteless concrete plinth. There were plenty of vender stalls, but by that time of day the place seemed nearly empty. Tired-looking men stood behind tables holding bags of curry paste or clothing or garish plastic housewares, while women sat beside blankets laid with vegetables and eggs. There were, though, few customers.

Martin found an open-air food stall. The old cook spoke little English, so Martin held up a hundred-baht note. The man nodded and waved him toward a low table.

He sat on a bamboo mat in a bamboo hut. The cook prepared a steaming bowl of stew with a tin spoon, and also passed him a platter of skewered meats. The meat smelled gamey, and Martin asked him what kind of animal it came from. He presumed goat, but the cook pointed to a rack where two monkey pelts were drying. Martin hesitated for only a moment, then dug in. The skewered meat was tough and tasted pleasantly of charcoal. The stew set Martin's mouth afire, but was delicious.

He caught the cook's attention, pointed to the stew, and gave a thumbs up.

The cook laughed. "Is okay?"

Martin nodded while eating fast with a ravenous hunger. He handed the empty bowl back to the cook and picked up another skewer. "Is the stew made from monkey?"

The cook bobbed his head up and down, smiling broadly. "Monkey shit stew."

Did I understand him right? Monkey shit? Martin couldn't believe it. He was sure this was some kind of linguistic misunderstanding—the lost-in-translation predicament. Yet, he was not entirely sure. "Did you say shit? This had animal shit in it?" His tone had an edge. He could feel his panic rising.

The cook's look of delight disintegrated. He used a bit of

pantomime mixed with limited English. "We take inside monkey. Very good. Very best health."

Martin was now in danger of chucking it all back up. He was about to demand his money back when the cook used more pantomime to ask if Martin wanted more. He was so delighted, so warm and gracious and proud of his stew, that Martin began to laugh, and the cook joined him.

Although the food he ate might have come from a monkey's ass, it was prepared in a tiny dirt-floor kitchen over an open flame, and everything seemed scrupulously hygienic. The cook, who finally introduced himself as Ko Ko Ni, was perhaps the friendliest man Martin had met on this trip. He seemed thrilled that a *farang* chose to eat in his stall. Martin had no doubt that this was a unique experience for both of them.

Two police officers wandered up and gave Martin a hard stare. The cook let go with a stream of indignant-sounding Thai words and began shooing them away. Martin suspected he had gained a friend, the first, and perhaps the only.

Martin held up his other hundred-baht bill. "Tiger beer?"

The cook snatched the bill and scampered off. He came back just as Martin finished his skewers, holding out two large bottles of beer. There were smiles and bows from both men as Martin tucked the bottles into his shoulder bag. He promised to return soon, and then began the long trek back to the *wat*.

As he walked, he became more than a bit proud of himself for going native, rather than eating at the tourist traps. It would give him a story to tell once he returned home. Yet, with the thought of home came the growing feeling that this journey was all for nothing. Since coming here, Tich had refused even to talk to him. It was clear that whatever they had shared was over. Halfway back to the temple, he decided to tell abbot tonight would be his last night. He would begin the journey home at dawn.

Back at the temple, he met up with Corbin and they led Soapsuds and Padre down to the stream for an afternoon bath. Martin opened the bottles of beer and they lay on the bank watching the old elephants play.

Corbin reminded him of several men back home who gathered in coffee shops to have earnest discussions about politics or the nature of the universe, who generally minded their own business but would visit a house to lend a hand if someone was in trouble. Corbin had a way of becoming quiet and looking serious, yet still maintaining a friendly poise. They both drank from the bottle. The beer was warm but it didn't matter.

Martin told about eating the shit stew, and Corbin began to chuckle. He explained that he knew the old cook, and the stew was made from the monkey's stomachs, not their excrement.

"Very heartening news indeed," Martin said.

"Those linguistic misunderstandings happen all the time," Corbin said with a wave of his arm. "You learn to roll with it."

"Looks like you're doing more than just rolling with things. What made you become a monk, if you don't mind my asking?"

"A few years back I tried to drowned myself, and ended up washed ashore at a monastery on Phuket Island. As a way to raise money to get my ass home, I started carving these damned elephant statues. After a few months, I got hooked on the artistry of it. Trouble was, I'd only seen pictures of elephants. How the hell can you sculpt something you don't really know? I traveled up north to surround myself with these animals so I could learn to really capture them in teak."

"If you're still trying to raise money for the flight home, I can help."

Corbin shook his head. "Thanks, but no. I'll never go back. The last thing I need is money."

"But why wear the robes? Why live such a meager life?"

"Meager? Boy, have you got a lot to learn."

"How so?"

"Where else can you find peace untarnished by commercialism or artifice? An agnostic like me, climbing before dawn into a dilapidated monastery, can be transported by the insistent chanting of monks, the beat of drums, and the chime of bells. A peace and sense of well-being arise out of that rhythmic droning. It has healing powers and gives a spiritual lift, much like the silence of a Pennsylvania Quaker meeting or a Gregorian chant in a European cathedral. And once you find that peace, you realize that inner harmony is far more important than outer comfort."

As Martin nursed his beer, Corbin explained how he had traveled to Chiang Mai, where he found Soapsuds and Padre. The animals had been mistreated by the tourist elephant camp that owned them. Both elephants were too old to be used daily, so they were letting them starve. Corbin took the animals off their hands with the promise to supply the camp with two hundred carved elephants to sell to the tourists. So far, he had sent them only twenty, but fully intended to keep his commitment.

They sat back and drank for a time, enjoying the beer, the smells of wood smoke drifting from the monastery, the resonating birdsongs, and the splash of the elephants.

Finally Martin finished his bottle and glanced at Corbin. "I envy you finding your inner balance here, but I'm leaving tomorrow. I came here to find Tich, and turns out he didn't want to be found. It's all been a colossal waste of time."

"What a shame. That will piss off the abbot."

Martin raised his eyebrows in question.

"The locals are fascinated by an American temple boy, so the alms take is massive compared to what it was before you came. There's been a steady stream of people at the temple today, wanting to get an eyeful of you. You are definitely good for business, and the abbot has plans to cash in on your rock-star status. It means he can raise more food and money for the refugee camp."

"How many people are at the camp?"

"That depends on the time of year. You see, during the dry season the Myanmar army makes a push into the eastern mountains. That drives the Karen hill-tribe people into Thailand. The camp nearest us has about two thousand refugees this time of year. When the rains come, they'll go back to their villages."

"I'd love to see the camp." Martin said.

"If you stick around you'll get your chance. The abbot wants you to give English lessons in the camp each afternoon."

"English? How can I teach if I don't know any Burmese?"

"That's up to you to figure out."

❖

That night, tucked under his mosquito netting and protected from the world, Martin reviewed the day, lingering over his decision to leave. Each time he began to drift into sleep, a stray noise would lift him into consciousness—the groan of a sleeping monk, or the incoherent mumbling of someone outside the window, Soapsuds and Padre becoming restless in their pen. Once awake, he fell back into his thoughts of the day. He didn't know how to feel about being "good for business." He was glad to be of service, to contribute more than simply sweeping out the temple, but he couldn't help but feel like a circus animal. And how the hell did they expect him to teach English? What on earth was that old man thinking? In the darkest part of the night, he came to the realization that he didn't mind being away from everything and everyone he knew. The journey to find Tich was turning into more than he'd bargained for, and was beginning to feel like a journey to find himself. He knew then that he would not leave at dawn. He was too curious to see what there was to find.

Long before dawn, the others awoke, and Martin followed them to the washroom. There didn't seem to be any rules about who used the toilets or the washing tub first or who waited. They all just naturally took turns and no one lingered too long. Everyone kept their underpants on, or a towel around their waist, as they prepared for morning prayers.

Martin noticed that some monks had their own prayer cushions, while other, like himself, sat on the hard wooden floor. He didn't try to join in the chanting, but rather, let himself drift with the sonorous cadence, still half-asleep and ravenous.

During prayers and the long ride into town in the back of the truck, he felt that the monks were treating him differently. His being there had, apparently, already lost its charm. Now they were treating him with blunt indifference, and some even mild irritation. He had to keep reminding himself that he was good for business, even if some monks, Tich included, treated him as in intruder.

Indeed, while making the alms rounds, many more people knelt beside the road with offerings, to the point that Martin's bag filled twice, and he had to run through the town to empty his heavily loaded bag at the truck, and then race back to find the line of monks. Their take was double what it was the previous morning.

Back at the temple, Martin gorged himself while helping to prepare and serve the morning meal. After the monks had finished eating yet another feast, Martin began to clear the dishes and carry them to the kitchen. As he came back into the dinning room to load up another tray of dishes, the abbot clasped him on the shoulder. Tich stood beside him.

"Tich tells me you are intelligent and trustworthy." Tich interpreted the abbot's words.

Martin nodded.

"I've have seen no evidence of either," Tich continued, "but I'm willing to give you a chance. Forget the dishes and the sweeping. Come with me."

Martin and Tich followed the abbot into the temple and behind the glass counter holding all the religious paraphernalia. With Tich still translating, the abbot showed Martin that every item on the shelves had a price tag attached. "When the villagers buy something, charge them half of the written price. If a tourist comes, charge them full price, and push them to buy more than they want."

So much for business integrity, Martin thought. His esteem for the abbot plummeted, but he nodded without comment.

The abbot left him behind the counter, and walked from the temple smiling. Tich, however, left as though in a bad humor.

A minute later Corbin walked up and slapped Martin on the back. "You've gotten a promotion, Slick. Congratulations. No more grunt work," he said and winked.

Martin nodded, not wanting to embarrass himself by admitting that he enjoyed the sweeping and washing the dishes. It was a way for him to earn his rice, and it brought him in contact with the others. He was not altogether happy about being stuck behind this counter.

"By the way," Corbin said, "that wily abbot has given you a new name: Hanuman, who was the son of the wind in Hindu mythology. He's very popular in Thai culture as well. Hanaman was a famous white monkey who ran faster than the wind but never tired."

"A white monkey? Sounds racist."

Corbin laughed and punched his shoulder. "Not at all. Hanuman teaches us of the unlimited power that lies unused within each one of us. He named you that because you show such power in bringing in donations, and by naming you that, he's ensuring that more people will flock to give. The abbot considers you a gift from the gods, a bringer of prosperity. You're in like Flynn."

"Yeah, well, Flynn was white too."

That day, several locals from the town wandered in to the temple to pray and ask for blessings. Each one would visit the display case after sitting with the monks, and more than a few bought amulets and small Buddha statues. There was also a steady stream of tourists, and each one bought two or three items at full price. Martin found it easy to talk to these people and show them something of value that they had overlooked.

In the center of the town, there stood a temple with an impressive white stupa, so it was unusual to see so many people making the journey out to this out-of-the-way monastery. Yet Martin was kept moderately busy. More than a few tourists asked a flood of questions about what it was like living with the monks. He tried to make it sound romantic, without actually lying.

In the midafternoon, the abbot climbed the temple steps. With Tich as translator, he asked to count the day's take. Martin opened the cash drawer and handed over a wad of bills. The abbot's eyes grew as large as goose eggs. He held the bills over his head for all to see, and he began to laugh, a deep, joyful sound that shook his slight frame from head to soles. Martin couldn't help but join him in a good belly laugh. The monks inside the temple began to shout, and the monks outside came running to see what the commotion was all about.

Soon, everyone was either laughing or shouting. Everyone except Tich. It seemed Tich's plan to chase Martin out of his life had backfired, and Martin began to feel sorry for his ex-lover. *How did he get to be such a sad and dejected man, wearing these robes and living such a difficult life? When did we commit our first mistake? How did things get so bad that I drove him here? I'm sorry with my whole heart, or whatever is left of it. I have no idea how I screwed it up. Had I been a better lover, I suppose I'd know.* Martin had seen Tich driven to paroxysms of glee by each improvement they had made to the mushroom farm, and also consoled him over uncountable disappointments, everything from backstabbing friends to expired pets. The fact that they were now at the point of not even being able to even make small talk showed Martin that the world was too unfathomable for his smallish mind. *How could this happen?*

As the general hilarity subsided, Martin helped load the day's extra food into the white truck. The abbot gave the wad of bills to Nook, and she and Martin raced off, heading west. Nook, as always, drove like Mario Andretti on amphetamines, bounding through huge potholes in the dirt track. They soon came to a valley cleared of trees, where several dozen wooden huts lined the road, and hundreds of tents and bamboo structures surrounded the huts. Martin felt his stomach drop. The conditions were grim, the poverty extreme. No running water or electricity, and thousands of people crammed into a very small area.

Outside the cab, pigeons clattered across the rooftops. A bearded man in a soiled white dress shirt and a *longyi,* a colorful full-length sarong, approached the truck.

When Martin stepped from the cab, he was greeted by the political leader of the camp, a man with short-cropped hair and a severe look, who introduced himself as Ko Song Aung. Wearing a sarong, however, did not make him seem the least bit feminine. He was unmistakably a seasoned soldier. They shook hands, and while a throng of young women unloaded the food, Ko Song led Martin to a fairly large hut. Inside, a candlelit table was laid out with bowls, and several men, all in their early twenties, sat waiting. Martin sat beside Ko Song near the head of the table. They waited in silence until teenaged women carried platters of food in. It seemed like a feast: steamed rice, vegetable soup, bean sauce, fried eggs, noodles, and even a bit of pork. Everyone dug in, and Martin was told to join them. It didn't take a Stephen Hawking to figure out that the Burmese believed strongly in hospitality, and as hungry as Martin felt, he was reluctant to eat too much, guessing that this might be the only meal of the day for these exiles.

He took a bowl of vegetable broth, a smidgen of rice, and a fried egg. While eating, a young man asked, in passible English, where in America Martin lived. When he answered, he realized that several of the men understood him. He went on to say that he had never taught English before, and felt a little nervous about it.

Ko Song assured him that his lack of experience would not be a problem. Even though he looked severe, he was kindness itself. "You will teach here, in our library," he said, pointing at the table they sat at. "You begin as soon as we clear the table."

Martin was stunned at the thought that this was a library. He scanned the hut, which in addition to the table, held a set of bamboo shelves that supported no more than fifteen moldy books.

During the meal, Martin learned that the camp held about two thousand souls: eight hundred children, four hundred women, and eight hundred men. Of the men, most were students-turned-soldiers on R&R. They were young, yet they were seasoned jungle fighters. They spent up to six months on the front lines fighting the *Tatmadaw* (Myanmar army) and then retired here to rest for a month or more. The guerrilla force was made up of several ethnic groups: Karen, Mon, Arakanese, Chin, Kachin, and the largest group in Myanmar, the Burmans. This fight, Martin realized, was not drawn along ethnic lines, but rather political lines: pro-freedom vs. totalitarianism.

As the meal ended and women came to clear away the plates, Ko Song Aung announced, in English, the lesson schedule: a one-hour "advanced" class following the meal, then a one-hour "intermediate" class, followed by a beginner class that would last ninety minutes. This class schedule would apply from Monday to Saturday. That said, one of the students produced a three-foot-by-three-foot blackboard and a single stick of yellow chalk. Everyone turned to face Martin.

Martin began to ask questions, starting with the man on his right and working his way around the table. That gave him an idea of each person's level of understanding. He realized that each student's grasp of the language was good, so he launched into a discussion, going back and forth between them and himself, like two kids on a teeter-totter, with Martin correcting their pronunciation. He wanted to keep it conversational for now, hoping he could somehow find a grammar textbook to base his future lesson on. He did, however, use the blackboard to write out some sentences, showing correct punctuation.

The conversation turned political, and one shy student raised his voice in obvious frustration. "If we were spotted owls or black rhinos, the world would care about us," he said, "but because we are poor humans, people can't see that we are an endangered species too." The others nodded. Martin could feel his embarrassment raising, for he too had not given them much thought until today.

Through the discussion, he found that the students were, to put it mildly, keen to learn. During the debate, he learned that knowing English meant they could communicate directly with international support agencies about their situation, tell their stories to the world media, and appeal to foreign governments for help. For these men, this meant survival for their families, their culture, their future. The hour was over in a flash, and everyone chatted gaily as the advanced students hurried out and twenty intermediate students hustled in.

The intermediate class was a mixture of teenaged boys and girls. Martin found the girls especially beautiful, with their silky dark hair and their cheeks decorated with *thanaka*. Two of the boys also had smudged *thanaka* on their faces, which make them look more like the girls than the other boys.

Through the next hour, talking with students not so fluent, the conversation stumbled into to all aspects of camp life, and Martin began to learn about these people and their history. He learned that besides a lack of food, the camp's big problems were dysentery and malaria, but there was no medical equipment and scarcely any medicine. The students struggled with pidgin English to tell of their hardships and the pain of being away from their villages for so long a time. Martin began clowning around to lighten the mood. He tried to make the lesson fun, and even in that short sixty minutes, he noted a marked improvement in their pronunciation. These kids were sharp and absorbed everything he said without needing to be told twice. Martin had learned so much information about camp life and beyond the border that he felt he was the student, and these excited pupils were really his tutors. Teachers throughout Asia are treated with great respect, and this camp was no exception. To Martin, that felt odd. He tried to return that respect in equal measure.

The beginning English class was the most fun, yet not as interesting. Martin had never had any experience with children, and he had no idea how to handle them. He was nervous and was sure the kids could see his discomfort.

The room was crammed with kids ranging in ages from five to twelve. Most had to sit on the floor. Earlier in the day, they had had classes in Burmese, math, history, and geography. Martin began by teaching them the alphabet song. He wrote out the letters on the blackboard and pointed to each one as the children sang out that letter in the song. Then he introduced them to the Simon Says game, only they had trouble with the concept of Simon, so he changed the game to "Ko Song Says." Soon he stood at the head of the table saying, "Ko Song says touch your nose," and he would touch his nose. "Ko Song says pull your ears; Ko Song says stand up…now sit down." Squeals of laughter erupted when half the class sat down without Ko Song saying so.

The laughter was so loud and came so often that Ko Song Aung poked his head inside the doorway, obviously wanting to see what the riot was all about. When he did, all the children shrieked, pointing fingers at him and laughing so hard as to nearly wet themselves. Ko Song seemed delighted, and gave Martin a thumbs-up.

Martin felt himself glowing as he and Nook walked through the camp, returning to the white truck. They passed a tent where a crowed of people stooped on the ground in a semicircle around the tent. Nook explained that a baby had died. The little girl had suffered from malaria, and chronic diarrhea had finished her off. Nook told him the camp would hold a vigil at the tent for the next three days, providing food and alcohol to the distraught parents. Martin's mood nosedived, and he was silent on the drive back to the temple.

That night he woke from a dream where he was playing the Ko Song Says game with several kids, but then they all began to drop dead. He was covered with sweat even though the room felt chilled.

He was no longer considering the possibility of flying back home. Indeed, he had to find a way to let the friends and company executives back home know he might be gone much longer than he had anticipated. He was no longer concerned about having to do menial work to earn his keep. He liked his new role as Hanuman, son of the wind, who helps bring food and money to the refugee camp. He vowed to double his efforts to raise money so the camp could buy medicine for the children. And, oddly enough, he enjoyed being a teacher, even though he seemed to be learning more than his students. As he lay in the dark under his mosquito netting, listening to the soft breathing from the others, the thought came to him for the first time that no matter what happened between Tich and himself, maybe everything was going to be just fine.

❖

A combination of hunger and anticipation kept him awake nearly all night. He took part in the morning ritual of bathing, prayers, and gathering alms in the town. The take was as plentiful as the previous day, and Martin looked forward to delivering the extra food to the camp. While staffing the temple display counter, he prepared lessons on grammar and vocabulary for his three afternoon classes. Whenever a customer would come to browse, he would lay his notebook aside and put everything into selling as much as possible. He tried to act friendly and helpful and encouraging, without being too pushy. There was a steady stream of customers throughout the morning and early afternoon, and he sold an impressive amount, enough to bring on another celebration from the monks, who shouted, "Hanuman, Hanuman, Hanuman."

Upon arriving at the refugee camp, he had a shock. While waiting for lunch with his advanced students, a group of seven men arrived. They generated copious excitement and were welcomed by everyone. They were dressed in fighting kit and carried AK-47s, M16s, GPMGs, belts holding ammo shells, and a multitude of hand grenades. To Martin, these guerrilla soldiers seemed fit, hard-boiled, and watchful, yet they looked exhausted. He learned later that they had spent five months at the front line, continually on the move, running from one fire-fight to another.

Martin sat in numb respect as all seven filed into his classroom and joined the others around the table. He was bursting with questions, but didn't dare impose himself on them. He smiled and nodded, hoping he didn't look too soft and ridiculous beside them.

One of the fighters, who introduced himself as Kublai, sat on Martin's left, their shoulders touching. He held the pungent odor of the jungle, carried two automatic rifles, a .45 sidearm holstered to his slim waist, and wore a vest with pockets bulging with clips of ammo. He was dark-skinned, with luxuriant sable-colored hair, and lean arm muscles hard as green fruit. His face looked boyish—protruding nose and big, attentive eyes that were slightly crossed, giving him a sweet, ever-questioning air—yet his ensemble seemed lethal.

The meal was served and everyone dug in without any conversation. The soldiers were as mannerly and respectful as the others, and ate no more than what they required. Once again, Martin beat down this hunger and forced himself to take only enough to be polite.

During the lesson, Martin tried to pull information from the newcomers. He learned that they had been fighting in the Karen state, and all seven were born there. Kublai, who spoke excellent English, proudly told how the Karen fighters had a long tradition for guerrilla warfare. During World War Two, he explained, the Karen killed more Japanese per head than any other nationality fighting in that theater. More than the English, American, Australian, and New Zealanders. "Our courage and skill are unsurpassed. Of course," he added, "today we are a few thousand up against the four-hundred-thousand-strong modern army."

Kublai had the ability to command a room. He was obviously respected by all who knew him.

As the discussion progressed into the second half hour, Kublai began to cough. It sounded rasping and loud, and afterward the young man gasped for breath and wheezed. He became quiet for a few minutes before starting to cough again. Martin wondered if Kublai smoked heavily, or perhaps he had some kind of illness affecting his lungs.

As the coughing continued, Martin slipped his hand into his shoulder bag that he'd draped over his chair and pulled out a bottle of water. He set the bottle before the young soldier and whispered that he should drink it all, that Martin had two more in his bag.

Kublai uncapped the bottle and drank deeply. Martin returned his focus on the lesson, but he could hear him gulping. It seemed to help. When Kublai set the empty bottle on the table, he dropped his hands under the table. He sighed, settling one hand lightly on Martin's thigh.

Martin, through his surprise, was sure no one in the room could see what was going on below the table. He moved his own hand over Kublai's, holding it in a tender grasp. It seemed burning hot, assuring Martin that he was running a high temperature and was indeed ill. But regardless, was this his way of thanking Martin, or was he secretly making a pass? Martin held that hand long enough for a bond to form between them, and then he reached into his bag and pulled out another bottle of water, setting it beside the empty. Kublai squeezed his thigh, but didn't remove his hand from Martin's leg.

At the end of the lesson, one of the other fighters draped Kublai's arm over his shoulder and helped the young man from the room. As the intermediate class hurried in, Martin stood outside the doorway, watching to see which hut Kublai was taken to.

For the next few hours he lost himself in the fun of teaching the younger students, but at the end of the day as the kids were running off, he marched to Kublai's hut. He softly knocked and entered. Kublai was naked under a blanket and stretched out in a hammock that was too short for him. His feet were sticking out, hanging in air. He was covered in sweat and the blanket was damp. As Martin approached the bed, Kublai opened his eyes. He appeared tired, weary, and as if in some anguish. When Martin asked if he needed more water, the fighter lifted the blanket to show he still had the second bottle of water Martin had given him. He hugged it to him like it was a puppy.

"That will do more good inside you than out," Martin said, trying for a note of humor. Kublai dropped the blanket and closed his eyes.

In the silence that caught, and held, Martin felt a need to comfort him. The tension felt awkward, as if Kublai didn't want to be bothered, yet Martin would not leave without some satisfaction.

"Right now you remind me of my mother," Martin said. "She always looked radiant and sad at the same time, like a candle about to burn out." He placed his hand on Kublai's burning forehead. "She gave me sponge baths to take my fevers down. She had some mysterious power to heal."

Martin walked to one of the community wash sheds, filled a pail with cool water, and found a sponge. He carried them back to the hammock and knelt over Kublai. He wet the sponge and gently swabbed that beautifully dark skin covering Kublai's brow, cheeks, and jaw. As the sponge caressed his neck, Kublai moaned.

Martin peeled back the blanket to expose a torso glistening with sweat. The compact square plates of his pectorals and the ribbed V of his torso showed every muscle in stark definition. There was zero fat on him. The vision gave Martin the sense that beauty is in fact the natural human condition, not some rare mutation.

Kublai lay quietly as Martin began to sponge his shoulders, arms, chest. After a time, Martin slid an arm behind his neck and lifted him into a sitting position, then sponged that narrow back. The warmth coming from him made Martin want to hold him for as long as possible, absorbing that delicious heat. It was the closest thing to intimacy that he'd experienced since Tich had abandoned him.

He didn't know if Kublai would allow him to sponge his lower body, but when he lowered him back into a lying position, he removed the blanket, exposing the dark bristle of pubic hair and the amber curve of his sex. Kublai didn't seem to care, even though he sported an erection. He appeared shameless, or more likely shame-free, offering himself, neither imploring nor aloof, simply present in the moment, naked, and real. Martin paused, thinking of that first weekend with Tich (striding naked together into the Point Reyes surf as the sun dipped below the horizon) until he realized he was standing there staring at Kublai's genitals.

Martin sponged that lovely stomach and crotch with infinite care. Kublai was not overly endowed, but there was no denying his penis was an object of beauty. Martin lingered over the crotch area, then worked his way down the legs. Both men seemed unembarrassed by the intimacy of the act, but Martin kept one eye on the doorway and listened carefully in case someone should come and he would need to cover Kublai quickly. He took his time, even knowing that Nook waited at the truck and she was no doubt concerned at what had happened to him.

When he had finished the bath, Martin found a dry blanket and covered his new friend. Before leaving, he leaned down and kissed Kublai's forehead. As he pulled away, Kublai's hand shot up to cup his neck and pull him back down for a tender kiss on the lips.

That kiss released the tension that had built up in Martin's shoulders and neck, making him love Kublai the way he imagined men loved their comrades in battle.

❖

On the ride back to the temple, Martin kept flashing on the vision of Kublai's nakedness, which continued to mingle with that refection of Tich at Point Reyes. The kiss had been brief. It seemed, nevertheless, passionate without being sexual. No tongue and no groping. Kublai's breath had been moist and somewhat sweet, and Martin had lost himself in the feel of honeyed warmth.

When Martin had finally pulled away, they had smiled at each other, simply smiled. No words were needed; the eyes said it all.

Riding next to Nook, remembering the image of that naked beauty, still feeling the touch of warmth on his lips, he didn't feel that he'd betrayed Tich, although there was no convincing Tich that it wasn't lascivious. Martin, however, felt no shame.

A rage rose up in him, as sudden as a panic attack, rage at himself for coming here, at Tich for abandoning him, at the abbot for allowing him to stay, even at the fucking elephant mahout for befriending him. His anger spread to everyone in this damned country except the one person he should be angry with, the lost naked soldier who had pulled him into that delightful kiss.

There was no telling how much or how little the soldier wanted from him. Martin was merely flattering himself thinking Kublai wanted a relationship. But pulling away from that kiss, Martin had seen desire in those eyes. There was no denying there was something there, something needful. But rather than feel grateful for being wanted, the memory of those eyes made him feel more hollow than mere sadness, more like a deep loneliness jumbled up with some under layer of jittery panic. He had no name for it, but it made him desperate to see Tich, to curl up with him under the mosquito netting and forget about the rest of the world.

❖

When the white truck pulled into the monastery compound, the sky had grown dark and the monks were already engaged in the evening prayers. Martin decided not to join them. His sadness had passed, and he felt almost happy that everything in his life, everything that meant something to him, was unresolved. Either Tich would come back to him or he wouldn't, either he would have an affair with Kublai or it would dissolve into nothing. Whatever happened would be something new, and the vagueness and uncertainty of the possibilities made him smile as he walked to the kitchen to see if the nuns had left him a snack to comfort him through the long night. He found at pot of cold rice with vegetable curry, which he ate standing by the window listening to the chanting.

When he strayed to his bedroom, he was alone in the dark. He didn't light a lamp. He could still hear the chanting, but it was strangely muted. Having the room to himself made him acutely conscious that he was isolated in the world and that he shared this room with a man he loved but couldn't hold. In this crowded space they slept only a yard apart, breathed the same air, perhaps even dreamed the same dreams. Martin grabbed his pillow and stepped to Tich's sleeping mat. He exchanged his pillow for Tich's and then carried it back to his own mat. He sat and ran his hand along the cool pillowcase. It held the scent of something earthy that belonged to Tich, that came from his sweat, from his breath. Martin hugged the pillow to his chest and lay back, keeping his eyes closed and pretending it was flesh softly pushing against him. Time seemed suspended, and he sank into a dream, a scene of him sponging Kublai's body. The image was every bit as vivid as the actual event had been, yet more exciting because of the way the light danced on that dark skin. The warm flesh and his kindness seemed to merge into a single feeling of affection. When Martin leaned in for a kiss, he felt himself flowing into those soft lips in liquid gushes, as though Kublai were consuming him, and then he surfaced enough to realized that he was having a wet dream. The next thing he knew, he was being shaken awake to attend morning prayers.

❖

Time passed. A day. A week.

Almost every Western tourist who came to the temple to buy spiritual knickknacks wanted more than they were buying. They came in ones and twos and asked questions about Martin's life at the temple. He wanted to confess that he wasn't on some spiritual journey, but rather, simply trying to woo his lover back to the States. And yet, there was something so earnest about them that it was clear to him that nothing more important would happen to them on their vacation, and perhaps in many years to come.

Their time with him, he began to realize, had nothing to do with need, or value for their money. Indeed, these people had gotten to a point in life where wealth was not so important. He recognized that these people dreamed of going on a spiritual quest, that their own lives lacked purpose, and they were searching for something to fill an empty space inside them. He began to tell them about the refugee camp, about the destitution of these people driven from their lands. The customers would try to draw him back into a religious discussion, wanting to discover a path to enlightenment, but he explained that helping people was a sacred act, perhaps the only one.

After one such discussion with an elderly American couple from Nebraska, Martin looked up to see Tich and the abbot standing a dozen feet away, listening intently, and for the first time since coming here, Tich smiled at him.

Tich came over and stood at the counter, eyeing the three thousand baht the couple had given Martin for a three-hundred-baht amulet. At first it appeared Tich was hesitant about speaking, but then he said, "The abbot is impressed that the tourists really connect with you."

Martin could feel himself getting nervous. "Some people are generous, other not so. If they could see the camp, we'd be rolling in dough."

Tich nodded and looked at the floor. "The temple hasn't had a good sweep since you started working the counter." As he spoke, he looked up; the expression on his face, Martin noticed, had turned sad.

It was well past three o'clock when Martin finished attending four tourists who had trouble making up their minds on what to buy and how much to spend. Nook sat in the truck gunning the engine. As soon as Martin hopped in, they took off like a rocket launching, leaving a cloud of dust.

Martin no longer minded Nook's lead foot. He was anxious to get to the camp, anxious to spend time with Kublai, to find out if there was something worth pursuing. The more time he had spent with him, the more he convinced himself that it had been a moment of weakness for both him and Kublai, and that he should not expect anything more to happen between them. Still...he couldn't help but hope.

At the refugee camp, some kind of celebration was afoot. In an open field off the main road, a four-foot-high stage had been erected on bamboo poles. Musicians played at the back of the platform while dancers dressed in elaborate costumes performed at the front. Several hundred people surrounded the stage, sitting on the ground.

The music was not something that he had heard before. Ching cymbals shimmered over the warble of a Pii oboe, and two Klong drums beat a frenetic pace. Women dancers moved from one classical dance pose to another that was unique to the Burmese. The audience cheered all through the performance, rather than only at the end.

Nook parked the truck near the community library. They sat listening for a minute as a song came to an end and the cheering erupted into shouts and vigorous applause.

When they stepped from the truck, Ko Song Aung was there to let him know there would be no English classes today. Ko Song asked Martin to join their modest celebration as his guest. As badly as Martin wanted to talk with Kublai in private, there was no way he could refuse Ko Song's generosity. He helped unload the food, then followed the camp leader toward the stage. They stepped through a tightly packed crowd, trying to find a place where he could view the dancers and also be able to scan the audience. The music started again, and a different set of performers, all male, began a more athletic dance. Martin recognized three of his students onstage, none of them the man he most wanted to see. The audience cheered, and no one was moving to make room for Ko Song and Martin. Everyone seemed settled, sitting with family and friends, and they had no patience for someone distracting them from the action onstage.

It struck him that there were thousands of people in the camp, many more than he had imagined. Up to now, he had assumed that these people were all from one area that lay somewhere across the border, but it seemed to be too many people for that. He was now certain that these refugees came from many different provinces.

He and Ko Song pushed their way between two families and hunched down so that they didn't block the view of the people behind them. He watched the dancers, who were splendidly physical. He could not relax and simply enjoy the performance. His eyes wandered the crowd, hoping to see the one man who, right then, mattered most to him. He wondered how long the show would last, and became impatient for it to end. He tried to focus only on the dancers, and also the musicians, who made a surprising range of sounds on just four instruments.

He saw Kublai moving through the crowd toward him, the expression on his face radiant and joyful. He was clapping his hands and moving his hips to the rhythm as he walked. Shirtless again, he wore his camouflage cargo pants, sandals, and a golden amulet hung from a leather thong around his neck. The amulet held two impressive rubies at its center, blood red and reflecting the light like the eyes of a demon.

Kublai knelt beside him and embraced him, the way soldiers do after a battle when they realize they have both survived something horrific. He felt Kublai's breath on his neck and the touch of lips pressing to that same spot. His breath held a strong scent of alcohol. When they pulled apart, Kublai's face settled into a youthfulness that wasn't as apparent when Martin had given him a sponge bath. As clichéd as it sounded, he could only think of that look as youth personified, made reckless by drink, yet still giving the sense of a young hero who poets and painters would aggrandize into saint and martyr for all the generations that would follow.

When Kublai remained kneeling, Martin realized how odd it must look, a gesture both penitential and reverent. How would Ko Song

Aung, or everybody else for that matter, interpret this gesture? Kublai pulled his amulet over his head and draped it around Martin's neck. He stayed close enough for Martin to feel the youth's breath on his face. Martin collapsed into a state of amazement, and could find no words. Kublai smiled with his eyes, and shrugged to intimate that no words or thanks were necessary. He laughed, and then looked up at the stage, settling in with his arm across Martin's shoulders.

They remained locked together. Martin struggled to understand how his feelings for Kublai had developed so quickly. He realized that, to him, Kublai was a young Tich incarnated: the youthful glow, the bold forwardness, those unreadable eyes that held you with an unspoken promise. It was all so familiar in some indefinable way. This had not been love at first sight; it'd been recognition of something he had already fallen in love with years ago. Tich had changed, had moved on, but here beside him, pressed to his side, was that dear perfection that he loved.

Martin had the overpowering urge to take Kublai's face in his hands and kiss him in front of all these people, to give them a show every bit as enthralling as the performers onstage.

Whoa. Slow down, he thought. Still, he wanted to taste those lips. It was not a desire to be erotic; not exactly. He wanted to savor that glowing perfection that wouldn't, couldn't, last, but was miraculously there beside him now.

He didn't kiss him, of course. He would not chance embarrassing Kublai in full view of his comrades. The music stopped, and the crowd cheered with a riotous sound. The woman came back onstage and a new song began. Now Martin was hoping the concert would last long into the night.

Still, Martin felt a little uncomfortable showing so much affection in front of the entire camp. He glanced around and found that only one person in the crowd paid him any attention at all. Unfortunately, that was Nook. She outright glared at them with disdain. Martin, however, would not push his friend away just to please her.

With this new song the crowd's mood shifted slightly. Kublai leaned even closer to whisper in Martin's ear, translating the words of the song, which was about a love between two people who barely knew one another. The chorus of voices rose and fell sweetly, telling of a love not from the heart, but from the soul, how souls who've loved in the past find each other again in the present. The sound rose tenderly into the night air, holding the crowd silent and still in its power to enchant. Martin felt a tremendous heat radiating from Kublai, his body pressed to Martin's and his arm holding him tighter as the song grew to a close.

❖

Later, when the concert ended, Kublai led Martin back toward the main street. They walked with Kublai's arm still holding Martin's shoulders. Now, in the crush and excitement of the crowd who were all moving back to their huts, Martin walked in silence, not wanting to draw attention to himself. He simply let himself be guided through the dirt paths between the shacks and tents, enjoying the warm touch.

He presumed they were walking back to where Nook had parked the truck, and was surprised when they came to the same hut where Martin had given Kublai a sponge bath. Neither of them spoke as Kublai ushered him inside and closed the flap. Martin stood in the dark not knowing what to expect while his friend lit three candles, which gave the room a semilight, romantic glow—a shadowy illumination that might just as well been emanating from the starlit sky.

This is it. The moment when I abandon Tich or not. He knew that if he wanted to stay true to his ex-lover, he needed to leave, now. Yet, once Kublai blew out the match, he began to remove his clothing, and Martin knew he would not leave.

Martin stood watching until his friend was naked, and a moment later, was in his arms, kissing him. The feel of burning skin over hard muscle was even more electrifying than the lips engulfing his mouth. Kublai opened Martin's belt and unzipped his pants, then began unbuttoning his shirt. He began caressing the skin on his back, and after a few minutes, moved under the elastic band of his underpants to hold his member and cup his balls, all the while their lips never parting, but rather, becoming more forceful, more needful. Martin's knees liquefied and he became afraid he would fall.

His shirt fell off his shoulders at the same time his pants and underwear fell to his ankles. He stepped free of his clothing while Kublai knelt, bringing his face level with Martin's crotch. He felt the heat of Kublai's mouth on the crown of his cock, and a heartbeat later, he felt the entire length of his member being swallowed and held, until Kublai began to gag. Kublai pulled back, releasing the now-glistening member, and began to lick it. He took the full length of it down his throat again, and began working with tender devotion.

Martin placed his hands on Kublai's head, touching his ears, his face, and lingering there. As he came close to climax, he gripped that head to hold it still and began bucking his hips. Kublai began to gag, but Martin was too close to stop now. He could feel a boiling in his groin and he knew he would shoot any second. At that point, Kublai pulled away and stood, and began kissing him again. They hugged as the boiling began to calm.

"Not so soon," Kublai whispered.

Martin realized his friend wanted something more than a quick blow job. He wanted to make love. He lifted Kublai in his arms and carried him to the sleeping mat. It had been so long since he had last made love that he felt afraid. Had he believed in God, he would have prayed: Please, Lord, let this be good for both of us. He wanted to please his new lover, to leave him glowing like a full moon in an unblemished sky so that they could begin their affair in a proper light.

"So many nights I needed you," he said, his voice a sigh.

"Shhh," Kublai said, lovingly nibbling an earlobe.

"I felt so alone, abandoned."

"Me too."

Martin pressed his face to his lover's neck and had to hold back tears, telling him over and over how deeply he needed him. They held each other for a time, and then he caressed that beautiful body with his fingertips and his lips, working his way from face to crotch. Kublai's body trembled so forcefully Martin couldn't tell if it was caused by distress or desire.

Martin had always tried to be an artful lover, but once his passion ignited he became a blunt force absorbed in fulfilling his own desperate need. He knew all too well that in intimate situations, a certain level of violence lurked just below the surface of his skin, and he had to force himself to keep that at bay. Kublai clung to him, pushing his head lower, as if that same violence simmered below his burning skin too.

Their bodies pressed together, rising and weaving, each push becoming stronger, harder, as the ferocity moved closer to the surface. He felt, for the first time in ages, wonderfully salacious.

This is how we begin, he thought, as Kublai moaned the sweet melody of his first ejaculation. A wave of gratitude shot through Martin, carrying everything away except the feel of skin burning beneath his touch.

They simply held each other for another twenty minutes, kissing softly without speaking. People were being hunted down and murdered across the border, Martin thought, even more people were starving in Darfur, a war raged in the Middle East while tens of thousands of victims suffered, yet somehow he had been granted this brief reprieve from the world's ills, this tiny cup of time, to experience a burgeoning love. He thought of the name they had given him at the monastery, Hanuman, and realized that he was as much a receiver as a giver.

At that moment, however, the tent flap was pulled aside and Nook stood staring at the lovers curled up on the floor. Her eyes bulged. She whispered something quick and breathless, then shouted something in Thai that Martin didn't understand, but assumed was an obscenity from the sharpness of her voice.

Martin struggled to his feet and slipped on his underwear and trousers. He grabbed his shirt and sandals and ran after her. He wanted to explain that it wasn't something sordid, that what had occurred was a thing of beauty. By the time he was back on the street, the white truck was racing toward him, leading a cloud of reddish dust. He stepped into the truck's path with his arms raised, assuming she would stop so he could explain.

At the last minute, she slammed on the brakes so hard the wheels locked up and the truck skated sideways as it plowed into Martin. He catapulted over the hood and tumbled to the side of the road as the truck came to stop. She watched as he tried to lift himself, and then she hit the accelerator again. The truck sped off.

Kublai came running after him, now dressed in his fighting fatigues. They sat in the dirt with Kublai holding him, watching the dust settle. Kublai began checking for broken bones. "You're hurt. I'll send someone to town to fetch a doctor."

Martin shook his head. He assumed Nook would rush back and tell everyone what she'd seen. Whether she told Tich directly or not, it would only be minutes before the gossip reached his ears. Martin wanted to face the music as quickly as possible, to put this drama behind him, and then see what cards he was holding once Tich and the others showed their hands.

Kublai wrapped his arms around Martin's neck and kissed him on the lips, a tender gesture in full view of his comrades. Clearly he had no intention of hiding his feelings from his people.

Martin struggled to his feet, stepped into his sandals, and began the long walk back to the monastery. Kublai argued he should stay but Martin was adamant.

Later, when he was a few miles from the camp, he realized he was seriously injured. His ribs made breathing painful and his right leg began to burn with each step. When he bent his arm to cradle his ribs, he realized that something was wrong with it was well. He felt excruciating pain any time he lifted the arm.

As night fell it became difficult to walk, and even harder to follow the dirt path through the rainforest. The canopy of trees blocked out all light. He hobbled along trying not to breathe too deeply, afraid to stumble and injure himself more, but as time passed, he became even more afraid of facing Tich. *Just what the hell do you think you're doing? How the hell can you have a relationship with a guerrilla fighter?* An excruciating pain shot through his gut and a moment later he leaned over and a stream of vomit flew from his mouth. He propped himself against the truck of a palm tree, hugging it for support while trying to steady his breathing. He felt lost. He couldn't see to move forward to the monastery or go back to the camp. Even if he could see, he wasn't sure his body would hold out on the long walk.

Hugging that trunk, which seemed the only solid thing in his life at that moment, he considered his options. It seemed to him that once Nook spread the news, he would be unwelcome at the monastery by Tich and the others. Buddhists still took a dim view of gay relations. He also knew, much as he had connected with Kublai, there was no way to make that work. The only reasonable thing for him to do was to limp into town, get bandaged up, then climb on the next bus for Bangkok, and from there fly home. But, of course, that would mean leaving Kublai just as something had kindled between them. He didn't know if being back home, alone, would be better or worse than being here. He imagined himself and Kublai boarding a plane for the States, but he knew the soldier would never give up his homeland, not while his family and friends were dying at the hands of the government.

In the end he realized he had only two options that he could act on. He could lie on the ground and wait for first light and hope someone came by to help, or he could continue feeling his way along the road in the darkness. Since he couldn't really walk with his hurt leg, his rib cage ached fiercely, and his right arm seemed to be broken, the idea of walking to town was out of the question. Still, what else could he do? No one would come to his rescue, and the longer he waited, the more painful his injuries would grow.

He pushed away from the tree and continued inching his way toward the monastery, clenching his jaw against the growing pain and hoping for the best.

❖

It was well past midnight when Martin bobbled across the temple courtyard and climbed the steps to his room. The complex was dark. No one was stirred.

During those last miles, a light rain had begun to fall. He was soaked to the skin and shivering by the time he shuffled to his sleeping mat, pulled off his clothing, and draped the mosquito netting over him. He wrapped himself in his blanket and trembled himself warm while outside the shutters were pelted with large raindrops.

The pain had grown monstrous, but there was nothing to do but wait until they could drive him to the clinic in town.

He heard movement in the room and a millisecond later, Tich lifted the netting and crawled onto his mat. They lay facing each other. Tich wore only his briefs and a pair of wool socks. Even in the darkness, that close, Martin could see that Tich also wore his profoundly soulful, listening expression.

The fact that Tich stayed up this late in order to confront him proved that Nook had blabbed the news. The only thing that was somewhat shocking was that Tich seemed so calm.

"What happened?" Tich asked.

"It just happened. I couldn't control it. I'm sorry."

Tich's nodding seemed to be more understanding than Martin was prepared to accept. *Okay, going out on a limb here, this means you don't give a shit if I've fallen for someone else. You totally don't need or want me anymore. It's truly over, for you, anyway.*

"It's okay, I understand," Tich said.

"The only question is where that leaves us."

"Uh-huh."

A heavy silence passed. He wrapped the blanket tighter around him, which sent funnels of flames through his injuries, but at least that gave him a bit of warmth. *Perhaps this will not be quite so monumental as I imagined.*

"She's jealous of us," Tich said. "Jealous of how much you love me, that you came halfway across the globe for me. The monks say she's always been like that. She's a woman who's never known love but has always yearned for it. I'm so sorry she's punishing you because of me."

Another silence, a long and terrible one, stretched through the pain in his ribs. Fat blobs of water hurled themselves at the shutters with more force, as if shot from a cannon.

Martin understood, somewhat, that in some stomach-wrenching way a miscommunication had taken place. Had he been wrong to assume the worst about Nook? In fact, they both were. He stared into Tich's doe-eyed expression as his ex-lover reached out and took his hand.

"I never stopped loving you."

"I thought I wasn't supposed to touch you?"

"You're not. I'm touching you."

And that, implausibly, was as far as anything progressed. Tich leaned closer while he lifted Martin's hand to his lips and he kissed it. Then Tich crawled from under the mosquito netting and returned to his own sleeping mat.

As exhausted as Martin felt, he was not able to sleep. He lay listening to the rain pelt the window while his body throbbed. He thought about his misunderstanding with Tich, and knew he needed to set things straight between them. Whatever they had, whatever kindness Tich was showing him now, was useless as long as they stayed at the temple. His mind went back and forth, first to Tich and then to Kublai, until the room began to pale with the coming dawn.

The temple gong rang out, calling the monks to prayer. Voices came to life as the men rose to the day. Martin wanted to disappear. He couldn't face the thought of explaining to everyone why that crazy nun had run over him. He lay still and waited.

"Time to bathe," said Tich.

He sat up, wincing at the pain in his ribs and arm. Tich was standing over him, pulling back the mosquito netting. He tried to raise himself off the mat and faltered, the pain in his side seemed to explode. With the dim light now coming through the windows, he saw that his leg had swollen to twice its normal size.

Tich knelt beside him. "Christ, you're hurt bad. You need a doctor." Tich moved to Martin's suitcase and pulled out clean clothes. He handed them to Martin and told him to dress while he went for help.

Martin didn't want to go to any damned clinic. Now that he knew that Nook had not spilled the beans and that Tich didn't hate him, all he could think about was getting back to Kublai. During that long night of comparing his feeling for them both, he realized he loved them both equally. The only difference was, Kublai still wanted him and Tich had abandoned him.

A few minutes later, Tich arrived with five others. They helped him dress, then lifted him onto a makeshift stretcher. Martin cried out when Tich grabbed his hurt leg. The men lifted him and managed the hallway and the stairs bit by bit. The rain had grown more forceful in the night and was now coming down hard. They crossed the courtyard to the white truck. Tich opened the passenger door and they lifted Martin into the cab. Tich sat with him while they waited for Nook to drive them.

It surprised Martin that Tich seemed more nervous and hurt than even he felt.

"I want you to do me a favor," Martin said. "This afternoon, can you go to the refugee camp with Nook and teach the English class for me? I don't want to let those kids down."

Tich shook his head. "No need. They're leaving today."

"Who?"

"The camp," Tich said. "Once the annual rains come, the government troops retreat back to the capital, so the refugees move back to their villages. By this time tomorrow, they'll all be gone."

Martin sat stunned. It seemed like his entire life was disintegrating. He glanced around the rain-shrouded courtyard, looking for any clue as to what to do now. Then his eyes rested on the keys sitting in the truck's ignition.

"Tich, the pain is getting worse. Run and get Nook, now. Drag her here if you have to."

Tich leaped from the cab and ran through the rain as Martin eased himself behind the steering wheel and reached for the keys.

The truck had difficulty navigating a road that was a sea of muddy clay, with foot-deep ruts cut by streams of runoff. During the last mile to the camp, the heavens opened up, making it seem as though sky and earth were at war. Martin had never known rain like it. Magnificently torrential. Humbling. It gave him hope of more time with Kublai, because it was impossible for anyone to travel in this weather.

He slewed about on the slick road, sometimes sideswiping trees. The jostling about the cab made his injuries explode in pain. He had to operate the pedals with his left foot because he couldn't move his right. There were moments when the agony became so overwhelming that he felt he might pass out. That didn't slow him down, however. He kept going, desperate to see Kublai.

The truck fishtailed up mud slopes and slid down the other sides. Channels beside the road gushed. The thick, warm rains washed the color out of everything: pale bamboo, brown mud, and overhead nothing but black.

When he reached the camp, he first noticed that the Thai army sentries that normally stood guard at the gates were missing. Inside the camp, people were on the move, carrying bundles and gathering in groups as if it were a summer's day and they were heading off for a picnic. He could see at a glance that he had misjudged them; the rain would not keep them here.

He plowed through the street and slid to a stop before the community library. He looked around, but could see little through the downpour.

As if by magic, Ko Song and Kublai appeared a dozen yards away, walking toward the truck. Kublai wore his full combat gear, carrying two automatic rifles strapped to his back. He looked as deadly as a cobra. Martin rolled down the window as they stepped to the driver's door.

"Our time has ended here, Hanuman," Ko Song said. "We thank you for your help."

"Take me with you."

Ko Song shook his head. "Impossible."

Martin stared into Kublai's soulful eyes. "Please, I can help. I'll teach. I'll fight. Whatever you need. I'll sleep in a hut. I'll—"

"No," Ko Song said with kind authority. "We are touched by your generosity, but Myanmar is our soil; we can die for it, but not you. It is time you returned to you own country. Continue the fight there, if you must, with your State Department."

Martin had no intention of dying, and he assumed if it was safe for women and children to return, then it must be safe for him as well. He would not give up hope.

He felt a spasm of pain in his rib cage from breathing so hard, nearly hyperventilating. "Kublai, please. Don't leave me." A moment of clarity came to him, and he realized that it was more than losing his lover, more than being left behind yet again. Working for the camp— gathering food, making money at the temple, teaching the children— made him feel like he made a difference. Back home he grew designer mushrooms for high-end restaurants, which served no crucial need except to give rich people something new to savor. Here he worked hard and made people more comfortable, happier; he helped fill their bellies and their minds. On the other hand, he knew Ko Song would not let him come because he would not take personal responsibility for Martin's safety.

Kublai reached inside the cab and cupped the back of Martin's neck. He said, "I will never forget you." He leaned in and gave Martin a long and meaningful kiss.

Kublai turned and began to walk away. Martin knew that for as long as he lived, he'd remember the anguished look on Kublai's face as he turned away. It was a look that was simultaneously penetrating and aching, fraught with hopelessness and regret, immense and profound as the silence that accompanied it.

Martin felt flattened and exiled, with nothing to do but step into the unknown. He felt his body grow larger, compelled. He flung open the driver's door. A moment later he unfolded from the cab and tried to hobble after Kublai. Agony skyrocketed to inconceivable levels. He clenched his jaw to stifle a scream. Still, he forced himself on. He would not be left behind with nothing.

His strength suddenly deserted him, replaced by the sensation that his muscle fibers were being incinerated from his bones. He felt himself falling. He heard shouts above him, and someone pulling his face from the mud. The next thing he knew, he was staring up at that beautiful face with those slightly crossed eyes. He tried to say, "I love you," but his body would not respond. The only thing he heard was himself sobbing. Whoever said that real men don't cry, he thought, has never lost anything more precious than life.

Everything went black.

❖

When he opened his eyes again, he lay stretched out in a bed in a white room. There was an utter void in his head, from everything shutting down. He didn't know if he was in the clinic in town, or perhaps a hospital in some larger city like Chiang Mai. The window blinds were drawn, so there was no way to tell.

The air had an antiseptic stench, reminiscent of cheap grappa and so strong he seemed to ingest it rather than inhale it. Six beds filled the room, with curtains that could separate one bed from another, three against one wall and three against the opposite wall.

He lay on his back in a middle bed. The beds on either side of him were unoccupied, but a Thai woman slept across the room, huddled in a fetal position with one arm dangling over the side of her bed.

Also, the abbot sat on a chair beside Martin's bed, eyes closed, either sleeping or meditating. As always, he was dressed in simple carrot-colored robes and his yellow woolen cap with that label that said "Aspire" in English.

Shadows came and went in the corridor. He heard footsteps resounding beyond the door, accompanied by voices speaking Thai. Two nurses hurried past the doorway pushing a gurney at a fast clip. It seemed as if all things existed in some parallel universe into which he'd been dropped without warning. He no longer recognized the world.

He felt nauseous, dopey, and devoid of strength. He had casts on his arm and leg, and bandages squeezed his chest. A nurse brought him a bottle of water and a paper cup holding three pills. She left them on the stand beside his bed.

He glanced back at the abbot, who now had his eyes open and wore his usual disarming smile that projected such empathetic warmth.

"Where's Tich," Martin asked with a voice that sounded like it came from a great distance. He knew better than to ask about Kublai, because he remembered enough to know that chapter of his life had closed. No doubt Kublai was now beyond his reach, forever.

The abbot spoke a burst of Thai.

"Oh, yeah, you can't understand me," he said. His voice rose to nearly a shout, "*Nobody* understands me!"

The abbot nodded, which reminded Martin of a dumb horse in a pasture.

"If I could only make you see," he said. "I came here because I was struck by Tich the first time I saw him. He was loving and kind, and he became the center of my universe. Every time he smiled at me, it was like a bolt of lightning illuminating the sky, and if he became sad or angry, then my entire world went black. When he left, it was like my soul separating from my body. I came to take him back home, where we lived as a couple. I came here because without him, I'm nothing. And then I found someone else who made me realize I can be someone, someone who makes a difference." There was no point in talking to this old man who couldn't understand, but Martin couldn't stop himself as the emotions began to build.

He closed his eyes and pictured their Northern California home—massive windows to let in the sunlight, oak shingles, verdant evergreens surrounding the three-story structure—that homey perfection that never seemed to change.

The abbot's face now carried a gentle scowl that disturbed Martin deeply. The abbot looked at him in a reflective way. He seemed to study himself as much as Martin. He said nothing, and in the silence, Martin assumed it was safe to continue.

He felt his face take on a peculiar inner smile, radiating from within his eyes, because he knew he could say anything. In this foreign place, the abbot was a man he could confide in. He felt grateful for the opportunity to tell his story, to say it one time, as a way to purge his pent-up frustrations. Words spilled out on their own, and what he said was about the two loves of his life, pure and simple, the kind of talk one doesn't make—or doesn't want to make—more than a few times every decade, or sometimes never. He described his being abandoned by Tich, about coming here and finding a sense of community with the Burmese, and about his finding unexpected love with Kublai.

It was a relief to talk about himself in a way that was meaningful, something beyond the sitting room recitations of small boasts and complaints. He didn't hold back, delving into how he felt about first losing Tich, then losing Kublai, which seemed like the point of the whole narration. It felt like slicing open his core to surrender a place that, well, that deep down determined everything.

Martin suspected the relief he felt came more from having someone who listened than from the talk itself.

"The sad part is, I'm convinced Tich needs me as much as I need him. And now I know that I have something of real value to offer him."

The abbot sat with his head bowed and his eyes bashfully down, as if trying to hide his own churning emotions. He listened without interruption and without any reaction. He had become a sponge, soaking up everything and giving nothing back.

At last Martin ran out of words and lay silent, staring at the little monk with the yellow wool cap.

The old man lifted himself from the chair, and stepped closer. He leaned over Martin and tenderly embraced him. Then he turned a shuffled from the room.

The pain in Martin's head began to intensify. He reached for the cup of pills and popped them into his mouth. Then he reached for the bottle of water.

Ten minutes, more or less, of obdurate wakefulness, and then the tidal pull of painkillers dragged him back into sleep.

❖

Over the next few days, he was fed three meals per day and helped to the restroom by orderlies. There was no TV and nothing to read, so he came to like the noises in the corridor, trying to learn a few Thai phrases. Doctors gave him injections and nurses fed him pills. Each morning Tich and the abbot visited him shortly after alms rounds and before he ate his breakfast. Even though he couldn't understand the staff, he managed to communicate by pointing to his plastered limbs and making faces. They would give him more medication so that he could drift off to sleep again. That pretty much summed up his time, eating, sleeping, sitting on the toilet, and lots of thinking.

The drugs made his memories at the temple and the camp begin to blur. On the fourth day they gave him a frame with wheels so that he could push himself to the bathroom unassisted. He had difficulty moving with the frame because he couldn't put weight on this injured leg and only had one good arm, but slowly he was able to stabilize himself by leaning hard on his good arm propped against the frame.

When Tich saw him moving on his own accord, he said, "I hope this means you'll be out soon, because the temple has a surprise for you."

Martin couldn't wait to leave the clinic. It was more than the boredom, he had become afraid of the silence. It seemed more like a morgue than a hospital, and he had a premonition that something bad might happen before he could escape. But he didn't want to return to the temple. There seemed no point. The temple held no attraction for him. There was nothing for him out there without the camp. It was useless to try to return to something when his heart was no longer in it. Still, he had to do something. He needed to crawl back up the grade. Lying at rock bottom was no way to live. With this kind of implosion, he thought, if you don't react swiftly, you become a bystander of your own collapse, and you don't realize that the abyss is slowly closing over you.

He needed to get to the bus station, and from there travel to the airport in Chiang Mai, to Bangkok, and home. The only things he wanted from the temple were his passport, money, and the necklace that Kublai had given him. He sat in that bed, hour after hour, imagining himself flying first class across the Pacific. He couldn't wait to down a couple of martinis and then tear into that steak he knew would be perfectly rare and nourishing.

Late at night, lying in the darkness unable to sleep, he thought of his two loves. But it was always Kublai who he remembered making love to, felt that sumptuous skin against his, the breath on his neck. Perhaps he envisioned Kublai because he had been the most recent lovemaking, or perhaps because he couldn't face the pain of Tich's indifference. Regardless of who he imagined, they were both with him through the long, dark nights.

On the afternoon of the fifth day, Tich, Corbin Edwards, and Martin's doctor came into the room. The doctor examined him and said he could leave the clinic. He would need to take the frame he used to get around, and he mustn't put too much weight on his leg, but he could finish his recovery anywhere.

Tich gave him shorts and a T-shirt, and told him he was being discharged.

"I don't want to go back to the temple," Martin said, knowing it would be too painful. "Can you bring my gear and just put me on the next bus?"

Tich's face fell. He tried to smile but failed. "We've arranged something different, something new. Trust me."

Martin didn't feel like insisting. He knew that the first step was to leave this damned clinic. Every move after that would be a step toward getting him closer to home. He gritted his teeth and pushed himself to a sitting position. He let Tich help him dress, and then slid into a wheelchair. It felt somewhat comforting to have Tich hovering only inches away. He could almost pretend they were a couple again. He knew he hadn't lost his love for him, which would make leaving difficult.

Because he was living with the monks, there was no charge for the treatment, the stay, a deposit for the walking frame, or the industrial-sized bottle of painkillers they gave him. Tich steered him through the halls and onto the covered front entrance. A warm rain came down in sheets.

Corbin walked Soapsuds up to the entrance and made the beast kneel so that Martin could climb on. Martin sat staring at the animal. "You're kidding, right?"

"You got a better idea?" Tich asked. "It's not like you can run a marathon in that cast."

"I'll look ridiculous riding that thing."

Corbin snorted. "When you drove off, we came looking for you, and 'that thing' carried your broken-down ass back into town."

Tich smiled. "Just pretend you're a maharajah out for a stroll through your kingdom."

They maneuvered Martin into animal's back, and Tich gave him an enormous umbrella. Martin was actually quite relieved that Nook was not driving him in her truck. No doubt she wanted nothing to do with him, which explained this means of transportation. Tich carried the walker, and he and Corbin flanked Soapsuds as they meandered along the slick, muddy roads. They walked through the town and along the road heading toward the temple. After being in a hospital bed for so many days, Martin began to enjoy the rhythmic swaying side to side as they trudged through the rainforest. He did feel like royalty.

Two miles outside of town, Martin said, "You said we weren't going to the temple?"

"You'll see," was all Tich would say.

Martin's leg was already throbbing under the cast, from just that little bit of walking to maneuver onto the beast. Whatever Tich had planned, he knew he would not be up for, and he began to regret leaving that clean, dry bed.

About a half mile from the temple, the road skirted the river, and there Martin saw a peculiar sight. At the side of the road, Nook and the abbot sat waiting in the white truck. Behind them, near the bank of the swollen river, stood two structures that had not been there before.

The two buildings were identical, thatched roofs supported by thick bamboo poles, covering two wooden platform, each large enough for a person to stretch out and sleep. Snowy white mosquito netting hung from each roof; sleeping mats, pillows and blankets were spread over the platforms. When Corbin pulled Soapsuds to a halt and made him kneel, Martin began to have a very bad feeling about this situation. He assumed he was no longer welcome at the monastery, and that he would be sleeping here, out in the open, until he was able to leave this damned country. He was too shocked to even be angry.

The next few minutes became a blur. Tich opened the truck's passenger door and helped the abbot from the cab. Corbin helped Martin off the elephant's back. The four men huddled under the umbrella for a moment, then Tich guided them all toward the platforms while Corbin held the umbrella over their heads.

When they reached the platforms, Martin stopped. His head had begun to clear and his panic was skyrocketing. "Dammit, Tich, tell me what's going on or I'm walking back to town!"

Tich stood silent as the abbot reached out and took Martin's good hand in his, and brought it up so Tich could take that hand and entwine his fingers with Martin's. Once they were holding hands, Tich said to the abbot, "Thank you, Khun Chompukeaw." He used the standard Thai honorific *khun* to show politeness and respect.

Tich stared into Martin's eyes. "I came back to Thailand because I wanted to live a more spiritual life, to build good karma for my family and myself. After your accident, Khun Chompukeaw convinced me that I don't need to live as a monk to be more spiritual. He said I can be your lover, and we can share the path to enlightenment, together. Tonight, we'll be together, sleeping side by side, while I decide which path to walk. Tomorrow I'll either go back the temple or return home with you. We've got a lot to talk about tonight."

Martin stood silent as puzzle pieces fell into to place in his mind. And then the most surprising realization smacked him square in the forehead. He turned to the abbot. "You understood me, in the clinic when I poured out my soul. You just let me rattle on thinking I was talking to the wall. You crafty old bastard."

The abbot chuckled. "Hanuman, your trouble," he said in passable English, "is that you make too many wrong assumptions. Better to make none at all than to make bad ones." He began to walk back to the truck. He called over his shoulder; "We'll pick you both up on our way into town at first light." When he reached the truck he collapsed the umbrella and crawled into the passenger side of the cab. A moment later, they were gone.

Corbin gave Martin a slap on the back. "Best of luck, Slick. Don't fuck this up." A moment later, he crawled onto Soapsuds's back and they began to lumber toward the temple.

There was nothing to do but crawl under the netting to get out of the rain. While Tich helped him onto the platform, their bodies jostled against one another, briefly and roughly. Now that they were alone, away from the temple, Martin felt their relationship evolving into something new.

Beside the sleeping mats, Martin found plenty of cold roasted chicken and steamed rice. Whatever the night would bring, he would not go hungry. Alongside the food lay the necklace that Kublai had given him, and at the foot of the platform, just out of the rain, were his backpack and suitcase. He assumed all his possessions were there and that he would be on his way home tomorrow. He also realized that having the necklace there meant that Tich knew about Kublai. Realizations were coming rapid-fire, and he struggled to keep up with his racing mind.

Just one more night, he thought. I can do this. The evening air was warm, and he knew the rain would keep the insects away. All he need do was to eat, sleep, and hope Tich would return with him in the morning. His arm began to itch, which caused his leg to itch as well. He knew he would have difficulty sleeping.

He watched Tich crawl onto the other platform and settle into a lotus position facing him. Tich seemed ready to talk, but waited for Martin to start the conversation.

"Can you tell me which way you're leaning? I mean, would you rather stay here?"

"When I first came here, I realized a peculiar thing. I found I had this noise in my head. I assume everyone in the West has it, and we're all so used to it that we don't hear it. It's a constant whine of information, and lots of misinformation, and it seemed to drive us. Yet, after a few weeks of scant diet, meditation, and no contact with the outside world, it went away. Silence. I experienced pure silence for the first time. I'm talking about inner silence. A deep calmness."

"I didn't get that. So what's it like?"

"Unadulterated boredom. The kind where you feel your life is going nowhere."

Martin was taken aback. He let go with a snort-laugh and he slapped the cast on his leg. "So California's looking brighter and brighter?"

"Living as a monk isn't for me. On the other hand, I don't want to go back to that life in the States. It would be different if I were a neurosurgeon or a great novelist, someone who makes a difference in people's lives. But going back there to grow mushrooms doesn't seem any more exciting than being here."

Sitting only a few yards apart, yet both shrouded by mosquito netting, it seemed bizarre they were have so serious a conversation. This was an environment neither had ever experienced before.

"Would it be too disconcerting if I asked what you think you want to do?" Martin asked.

Tich frowned.

Martin couldn't stand the silence that followed. "Come on, you must have some idea."

"Right now, I want to enjoy our night together and see the sunrise."

Martin lifted himself to a sitting position, trying to determine where the sun would rise. The breeze rummaged around under his shirt and tousled his hair. He lifted his good leg, wrapped his arm around the knee, and delicately placed his chin on them. He stared unwaveringly at the river, hearing more than seeing the flow of water.

The rain slackened into a heavy mist, which made the sound of the river seem louder. "Let the song of the river drown out all that noise inside you," Tich said, surprising Martin by easing himself down behind him. Tich caressed Martin's shoulders, neck, and the back of his head with aching tenderness, his fingers flowing silky as a stream over smooth stones.

He listened to the water gurgling in the hollow of a rock, and he realized he didn't want to think about anything. His time at the temple, California, even Kublai, seemed nothing more than old sorrows and old ghosts. The memories were still very much intact, yet he wanted to move past them, to somehow rises from his own ashes. But arise as what? Wasn't that what they were both trying to do?

Just then Martin could only feel an unspeakable distress. He tried to let the sound of the stream wash it away, but without luck. What tore into him was the idea that we only had one short life, and yet, what had he done with his? Tich was spot-on, he had flittered away his time. It wasn't so much that he was hurting anyone, it was every missed opportunity to comfort others. Surely teaching at the camp had taught him how wonderful it was to help people. That experience had allowed him to love those refugees, and some of them had loved him back. For the first time, he saw his life in a stark white light, and he was sick that his life to that point had been too busy, too self-absorbed, and too distracted by trivialities.

His mind bombarded him with excuses, and as quickly as they few into his head, they fell away like chaff. Millions of men and women and children, he knew, were living in inhuman conditions. Children starved while people back home threw food away. People died of curable diseases while Americans plowed billions into cosmetics. People just across the border were living in soul-destroying fear of brutal men with guns, being thrown into prison, and worked to death while America does trade with their oppressors. Hell, Martin realized—while listening to the river flow and feeling Tich's finger kneading tense muscles— was understanding that one didn't help when one could have. The old *Schindler's List* syndrome. True torment was realizing how little one truly loved beyond oneself.

For the first time, Martin knew why Tich had fled, and why he couldn't declare the reason in words. Words couldn't really express that deep humiliation.

How crazy I was, to ever think that I had anything to offer Tich. It's time to start really loving him, and everyone else.

They sat in silence while a rage inflamed Martin's chest. When it began to cool, he leaned into Tich, to feel the luxury of them being together, alone. Reality and fantasy bled back and forth: one second they were recapturing their first blush of desire; the next they were lost in a dark and mysterious rainforest where ancient gods and dangerous animals roamed at will.

Martin took one of Tich's hands and pulled him around so they could sit face-to-face. "So you don't want to be a monk, yet you want to live a spiritual life helping others? If I don't go back tomorrow, if I stay in Thailand, is there room for two in this dream you're inventing?"

Tich sighed, obviously in no rush to respond. He relaxed his shoulders and showed the hint of a grin. He became an enigmatic Buddha offering more than enough presence with his silence. His aim, Martin finally understood, was to make Martin answer his own question.

Something passed between them. Martin realized something he suspected Tich had understood all along, that they were both doing the best they could, and both were failing. Now here they sat in the middle of a jungle, in each other's arms, and a little unsure about how exactly they got there and entirely unsure about what to do next. All Martin knew for sure was, neither could go back to what came before.

Martin leaned into him, offered a wet-eyed smile, and he kissed Tich on the lips. It was not an act of passion, but one of searching, and done with such profound tenderness that even Martin was stunned. His heart began to thump.

He pulled away, not so far as to lose the scent of Tich's breath, and he stared into those lovely eyes. There was nothing either of them could say.

DEATH OF A STRANGER

As a child I had never doubted "the system" or the people who controlled it. I had absolute trust in parents, teachers, police, government, even the Church. As my peers were protesting authority at every opportunity, I held, with an alarming naivety, the belief that everyone in power was honorably devoted to the welfare of society. By the time I joined the priesthood, I understood that the system was flawed, that people put their own interests first and only helped society whenever they themselves benefited as well. The system, be it the Church or school or government, gave power and honor where none was due, and crushed those trying to help the needy.

I know this firsthand because I am one of the crushed. I tried to help a young man who had fallen in love with me, and I spent two years in a Texas prison because he was a few months shy of eighteen. Luke, the light of my soul, was crushed as well, only he never recovered. I came to Thailand while pitifully trying to rebuild my life, my dignity, and found an aged, blind monk who carved beautiful statues of elephants. Upon his death, he willed me his carving knife and a budding love for the beasts he carved.

But this story is not about me; it started long before I came to this temple, even before I became a mahout, a caretaker of elephants. I mention my childhood naivety only because it was during the unfolding of this story that I truly began to understand what evil "the system" does to the innocent and weak.

How does one create order out of a jumbled memory? My spiritual master would suggest: begin at the beginning, attaching the first thread to the loom, and proceed, patiently, like a weaver at his craft. He adored similes. I know which place to start this tale; in truth there can be no other.

His name was Archer, and I knew the moment I laid eyes on him that I would love him, even though that love would never be returned with the same intensity. That was our destined roles, he the loved and me the lover. He was unusually tall, even for a Caucasian male, old enough to be a man yet young enough to still be as slender and supple as a young willow. He moved with extraordinary grace, and whenever he spoke, which was seldom, I could swear he was singing a love song that would open even the cruelest hearts. A voice so melodic, birds in the trees were silenced by envy.

He arrived at our temple with a companion, Annop, a monk of little esteem at Wat Phra Singh, the chief temple in Chiang Mai, Thailand. Annop's body was the size of a twelve-year-old. He dressed in the orange robes and needed a wheelchair to move about. His shaved head was handsome, but hard for him to control. It rolled to the side every time his mouth spread into a grin, which was often. His was not quite a man's voice, even though he was in his mid-twenties. It wasn't easy for Annop to make his hands go where he wanted them. They strayed every which way, as if having a will of their own.

I first saw Archer at the temple gates. I had been down at the river giving the two elephants I cared for, Soapsuds and Padre, a cooling soak. As I led the beasts back up the path to the temple compound, there on the outside of the walls stood the abbot beside Archer and Annop. Archer knelt beside the monk in the wheelchair, gently pulling bits of dirt and lint from Annop's robes. He was utterly absorbed in his task, and showed a devotion to the young monk that left me stunned. In that moment I witnessed him stripped bare of all the superficial trivialities that we in the West judge each other by. What I saw was a simple man who was born as innocent as me, who wanted peace and comfort and freedom and respect like me, and who was not too lofty to devote himself to another. My heart went out to him. I wanted to show him that we were brothers, and to give him that same devotion that he gave Annop. I was filled with tender compassion.

The abbot introduced us, and I learned that Archer had been a prevalent television personality back in the States. What brought him to Thailand, he wouldn't say. Everyone had his or her unique reason for coming here, and his purpose seemed to be service to Annop. The young monk had some kind of mission, and Archer was helping him.

They had arrived at the temple by taxi that morning, about three weeks after the start of the rainy season. They were trying to make their way into Myanmar, but not by the main highways, which were guarded by both the Thai and Burmese arms. They wanted to slip into that country unnoticed. There were trails, of course, leading through the rainforests. They started out boldly enough, but grew narrow and rough after a dozen miles, dwindling into deer paths and finally losing themselves within the steep hills and mountains. This time of year, the highland trails were muddy tracks, and unusable by any kind of vehicle. To travel on anything other than oxen or elephant was optimistic to the point of sheer whimsy.

So it fell to me and my elephants to take Archer to a village across the border, Toungoo, a place forgotten by the world outside of Myanmar. It was no more than a starveling outpost of temples and huts sheltering refugees fleeing the atrocities by the military government on its people. It was a place of sweltering heat, malaria, blackwater sickness, and utter lack of communications except by foot through forest trails. Simply put, it was a place no Western person would bother with.

I had no idea what these adventures had in mind, but I felt that they both had flippantly overlooked the conditions of the trails, coupled with the fact that a hundred miles of rainforest, river crossings, and steep mountains lay between our temple and Toungoo. What I did know was that they were willing to make a sizable donation to the temple if I could take them safely to their destination. I had no idea how I would manage to guide them through miles of dense jungle to find Toungoo, but that much money for the temple was too tempting to refuse.

The temple needed money to buy rice for Burmese refugees. There had been two years of poor rainfall in the region. Ordinarily that would not have been a disaster for the rice harvest, but the *Tatmadaw* (Burmese army) near the border didn't carry rations; they seized rice and livestock from the local farmers, and sometimes burned a village's supplies. In many areas, the locals were starving. Our temple stockpiled sacks of rice, paid for with donations. The Burmese would slip across the border, sometimes walking for several days, and carry this rice back to their villages.

A tingle of fear rose up my spine. It was more distress of getting lost than getting shot at by the *Tatmadaw,* but I would be lying if I said I wasn't concerned by both.

The abbot must have read my mind. He touched my arm, which steadied me. "You have everything you need. I have confidence in you."

I bowed and stayed silent. I didn't want them hearing the fear I was sure would shade my voice. We agreed to leave at dawn, taking the main road west and then veering off the roads before we reached the border. We would enter Myanmar's Karen state and then travel northwest into the Karenni state.

That night I couldn't sleep. Waiting was dreadful. As much as I didn't want to do this, I couldn't concentrate on anything other than getting the ball rolling. I felt that was the only way to relieve my growing apprehension.

When roosters began to crow, I rose from my sleeping mat, anxious to start the day. The sky was cloudy with a mist steadily falling. I assumed it would later turn to rain. I slipped into my orange robes and strolled out to the elephant's pen to give Soapsuds and Padre a good feed before our journey. To my surprise, two soldiers of the Karenni National Progressive Party were waiting for me. They were dressed in fighting kit. These guerrilla soldiers seemed hard-boiled and alert.

One of the fighters introduced himself as Kublai, using excellent English. He held the pungent odor of the jungle, carried two automatic rifles, a .45 caliber sidearm holstered to his waist, and wore a vest with pockets bulging with clips of ammo. He was dark-skinned, with sable-colored hair, and lean, hard muscles. His face looked boyish, yet his ensemble made him seem lethal.

He shook my hand. "Boss, I'm your guide," he said. He pulled black shorts and a pullover shirt from his buddy's backpack and held them out to me. "You need to lose that orange. It makes too good a target in the forest."

I assumed our wily abbot had sent a runner across the border, asking for help. A sea swell of gratitude washed through me. I would have an armed escort. Still, I was not thrilled about abandoning my monk garb. I had grown to love the swish of cloth about my body as I walked, the quiet dignity I felt while dressed in them. I was less thrilled at the possibility of someone shooting at me. I was merely a mahout delivering cargo, not some guerrilla fighter trying to overthrow a government. Still, if there were soldiers out there who would shoot at me, wearing black as apposed to bright orange did make sense. I stripped and carefully folded my robes, then donned the black clothing. I had the distinct feeling that Kublai enjoyed my discomfort, and he seemed to silently appraise my nakedness. Years of a scant diet had made my muscles almost as lean and hard as his. Even so, I outweighed him by thirty pounds.

The material was coarse and too snug to be comfortable, but I was in no mood to complain.

Kublai held out his AK-47. "Have you ever fired a weapon?"

I found it odd, given that moments before I had been dressed as a monk and had a shaved head, that he offered me a rifle. Did he think that Caucasian monks were any less compassionate than Asian monks? Or in his country, were monks expected to fight? I held up my hands. "No. And I don't want to carry a weapon. I might accidently shoot myself. Hell, I might even accidently shoot you."

He smiled. "If we stumble into a tight spot, boss, you may have to defend yourself."

I dropped my hands but not my resolve. "Let's stay away from anything tight, shall we?"

He chuckled while nodding. "How soon can you be ready?"

"Would it be too much to asked to wait until after breakfast?" I was interested in eating as much as possible before our departure. I assumed there would be scant rations once we entered Myanmar.

He stared at me, no doubt weighing me up. I think my suggestion of food pleased him, showing him a practical side. I assumed, however, he would not drop his barriers until he saw firsthand how I coped with rugged country, hunger, and hardship. It would take a lot to impress him, I knew, and I held little faith I would measure up.

After sunup, the other monks returned from their morning alms gathering. The nuns used that food to cook rice gruel, vegetable curry, and fried eggs. Archer, Annop (now dressed in the same black clothing as I), and our two armed guides ate their fill in silence, as did I. We then gathered at the elephants' pen. We would travel as light as possible. The only luggage was a large gray bag slung across Archer's back. I hoped it carried food and medical supplies, but I didn't ask.

We determined that Archer would ride behind me on Soapsuds, Annop would ride on Padre, and our guides preferred to walk, one leading and one following. I was skeptical that Annop, with his disability, could handle Padre, but he assured me he was a capable mahout.

Archer lifted Annop from his wheelchair and placed him on the kneeling beast. Annop leaned over the animal's head and drew his face against that thick hide. He stroked Padre's cheek with as much tenderness as his uncoordinated fist would allow.

As Padre lumbered to his feet, my fears vanished. Annop wheeled the beast around, using a combination of whistles and patting the beast's neck with his hands. The language used by mahouts to communicate with their elephants comprises sounds, words, and body language. You could fill a dictionary with the many commands, and it seemed that Annop had written much of that book. He seemed balanced and in control, a maharajah out for a joyride. He was visibly thrilled to be out of that chair, yet still as mobile as any of us.

Annop laughed, a loud strangling sound. When he spoke, his words came haltingly and loud, but with the Thai singsong accent. "I'm...king of...the world," he said. The ecstasy radiating from him outshone the cloud-veiled sun.

I stepped to Soapsuds and gave that gentle beast the command to kneel. As he did, I gave his head a loving pat and playfully pulled his left ear. He shook his head and let go with a blast of his trumpet. He and I had developed a mutual affection, I can think of no other word for it. Had he been human, I suppose I would have called it love. I crawled onto his shoulders, and Archer shimmied up to sit behind me. I gave a whistle, and Soapsuds rose to his feet. I gave the command *pai,* and we were off to Toungoo—a silly name for a nothing place. A place of trifling hopes and smaller disappointments. A place inconsequential to the world, out of bounds and well out of most men's thoughts.

A hundred miles can be nothing for a plane or a truck on good roads, but it can seem like the end of the earth by the slow plod of elephants. Our journey was not heroic, not even romantic. It was a delivery job, uncomfortable work, to be started at an hour with sleep in my eyes and a half grumble on my lips. I was unhappy, to say the least, about leaving my cozy monastery and venturing into the unknown just because two fools with money wanted to demonstrate their stupidity.

Kublai took the lead, armed and serious. We turned west and began to plod along the road with Archer's arms wrapped around my waist, clinging to me. I could tell it was his first time riding on an animal's back, and he was visibly terrified. Lay people like him are not allowed to touch a monk, even a Caucasian one. For him to relinquish that custom spoke volumes. Truthfully, I didn't mind. After those first few miles, his clinging relaxed into a gentle embrace. His hands gripping my torso were both comforting and exciting. They were hot hands, as if he had so much energy in him that he discharged radiation.

Soapsuds was an old brute, past his prime and past the point of hauling tourist up into the rainforests. That's why he was put in my care. I hoped he could endure this mission, not only because I didn't want to walk back on foot, but because I couldn't bear the loss of another good friend. He was a living creature and he spoke to me; through my thighs around his shoulders I understood the strain and flex of his muscles.

To get to the border we took the main road, but had to avoid a couple of Thai checkpoints by circling around them through the forest. The road was muddy, and often looked more like a river. We had to keep an ear and an eye out for anyone coming our way. It would not do for anyone to see white men on elephants in this part of the world. There was a network of informers, Kublai informed me. And because of the elephants, it would be nearly impossible to hide.

We veered off the road and used forest paths, climbing steep hills and traveling along the ridge that formed the border between Myanmar and Thailand.

Before plunging down the mountain, we took a long break to feed and water the animals. There I learned from Kublai that there are over six million Karen. To the north, another 150,000 Karenni. A vast strip of the Karenni State, that section sandwiched between the Thai border and the Salween river, had been taken over by the army as part of their *pya ley pya* (four cuts) campaign. They cut off supplies of food, money, information, and recruits to the ethnic resistance armies. The junta had forced the population of that area west into "relocation centers" and then destroyed all the villages, making it a free-fire zone. Any non-army persons spotted there were shot on sight, which was why we were crossing into the Karen state first, before turning north.

As we mounted our elephants again, I stared out to the west over ceaseless waves of ridges and valleys, green fading to gray. I could see three hilltops where the *Tatmadaw* had built fortifications, conspicuously white surrounded by the cleared red earth. I knew then we would be running a gauntlet between these camps, ever under threat of ambush. It had begun to rain in earnest, and I felt a chill as we moved along the trail. Even the heat radiating from Archer could not warm me.

We snaked along the ridge for a few kilometers and then plunged into a valley. When we abandoned the ridge we also abandoned the view. I could see only short distances through the wall of trees and thick vegetation. Now both guides walked out in front with their heads down. Every once in a while, one or the other would stand still and wave us around him, to avoid the landmine he was standing near. It was not clear to me who had placed the mines in the trails, the junta or the freedom fighters, and it didn't make much difference. What mattered was that we were in danger, and without our guides, we might have already been dead.

Sometimes the vegetation was so thick that I could only see the back of Kublai's head moving though a sea of green. If there was a path at all, it was lost to me. Occasionally all I followed was the leafy bushes still swaying from the men in front of us. Further on, below the crest of another ridge, we came upon a forest of sturdy hardwood trees so tall and lush I could only see the trunks and lowest branches.

We were silent all day, by necessity. Any bit of noise could land us in prison, or worse. Riding on elephants can be a lonely business, but to ride through unbroken forest with no more than the companionship of Soapsuds or the knowledge that somewhere ahead were lights and warm food and a comfortable bed was something more than simply lonely. It was at times unreal to the point where the existence of other people seems not even a reasonable probability. Thank goodness for Archer's hands clutching my waist. That human contact helped anchor me. The trail, the hills and valleys, the dense jungle all form a kind of darkness, and that absence of light seemed infinite. Soapsuds became a planet lumbering though dark Space, hoping to find the gravitational pull of some star; any bit of light would do. Finally I couldn't take the silence a moment longer.

"What brings you here?" I whispered over my shoulder.

After a long silence, Archer said, "I guess I'd have to say love brought me here."

His deep, yet soft voice in my ear was both tantalizing and comforting. He went on to explain that Annop had lived with a Caucasian monk in Chiang Mai, Philip Mann, who had been a fireman during the attack on the World Trade Center on September 11, 2001. Annop had fallen deeply in love with Philip, but when the ex-fireman returned from the States a few months ago, he and his son began helping an NGO smuggle medical supplies and food into Myanmar. They were both caught, of course, and were sentenced to twenty years in a Yangon prison.

"You're going to free them from prison?" I asked.

"More or less."

"And why are you involved?"

Another long silence. "I guess you could say I'm here for love as well."

I turned my upper body so that I could search his face for what it might unwittingly disclose, and I listened for nuances and clues into his relationship with Annop. What other love could he possibly be talking about?

I waited for him to elaborate, but he said no more. I turned to face the trail again, annoyed that he refused to discuss it. But I knew then that he loved Annop, and my admiration for this beautiful man blossomed. He was obviously a man who saw past outward appearances and connected with the inner person. How I longed to do that very thing with him.

Long after the sun had set and the light had faded, we came to a deserted village, a few dozen huts beside a wide but shallow stream. The air was dank. The ground was bare, wet earth and mossy rocks. I watered the elephants, let them graze on what foliage was available, and then tethered them to a tree. Kublai announced we would have no fire, which could have alerted the *Tatmadaw* of our presence. He and his companion would only smoke their cheroots inside a hut. We ate cold rice that our guides had brought from the temple, and also tins of Spam that came from God knows where. After twelve hours of not eating, it seemed like a feast.

It had drizzled all day, but that night we slept under a thatched roof. We all huddled on the wooden floor under two blankets. Our clothes were soaked, so it was not warm, but neither was it unbearable. I slept only a few feet from Archer, with only Annop separating us. As sleep took me, I longed to reach over and touch Archer, hold his hand, try to give him comfort. I knew, however, that Annop had beaten me to that task.

The dawn came with gray light and heavy clouds to the east, but the rain had stopped. We all seemed confident it would bring a better day. As soon as I had watered the elephants we were off again, this time without breakfast. My hopes of a better day began to fade.

We crossed range after range of hills and passed through lush valleys. Occasionally we crossed streams deep enough that even the elephants had to swim. Every now and then we passed through a deserted village, rotting, dilapidated, or burnt to the ground. The rains held off, yet the air was so muggy that it became difficult for me to breathe. It often felt like I was trying to suck air into my lungs through a straw. I suppose that could have been fear constricting my lungs, more than humidity.

Five hours into the day we came to another village, this one inhabited. In the center of a dozen huts sat two ancient women and a young girl tending a cooking fire. They seemed to be alone. Kublai spoke to them, then he jogged to the far end of the village and called out. Minutes later, a knot of about thirty men and women emerged from the surrounding forest. They seemed wary at first but relaxed after chatting with Kublai.

I didn't need an interpreter to know they had seen us coming and thought we might be government soldiers. They must keep a constant vigilance, afraid that every hour of every day the *Tatmadaw* might steal their food and enlist their men, or worse, herd them into the labor camps. How could they stand to live like that, I wondered. And what courage it took for them to resist the government to maintain their freedom.

Kublai waved for us to dismount. The villagers had, apparently, invited us to a meal. I tethered the elephants in the forest where they could graze on leafy plants, and we sat in the protection of a banyan tree while the women prepared what must have seemed a banquet to these poor villagers. Apparently, while they hid in the forest, one of them had come across a snake, about five feet long and as thick as a man's wrist. As we relaxed, I watch him skin the snake and remove the meat from the bone. The women cooked that meat with vegetables in a curry stew. Also, they wrapped damp rice in great green leaves and buried them in a shallow hole, then built a fire over it. Soon, the spicy aroma of curry wafted on the air.

Three elderly men and a toothless old woman hunkered around us. They squatted on their haunches, and I emulated them. One of them, Kublai informed us, was the village chief. He was dressed in a maroon *longyi,* thetraditional sarong that is tied at the waist and drapes to the ankles, and a collared check shirt. He had mahogany-colored skin below his frizz of white hair. He spoke a few sentences to Kublai, who replied, then took my hand, lifted it to his lips, and kissed it.

Comprehension lit up the villagers' faces. The chief leaned toward me and caressed my cheek. He nodded and smiled, then he winked at Kublai.

The mood turned lighthearted.

"What the hell did you say?" I asked.

"He asked why we traveled with white men. I told him that Annop and Archer were lovers, and that you are my boyfriend. He approves of you, says your big bottom must make you a fine mistress. He even suggested that we use his hut while we wait for the food to cook."

I was dumbfounded. When I found my voice again, I asked Kublai why he lied.

It's better to tell them something simple that they can understand, rather than something they may find distrustful." He smiled at me and seemed a little embarrassed. "Or maybe it was just wishful thinking."

I was sure Kublai was merely pulling my chain, but even so, I felt a sense of enjoyment that these villagers all assumed I was his lover. I hadn't given the idea much thought until that moment, but it not only seemed feasible, it somehow felt suitable.

After forty minutes, we were served snake curry over fluffy rice, and shredded green mangoes mixed with tea leaves and ground nuts. Everyone ate, the women more shyly than the men.

For the first time, Kublai seemed in no rush to get moving. We lounged over our meal, eating slowly, savoring each bite. To rush would have been a show of terrible manners, and there was no way we would display any disrespect to these people who gave everything they had to give.

They tried to push a second helping on us all, and there was nothing my belly wanted more, but we declined, claiming we were stuffed and couldn't eat another bite. We had remained silent through lunch, but once the plates had been whisked away and replaced by mugs of *cha,* green tea, the talk livened up as we sipped. The lunch would not have been complete without tobacco, so the elders offered us cheroots. There was a pause in the conversation while the elders, Kublai, and his partner lit their cigars with a burning brand brought from the cooking fire. They sat blowing smoke into the branches of the tree and sipping *cha,* seemingly as content as a body can be.

"A little food in your belly makes you a happy man?" I said to Kublai, trying to tease him. I was hoping that he would bring up the topic of my being his mistress again. It was not too late to use the elder's hut.

He nodded. "When you don't know if you will be alive at the end of the day, it's a blessing to sit with men you respect and talk and smoke and enjoy their company. Blessings like this must be savored."

"Since you put it like that, maybe I will have a second helping of curry."

He laughed and slapped my back. He translated our conversation to the elders, and they laughed so hard tears ran down their cheeks. One called to a pretty girl, and a minute later she came running with another plateful. I had only been joking, but it would have been even worse manners to refuse, so I ate with relish.

After the cigars and a second mug of tea were finished, Kublai waved and we all stood. We bowed low to the chief, and I said, "We thank you for your hospitality." Kublai translated.

The old man waved a hand.

The clouds had faded and the afternoon sky blushed a pure shade of cerulean. The villagers gathered as we mounted our elephants and continued our journey. There were many smiles and waving of hands. A few minutes later, we trudged through thick vegetation once again. With our bodies swaying to Soapsuds's lumbering movement, and trying to keep up with Kublai and his partner, who were now anxious to make up lost time, I said over my shoulders to Archer, "These villagers are amazing. To live in constant fear, but still maintain their dignity and sense of humor."

"They will never give up their land," he said, "the place their ancestors are buried. This is their life, they want no other. They will defend it to the last man, woman, and child."

"I pray it doesn't come to that," I said, finding the strength of these Karen people more inspiring than anything I'd ever experienced before. *They require so little, yet they will not let anyone rob them of what they have, and what they have is dignity. Their freedom and their dignity is everything.*

❖

As the sun sank toward the horizon, I began to hear a faint sound. "Dah!...Dah!...Dah!" Both Kublai and his buddy stopped, and I brought Soapsuds to a standstill. Kublai turned to look up at me. That's when I realized that the sound was gunshots somewhere up ahead. It was also the moment when I realized we had plunged into the deep end of the shit pool.

I heard long bursts of automatic fire. Smoke drifted on the air, becoming thicker each moment. The smell of burning grew strong. I could tell Soapsuds had become nervous, which was a bad sign. I had the urge to turn him around and put the spurs to him, if only I had had spurs on my sandals. I had no idea what to do, and I waited for Kublai to tell me. Luckily, he seemed calm and poised. He waved in a direction off the trail, and led us to an outcrop of boulders about a hundred yards south, well out of sight should anyone come along that same path. Archer and I jumped down, and while he helped Annop off Padre's back, I tethered the elephants to the nearest tree. We all crouched down, with Archer holding Annop in his arms like a squirming puppy.

Kublai shoved his AK-47 into my hands. He ripped his .45 handgun from its holster and gave it to Archer, and then swung his M16 off his shoulder and clicked the safety to the off position. "If we don't return by sundown, boss, go back to the village. Someone will lead you back across the border."

I stared at the weapon in my hands, knowing that I could never kill a human being in order to save myself. The question was, could I kill to save Archer and Annop? I had no answer. "You can't leave us," was all I could think to say.

Kublai did something totally unexpected that left me dazed. He leaned into me and kissed me on the lips. It was a sensual kiss that lasted a long time. A moment later, he and his partner were moving off at a fast run.

"What the..." I mumbled. I knew then his comments back in the village had indeed been wishful thinking.

The noise ahead intensified, with three quick explosions that I assumed were grenades. We three stared at each other, and it seemed I was the only one afraid. Archer and Annop were so calm they could have been sitting back at the temple waiting patiently for prayers to begin. It unnerved me that they were both so composed. "What if they find us?" I asked Archer.

"We give ourselves up, of course. We're not soldiers. All we've done is enter the country illegally."

"Right." I tried to sound encouraged, but I couldn't feel anything of the sort. "What if they shoot first and check out passports after?"

He shrugged.

The sound of gunfire grew louder, which made me wonder if the fight was moving our way. More explosions erupted. Booming sounds echoed off the rocks and trees, making it seem like the battle was all around us.

I couldn't believe I had been so damned stupid as to let myself fall into this situation. And for what? To break two men out of prison? I didn't even know what the hell the plan was for the jailbreak. I had been duped. I was supposed to be the delivery guy, a mahout, nothing more, and here I was in a firefight in the middle of a jungle. My mind raged, and I knew I had to calm down. I focused on my breathing, trying to ignore the sounds echoing around me.

I told myself that Archer was right. The only thing to do was surrender. I wasn't about to do anything heroic.

I expected the fight to last several minutes, ten or fifteen at the most. But the sounds of battle stretched on for twenty, thirty, forty minutes. This was no skirmish where a *Tatmadaw* patrol was surprised by a band of freedom fighters, where both sides ran for safety after the first few shots were fired. This was real, very real. The kind of real that turns deadly for both sides. After that long a skirmish, I held no hope that our guides would return.

Then the air grew silent. Smoke still billowed through the trees, but the fight eventually ended.

I had no doubt who won. I knew from our guides that the freedom fighters had great courage, but they were poorly armed. The AK-47 I held was at least thirty years old. I also assumed that the *Tatmadaw* had modern weapons. It was one thing to debate the rights and wrongs of armed struggle. It was another to see underequipped men fighting heart and soul for their land against monstrously superior forces.

"I think we're done for," I said.

Archer shook his head. "These Karen and Karenni fighters know the land and have more reason to fight for it. Man for man, they're unbeatable. Most of these government soldiers are teenagers, press-ganged into fighting with a rifle in their backs. They're victims too. Have faith."

We waited. As frightened as I felt, I had almost drifted off to sleep when Annop tapped my shoulder. His arms waved about, trying to point back to the trail, which was about a quarter mile away. By that time the sky was deep into twilight, and there was no way I could see the trail. Annop pointed to his ear, indicating that he had heard something. I motioned to him and Archer to remain hidden, and I began creeping closer to the trail.

About halfway there I saw something move. In the fading light, the figure of a man stood on the path. He was young, early twenties, with a middleweight boxer's build, short hair and clean-shaven. He held an automatic rife at the ready. By the time I blinked, another soldier joined him. Moments later, two more ran up. To me, they all looked like they chewed granite bricks for breakfast.

They huddled in a tight group, then began to comb the ground on both sides of the trail, no doubt searching for tracks in the shadows of the trees. *How difficult will it be to find elephant prints?* I clicked my AK-47's safety off.

I felt a pressure on my leg. I turned to see that Archer had crawled up alongside me. He was trembling, and I saw the fear in his eyes. He hugged me. How many hours had I longed for this man's touch, to be this intimate?

"If we're lucky," he whispered, "they won't find our tracks."

"And if we're not lucky?" I whispered.

"Then we're dead."

I instinctively knew he was right. Giving ourselves up in this darkness was madness. They would surely blast anything that moved, fearful of an ambush.

"I guess we'll have to get lucky," I whispered.

"I'm sorry. I didn't know it would be like this."

"I wouldn't have missed this for the world," I said with a joviality I didn't feel.

"Atta boy."

We watched the soldier gather in a circle again. They argued for a few minutes. At that point, I knew they had not found our prints, or if they had, they were not willing to follow into what might be a trap. I held my breath until I became dizzy. As I exhaled, the soldiers hurried down the trail and vanished in the dim.

As soon as they were gone, Archer hugged me harder. I felt hot tears falling on my neck, and my eyes burned as well. We shared raw emotion, and it felt erotic.

I said, "We'd better get back."

"Okay," he said with the voice of a lost child.

Moments later, a nameless dark enshrouded us. He began to crawl and I followed.

My only recollection of that night huddled in the boulders was that it felt miserably cold and interminably long. The temperature dropped lower than the previous night because we were at a higher elevation. Cold enough to crack bones until you bled marrow. The blankets were still, no doubt, in our guides' backpacks. I huddled with my arms around Archer's shivering body, with Annop sandwiched between us, trying to avoid freezing while at the same time concentrating on hearing anything that happened around us. I had no energy for any other feelings or reflections. At the sound of a snapping twig or hushed footfall, I would raise my weapon, feeling a jolt of electricity run up my neck.

The blackness grew so dense that it hurt my eyes staring into it. At the temple, I often stared up at the stars, but here the stars did little to illuminate the landscape. Hours later, the moon showed its face. It made me wonder what the hell I would do at sunrise.

The only thing to do, I knew, was follow Kublai's last instruction, make our way back to the village and pray someone there could lead us home.

I listened to the breeze moving through the branches. I tried to shake my fear, tried to act like Kublai, but I was not him and never would be. Fear is a vampire. Once it sank its teeth into me and began sucking my blood, I felt powerless to fight it. *If only my heart were made of stone, my nerves steel rods. If only I had the resolve of these Burmese people fighting for their land.* But what the hell was I doing? I had no idea. I had spent years holed up in one temple or another, hiding from the world while I carved my elephant statues. Now I had been dragged into a battle for life, and I didn't know what the hell to do.

All I could do at that moment was wait for dawn.

With the first gray light I flipped my weapon's safety to off, and slipped through the opaque woods to have a look-see. I heard coughing behind me, and knew it was Archer. He coughed for a long time, long enough for me to reach the trail.

I knelt on the path, raised my face to the paling sky, and prayed hard that Kublai would somehow miraculously return. I knew all too well that he was the only thing standing between our little band and death.

"Are you there?" I whispered, talking to Kublai, not God, although I would have been equally happy if either had answered. "Are you still alive?"

Through the raw, cold light, I saw movement up the trail—a man ambling toward me. I raised my rifle, and thought that I should have left my weapon with Archer. *If I die here, they'll need it.*

As the man drew near, I realized that he was Kublai's partner, and that he was carrying a bundle over his shoulders. That bundle turned out to be a wounded Kublai. My prayers had been answered.

Kublai had been shot in the left thigh, four inches above the knee, and was in obvious agony. His partner carried him off the trail to the place where Archer and Annop huddled against the cold. Once the soldier laid down his load, I was able to get a better look. Kublai's left leg had swollen massively around his shattered femur. There was already a field dressing on the wound. His tattered pants were covered in blood. Fortunately, the bullet had come from a small caliber rifle and had missed the artery.

I held Kublai's head while the other soldier stripped away the bloody dressing and cleaned the wound. He pulled antiseptic powder and a new field dressing from his backpack, sprinkled the powder over the bullet hole, and then applied the fresh dressing.

Sweat covered Kublai's face and body. While his partner dressed his leg, he stared up into my eyes. His face held an expression of intense determination, and I assumed he was struggling against the pain. I felt my heart crack open.

His body went limp, as if he had exhausted all his strength. Only his eyes appeared to be alive. They grew enormous, seeming to move in their sockets independently from the body they occupied. They stared up at me from a bed of pain, but they also held a glint of humor. They seemed to say, "I've held off death this long only to be held by you. At last I can die happy."

"We need to get you to a hospital," I whispered.

He waved a hand to silence me. "Too far. The others…dead. Soon, me too."

We were two days from the Thai border. We could run him back to the clinic at Huay Sa Tao. "We'll take you back."

He shook his head. "Leave me. Deliver them to Toungoo, and bury me on your way back."

I tried to speak but my mouth had dried. I managed a swallow, and tried again. "I'm not leaving you."

He smiled. "I could have loved you. We could have been happy for a time. I have a soft spot for lost puppies."

The other soldier finished dressing the leg. He spoke a rapid sentence I didn't understand, and Kublai nodded.

"You can travel on elephant back," I said. "We'll have you at the clinic before infection can set in."

"The mission is more important. Ko Ruta will lead you there, and back. He's a good man."

"I'm not leaving you."

He reached for the rifle slung over his shoulder and pointed it at Soapsuds. "If you're not mounted and moving out in two minutes, boss, I'm killing the one thing in the world you love."

"I have…a…propo…sition," Annop said in a halting voice.

The rifle didn't waiver. "Talk fast," Kublai said, "you don't have much time."

Annop proposed that Ko Ruta lead me and Archer to Toungoo to complete the mission while he and Kublai rode Padre back to Huay Sa Tao for medical help. Defiance drained from Kublai's face, turning it into a mask of intense interest.

"You can kill Soapsuds," I said, running with what seemed a workable idea, "in which case we're all fucked. Or you can go back with Annop while we soldier on."

Kublai's voice was soft and controlled, and very weary. "Why can't you just leave me?"

I bent my head and kissed him on the lips. When I pulled away, I said, "I want you and me to experience that happy time you talked about. Right now, that's all that matters to me."

He lowered his weapon and scratched his chin while pondering the possibilities.

More beads of sweat swelled on his forehead. He was feverish. I couldn't help wondering how much time he had before the inevitable delirium overtook him.

He gasped with weak laughter. Tears streamed down his face. When he recovered, he said, "You, boss, are a romantic. A dying breed, I'm afraid. But I like your optimism. Will you promise to deliver Archer?"

"If you lead Annop back to Huay Sa Tao, I'll do whatever you wish."

He gathered his pride around him like a cloak. "The journey will undoubtedly kill us both. Even from that first day, I gave us slim odds of ever getting this far."

I attempted a smile. "Perhaps a couple of foolish romantics can beat the odds by sheer dumb luck."

He nodded. "Yes, here's to dumb luck. We have a deal, Corbin Edwards."

For the first time, he had not called me boss, letting me know our relationship had changed. We were now equals.

He lifted my hand and squeezed it. I kissed him again, longer this time, with even more feeling. Then we looked eye-to-eye without any attempt at evasion. The bargain was struck, the die cast. We both understood that us both surviving this was a million to one; there was no need to say any more. But I hoped that, if he moved fast, his odds were far better than mine.

I untethered Padre and made him kneel. Archer lifted Annop onto Padre's shoulders, and I cradled Kublai in my arms, sitting him directly behind Annop. As the elephant rose to his feet, I said, "I'll see you in four or five days. We can fly down to Bangkok and live it up while you recuperate."

"Oh yes," Kublai said. "And after Bangkok, why not fly to San Francisco?" He smiled. "After that we might try New York, Buenos Aires, Paris, Rome. Our future is looking brighter and brighter."

"You forgot Hollywood," I said. "We'll want to see Brad Pitt."

"That was too much to hope for. At least for today."

I noticed that despite his spirit and courage, his voice had grown thin and less certain of its strength. He fought off the agony by sheer willpower, and the effort was becoming too great for him. I prayed we would both live long enough for me to show him city life.

I bid Kublai good-bye as Padre carried him out of camp. A few minute later, Archer and I rode Soapsuds west, following Ko Ruta. I was happy to finally know the soldier's name, but not so thrilled that he spoke no English. All our communications would be via pantomime and hand signals. He had a soft voice and a lean-boned, sun-beaten face. He seemed to have the fullness of a morning sunrise and the quick finality of death. His skin held the sheen of used copper, and his posture capable arrogance.

Indeed, with the absence of Kublai, Ko Ruta became supercilious, holding his weapon across his chest to ensure we knew who was in charge.

Two miles up the trail we came across a sight that will live with me for the rest of my days. Yesterday's battle had centered at a village, and as we approached that area, we had to cover our nose and mouths to keep from ingesting the foul-smelling smoke. What had been a thriving hamlet only twenty-four hours ago was now mounds of smoldering ash, with dozens of bodies still lying in the mud. Many were *Tatmadaw* soldiers, but the majority were villagers and freedom fighters. I saw several women and children among the dead. I've never witnessed, before or since, a more heartbreaking scene. Sadness and anger began battling for control of my head, and in the end, I could only cry. Ko Ruta wouldn't even let us stop to bury the dead.

After leaving the village behind, Ko Ruta turned us north, to enter the Karenni state. He set a fast pace. Little sleep the previous night combined with worrying about Kublai had exhausted all my remaining strength. It was all I could do to keep from falling off Soapsuds as he lumbered along. Luckily, Archer held me to him in a tight grip. That alone, that human touch, kept me going. I wondered over and over if I could have made a difference to that village. That is, had I gone with Kublai and Ko Ruta, adding my AK-47 to the fight, could I have saved a child or two, perhaps an elderly woman? Or would I have died making no difference at all? There was no way to know, but I couldn't let go of that thought. It gnawed at my brain like a dog worrying a bone. And for the first time, I wanted know exactly what our mission would accomplish. I needed to be part of something that struck a blow to these generals who saw fit to destroy the people of this country, who ruled with bloodshed and by instilling fear. I wanted to take part in some kind of revenge.

No, some deeper part of my mind argued, it had nothing to do with simple revenge. It had to do with accountability, the rule of law, and justice for the people least able to defend themselves.

At that point, I only knew the plan was to somehow get two men, Philip Mann and his son, out of prison. But how, and what the hell difference could these men make? To my weary mind, the pieces didn't fit together.

As we traveled north, we came across many other destroyed villages. Some I hardly noticed because they were so overgrown. With each one, like the first, I experienced a feeling of absolute finality. The scheme of things within which I had always lived ceased. We didn't see one village that was not demolished. This genocidal campaign seemed to have been utterly successful.

We kept marching and had few rests, moving fast, striding hard. I could tell the pace was weakening Soapsuds, but I wanted to put that battle scene as far behind me as possible.

We quick-marched for nineteen hours that day, reaching the outskirts of Toungoo. We stopped at a hut with corrugated tin walls, a dirt floor, and thatched roof. A short, chunky man stood in the open doorway, frame by the uncertain light from within. He had a flabby face under a patch of graying hair, and his eyes seemed trapped in a spider web of weary lines.

Soapsuds knelt, and we dismounted.

The man held out his hand. "You made good time," he said in passible English.

"All part of the platinum service," I said, shaking his hand.

"I'm Dr. Kengtung." He wore a gray, blood-stained shirt and loose military trousers. He spoke apologetically, as if I were a dignitary visiting from another, more glamorous civilization, who would certainly find the conditions less than satisfactory. He jerked his head toward the hut. "Come inside. There's tea, food, whatever you need. I'll water and feed your fine elephant."

Before I could answer, he stepped to Soapsuds, grabbed the halter, and began leading him to the back of the hut. Ko Ruta busied him at a fire pit in the front yard, where a teakettle and a soup pot sat on the coals.

Archer and I entered, and I sank into the nearest chair. I saw no women and no children. A dog, hollow-bellied and dispirited, sprawled in one corner. This place held no human warmth, a home without comfort, color, even laughter.

As I waited for tea, I thought of Kublai again, wondering if there was any chance he would make it to a hospital, and if so, could I find my way back to him? I couldn't think beyond that, about what kind of life we could have together, because just seeing him again seemed impossible, the odds against us too great. All my life I had had prodigious dreams, only to watch them smashed one after another. It was all too much to hope for.

A hurricane lamp with a cracked, soot-smeared chimney spluttered in the center of a long plank supported by two upended barrels that served as a table. Beside the lamp lay a covered platter of food. Archer placed his shoulder bag on the table, opened it, and checked that the contents were still undamaged.

I wondered for the first time what the hell that bag held. What cargo was this beautiful man carrying that could break someone out of jail?

Ko Ruta came through the doorway carrying the teakettle in one hand, the soup pot in the other. He set them on the table. He filled three tin cups with tea, and handed one to Archer and one to me. The drink opened my eyes, both from the heat and from the sweetness, which was sure to give me a sugar high. My first thought was to spit it out, but I swallowed while scrunching up my face. *This stuff will dissolve my fillings,* I thought, but I was grateful for it anyway. No matter how bad it tasted, I wouldn't have traded that drink for a million bucks. Sipping more, it seemed to clear my head and warm my insides the way whiskey can do.

As I drank more, Ko Ruta pulled three bowls from a shelf and set them on the table. He uncovered the food platter and grabbed handfuls of already-cooked noodles and tossed some in each bowl. He added bits of meat that looked like chopped-up organs, tendon, and cartilage, and also green leafy vegetables, then ladled broth from the pot to fill each bowl. He let them simmer for a few minutes, then set a bowl and chopsticks before each of us.

Only then did I realize I was ravenous. I set my tea aside and dug in. Gobbling each bite, I felt myself returning to something resembling human life. After the meal I dropped like a stone into unconsciousness. I slept through the night without stirring. Before dawn, I was shaken awake and dragged to the table for more tea and noodle soup.

This time I ate slowly, wondering what the day would bring. Dr. Kengtung joined us. "Eat up," he said to Archer. "There's lots more. We'll hit the market place just after dawn. The whole town will be there to witness. So eat as much as you can. This could be your last meal for many days."

My curiosity over came my hunger. "What, exactly, are we talking about? What happens in the market?"

Dr. Kengtung shot Archer a puzzled glance.

"His job was to deliver me here," Archer told the doctor. "We didn't tell him any more than that in case we were captured along the way."

"Great," I said. "But now that I've done my job, what the hell is going on? Will someone please explain how you plan to break these Americans out of jail?"

"My dear young man," Dr. Kengtung said, "we plan to break someone into prison, not out."

"What?"

Archer set his noodles aside. "Corbin, I'll be arrested for passing out pro-democracy information. The good doctor here will record the whole thing, and you are going to take that video back to Thailand and email it to my network in Hollywood. Our plan is to call attention to what is happening in Myanmar, and we think this will get our State Department working on freeing all the Americans in government prisons. This could help hundreds of political prisoners, not just Philip Mann and his son. This could be the start of something that can change millions of lives here in Myanmar."

"What makes you think they'll pay any more attention to you than they did to Mann?"

"Corbin, I'm a huge television celebrity in the States. I'm bigger than Oprah, bigger than *The Tonight Show* and *Saturday Night Live* combined. Thirty-four million viewers watch my show every day. Once they see me arrested, they will force the State Department to act."

The plan seemed simple enough, but it still didn't make sense. "If you're such a hotshot, why don't you just go to Washington D.C. and kick some butt? Why don't you stand before your millions of viewers and tell them what's happening? Why suffer in a filthy prison?"

"Because people don't care unless it's happening to someone they love or admire. People don't care about millions of Burmese or a handful of Americans they've never heard of. They will care what happens to me."

"There has to be a better way than having you rot in a cell."

"Trust me, I won't be there very long. And this is not about me being in a cell. That's all I can say. Look, I don't ask that you approve, or even understand. I want you to let Ko Ruta lead you back to Thailand, and then email what's in this camcorder back to the address I'll leave with you." He pulled a camcorder out of his shoulder bag. "Will you do that for me?"

I wanted to argue, but I realized he would not be swayed. Everything had been worked out before we left Thailand, and I had been kept in the dark.

"Sure, I'll do my best."

"Atta boy." He pulled a piece of paper from his bag, signed it, and handed it to me. "This is a cashier's check that you can cash in any Thai bank. It will get you back to the States and keep you going until you're on your feet again."

I check the amount, counting five zeros. "I can't accept this."

He smiled. "You risked your life. Hell, you're still in grave danger. I think that deserves twice that amount."

I was a bit stunned, and I didn't like this situation, but I folded the check and slipped it into my pocket.

They wanted me to stay at the hut, but I insisted on going to watch what happened. They dressed me in a traditional *longyi,* collared long-sleeved shirt, and a straw hat that partially hid my face so I could blend in with the locals. Then I followed Archer and Dr. Kengtung into Toungoo.

It was a small town where the misery of poverty and oppression were on full display. At the market, men stood behind stalls of fish paste or clothing or tools, but few customers were buying. Women laid vegetables out on sacks and breast-fed their babies while attending customers. Everyone, vendors and customers alike, carried that same exhausted look about them.

I squatted down and leaned against a building, trying to become invisible. A dozen yards away, Dr. Kengtung held the camcorder pointing at Archer, who stood in the middle of the crowd. I became sick with apprehension as Archer pulled letters and CDs out of his bag. *"Kyaungtar khaung zaung Min Ko Naing hnit naing ngan yey a kyintha, lut myowt yey!"* he shouted, and began hurling the first fistful of letters into the air. At that moment, my heart plunged into by belly. I could do nothing to stop this.

He began walking through the market stalls, handing CDs of

pro-democracy songs to vendors and shoppers. At short intervals, he tossed more letters into the sky to be carried on the breeze. People snatched them out of the air.

"Release all political prisoners!" he yelled in English. Many of the locals stared in astonishment. "Reopen the universities!"

As he moved through the market, the good doctor followed from a safe distance with the camcorder trained on him. Dr. Kengtung did his best to keep the camcorder hidden, but there was no way to record everything and not have it held high enough for people to see. I believe that was why Archer was making such a loud spectacle of himself, to draw attention away from the doctor.

Most of the locals pretended Archer wasn't there. It was not safe for them to show interest, especially if someone was filming. But of the ones who did, I clearly saw a thirst in their eyes, to have something to read that had to do with freedom, something to do with the fight against the military junta. For a moment, while watching, my heart pulled itself back into my chest and began to sing. Yes, Archer's demonstration meant something to these people. Even this little display brought them hope. What we were doing was right. I could only hope that the camcorder would expose their hunger.

"*Demokrasi! Khinmya doh ayey-ha, janore ayey bar heh!*" Even I could tell his pronunciation was appalling, and I wondered if the locals could understand his Burmese any better than they understood his English. It didn't matter. All the information was no doubt recorded in those letters. He was not trying to start a riot or revolution. He was merely trying to get arrested for the crime of speaking the truth.

He made his way to the end of the marketplace and then doubled back, working his way toward me. Several minutes had passed and Archer had run out of handouts. He stood in the center of the market, shouting, "Democracy now!"

The people moved away from him. Each face in the crowd became a sketch of sorrow and alarm and mistrust. Then two uniformed men appeared, shouting Archer down. They spoke Burmese, so I had no idea what they were saying. Archer tried to walk away, continuing his shouts, but one of the officers grabbed his arm, holding him back. They seemed uncertain how rough they could be with a foreigner, but they were obviously intent on stopping any more demonstration.

"Free the political prisoners! Democracy now!" Archer shouted, and again I believed it was to draw attention away from the camcorder.

He was silenced, however, when one of the men slapped his face, hard. A half dozen uniformed men came running up, surrounding Archer. For a moment, I wished I had demonstrated with him. I began to cry, knowing that I was witnessing the bravest, most selfless act of my thirty-five years. I wanted to hoist him on my shoulders and parade him around like a hero. I knew then that it was more than simply admiration. I had fallen in love with this man for showing me the human face of true compassion.

"Lut lat yey! Freedom!" he yelled a last time before they began beating him about the head and shoulders. He sank to his knees. Two men flanked him, each one grabbing an arm, and dragged him through the streets. The only things missing were a wooden cross and a crown of thorns. They moved fast, whisking him out of sight in seconds.

In the stunned silence that followed, Dr. Kengtung came and sat beside me. His hands trembled with excitement. He handed me the camcorder and told me to follow the main road back out of town to his hut. He would go to the police station and make sure Archer was physically okay. I assumed he also wanted to gather any information about what the police planned to do next.

I had no trouble walking back to the doctor's grim hut. I busied myself with watering and feeding Soapsuds. A war waged inside me; one side held the thrill I felt while watching Archer's bravery, the other side was devastated that now he would rot in prison until the US State Department could arrange his release. That could take months, even years.

Ko Ruta made tea, and we sat at the table to wait for Dr. Kengtung. We had what we had come for, and every minute we waited to depart put us in deeper peril, but neither of us would leave before learning about Archer's condition.

We waited several hours. When the doctor finally appeared, he told us that Archer had been arrested, tried, and sentenced to fifteen years of prison for distributing anti-government literature. He had no lawyer, was not given the opportunity to defend himself, and at no time during the trial was the anti-government literature produced or read out loud. They would transport him to Yangon the next morning.

Listening, I realized that words like "arrest," "trial," "judge," and "law" had no meaning in this place, because no such things existed. I was speechless, and anxious to climb onto Soapsuds and get my butt back to Thailand.

When I stood up to get started back, Dr. Kengtung waved me back down. "Stay the night," he said. "There is no hurry."

A flash of anger surged through me. "The sooner I deliver this file, the sooner Archer will be free."

The doctor shook his head. "I'm sorry, didn't you know?"

"What the hell are you talking about?"

The doctor paused. "He has an inoperable brain tumor. He'll most likely be dead within a few weeks. A month at most. There's not enough time to get him out."

I sat at the table, feeling a panic rushing to my head.

Dr. Kengtung patted my shoulder. "My friend, his dying in a Yangon prison will spark an international outrage. He knows this. He's the one who suggested it. It will force America to do something, it will force the International Red Cross to do something, and most importantly, it will force the military junta to give up their political prisoners. It's a brilliant plan."

I tried to be as brave as Archer, but my insides were imploding. Now there was only one thing I could do, finish the mission. We left as soon as we filled our water bottles and Dr. Kengtung prepared food for our journey back.

The passage across the border took three days, then another day to the temple. The delays were mostly because of Soapsuds. He was exhausted, and I refused to push him hard. We stopped often for rests and feeding. Once we reached the temple, I waited only long enough to bath and change clothes, then rode Soapsuds into Huay Sa Tao.

I visited the only Internet café, emailing copies of the video showing Archer's arrest to his television studio and also the Associated Press. I included a long text detailing our entire trip, and the mission that Archer had taken to free all political prisoners in Myanmar. That done, Soapsuds and I made a beeline for the only medical clinic in town.

On a wide sloping lawn, tucked into a grove of coconut palms, stood a white building with a large red cross on the wall. It had a covered porch, and a line of women holding infants snaked out the door and along the wall. Padre was tethered to a palm tree. The two elephants seemed overjoyed to be together again. I tied Soapsuds's harness to the same tree and hurried inside.

There were twelve beds on the ward, and Kublai's was at the far end. As I walked down the ward, I saw that he lay on his back with his injured leg elevated and in a cast from toes to hip. Beside the bed, Annop sat in his wheelchair, and on the bedside table was a chessboard. They were in the middle of a game. Kublai's eyes seemed sad, and he obviously was not interested in the game. I assumed he was feeling the effects of drugs, but when he glanced up at me, his face, his being, subtly altered, becoming more defined, livelier. A soft light grew around him.

His shoulders looked wider than I remembered, more muscular. But as our eyes drilled into each other, those shoulders sagged, and his expression turned into a comical blend of fatigue and delight. My throat grew dry as my pulse went haywire.

I hurried to his bedside, and he grabbed my arm and pulled me to him until our lips pressed together. I found myself releasing emotions that had been building up in my heart. We hugged and kissed and hugged more, all without words.

I pulled away only far enough to look him in the eyes and whisper, "I didn't think I'd see you again."

He kissed me once more, and I could tell from his silence that he had felt the same.

"Per...haps I can arr...ange a private...room," Annop said.

"We got it all on tape," I said, "and I emailed the files to the right people. Let's hope it works."

"Thank you," he said, his voice hoarse. I wasn't sure if it was drugs or emotions that made him sound funny, and I didn't care. I was so damn glad to see him lying there smiling.

"Yes...Thank...you," Annop said, and I heard genuine gratitude in his voice.

I glanced at him. "I wish you'd have told me what the hell was going on before we set out. It was quite a shock watching it unfold and not knowing why."

"Peo...ple like...you can't...understand," Annop said.

As soon as he said it, I understood. People like me are the ones who hide from life and its problems, sitting in a monastery carving elephant statues. People like me are too caught up in their own drama to devote themselves to helping others. People like me would not have gotten involved had we known the dangers ahead of time. People like me.

"What's done is done," Kublai said. "Archer knew that there is evil in all of us, and if we are to fight against evil, then we must fight that wrong within our own being. His evil is locked in his head, and it's killing him. He found a way to use that to help my people, which beats the hell out of lying in a hospital bed feeling sorry for yourself."

"I get it, I just hate the thought of him locked in a dingy cell for the last few weeks of his life."

"The freedom which counts is one which none can take away, just as none can give it. Inner freedom overcomes fears and hardships, and Archer has that in spades. His death will show the world that the courts, judges, and legislation in Myanmar are a charade. With his arrest, they will not be able to hide the gross injustices that have become the norm. The regime will be weakened, and hopefully back down and free the other political prisoners."

At the temple, I had often meditated on death, as a way to prepare myself for my own demise. Most Buddhist monks do. But the idea of Archer's beautiful, lifeless body—its coldness, the rubberiness of the skin, the death smell, and the utter absence of life—was sobering and too hard to accept.

The teachings of the Lord Buddha were often simplified into what are known as the Four Noble Truths, and it was the first of these that struck me, the truth about suffering. We all suffer. Birth is suffering; aging, sickness, and death are suffering. I glanced across the bed to Annop, and knew that being separated from those we love is also suffering, and he must be in a constant state of pain while his lover sat in prison. I saw it in his face, in that vacant stare. There's physical suffering, but also mental suffering, which is oftentimes worse. We had all risked our lives in order to end Annop's suffering, and the pain of an entire people. His pain, however, was still etched on his face and would be until his lover was back with him. I knew then that my job, this mission, was far from over. Annop needed help, and I was seemingly the only one who could give it.

I stayed at Kublai's bedside holding his hand for the rest of the afternoon and into the evening, contemplating the debris that was now my past. I knew I could no longer go back to carve elephant statues. I was no longer content to hide from life. From this point on, and with Kublai's help, I would build a new life, like building a bridge stone by stone. I felt a different person, positively reborn.

I would start by doing what I could to make sure Annop was comfortable while we waited for Kublai to be released from the clinic, and for Philip Mann and his son to be released from prison. I would devote myself to this monk as Archer had done. Then I would see what came next. When Kublai fell asleep, I kissed his forehead and ran my fingers through his hair. Then I wheeled Annop out to the lawn where the elephants stood waiting. I untethered them and had them kneel, and I lifted Annop out of his chair and placed him on Padre's shoulders. Annop's arms were flying every which way as Padre lumbered to his feet. As I climbed on to Soapsuds, Annop yelled, "I'm...king of... the...world!" and Padre began to scurry away at a fast pace, heading down the road that led to the temple. I whistled for Soapsuds to rise, and then I had to hurry after Annop.

❖

In the weeks that followed, I came to town every day to visit Kublai and to check the news at the Internet café. I searched for articles about Archer and found a firestorm of controversy back in the US, and plenty of saber rattling (no surprise), but no information on his release or his physical condition. I knew I would never see him again, even if the State Department managed his release before his death. While on the net I also searched for any English word that encapsulated my feelings for him, that blending of my love and my sorrow. I uncovered nothing. I discovered, however, a Portuguese word—*saudade*—that seemed to fit. It means that the memory of someone brings great joy, but shackled to that joy is a profound melancholy, because you realize the one you long for will never return. It's a ravenousness craving, a heartfelt nostalgia for what can never be again.

Saudade...it's the love that lives on. That feeling, a deep affection for Kublai, and a desire to be involved with others, are all I carry into the future.

About the Author

Alan Chin enjoyed a twenty-year career working his way from computer programmer to director of software engineering, but he lost interest in computer science when he began writing fiction. He walked away from corporate America in 1999 and never looked back. Since then he has traveled to over fifty countries, scuba-dived the Great Barrier Reef, tracked black rhino in the Serengeti and Bengal tigers in Nepal, and dined in most of the capitals of Europe. Oh yes, and he's published nine novels and three screenplays.

The Plain of Bitter Honey was a finalist in the 2014 *ForeWord Review* Book of the Year Award in the Science Fiction category. Alan's novel *The Lonely War* swept the 2010 Rainbow Awards, taking top honors in Best Fiction and Best Historical. Alan's novel *Match Maker* won the 2011 Rainbow Award in Contemporary Fiction. *QBliss* magazine awarded their Pride In Literature award to Alan for his debut novel, *Island Song*.

Alan currently spends half of the year traveling the globe and the other half writing at his home in Palm Springs, California.

You can visit Alan's website at alanchinwriter.com and his writer's blog at alanchinwriter.blogspot.com. You can also email Alan at Alanhchin@aol.com.

Books Available From Bold Strokes Books

Buddha's Bad Boys by Alan Chin. Six stories, six gay men trudging down the road to enlightenment. What they each find is the last thing in the world they expected. (978-1-62639-244-1)

Play It Forward by Frederick Smith. When the worlds of a community activist and a pro basketball player collide, little do they know that their dirty little secrets can lead to a public scandal…and an unexpected love affair. (978-1-62639-235-9)

GingerDead Man by Logan Zachary. Paavo Wolfe sells horror but isn't prepared for what he finds in the oven or the bathhouse; he's in hot water again, and the killer is turning up the heat. (978-1-62639-236-6)

Myth and Magic: Queer Fairy Tales, edited by Radclyffe and Stacia Seaman. Myth, magic, and monsters—the stuff of childhood dreams (or nightmares) and adult fantasies. (978-1-62639-225-0)

Blackthorn by Simon Hawk. Rian Blackthorn, Master of the Hall of Swords, vowed he would not give in to the advances of Prince Corin, but he finds himself dueling with more than swords as Corin pursues him with determined passion. (978-1-62639-226-7)

Café Eisenhower by Richard Natale. A grieving young man who travels to Eastern Europe to claim an inheritance finds friendship, romance, and betrayal, as well as a moving document relating a secret lifelong love affair. (978-1-62639-217-5)

Balls & Chain by Eric Andrews-Katz. In protest of the marriage equality bill, the son of Florida's governor has been kidnapped. Agent Buck 98 is back, and the alligators aren't the only things biting. (978-1-62639-218-2)

Murder in the Arts District by Greg Herren. An investigation into a new and possibly shady art gallery in New Orleans' fabled Arts District soon leads Chanse into a dangerous world of forgery, theft…and murder. A Chanse MacLeod mystery. (978-1-62639-206-9)

Rise of the Thing Down Below by Daniel W. Kelly. Nothing kills sex on the beach like a fishman out of water…Third in the Comfort Cove Series. (978-1-62639-207-6)

Calvin's Head by David Swatling. Jason Dekker and his dog, Calvin, are homeless in Amsterdam when they stumble on the victim of a grisly murder—and become targets for the calculating killer, Gadget. (978-1-62639-193-2)

The Return of Jake Slater by Zavo. Jake Slater mistakenly believes his lover, Ben Masters, is dead. Now a wanted man in Abilene, Jake rides to Mexico to begin a new life and heal his broken heart. (978-1-62639-194-9)

Backstrokes by Dylan Madrid. When pianist Crawford Paul meets lifeguard Armando Leon, he accepts Armando's offer to help him overcome his fear of water by way of private lessons. As friendship turns into a summer affair, their lust for one another turns to love. (978-1-62639-069-0)

The Raptures of Time by David Holly. Mack Frost and his friends journey across an alien realm, through homoerotic adventures, suffering humiliation and rapture, making friends and enemies, always seeking a gateway back home to Oregon. (978-1-62639-068-3)

The Thief Taker by William Holden. Unreliable lovers, twisted family secrets, and too many dead bodies wait for Thomas Newton in London—where he soon discovers that all the plotting is aimed directly at him. (978-1-62639-054-6)

Waiting for the Violins by Justine Saracen. After surviving Dunkirk, a scarred and embittered British nurse returns to Nazi-occupied Brussels to join the Resistance, and finds that nothing is fair in love and war. (978-1-62639-046-1)

Turnbull House by Jess Faraday. London 1891: Reformed criminal Ira Adler has a new, respectable life—but will an old flame and the promise of riches tempt him back to London's dark side…and his own? (978-1-60282-987-9)

Stronger Than This by David-Matthew Barnes. A gay man and a lesbian form a beautiful friendship out of grief when their soul mates are tragically killed. (978-1-60282-988-6)

Death Came Calling by Donald Webb. When private investigator Katsuro Tanaka is hired to look into the death of a high profile lawyer, he becomes embroiled in a case of murder and mayhem. (978-1-60282-979-4)

Love in the Shadows by Dylan Madrid. While teaming up to bring a killer to justice, a lustful spark is ignited between an American man living in London and an Italian spy named Luca. (978-1-60282-981-7)

Cutie Pie Must Die by R.W. Clinger. Sexy detectives, a muscled quarterback, and the queerest murders…when murder is most cute. (978-1-60282-961-9)

Lightning Source UK Ltd.
Milton Keynes UK
OW04f0815010216
445UK00014B/23/P